Lilith

Lilith

❨ *A Novel* ❩

Nikki Marmery

alcove
press

Published in the United States by Alcove Press, an imprint of The Quick Brown Fox & Company LLC.

Alcove Press and its logo are trademarks of The Quick Brown Fox & Company LLC.

Library of Congress Catalog-in-Publication data available upon request.

ISBN (paperback): 978-1-63910-571-7
ISBN (ebook): 978-1-63910-572-4

Cover design by Sarah Whittaker

Printed in the United States.

www.alcovepress.com

Alcove Press
34 West 27th St., 10th Floor
New York, NY 10001

First Edition: October 2023

10 9 8 7 6 5 4 3 2 1

For women everywhere.
Be your own gods.
Your Mother commands it.

Lady Lilith

Of Adam's first wife, Lilith, it is told
(The witch he loved before the gift of Eve,)
That, ere the snake's, her sweet tongue could deceive,
And her enchanted hair was the first gold.
And still she sits, young while the earth is old,
And, subtly of herself contemplative,
Draws men to watch the bright net she can weave,
Till heart and body and life are in its hold.

Dante Gabriel Rossetti

Part One

PARADISE

4004BC

Then the Lord God said, "Behold, the man has become like one of Us, to know good and evil. And now, lest he put out his hand and take also of the tree of life, and eat, and live forever"— therefore the Lord God sent him out of the garden of Eden to till the ground from which he was taken. So He drove out the man; and He placed cherubim at the east of the garden of Eden, and a flaming sword which turned every way, to guard the way to the tree of life.

Genesis 3:22–24

In the Beginning

At first, I loved him. How beautiful he was in those days.

There he stood: legs planted wide in the rich soil of our Paradise. Hands on hips, his muscled arms firm and knotted as a young fig tree. His hair fell shining, raven-feathered, to his shoulders. His dark eyes beckoned.

The musty, coupling scent of him unmoored me. He made me giddy.

And I, him, I suppose.

At first.

When did it start? It seemed to come out of the blue. But now I see the signs I brushed away, as ripples on the surface of a pool, sending them far from me, as if that would be the end of it. The fool I was! How could I not know they would come surging back, a hundredfold!

He started to have *ideas*.

He watched me watering the grainfields with the rain I had stored that was plentiful and sufficient.

"If we dig here," he said, "we can channel groundwater. We needn't wait for the rain. We will direct the water toward the wheatfield and master it. I shall call it *irrigation* and it will be good.

"As for your hoeing," he said, as I broke the ground one day, "it is too slow. We shall hitch a curved and sharpened stick to an ox to bear the burden. I shall call it a *plough*." He nodded sagely. "And it will be good.

"We shall tally our labor," he observed, as I weeded the Garden. "When there are more of us—I have a feeling there will be more of us!" He winked. "We shall exchange our work, surplus food and so forth with a worthy item as a symbol of its value. I shall call it *money*—"

3

"And it will be good?"

"Don't interrupt, Lilith. I'm talking."

He paced the meadow, fretting. "We will need records of the money. We shall make marks in wet clay, and those marks shall have meaning. When the clay is fired, the meaning will be set forever, as if in stone."

"Like this?"

I showed him the marks I had carved on the rib bone of a goat. A calendar for marking the coming and going of the moon, the wax and wane of my own blood that tracked it.

"No, not like that. Not like that at all." He frowned. "I shall call *my* marks *writing.*"

He was dissatisfied with the bounty we had. He must have more of it. So, he experimented, crossing the various trees in our Garden to create a new fruit. After he noticed how the creatures in our care multiplied, it was the same with the animals.

"We shall build fences," he mused. "I shall separate the rams from the ewes, and the boars from the sows. I shall permit the ram to know the ewe, and the boar to know the sow, when I wish them to breed. This way I shall bring forth more rams and ewes and boars and sows as we require them."

They were fine plans. I admired his ambition.

Only that it changed us. Subsistence was no longer enough. Always, he wanted *more.* Always he wanted to *control.*

With the marks on his tablets, he became the Law.

"See here." He pointed to his mystifying wedge-shapes and arrows. "This is how it must be."

I could not argue with that, for he had not revealed the meaning of his marks. To me, they were as a sparrow's feet crisscrossing the clay in search of a worm.

He became the owner of these innovations: at once in charge of them, and benefitting from them most. As he tallied our labor and assigned it a value for his *money,* he judged his work as higher in merit and necessity than mine.

A strategic director, you might call him in these modern days. It suited him. The knowing arch of his brow. The forthright crossing of his strong arms. The way he nodded when he dispensed his edicts and orders. He was good at it.

☽

His final plan was the clincher. The deal-breaker. The world-changer.

"When there are more of us," he started one day—it had become his obsession, *more of us*, though I wasn't sure where he thought they'd come from— "we will need to protect ourselves from the Others."

He produced two small hard rocks: one reddish-brown, one gray, salvaged from the riverbed. "We shall melt these metals. When they combine, they make a harder, stronger substance, which we will use to make swords and knives, axes and so forth."

"What will you call this new material?" I asked, to amuse myself.

"Bronze," he said, unsmiling. "Naturally, I shall wield these weapons, for I am bigger and stronger than you, and I would protect you from harm."

"Naturally."

It made sense—at first. Whatever made him happy.

I had no need for weapons. Let him have his sword and his plough, his writing-tablets and money. I didn't look to the future. I lived happily in the here and now, rooted in the cycle of our daily lives. I tended my roses, I cared for the animals, I gathered the grain. I made clay pots to store our food. I made music to mark the rhythm of our lives. I beat a tambour to welcome the new moon. I danced for my own delight.

One day, I had been assured, I would be the mother of all mankind. All in good time.

I was in no rush. I had my own purpose: the Secret, entrusted to me alone. Its gift was finer than rubies; better than gold. I cherished and nurtured it in my belly, for it was mine, the gift of our Holy Mother solely for me, the First Woman.

Nor did I mind his mania for progress, for I loved him. And after the smelting and the forging, the harvest and the grinding, the

winnowing and the milling, the baking and the cooling, the music
and the dancing, we would meet under the Tree—the one from which
we Must Not Eat—and we would roll upon the moss and laugh and
kiss, and by all that is sacred and holy, he would plough me like a field
of barley, and it was *very* good. ·

I Am Your Lord!

The day it changed was like this:

We were beside the pool. The sun burned dazzling bright. The waterfall churned, sending forth little waves, crests shimmering gold like nectar. We lay on a sun-warmed rock and breathed in the drowsy scent of myrtle.

What glory there was in our Garden. All that was pleasant to the eye and good for food. Hard rosy apples and blood-red oranges. Lemons as fat as quails that dropped from the branch if you so much as looked at them. Walnuts and pears, over-ripe figs, almonds, and olives. Jewel-seeded pomegranates and sharp-tasting quinces. Everything always in season, no tree ever bare. The sweet heady scent of blossom at all times, even as there was fruit.

Now I come to think of it, it never grew. The fruit was merely there, ever ripe for plucking.

I did not know that was not usual. How could I?

Beyond the orchards lay the grainfields: the golden barley and swaying wheat. Adam's irrigation, his basins and levées, taps and dams, ran through them, bringing life-giving water from the four rivers that bounded our Paradise. The chest-high stalks bowed low with the wind. Always full-grown. Eternally ready for harvest. Since the first planting we had not sown new seed.

Looking out over the fields stood our sturdy cabin, crafted from the trunks and boughs of tall cedars and graceful pines, roofed with date-palm thatch. Beside it, my rose garden. The sweet scent welcomed me every morning and sent me joyful to sleep at night.

The animals came to drink from the pool. We had many rams and ewes, boars and sows by then, thanks to Adam's breeding regime.

Sturdy bulls and sweet-eyed cows. Bearded goats. Plump-breasted ducks, feathered fowl of all kinds. We looked at them, and they were good.

The heat was thick in the air like honey. The lilies danced on the breeze. The sun beat upon the glittering water and reflected into the sapphire sky.

Adam turned to me, his lips wet with lust. He put my hand to his thickening part and it reared with life and vigor. I climbed onto him, my fingers rooted in the black-curls of his chest.

"No." He squeezed my wrists. "Lie under me."

"I don't want to." I lowered my hips, enfolded him deep within the core of me, to prove my point. I proved it well enough.

He groaned with pleasure, then pushed at me again.

"I said, *lie under me!*"

"No! You lie under me!"

I thought he was joking. And truly, I was very content where I was, filled with the joy of him. But his eyes weren't smiling.

"I am your lord and you shall lie under me!"

"You are my *what*?" I laughed and felt him shrivel like a prune.

Oh, he was angry then. "I am your master!"

I rolled beside him and shut one eye against the blinding sun. Lord and master indeed!

"We were made together, you and I, and I am your equal." I caressed his broad chest and kissed his plum-red lips. He softened. "And while I'm at it," I laid my head in the hollow of his shoulder, "I've had it with your edicts and orders, your zeal for improvement. Let us return to how things were before. Let us live and work together in harmony once more."

He squeezed my hand and my spirit soared.

"Shall we not have more time for leisure? Must we toil all day under the hot sun, for more bounty than we need? What call have we for surpluses to trade, money to exchange? Let us rest and enjoy what we have been given, for we are blessed indeed."

He smiled and my heart leapt with love for him.

"As for your weapon—" I eyed his great bronze sword laid beside us. "Is it really necessary? I am the only one here. The animals are tame and do our bidding. Why do you carry it?"

Well, he did not like that. The tenderness drained from him like blood from a sacrificed lamb. He slammed a balled fist into the rock.

"Do not question me!" he roared. "It is my strength, my right hand. I carry it to protect you because you are mine! I wield it to remind you of your weakness!"

I froze to hear these words. Why did he think I was *his*? Why did he want me to feel *weak*?

As it turned out, the sword he claimed was for my protection was no defense against that which hurt me most. His body that I loved so much, he used against me. His oak-strong arms held me down and his tender hands crushed my wrists. He forced me beneath him and pinned me with his legs, a knee bruising the inner flesh of my thigh, his foot pinioning my ankle. The hard boulder bit from below and he pummeled me from above and within. He smothered my mouth to stop me cursing and looked over my head as if I were not there. Where once we had pleased each other, now I was but a vessel for his desire. With violence he had his joy of my body and there was no joy for me in him.

Was it worth it, Adam? You took by force what you had always had by love. It cannot have been sweeter.

His Name

Perhaps you have been told I was banished because in my anger I cursed and said His name.

But that is not what happened.

In truth, He is a jealous god. He was angry because it was not Him I named at all. In my fury and despair, I called to Her. To the Holy Mother who loved us, who nursed us, who should have protected me.

"Asherah!" I cried, when Adam had slunk away among the barley-stalks, shame-faced at least, the tip of his ridiculous sword trailing behind him. I wiped his dew from my bruised thigh with a bulrush.

"Mighty Asherah, Giver of Life and Queen of Heaven, why have you forsaken me?"

There was no answer. She had been quiet a long time by then. I had seen Her only once in recent weeks, when She came to the Garden to bequeath to me the Secret.

I washed Adam's stain from me in the pool. I stayed a long while under the waterfall. Its rumble filled my ears, its icy embrace numbed my senses. All around me, water tumbled and churned.

I dived below the surface where there was stillness and peace. I scrubbed the blood from my limbs with silt from the very depths. I scoured my insides clean of his seed.

When I was out and warmed again by the sun, I crushed the leaves of soothing aloe and healing comfrey and bathed my bruises in the sap. I sat on the rock and cradled myself. The myrtle drooped in sorrow. A bearded dove, perched on a carob tree, wept. Fat drops fell from his beady eyes, his head tilted in sympathy.

In the distance, thunder rumbled. A cloud rolled in, low and black. The dove took wing and soared. Here He comes. I steeled myself.

He boomed my name. "Lilith!"

It was as if the mountains cracked and spoke. It echoed in the plains and valleys, blasted from every crevice and cave. The leaves whispered it as they rustled in the wind. The bulrushes wailed it, bowing low to the tempestuous pool. The waterfall thundered it, *Lilith! Lilith!* as it cascaded down the rockface. The river babbled it, splashing around boulders, rushing onward to the sea.

The sound came from all around, at once inside and outside of my head. The word throbbed and pulsed through my veins. My temples bulged.

LILITH!

☽

I misled you. I did say His name, too.

It is forbidden, but words do not scare me, for I have eaten of the Tree of Knowledge, which grants mortals the Wisdom of gods, and I am Wise.

And I know the Secret.

I know that like a ram, a bull or a boar, He cannot create life alone. He did not birth us.

Asherah did.

But since She has been silent, (where did She go? Why did I not notice when She went?) He tells us that naming is Creation.

He names and it is so. He breathes and gives it life. It's why Adam loves to name things too. Naming is to man what birthing is to woman.

They can name things all they like, it does not change the truth.

Life comes from a Mother.

He cannot fool *me* as He has deceived Adam!

What can He do to me now? He is not *my* god, no Father of mine. He did not protect me! He did not avenge my violator! He thinks to punish *me* for Adam's sin! I will say His name whenever I please.

"Yahweh, Yahweh, YAHWEH!"

I screamed it from the mountaintops, I hurled it against the cliff so it rebounded one hundred times in number, but not a gnat's wing more in strength.

The Red Sea

I fled south to the ocean. Asherah was Lady of the Sea. Perhaps I'd find her there.

He sent three angels after me. Those who always delivered His pronouncements. Tearing down on beating wing, tripping over their clumsy feet in their glee to report the Shalts and Shalt Nots.

The angels found me on the shore, toes in the cooling surf.

"What have you done?" asked Senoy, wrapping his gray wings around his shoulders like a cloak.

"What any woman would."

"Return to Adam," barked ugly-browed Sansenoy.

I burrowed my feet deeper into the sand.

"It will be death to refuse," said Semangelof.

"What is death?"

"You stupid woman!"

Semangelof was by far the scariest of the three, with frown lines like cracks in granite marking his huge, bulging forehead. His thin hair bristled like an angry cat. "Death is when life's joys end. Your body will go to its grave and your soul will descend to the dark pits of Sheol, the Underworld. Never will your eye see happiness again!"

I mulled it over. "So be it."

They turned and whispered among themselves. Senoy pointed upward and grimaced. Sansenoy shivered, his feathers rustling in the wind. Semangelof bared his teeth at me like a wolf.

I laughed. They left.

The sand tickled my feet. Crabs pinched my ankles. The surf rushed back to the sea, streaming between my toes.

Above me, soared a kite. Fast and sleek, unstoppable. How easily the angels had found me. How quickly they covered that rough terrain. It had taken me weeks to reach the shore, crossing parched deserts and climbing scrabbly peaks. I had forded watery marshes, scrambled along the rock-beds of dried-up streams, grazing my knees, cutting my elbows, ever searching for the sea.

As I remembered the angels swooping down on me in their ease and audacity, there came the strangest sensation. A glowing, a budding, a humming in my back. A searing, stabbing pain, rippling outward, then folding into itself, intensifying into two distinct points, low on each shoulder blade. From each wound, something sprouted, tearing through my flesh like spears. Blood dripped heavily onto the sand. Spiny quills lengthened into silken, ivory feathers.

I plucked one and brushed it against my lips. Soft as down. Pure as a dove. The faint scent of duck eggs.

As they unfurled into their full majesty, I bowed to balance the weight. I put out my hands to break my fall, but I never reached the ground. I hovered, my glorious wings bearing me up. I cricked my neck, I arched an arm. I lurched, I staggered, I bounced. It was not elegant. But oh, soon it came to me, and I soared.

Such speed, such thrilling release! I had not found Asherah, but surely, I had won Her blessing here beside the sea. I felt full to bursting with tremendous power.

Through rushing clouds I flew. The rain yet to fall misted on my cheek. Fury and sorrow fell from me like crumbs.

High in the noontime sky I looked back upon the earth. Whales breached in the ocean, dolphins spiraled at play. Hippos hunched in shining rivers like rocks. Crocodiles basked on lotus-flowering banks. Camels loped across the desert. Horses galloped the arid plains. In the savannah, a lioness dragged a mangled gazelle to her waiting cubs.

Snow dusted the peaks of purple mountains. Wind ruffled vast forests of oak and cedar and pine. In the meadows, I saw each sharp-edged blade of grass, each tiny-petalled flower, each ant in well-kept line.

Nestled between four sparkling rivers I saw the Garden of Eden, its orchards and farmed fields. In the midst of it, both trees, the Tree of Knowledge and the Tree of Life, separate from all others, within two airy glades. The waterfall thundered into the glistening pool. A shaggy ram drank deeply from the bank.

I saw our cabin and my beloved rose garden.

There was Adam, the wicked man. He sat upon the deck of our dwelling cradling his head in his hands. His curls hung down at his shoulders, exposing the nape of his once-loved neck. Ripe for the blow of a sharp, bronze blade.

I cursed him for all the days of his life. He would be lonely now.

And I? This was my punishment? Freedom!

Bone of My Bones, Flesh of My Flesh

I circled the mountain-tops, delighting in my wings. I swooped and soared, I plummeted and plunged. Such delicious speed. I rode the currents, the warm air rushing from the south, the westerly wind that swept me toward the rising sun.

I saw things you would not believe.

Lands so green they put our Garden to shame. Prairies of swaying grass as far the eye can see. Frozen northlands, the very sea turned to tumbling ice. In the east: vast mountains so high my breath failed me. To the south: dense, boiling jungles that steamed when it rained.

I saw fish shaped like stars. Parrots that talked. Animals that jumped on hind legs, carrying their young in pouches at their belly.

I saw the earth is round. That the sun does not set nor rise. Instead, we on this giant globe rotate around it, spinning as we go, the moon in turn circling us.

I saw that we were not alone.

There were Others—everywhere. Skins darker, lighter, hair of every hue—fair like a lioness, black as ripe olives, red like amber. They were young and old, tall and short. Mothers cradled babies as helpless as newborn lambs. My stomach lurched. Once, that was my destiny. Would motherhood now be denied me? I saw old people, hunched and gray, children who stumbled and crawled. Men in their strong-armed prime like Adam. Women full and ripe like me. They were everywhere, on every continent, sailing every river, crossing every sea.

So He had lied: we were not the first. We were not the only.

The people went about their business. They harvested crops I did not know, in landscapes wild and alien to my eyes. They lived in stilted houses above marsh that was neither land nor sea; they dwelt in huts of ice. They covered their bodies with garments fashioned from animal skins, grasses too, from cloth woven and dyed in many colors.

They did things differently.

They did not worship Yahweh. All manner of gods and goddesses they praised in temples and shrines, in forests and plains, on mountaintops and in caves. They burned sweet-smelling herbs to honor their deities, made images of gods with heads of jackals, with bodies of bears, gods that looked like eagles, fish, and frogs. They wore masks and headdresses, antlers and hooves. They danced and drummed and sang. They made offerings of wine and blood.

But nowhere among this multitude of people and their gods did I see Asherah.

☽

In the Garden, Adam continued as before, believing himself the First. He carried on, obliged now to do all the work himself. He harvested the wheat. He winnowed—badly, mixing the husked and unhusked grains. Such a look on his face like thunder. He carried his bronze sword everywhere to fight his imaginary enemies, those Others I'd now seen myself, who hadn't the least knowledge or interest in his existence. How I laughed to see him earth-bound and at toil when I was so blessed.

One day, I came lower than usual, alighting on an ancient olive tree. I folded my wings and preened the feathers. They tasted delicious: of sweet nectar and freedom.

A footstep roused me. Someone stepped out of the cabin.

Another woman.

Where did she come from?

She walked, pale and clumsy, carrying an empty wooden pail listlessly at her hip. Her eyes were cast upon the ground. Her hair was the color of rain running with mud: it didn't fall in dark and lustrous coils to the small of her back like mine. She was wan and looked like she might melt. I did not think much of her.

Adam followed. "Eve!" he called from the steps of the cabin.

She turned, unsmiling.

"That's your name," he said. "I have named you Eve."

She nodded.

"Eve," he said again. He could not get enough of saying her name. "You are a woman. I named you Woman since you were from Man—me!" he grinned—"extracted."

She dipped her eyes.

"Today you must mill the flour. I will show you. I'll show you everything. Bone of my bones. Flesh of my flesh." She stared at him blankly. "You are my helpmeet." He winked.

Bone of my bones?

Flesh of my flesh?

Helpmeet?

Is he *demented*?

How can woman be made of man? Man is of woman born! He knows this, for he has seen the animals birthed. Is *he* now her *mother*?

She inclined her head and went to fetch water.

Eve, you insipid fool!

She was lucky she had me to rescue her.

☽

I found her at the pool.

She was sitting on a felled log gazing into the limpid waters. Perhaps she was looking for her reflection. If so, she was disappointed. So unremarkable was she, even the waters failed to mark her presence.

"Eve." I touched her shoulder.

She turned slowly. Every gesture she made was effortful, as if she moved underwater. She said nothing. I seemed not remotely surprising to her.

"Eve," I said again. "I have something important to tell you. Leave this place. Come with me."

She touched my wing. "Who are you?"

"Lilith," I said. As an afterthought: "An angel."

Whyever not? I, who was hereafter proclaimed a demon.

"Can women be angels?" She stroked my feathers with the back of her hand.

In answer, I unfurled the full glory of my wings and she fell backward off the log.

"Most assuredly." I helped her up.

"I cannot leave. I was made for him. I am his helpmeet."

That word again. By the power of Creation, it sparked my fury!

"No!" I shook her drooping shoulder. "You were not made for him! You were made for yourself!" She shrank and cowered on the ground.

"Eve!" Adam called, from the cabin beyond the olive grove. "Where is that water?"

"Don't go!" I urged. "There is something you must hear. He's lying to you."

But she ran, as fast as her sorry legs would carry her.

I soared west. Into the desert, where jackals roamed and owls screeched. Night fell around me. Under a solitary date palm, I brooded.

She was right. I saw it then. She *was* made for him. *Created*— somehow. *Stolen* from the outside world?—because *I* refused him. The blame for her wretched state lay heavy on my shoulders. I would have to find another way to bring her to Wisdom.

The Snake

They say He made me a demon as my punishment. But if I am a demon, it is like no other. No. I believe He had no power to thwart Asherah's design. For my wings were Her blessing. I wanted Freedom, I ached for it—and lo, did they not arrive?

I took myself away on the rushing easterly wind to wave-washed Alashiya, a sweet-smelling island cradled in the emerald sea, copper-rich, with ancient oaks and shady planes, cypresses that brushed the very heavens. A land of fishing folk and winemakers.

Though time stood still in the Garden of our Paradise, it was the season of new growth here. The hillsides flamed with golden euphorbia. Fragile narcissus and pale anemones carpeted the olive groves. Bold orchids bloomed in the meadows.

Eve had resisted me. She would not listen. If I had any hope of gifting her the Wisdom Asherah had entrusted to me, it would have to be in another guise. Among tall pines on a mountain slope, I practised. I imagined myself in other forms, as I'd been thinking of wings when they first arrived.

At first, I could only summon different body parts. Cloven hoofs that replaced my hands. An ass's tail, which pleased me, trailing in my wake, a switch to ward off flies. But it was not enough. I needed to see that which I would become, as I'd seen the angels in flight. I thought away my wings and wandered onto the hillside.

Wheatear chicks trilled from their nests, calling for food. Tender herbs sprang from the earth. The sweet and heady scent of almond blossom lured the bees from their hives. We had no bees in the Garden of Eden. We had no need for them.

Beside the blooming orchard, a stream carrying snowmelt from the mountains tumbled to the sea. The sense this aroused in me: of change and onward motion; the rightful torrent of time. You cannot imagine how I, who had never seen a honeybee before, never known the passing of seasons, let alone the full majesty of ripening spring, was dazzled by all this.

☽

The trees thinned. I emerged into a grassy field dotted with carobs. Beyond, the sea sparkled. A boat rode the gentle surf: a simple craft, painted in zigzags of white and blue that mirrored the waves. A handsome fellow stood at the helm, naked to the waist, hair slicked down his back. My blood thickened. What a trick it was to tell me Adam was the only man! This man was a thousand times more comely than he!

I watched him, tossing silver, flapping fish over his shoulder onto a growing pile in the stern. His wide shoulders glistened. As he stood to haul a net, the cloth around his loins strained taut.

I was still naked. Glorious, undoubtedly. Firm and strong. But it would not do. I needed a garment, like those I'd seen since fleeing the Garden.

My eye followed a goat-track to a pink-blossoming tamarisk tree beside a wooden hut near the shore. Linen cloths, pegged to its branches, fluttered in the wind. I stole one, wrapped it around myself as I'd seen other women do, knotted at the shoulders, tied a sash of red wool around my waist.

I smoothed the pleats of my new robe and called to the man. He continued picking out the small fry trapped in the mesh. Each tiny fish he sent back, wriggling, into the sea.

"Hail, boatman!" I called again.

This was before Babel, you understand. There were no foreign tongues. For all the good it did, because he did not answer. He continued at his work, frowning at a gash torn in the net.

Finally, he looked up, transferred his frown from the broken net to me, and, throwing the net into the hull, he began to row towards the shore. What a sight he was! His strong arms rippled, his long hair danced. The season of new life sprang up in me, made merry in my loins, and swept throughout my tingling body. As he neared the shallows, he leapt from the boat, tied it to the trunk of the nearest tree, but still he did not greet me.

I tried again. "What is your name?"

He grunted. No matter. I had not learned nothing from Adam.

"I shall call you Yem," I said. "And I am Lilith."

He brought out his catch in a reed basket, still frowning. I liked it. It said he had places to be and no time to exchange pleasantries with strangers. Adam grinned perpetually, so pleased was he with his accomplishments. It lent him the appearance of a simpleton.

Yem marched down the beach, towards a path leading to a valley between two hills. I tripped after him, struggling to keep up with his stride.

"What have you caught today?"

"Fish." He was not gifted at conversation.

"What sort of fish?"

"Big fish."

I gave up.

The track wove through low scrub of prickly gorse and sun-warmed rocks. The sea-breeze blew fresh on my back. I was not sure why I was following Yem, save that I felt compelled to draw as close to him as possible. He would show me something of the world, I was sure. If he should show me to his bed as well, so much the better.

We came to a settlement of ten or twelve huts, surrounding a stone altar. Smoke curled from incense burning in a shining metal bowl. A tall woman wearing a head-dress of crescent moons presided over a young couple. Around them, perhaps two dozen villagers.

Yem laid down his basket of fish and watched reverently. He placed his fist across his breast and chanted in time with the others.

Since my departure from Eden, I had seen many ceremonies and rituals, but none so close at hand. From afar they seemed incomprehensible, the meaning lost in symbols I could not understand. But now I felt the power of close-drawn bodies, their common purpose and goal. The beat of a drum pulsed through me as through them. The incense altered my senses; my limbs and voice joined as one with the crowd. We swayed and we nodded as to one heartbeat.

The priestess beckoned an attendant and from her basket brought out two wiry, green snakes. She held them high above the young couple's heads. She chanted, the youngsters bowed, the serpents writhed and hissed. The villagers dipped their eyes in devotion and beat fists against their breasts.

It came to me in that moment. Of course! I would bring Eve to Wisdom in snake form. Are snakes not sacred to Asherah? Are they not harbingers of Wisdom? They live their lives in cycles, in accordance with Asherah's Law. They shed their skin and are reborn anew—as Eve will shed her ignorance and step into the light of understanding. She would listen to me then, perceiving the meaning of what I had to say before I even formed the words.

The ritual completed, the young couple were crowned with fragrant stephanotis and kissed by every man and woman in the village. All dispersed to the budding vines in the fields, to a long table dressed for a feast.

Yem and I stood alone amid the whirling incense. His countenance changed. He looked at me afresh, put out his hand for mine and led me towards the feast. He set his basket beside the fire, where perspiring men turned roasting meat on a spit, and we sat at the table.

I had never drunk wine before. It was delicious; sweetened with honey and spiced with herbs, mixed with water in wooden bowls. I savoured it. Perhaps overmuch.

The villagers fell to dancing and singing. First the young couple, then them all. The men hopped and kicked, leaped, and turned. The women bunched tunics at the knee to whirl and skip in answer.

Meat was brought: salted, exquisite, fat glistening. Yem's fish arrived: charred and dressed with lemon and thyme-oil. There came flatbreads; fluffier, more delicious than my poor attempts in Eden. Fruits I had never seen before. Cakes made with honey. Nut-filled desserts. Wine flowed endlessly from patterned clay jars.

Reddening clouds breezed to the horizon, as the villagers laughed and sang. Dancers snaked around the vine, children played beneath ancient fig trees. An elderly man took up a melancholy air, accompanied by lyre and flute and drum.

The evening star had long set by the time Yem led me from the bountiful table back into the village. Beyond the flickering torches, it was dark as pitch. I clung to him, happily intoxicated by the wine, yearning for the sturdy frame of his body.

The wine had not improved his talent for conversation.

No matter.

As we fell entangled on the sheepskin of his bed, I felt it.

First in the tongue: a splitting of the tip. I hissed in his ear, my forked tines rasping against the bristles of his cheek.

The smell of him deepened. It ripened into hills and valleys, peaks and furrows. His indistinct briny aroma contracted into separate, knowable scents. Crabmeat, freshly shucked. Barnacles clinging to rotten timber. A sea-urchin blanched by sun.

As his scent overwhelmed me, my sight dimmed. I saw him in blurred shades of black and white, his strong jaw fuzzy, the heat of his body now visible, trapped in the hairs of his skin.

I stretched beside him in my lust and lengthened. My bones were crushed, breath squeezed from my lungs. My fingers fused, my arms merged into my body. My toes and legs conjoined. I was nothing but pure, hard muscle, tense with the thrill of his touch.

He seemed not in the least surprised. Nor put off. If anything, his passion swelled. I had nothing to caress him with save my smooth scales, a darting tongue, the coils of my serpentine body. I had no warm and welcoming haven for him to enter and yet . . .

It worked. I pleased him well enough, and he found ways to delight and pleasure me. That is all I have to say.

Eat and Ye Shall Be as Gods

It took a long time to find Eve alone. Adam was always there. Directing her. Critiquing. "Not like that, Eve. Like this! Knead the dough harder. You've put too much water in it, you dolt! Fan the fire. Don't let the flame die! What were you thinking?"

They were still naked, but Adam had taken to wearing a string of coral beads around his neck that clattered as he moved. I cannot say where he found the time to fashion such a thing when there was so much hoeing and herding, harvesting and husbandry to be done— nor where he'd found the coral, this far from the sea.

While Eve made the bread, he watered the Tree of Life, pouring spring water from a bronze ewer. That had been my task—not his. It was my birthright. Woman shall nurture all life, Asherah said, when She showed me what to do. Why had he taken this, of all the daily tasks, from Eve?

I watched them coupling in the manner Adam had tried to impose on me. He, holding her down, enjoying. She, underneath, enduring. Eve's unleavened bread cooled on a rack beside them, flat and dry.

The sooner I got her out of there the better.

☽

On the third day of my surveillance, she rose from one of these dismal bouts of fornication. Leaving Adam sated and snoring, she crept from the hut. She hugged herself, covering her breasts, as if she knew already the fact of her nakedness.

It was a sultry afternoon, just after noon, close and hot. The Garden hummed and dripped and drowsed. She tiptoed past the figs and palms, through spiky acanthus, crushing dusky violets underfoot. She

25

aimed for the Tree of Life as if it pulled her by a cord. I followed, slipping into the shadows whenever she glanced back to the hut and sleeping Adam.

At the Tree—a beautiful, towering date-palm—she lay flat on her belly. I transformed myself into a cormorant and flew into a low bough, to see for the better.

Sharp-eyed, open-beaked, I watched. After a while, she looked up and about in confusion, unsure what to do now she found herself there.

I swooped to the ground, exchanging the cormorant's guise for a regal asp—mid-flight, I might add, so skilled was I now in the art of transformation. I landed on the tip of my tail and reared to full height.

"Eve!" I called. She opened one eye and looked around.

"Fair Eve, resplendent Eve!"

At that, she got to her knees. To her credit, she did not recoil.

"What is this?" she asked. "How came you to speak with human voice?"

I blinked as if to say: *ah, it's nothing*. "I ate of a fruit," I said. "A fruit that gifts reason."

"Where is it?" she asked, as surely anyone would.

"Yonder." I dipped my head. Her eyes followed, across the grove, to the Tree of Knowledge, laden and heavy, boughs ripe with clusters of shining, red pomegranates.

"Oh, *that* fruit." She mimicked Adam's hectoring voice. "Thou shalt not eat that fruit, or even touch it. Lest ye die."

As I circled her, she turned on her knees, to keep her eyes on me. I raised myself to within a forked tongue of her face.

"And yet, I live. I, who have touched and tasted it many times."

She frowned at that. She was quite pretty close up. Too pale. But delicate, with a lovely arch to her brow. Sharp cheekbones and a pointed chin.

"Who told you you would die?"

"Adam," she said. "My head and guide. My bone is of his bones, my flesh of his flesh. I am his help—"

"Yes, yes, I know." Derision in snake form is hard to muster. It felt like a bone choking my throat. "And from where did he learn this warning, the man Adam?"

"From our Maker, the Almighty."

The Almighty. How quickly the lie takes root: that there is only one.

"I regret to advise you that the man, your head and guide, has been misinformed." I coiled up her body and she held me from her face as far as her arm allowed. "You have been told to shun the fruit to keep you base. The fruit brings knowledge, of what is and what must be. Of all that is good and all that is evil. It is a desirable fruit, which makes one Wise. Myself, I eat of it daily."

She looked from me to the fruit, which was so very red, so very alluring.

"It does not bring death. Far from it. Rather, it brings freedom. The eye of your mind will be opened. It will show you how to live and how to live well."

"Then why would the Almighty wish us to shun it? He is our Father. He would have us free. He would see us live well."

"Not exactly. His plans for you are . . . quite different."

I slipped from her arm and coiled upon the ground. "Have you never wondered, dear Eve, why Adam is the head and guide, while you are (I regret the insult)—the *help?*"

She shrugged her thin shoulders. "Such is the lot of women."

"Another thing you have perhaps contemplated: how is it you have a Father but no Mother?"

"What is a Mother?"

"Oh, Eve," I sighed. "This is why you must eat the fruit. You know so little. It is foolish—dangerous—to go into the world so bereft of understanding."

"Who are you?"

"A friend."

She cast her eyes to the fruit.

"Come. See it, at least. It can do you no harm."

She consented to that and padded after me twenty paces to the Tree of Knowledge.

"Eat, and ye shall be as gods, knowing good and evil," I proclaimed, as we stood (one on legs, one on tip of tail) admiring the bounty of the Tree.

"Gods?" she asked, not taking her eyes from a thick cluster of fruits weighing down a bough directly before her.

"Oh, yes, dear Eve. I have travelled the world and seen many. He is not the One and Only. Nor are divinities elsewhere all male. Has He never mentioned that?"

She shook her head, never shifting her gaze from the fruit.

"I suppose not," I sighed. "It is not convenient if you are to be—" I mouthed the distasteful word—"a *helpmeet*."

She looked at me now, our eyes level. She plucked a pomegranate. Turned it over, admired its sheen, the perfect calyx, a bloom unfolding. She plunged one sharp thumbnail into it, tearing apart the stringy flesh. Ambrosial scent flooded the air. The rubied seeds sat plump and glistening within. She devoured them, crimson juice dripping from the corners of her mouth like blood.

She ate like she was possessed.

And as she ate, I saw the light of reason flicker in her eyes. A rash of understanding spread, as she became possessed of Wisdom. I knew what she was feeling. I'd felt it too, when I first tasted the fruit. I knew the cold waves of truth that were crashing upon her like surf on the shore. The cool, clear current of logic that swept away the chaos of her mind. She, like I before her, was emerging from the ocean depths, gulping for air as the waves retreated.

She blinked. "You are a woman too!"

I shuddered out of my asp's guise and became myself once more.

"It's you!" she gasped. "The angel, Lilith!"

"Indeed."

"Woman is not made from man!"

"No. It was a lie."

"Rather, man is born from woman!"

"Indisputably."

"Adam is not my lord! I am his equal!"

"Absolutely!"

She looked at my tunic. "I'm naked!" She panicked, covering her breasts with one arm, her sex with the other.

"It doesn't matter. There is nothing sinful about your body." I wiped the morbid juice from her mouth with the hem of my gown.

"Good and evil are not separate nor external!"

"No," I sighed. "Both abide in all of us."

"We are not masters of this world!"

"We are born of it. We must cherish and protect it as it sustains us."

"And where is She?" She looked about, sweat gathering on her brow, beading on her nose. "Where is the Holy Mother? From whom all life and Wisdom flows, our Creator. Where has She gone?"

"All in good time, Eve. That's why I'm here."

The Temptation of Adam

"I must tell Adam," she whimpered.

"What? Why? This is not for him!"

"Because he needs to know. About everything. These truths should not be secret! How can we live in harmony and balance, if he knows nothing of it? How can he know I am his equal? That we are of this world, not set above it? That together we must protect it, as it nourishes and sustains us! That death is part of life. One day we shall die, that our children may live? That we are given reason, and must use it to question, and come to Wisdom, that one day, we shall be wise enough to become our own gods in this earthly realm!"

"He won't believe it! He has his reasons. Don't tell him you've eaten the fruit. Come with me."

"Lilith!" A single tear streamed down her cheek. "How can you be so *unkind*? I must save him as you saved me!"

"He does not want to be saved! He likes his ignorance. It suits him."

"What have you against Adam?" She narrowed her eyes. "Did he spurn you?"

Wisdom begets wisdom, and she gulped as the obvious truth washed over her. "He was yours before mine! I am not the first woman!"

"Look, Eve—we don't have time for this. We have to leave before Yah—"

"Don't say His name!" She fanned her fingers to cool her burning face. "Oh, heavens aflame, I forgot about Him! What will He do?" She pulled at the roots of her hair like a wild thing.

"Calm yourself, Eve! That's why we have to leave. He has no power beyond this Garden. He has a following of one, if you will only come

30

with me." I tugged her arm, but she pulled it back to cover her body once more.

"Listen, Eve." I took her shoulders. "I hardly understand the compact between this man and his god. Who is leading whom, what conspiracy they have dreamed together. But their plans come to nothing if you walk away. Our heavenly Mother is missing. Adam tried to rule me—and he will crush you too if you stay. What can they make of Creation with no Woman? Show them what it means to scorn and degrade us! To tell us we are helpmeets, fit only to serve and lie beneath. I will find you something to cover yourself if it bothers you so much. But we must leave—now!"

She stood there, arms wrapped around herself, rigid with fear. And then she ran. Streaming through the thicket, uncaring of bramble or thorn, scratched by low-hanging boughs, tripped by trailing vines, trampling buds underfoot, straight to the cabin where Adam slept.

By all God's demons, the stupid girl.

Now she was for it.

☽

Now what, now what? Oh, He was coming, I felt it in the air. Taut as the gut-strings in a tortoiseshell lyre. Tense like a July thunderstorm.

The blossom on the trees withered and fell to the ground. The animals withdrew, tails trailing.

Abandon Eve to her fate, or remain and face His wrath?

I stayed, more from curiosity than loyalty. There was nothing I could do for her now. I had delivered her to Wisdom. Led her to the forking path. She had chosen badly.

I assumed an asp's form once more and slithered after her.

☽

Adam was on the porch, bleary-eyed and confused.

"You *what*?" he said, over and again. "You ate the fruit? That thou shalt not touch?"

"Yes!" she cried, not knowing whether to cover herself or wipe away the snotty mess streaming from her nose. "But it's not as you said! It brings truth and freedom. Knowledge of death, not death itself. There is so much you must learn."

"*You* presume to tell *me* what I must learn? You came from me! Bone of my bones. Flesh of my flesh." He brought an accusing finger to her breastbone. "You *belong* to me."

"Oh, Adam," she sniffed, pushing him away. "Don't be so stupid. I didn't come from you. Look at me! I am a person, of woman born, just like you. How could I be made from your rib? Open your eyes! This is why you must eat the fruit, your head is filled with falsehoods and superstition."

"Me? No way." He paced the deck. "You can't trick me that easily. He said, thou shalt not eat, and I shalt not eat. I can follow basic instructions." He kicked her shin and she stumbled aside. "Not like you."

"I will tell Him," she pleaded. "I will tell Him it was my idea."

But Adam continued in his rage, kicking the timbers of his house. "Perfidious woman! Treacherous female! What is wrong with you all? I have plenty more ribs. He shall make me another woman!"

From my hiding-place amid the boughs of an oak, I stifled a laugh. How many more wives can he get through? Eve hadn't yet seen out a week! The man was wife-repellent!

Eve drew herself to fullest height, abandoning all attempts to shield her naked breasts. "Then I suppose," she said haughtily, "you shall have to accept that I will always know more than you. You shall remain forever like a boar, wallowing in the mud of your ignorance, while I walk the bright vale of righteousness, in the full noontime of understanding."

The fruit had lent her a poetic turn of phrase, I'll give her that. I felt something like motherly pride.

She descended the steps of the cabin. "And Adam," she called over her shoulder. "You have no idea how ridiculous you look, walking around naked like that. No one wants to see that thing swinging about between your legs. Put it away!"

Banished

He followed her—of course. He ate the fruit—of course.
It had a strange effect on him. His eyes didn't light up, as had Eve's and mine before her. He gulped as if the pomegranate were hard to swallow. He blinked as if it tasted bitter.

"Well?" demanded Eve. "Do you see? Now do you understand?"

"Oh, I understand alright." He dashed the fruit to the floor. "You have tricked me! Seduced me to commit this mortal sin. Now I too will face His Almighty wrath!"

Eve's eyes narrowed. "What did you learn? That we are equal, two halves, who must live in harmony? That we are of this world and must cherish it, as it sustains us? That we must use our reason to question and come to Wisdom, to live one day as gods ourselves?"

He looked shiftily to one side. His thumbs worked circles on his thighs. "Not that mumbo jumbo," he spat. But none of what she said surprised him.

He fixed his gaze on a drooping cedar limb behind her. "I learned that our bodies are sinful. We shall never be gods! For there is but One, who must be obeyed. I learned His authority flows through me—and only me!—for I am the lord of all. Master of the creeping things, the flying things—" His eye fell on my serpentine form. "And slithering things." I ducked from the stick he hurled my way. "And you!" he pointed at Eve. "Most of all, I am master of you, because you are Woman made of Man. All these things are mine to do with as I will, because I am foremost of God's works. My seed and my seed alone shall populate the earth! I shall fill it and subdue it! I shall have dominion over every living thing that moves!"

She nodded, though her face betrayed little in the way of agreement. "God, you say. Just the one?"

"And I learned," Adam went on, "that death can be overcome, for we shall have life eternal if we live by His law. We shall cast aside these sinful forms and live forever alongside He who made us in the kingdom of heaven."

"Sinful forms?" Eve scoffed. "*He* who made us? Where did you get this nonsense? Whose purpose does it serve?"

Adam looked sheepishly at the ground.

"And what of Asherah?" Eve continued. "What did you learn in the fruit of Her?"

"Asherah!" he jeered, overly dramatic as ever. "There is no Asherah! Never was. Woman cannot be divine! Have you gone mad?"

Eve turned on her heel.

Adam was lying. He had known Asherah, as I had. In our earliest days, She was more than a heavenly presence. She had been an earthly Mother too. Like me, he had felt Her enveloping warmth, had suckled at Her breast. Why did he deny Her now?

He kicked the ground, like a petulant child. Then he picked up the half-eaten pomegranate and threw it as far as he could. It landed with a splash in the pool.

☽

He rumbled in, as I knew He would. It was the cool and breezy time of day, but the rustling leaves were silenced, the birds were stilled, the pool was flat. He came: a blazing ball of light that burned the eye, a humming felt sharp in the roots of my teeth.

"Adam!" He called. "Adam, my child, where art thou?"

So much for all-knowing. How can He not see the man there, trembling, crouched within that gnarled and ancient juniper tree?

In asp's form, I hissed to draw attention to him.

Adam jumped. He covered his nakedness with both hands. What did he think? That his organ was so mighty, it would offend its Creator?

"I hid," Adam mumbled. "I heard You coming and was afraid, since I am naked."

"Who told you you were naked?" He boomed. "Hast thou eaten of the fruit of the Tree I commanded thee to shun?"

"The woman! She whom you made for me. She jabbers and whines so like a never-silent bell. She gave me the fruit and bade me eat."

Yahweh sighed, a great tornado of a sigh that whisked the leaves from the trees and sent them spiralling into the air. "And if the woman told you to jumpeth off a cliff," He thundered, "would you?"

In desperation, Adam pointed to me. "The serpent," he whimpered. "The serpent beguiled the woman."

I felt the force of His blinding gaze upon me. "Thou!" He roared. "What hast thou done? Thou art cursed above all creatures. More than cattle and wild beasts! Thou shalt go upon thy belly, and eat dust all the days of thy life!"

As He said it, I slumped to the ground, no longer able to hold myself upright with dignity.

"I will put enmity between thee and the woman, between thy offspring and hers. They shall bruise thy head, and thou shalt bruise their heel!"

I wasn't sure what that meant but it hardly mattered. I did not intend to continue much longer as a snake. I would bruise no one's heel and permit no one to bruise my head.

There was a rustle in the bushes behind us as Eve emerged into the clearing. She was wearing a garment fashioned from fig leaves and vines. The dark green suited her. She seemed taller. No longer did she dither and droop, she trod firmly, chin angled in dissent.

"The serpent meant only to help," she said.

Oh, Eve.

"She wanted only to tell us how to live. To give us Wisdom, Asherah's eternal truths, that one day we might become wise enough to be our own gods."

The Garden fell completely silent. Every living thing held its breath. The distant flow of the four sparkling rivers was stilled. There was a rushing of the winds. An intake of His breath. The roar of it released.

"Do not tell Me what the serpent meant! I will multiply thy sorrows!"

His voice was shrill. The volume deafening.

"I shall make your pains in childbirth most severe! In sorrow and grievous torture thou shalt bring forth children! Thy desire shall be to your husband, and he shall rule over you!"

The Voice turned to Adam. "Why hast thou listened to this woman? Art thou not the man? Cursed is the ground for thy sake! In sorrow shalt thou eat of it all the days of your life! Thorns and thistles it shall bring forth! In sweat you shall toil until you return to the ground, for dust thou art and to dust you shall return!"

"Behold!" He screeched, hysterical now—a god of such passion. "The man has become like one of Us, knowing good and evil!"

"Us?" dared Eve.

"I meant *Me*!" He roared. "Now, lest he put out his hand and take also of the Tree of Life and live forever, send them forth! Let them till the ground whence they were taken!"

I was not sure at whom this order was directed, but now I saw the angels Senoy, Sansenoy, and Semangelof hovering at the edge of the blinding light, nodding grimly. The light brightened to pierce the eye, then diminished. The hum ratcheted to an ear-splitting shriek, before extinguishing entirely.

The angels alighted on the ground before us.

Fists clenched, jaws set, Senoy and Semangelof entered the cabin. From within came the crash of pots breaking, timbers splintering. The urns and jars I had crafted with such care were thrown from the window, smashing into a thousand pieces on the stony ground.

Sansenoy picked up a fallen juniper bough and beat it into his palm as he advanced towards the unhappy pair. He drove Adam and Eve from the clearing, through the groves of olive and carob, out of the Garden to where the wild oleander grows. They left with nothing but Eve's leafy gown, the necklace of coral at Adam's throat, and the welts on their backs from Sansenoy's switch.

Semangelof emerged from the cabin bearing Adam's great bronze sword. He sliced the bloom from every stem in my rose garden, then marched to the Tree of Life and drove the sword into the earth before it. How it shone and glistened in the sun; it seemed to blaze with flames! The angels took up sentry posts around the Tree, their backs to the trunk, faces marked with thunder. They paraded around it, a march of ludicrous precision.

No one took any notice of me. I slunk off, condemned to travel on my belly until I was away from that cursed place.

☽

Adam and Eve fled Eden to the east, so I went west. Beyond the Garden I resumed human form. I put away my wings and walked as penance, for I had failed.

In the time to come, Eve would be reviled. Her disobedience, so it was claimed, the root of all Sin—the origin of Death itself. What power this one woman had! What an achievement—to invent *Death* against the wishes of an ever-loving god! So, Eve's sin would justify the abuse of women thereafter. As she succumbed to temptation, so would her daughters. As she led man astray, so would all women who followed. Henceforth, all women would be punished for the sake of Eve. All must be ruled and restrained, kept close by their lords and masters. For females are the devil's gateway. Evil and duplicitous, gullible, untrustworthy.

To me, her one act of disobedience was her saving grace. Not sin, but Wisdom and consciousness were her gifts to mankind. Knowledge of death, not death itself. But she threw it all away. That is why *I* reviled her. She chose the peacock Adam over me. Servitude to a man for all the days of her life instead of freedom. And her reward? From He whom she tried to appease? She was cursed, with all her daughters thereafter, to bring forth children in agonising childbed, to be reduced beneath her husband's authority to his servant, his *helpmeet*. She had no one to blame but herself.

I shunned the people who lived in these lands, keeping far from the fertile meadows and water-fed valleys where their black tents huddled like wolves. My path lay otherwise, through barren deserts and rocky canyons, bereft of tree or shrub or herb. I did not eat, nor did I wash. My hair grew lank, my muscles weak, my tongue was parched. By day the whirling eagle and spitting cobra were my only companions. By night, the screeching jackal and swooping owl stalked me from the rear.

Onwards I walked, in blistering heat and biting wind. Scoured by sand, feet burned by scorching rock. Until, one day, I came to a vast chasm I could not cross. Too deep to descend, too wide a void to leap. I considered my wings, but I did not deserve them. I, who once was human, had failed all of those to come.

I lay and felt the solid ground beneath me. I watched the wisps of cloud scud past. The veil of night fell. Thousands of stars, like so many watchful, judging eyes, winked upon me.

Countless days and nights passed like this.

I don't know how long I remained rooted to this lonely spot. I cannot say how many times I charted the sun's path across the sky or traced the bright stars wheeling through the heavens. I lay and I observed. Until one day my view was disturbed by something most unexpected. Something feather-scented, shining, heavenly.

Someone, I should say.

He had found me. At last, he had found me!

Part Two
SHEOL
2650BC

Her ways are ways of death
and her paths are paths of sin.
She steps out towards Sheol.
None who enter there will ever return,
and all her successors shall sink into the Pit.

Dead Sea Scrolls

Edom Desert

His face hove into view, blocking the light.

"There you are!" a bright voice said. The sun shone a halo around dark curls.

"Here I am." I did not move.

He shifted onto hands and knees to lean over me. "Is it—perhaps—time to get up? You've been there a goodly long while." He held his head, cat-like, to one side.

"What do you care?"

"I've been looking for you."

"Who are you?"

"Come now. You know me, Lilith."

His face was shadowed, it was hard to make out his features. At his shoulders, the sun reflected off the tips of folded wings. But he was none of the angels I knew. He had not Senoy's grim face nor Sansenoy's brutish brow, none of Semangelof's sharpened, wolfish teeth. I took the arm he offered to help me to my feet.

No, he was entirely unfamiliar. How could anyone forget such a face? A straight nose, eyes like honey, unkempt stubble on square jaw. A prominent, divine bow on his full and godly lips. He was sublime, an image of incomparable beauty.

"Why have you been looking for me?"

"We outcasts must stick together." He grinned.

"You are an outcast?"

"The very first." He lifted his chin with pride.

I looked at him again. A flicker of recognition, nothing more.

"If you can't remember me, surely you've heard of me? It is I," he winked, "Samael—Angel of Death!" He crossed his arms over his bare, and frankly magnificent, chest.

I shook my head.

"Look, do you think we could continue this in the shade?"

He blinked against the sun and nodded towards a solitary, ragged cypress tree I had not noticed before. I followed him. Once we were planted, the spiny trunk scratching our backs, he kissed my hand.

"I'm sorry," I said. "I know no Samael." Such a pity to disappoint his eager, puppyish eyes.

"Lilith." He sighed. "Stop toying with me. I've been searching for you for centuries. Now that I've found you, don't make me turn away again and leave you to your lonesome misery."

"Centuries?"

"A millennium and more! Since you—and I for that matter—left Paradise."

How could this be? Two weeks, possibly. Maybe three. But centuries? "How can this be true?"

"Time runs differently for us, surely you know that? Hundreds of mortal years may pass in one celestial day."

"How many celestial days has it been?"

"Oh, a handful."

"And how many mortal years?"

"Ye gods, Lilith, I don't know. I don't keep score for the little people."

"Then am I now . . . immortal?"

"You and I both." He winked.

"How—why?"

"Because you left. You escaped God's curse. *Unto dust shalt thou return*, He said. For all mankind. But not for you."

I licked my teeth. Tasted satisfaction there.

"Might He not curse me still?"

"Oh, He'll try." Samael flicked a lock of ill-behaved hair from his sparkling eyes. "But He's a local god, with little reach. He has few believers beyond this narrow realm."

I pondered his words. Contemplated the dust at my feet.

"Then tell me: what has gone on in the world, since I came here?"

He picked up a fallen cypress spray and brushed the feathery leaves against his upper lip.

"Not much," he mused. "Adam found sorrow in the world outside Eden. He tilled the earth, bringing forth thorns and thistles as much as crops. No more magical fecundity for him! He ate only what he raised by the sweat of his brow from his toil in the fields. Then he died."

"He's dead?" I surprised myself. There was not the sweetness of revenge I might have felt.

"Oh, don't worry," said Samael. "He reached a good age. Nine hundred and thirty."

Nine hundred and thirty? Despite what he'd said about celestial time, I hadn't taken it in. I looked about me. Merely desert and canyon, the same red sand and blue sky, just as before. A flash of green in the distance betrayed the odd tree. A mountain range shimmered, hazy in the heat. It was no different from when I arrived. There was no sign of human habitation or advance.

"And you," Samael said. "I see you've given up grovelling on thy belly, eating dust all the days of thy life."

I ignored that. "And Eve? Does she live still?"

"Oh no. She died before Adam. Who knows how old she was, though. No one remembered. She's merely the mother of mankind. Her sorrows were greatly multiplied. In grievous pain she brought forth her offspring."

"A mother? They had children?" The thought burned like fire.

Samael reclined on his side. He tucked his wings neatly behind him and propped his head casually on one elbow. Angels had started wearing loincloths, I observed, since the days when Senoy, Sansenoy, and Semangelof roamed the skies as God's hired thugs, brutish, and naked.

"You'll like this," he smiled. "They had two sons: a farmer and a shepherd. As oafish and vain as their father. Always fighting. Then the shepherd made a better gift to Yahweh: a firstling of his flock. So his brother killed him and was cursed."

Samael roared with laughter. Really, he was very comely when he laughed. His eyes twinkled, his perfect ivory teeth glinted. His chest rippled with each hearty guffaw.

"No—" he recovered himself and raised three fingers. "Three sons. Later, there was a third. And it is from he, Seth, that the tribes of men are now descended."

"From him," I asked, "and whose womb?"

"Oh, who cares about wombs," said Samael. "That's not why I'm here. I didn't spend this long looking for you to chat about mankind's family history."

He held my eye and exploded with fury. "I can't believe you don't remember me! I used to watch you in the Garden. With that clown, Adam. No wonder you left him. You were the height of Creation from the very first. Never bettered, never equalled. Not since has there been a woman like you. This lot," he waved dismissively into the distance, towards the unseen valleys filled with goats-hair tents, the flocks and shepherds I had left behind, "they're meek and dull. I'm bored, so very bored, of tricking these women—and the men, for that matter—into lying with me. They age so quickly and so terribly. Exquisite young maidens one day, dumpy matrons the next. Lithe youths become paunchy men. They sag and they droop, Lilith. They bloat."

He stroked my leg lazily with his foot, vast disappointment clouding his face. "But look at you. Still in your prime. Your beauty will never fade. I've never forgotten you. How could I?"

His foot strayed to my inner thigh, tracing a tender path from ankle to my loins. "Never will your fruit wither on the vine. Your blossom shall not rot and fall. Forever will *your* fig remain ripe and alluring."

He pressed at the place that burned at the parting of my legs, to make his point known. "Come with me, Lilith. What a life we could have together. What games we shall play!"

The nearness of him excited me beyond all measure. It had been a long time since I had known Man—and this one truly was the exemplar of his sex. I breathed him in. He was musk and ambrosia, honey and sweat. His wings rippled in thrilled anticipation, his loincloth peaked.

He kissed me from ear to toe, lingering, much occupied, at my sex.

"Imagine, Lilith!" His voice came furred with lust. "What glories of angelic fornication might we attain together? Forever!"

Must I be honest?

He had me at "height of Creation."

Let There Be Light!

"I do remember you," I sighed.

We had indeed attained glories of angelic fornication, as he put it, right there, under the cypress tree. Celestial passion soars to heights that cannot be scaled by mere mortals. It is sharper, more sublime and blindingly ecstatic, than man or woman can ever know. I found myself, there and then, wedded to Samael, irretrievably; the unrelenting delights of his body, his lips on mine, my breath and my bread, thereafter.

"I saw you once," I said. "In a carob tree. I mistook you for a bird. But you were weeping."

Samael shifted under me, moved his arm. "I wasn't crying!"

"You were."

I thought it odd. But everything was odd in that place. A weeping dove with handsome, bearded face, no more nor less astonishing than the wheat, which grew without seed, or the apple trees eternally in fruit, but never in bud.

"I knew I was leaving," said Samael. "I knew He was coming for me. I feared I'd never see you again."

"Why did He come for you?"

"Oh, the usual. You should know as well as anyone. I defied Him."

"How?"

Dusk was gathering. In the distance, the mountaintops glowed. The setting sun lit a streak of green-glowing malachite in the tallest peak. The evening star—Asherah's own—flickered as it rose.

"It's a long story," Samael said. "Are you sure you want to know?"

I settled into the crook of his arm and urged him to continue.

☽

46

"In the beginning," he said, "I was alone. When the Earth was unformed and void, before the heavens were made firm, before the horizon was fixed, I was the darkness on the face of the waters.

"For aeons uncounted, for epochs immeasurable, nothing changed. Time itself stood still. You cannot imagine the boredom! Then from the depths, something stirred. Rock cracked. Scalding vapours bubbled to the surface. Forged in fire and water, wrought from opposites: from light and dark, from heat and cold, from wet and dry, something emerged. A Spirit lay, exhausted, hovering over the waters. From formlessness, matter coalesced. The Spirit of Creation cried: *Let there be light!* And there was light, wrenched from me and of me, thereafter forevermore apart.

"I watched as the world was made. As the fountains gushed forth and the mountains sprang up. As the limits of the seas were assigned and the foundations of the earth were set. I saw the making of the grass, the herb-yielding seed and the fruit-bearing tree. The first creatures arrived: those tiniest life-forms, invisible to the eye. Then the jellies, the sponges, the snails. I saw the great lizards that lumbered across the earth. Later, the coming of the beasts, both the clean that chew the cud and the unclean with undivided hoof. The fowl and whales and every living creature that moveth. The cattle and the creeping things. The winged birds that fly across the firmament of heaven. The breathless fish that swarm and aboundeth in the waters. A long time after that, I saw the first people. Not you," he put a hand to my arm. "Not yet. They were different. More like apes than men. They hooted and grunted rather than spoke, but grew, in time, to walk and talk in their own way.

"Throughout all this, I watched as the Spirit altered and dissembled. No longer ineffable, but personified, as the first humans emerged. Manifest in an infinite variety of forms, coexistent, in different places, all at once. For countless ages, in every mind that conceived of a Maker, She was the Creatrix. The heavy-bosomed, wide-hipped Mother of All. As humans discerned the role of a father in generating new life, She acquired consorts: the first male gods, junior at first, then growing in seniority. As human life and experiences advanced, She expanded into pantheons. She manifested as goddesses of the earth, thunder gods of the sky, shimmering water divinities of the sea. She became deities of Wisdom, Nature, and Mischief. Of Memory, War and Music, called and moulded into being from the divine essence of that first Creative Spirit by the people who needed them. Of different natures and qualities, according to the time and place, each of varying importance, as their virtues met the needs of the people they served.

"At Eden, the Spirit settled into the Lady Asherah and the Lord Yahweh, separate and equal—not yet at each other's throats. They created you and Adam both, in the mirror of Their own images, and a Paradise for you to live in. You were to be a new start. The pinnacle of Creation. For the first time since the light was torn out of me, I was not alone."

I felt breathless, as if I were reeling through the vastness of the universe. Everything I thought I knew toppled in the spinning wheel of my mind. Since leaving Paradise, I had learned the world was far wider than Eden. That people elsewhere lived and thrived. But the enormity of Samael's revelation hit like a hammer blow. As Adam and I had not been the first, neither was Yahweh—nor even the Holy Mother Asherah! They too were born of something else: the Spirit of Creation birthed from the very earth. How much had existed for so long before humans ever breathed! Eden, and all that I'd known, merely one corner of this world—one thread!—in the vast tapestry of Creation. It baffled the mind!

Samael perceived my bewilderment. "I haven't finished." His fluttering fingers drummed my back. "Indeed, I have barely begun."

"Go on. Tell me of your defiance."

He took a deep breath and continued.

"As you grew into womanhood, I ached for you. I wanted you. I rejoiced in you. I desired you. But you, too, were kept from me and I was suffered only to observe. I watched as Adam corrupted the natural state of your Paradise. As harmony was disrupted and balance overturned. As he started on his path to exploit all he had been given, to control his mate and dominate his world.

"They had made me the first angel. It befitted me, as Darkness, to take my place as the Angel of Death. This was my allotted role. I would attend to you and Adam, to your offspring, to prepare and comfort you at that hallowed time. But I was ousted long before that. For all angels were made to bow before Adam. Forced to grovel to a mere man. You, I would have bowed to." He kissed me. "No question. But not that vain and boorish man. To put Adam above me, alongside a woman he did not deserve and treated so ill! I could not bear it."

He picked up a cypress cone and tossed it angrily from hand to hand.

"I sought God, and I asked: "Why have You set him above me? I was here first and yet You favour the man Adam over me!" You can imagine how that went down. He was wroth, Lilith—mighty wroth. His lips were filled with fury. His tongue was a consuming fire. There was storming rain, blinding lights, hailstones, brimstone—the works. You know what He's like.

"He demoted me. Darkness, from which light was conceived—can you imagine? Now I was nothing. A fallen angel, shunned by all." He crushed the cypress cone and threw the shards far into the distance.

"Not by all." I kissed his full lips. "Could Asherah not have spoken for you? She understood darkness. She knew your import."

"Oh, it was far too late for that."

A shadow passed over his face. He mastered a smile.

"What do you mean?"

"I did something foolish, dear Lil. Something rather—in fact, very—ill-advised."

"What did you do?"

He blew a coil of hair from my face. His breath smelled of honey and wine, of all things sweet and good.

"I planted a tree."

They Shall Be as Gods

"I see," said I. "A tree, perhaps, of Knowledge?"

He nodded. A mischievous smile.

"A tree with luscious and alluring fruit, ambrosial in aroma, divine and irresistible to the eye?"

"That's the one!"

"A tree to make one Wise? That bestows knowledge of good and evil and all else besides. That grants mortals Wisdom. The gift of Asherah, Mother of All, Incarnation of the formless Spirit of Creation, Keeper of all Natural Law?"

"Yup!" He jerked both thumbs towards his grinning face. "That was me!"

"Why didn't He uproot it?"

"He can't. It has Her protection, still."

"Did She give it to you?"

"Not . . . exactly."

"Then how did you come by it?"

"Don't get mad at me, dear Lil . . ."

"*Where* did you find it?" I pummelled his ribs.

He coughed and pushed my fists away. "Well. It was like this."

☽

"I was walking one evening, in Eden," he said. "I'd been watching you as usual with the bonehead Adam, disporting yourselves in delight. It was torture to me. Mightily heartsick and lonesome, I walked up the hillside to the parting of the rivers.

"Near the top of the hill, in the meadow where the wild sage grows, I heard Them. At first, just the clear strings of Her lyre picking out a three-note melody. His low voice, alongside it. He was pestering Her to sing His favourite song. You know, the one about the stars and the moon on water. She was annoyed, resisting. I crept close enough to see Her lay the lyre aside and say: 'It is time, dear One.'

"'It certainly is,' said He. There was a rustling and some laughing, then She said, 'No, not time for that, thou horny old Goat. It's time to give our children the greatest gifts.'

"'Not this again!' He thundered. 'Those gifts are not for them. Would you have them be as gods, like Us? All-knowing and as Wise?'

"'Perhaps not *so* wise.' She smiled. Do you remember Her smile, Lilith? As bright as the noontime sun." He looked down, wistful.

"Anyway," Samael continued. "She said: 'Why else create them, if not to see them grow? To advance—and yes, perhaps, in time, replace Us. To choose to live well, in balance and harmony. To bring forth new life themselves, to create their own children, conscious of their actions, responsible for them. They shall be their own gods, with judgement and reason. They shall have free will.'

"'They're not ready,' He grumbled, then shrieked: 'They will never be ready!'

"'Dear Heart.' She stroked His whiskery cheek. 'It is their birthright. What loving parent would not step aside in time?'

"'This one.' He pointed at His vast chest, then grabbed Her lyre and cast it into the sky. Up it soared, retreating to a shining pinprick. There was a pause, in which the fate of humankind turned. Where other possibilities danced; different destinies bloomed. Then gravity prevailed. The lyre fell and smashed upon the ground, the tortoiseshell broken beyond repair, the horn keys split, the strings curled and broken, never more to play.

"She said nothing, but rose and walked away. Out of Eden, towards the river. I followed Her, of course. She travelled south, by the willowy banks of the Euphrates. I kept a safe distance on foot. And before long, I realised She was being followed."

"By whom?"

"Guess!" said Samael, grimacing. "One grim, one ugly, one wolfish."

Those three! Found wherever my peace is disturbed. "And what did you do?"

"What could I do? There was one of me and three of them, and Semangelof is terrifying, as you know."

He gave a passable impression of Semangelof baring his sharpened teeth and I laughed. Samael went on. "I watched, hidden behind a rock. They took Her. They bound Her hands and feet with hemp and gagged Her with a filthy cloth. They held a rag soaked in valerian to Her nose to make Her drowsy. Then they carried Her away, flying south."

This, I should have expected. Of course, *He* was at the root of Her disappearance. "So how did you find the Tree?"

"I knew where She was going. I'm not just a pretty face, my love. Don't forget I was here first. Long before these upstart gods. Before any of these man-summoned deities dared to eff the ineffable. So I knew where She came from. Before."

"Before what?"

"Before She was Asherah, Lilith. Keep up! All gods have a local place, from where they draw their power—from the people who called them into being. He is from round here, but She's not. She's much older. She came from elsewhere, at the cry of an earlier people. At Uruk in Sumer."

"Uruk?" I'd never heard of it.

"The cradle of civilisation. South of Eden. A princely city between the wide Euphrates and the mighty Tigris. That's where She was going when the angels took Her. What's more, I knew exactly where in Uruk She was headed. To Her famous garden. You've heard of that, surely?"

I had not.

"By all the gods, Lilith! For someone who has tasted of the Tree of Knowledge, you know virtually nothing. So," he shook his head at my ignorance, "that's where I went.

"It's a beautiful city, Lilith. A shame you never saw it. Vast gates as high as heaven mark its entrance, flanked by lions and gigantic pillars. Within: a maze. Houses, workshops, and stalls skirt the temples of limestone, one for every god there adored, each with a holy ziggurat rising to the sky. Canals weave through it all, glistening in the sun.

"Outside the city, surrounded by towering walls, lies a garden. Aqueducts, bringing water from both great rivers, give it away. Inside, it's impossible to mistake for any but the garden of a god. The heavenly scent of jasmine cloaks the air, so thick you could cut it with a knife. Figs and all sweet things in plenty, always ripe. You'll remember that trick of the gods from your Paradise, Lil. And the jewels—you should see them! Fruits of carnelian, leaves of lapis lazuli, bushes bearing emeralds and pearls. It puts your rustic Eden to shame."

"And the Tree?" I urged him. "Tell me about the Tree."

"It stood in the centre of the garden. The crowning glory. She watered it. She kept it safe. I didn't like to take it, Lil. Nothing good comes from stealing from the gods. But it was *yours*. Asherah was taken to stop you tasting that fruit. It was your inheritance. You know, I'd do anything for you. So I dug it up and brought it to Eden."

It didn't make sense. "But She came to me and told me to eat from it. How is that possible if She was already gone before the Tree was planted?"

Samael smiled. "That was me. Not bad, eh? Did you think you were the only one with a gift for transformation?"

I was angry then. The dented pride of being tricked, as I'd fooled Eve. "Why did you never tell me this before?"

"Because you're like smoke on the wind! First you ran away. By the time I found out you'd returned, you'd already caused the Fall of Man—which, by the way, I knew at once was your work. It had your fingerprints all over it. Then you were gone again. Slithered away," he laughed. "I've been looking for you ever since. Now I've found you, I've told you all. You're entirely up to date."

"I wish you hadn't told me!" I cried, shamed, like a child. "I should have known all this. I knew She was gone. What use was my understanding if I didn't even question it? How did I profit from the Wisdom granted by Her tree? It was wasted on me."

"You didn't eat the fruit until after She disappeared," he pointed out.

But I was lost in self-pity. "How did I go on, occupied with my own petty concerns? My revenge on Adam—a mere mortal, now dead and gone. Saving Eve, who would not be saved. None of it mattered."

"You're too hard on yourself." Samael wound his fingers through mine. "Mortals can be delightful. Diverting—for a while. But you should leave them behind now. You belong with me."

He pulled me to him.

"And do you belong with me?" I asked.

"Absolutely. You're all I've ever wanted since I first caught sight of you."

"Then come." I pulled him to his feet. "We've no time to waste."

"Where are we going?"

"To rescue Asherah, of course! To restore Her to Her rightful place. Then no longer will we be outcasts. You and I, my fallen angel, we shall regain Paradise!"

Return to Eden

"This is not what I had in mind," Samael said, as he tripped along beside me. "I hadn't planned a quest."

We journeyed east on foot, putting away our wings for fear of attracting attention. Beyond the valley I'd withdrawn to for so long, the world had changed. It was busier: the flocks of goats roaming the hillsides more numerous, the tents sturdier, more widely spread out along the valleys. As we neared the fertile land beside the Euphrates, we saw low buildings of stone, wells at the meeting places of dusty roads, fields of barley and corn watered by a grid of canals Adam could only have dreamed of.

"I thought we might elope," said Samael. "Enjoy eternity together. Make up for lost time. A thousand years; that's a lot of lost time."

"Yes, yes. We will. After this great wrong has been righted. When we're restored to our rightful places. We can't let Him get away with it."

"Why do you care? We could go anywhere. We never have to see Him again. He has no power beyond His believers. We could go to Harappa—you'd love it there. It's the very latest in modern living. We'd punt on the Indus, hunt antelope, live in luxury. Or go to Caphtor, to Dicte's isle, and the shining palace at Knossos. You should see it, Lilith. They know how to live! Drinking and dancing, loving and feasting. You can sleep in a bed, Lilith, imagine that! No more reposing on the stony ground. Clean linen every day, perfumed oil to scent your hair."

"She chose *me*, Samael. *I* was to be granted Wisdom above all others. How can I let Her down? My own *Mother*! Taken—because of me!—and banished who knows where. If I don't find Her, who will?"

"But—"

"And in Her absence, He has broken natural law. Put woman under the yoke of man! What will happen to a world ordered and ruled entirely by men? She must be restored!"

He sighed. "So what's your plan? I can't help but notice we're heading to Eden. You know I hate that place."

"The angels are there. Or at least—were. It's where I last saw them. They know where She is."

"They're hardly likely to tell us."

"No. Some trickery will be required. That's where you come in."

☽

Eden was utterly transformed. Without human hands to tend the weeds, the Garden was overgrown. The paths were gone. I wept for my roses, for the vine-dappled carpet of primrose and violet, for the sweet scent of evening jasmine, now choked by bitter briar.

The pool had dried. Over the years, the river that supplied it had diverted far to the east. The fields we farmed had returned to the wild. Blood-red poppies and golden yarrow swayed among the barley. Nothing at all was left of our cabin, the planks rotted to mulch over a thousand years.

Only one remnant of our lives here remained; the glinting curve of a copper bowl caught my heel. I dug it from the soil and wiped the crusted mud. Adam had made it before he turned his mind, and all his metalworking skills, to making weapons for imaginary warfare. Around the edge he had engraved an intricate rolling pattern. In the centre was the image of a woman—me—with cascading hair, sitting in calm contemplation beneath a tree.

It moved me to profound melancholy. He had loved me once. How different might it all have been had we continued like this, in delight of each other? I would have been a mother. I would have been *the* mother. No compliant Eve, but bold Lilith the mother of all mankind.

Beating back bramble and thorns, we spied the grove where the Tree of Life stood. I gasped to see they were still there—Senoy, Sansenoy, and Semangelof, parading in military precision around the scaly trunk of the majestic date-palm. At their feet, Adam's bronze blade—tarnished, no longer bright, but upright—still plunged into the earth.

"Remember the plan?" I whispered. Samael nodded.

☽

Samael entered the grove from the east, dawdling idly. "Alright lads?"

They turned as one.

"Thou!" seethed Semangelof. "What dost thou here, foul outcast, polluted one?"

"Oh, haven't you heard? I'm back. Admitted once more to the gates of Paradise." He bowed low.

The angels turned and muttered among themselves.

"But maybe you didn't know." Samael examined the dirt beneath his fingernails. "I doubt you've heard from Him in a while. Been a bit silent, hasn't He? Perhaps that's why He's given you this non-job, guarding a tree from nobody. To keep you out of the way."

"This is not a non-job!" cried Senoy. "We protect the Tree of Life from human hands, lest they eat of its fruit and live forever!"

"Yeah, right," sneered Samael. "And how many humans have come looking for it in the past millennium?"

"Millennium?" ventured Sansenoy, fingers darting to his unruly hair. "Has it really been that long?"

"We are His trusted envoys!" snarled Semangelof. "He comes to us to perform all His works."

"Not any more," said Samael. "Not after the mess you made last time. That's why I'm back in favour."

"What mess?" Senoy's wings bristled.

"Come now," said Samael. "We all know of it—out there in the real world. How you stole the Queen of Heaven. Bruised and beat Her. Drugged Her and carried Her away, imprisoning Her far from all Her children. Shame on you!"

"Who told you that?" growled Sansenoy. But he was on edge. His fingers fluttered like reeds in the wind.

"Everyone knows it." Samael shrugged. "Since She fled Her prison."

"She's escaped?" Senoy's hands flew to his cheeks in alarm.

"Oh yes," said Samael. "And rumour has it—I haven't seen Her myself yet of course, I heard this only from two-faced Isimud, messenger of the Lord Enki—"

"Do not speak to us of false gods!" screeched Semangelof.

Samael waved away the objection with his hand. "And Isimud tells me She is apoplectic with rage—absolutely *livid!*—with the three goons who carried Her off, for whom she is now searching with a growing army of furious, blade-wielding acolytes."

"It's not possible!" cried Sansenoy. "Her sister would not allow it!"

Semangelof flashed a warning glance, put out a hand to silence him. "It's not true," said he, coolly. "We don't know what you're talking about. Be gone, angel of iniquity, elect of all evil!"

"Right you are then!" Samael breezed to their amazement and consternation. "Cheerio!"

$$)$$

We left the angels in much commotion, bickering about whether to stay and guard the tree, or take themselves off to hide with no time to lose.

"Well, that was interesting," said Samael, as we passed through the squeaking, rusty gate leading out of Eden.

"Most enlightening. Did you know She had a sister?"

He shook his head.

"Curious," I mused.

"Illuminating!" said Samael.

We set our faces to the south and off we strode, down the trail lined with death-bringing oleander. The same path of shame that Adam and Eve had trodden a thousand years before.

Daughter of the Moon

The answer, Samael assured me, would be found at Uruk; the domain of the old gods, where Asherah had first emerged out of the watery fruitfulness of the delta. And, he winked, he knew just the person to help us.

We sailed the swift-flowing Euphrates by bowl-shaped kuphar, stolen from a merchant loading his wine outside white-walled Mari. A mule, our unwilling passenger, was already boarded.

Shall I recount the gleaming cities we spied from the boat? The nomads beating up dust-storms on their horses in the distant plains? No, my story is long and time is short. I shall linger in my tale only once: at Babel, where we anchored among the bulrushes to shelter from the searing noontime heat. There, assailed by a frenzy of mosquitoes, we saw a tower in construction, a ziggurat rising level by level to the very sky, defying gravity and sense. Workers toiled like ants carrying hods of newly-baked bricks up steep ramps.

"That will never last," observed Samael. He unstopped yet another jar of the merchant's wine and we lay back, dodging the mule's sweeping, fly-switching tail, in the cradling, rocking cramp of the hull.

☽

Dawn broke as we arrived at the princely city of Uruk. From the riverside marshes, the city walls rose shimmering pink. At the harbour, an army of merchants unloaded wine, honey, dates, and oil from unsteady kuphars, like so many upturned turtles among the reeds.

We transferred what remained of the wine into the mule's packs and followed the throng through the vast wooden gates leading into the city. Inside, Samael plucked me into an alley. He led me past doorways giving onto dark rooms, where women wove at looms in the low light. Past window ledges where cats idled on cool stone. At a corner, we turned into a wide square full of people. It was market day. Quails whistled from overcrowded cages. A dog ran past with a scrap stolen from the butcher's block. The heavenly scent of baking drew my eye to the vast communal ovens lining one side of the square.

"There!" Samael pointed to a flight of broad steps rising beside the ovens. "That's the temple."

It was as if we had stepped into another world: a city within the city. An immense ziggurat rose from the centre of the compound, surrounded by low, limestone buildings and shady courtyards. Attendants everywhere swept shining marble flagstones. From some unseen quarter came the beat of a kettle drum and a woman singing. Above it all, the scent of lilac smouldered.

Samael knew exactly where to go: past a line of worshippers bringing offerings, past workshops of pot-makers and cloth-dyers, into a vast storehouse. Pyramids of grain towered above us. Barrels filled with pomegranates, figs, walnuts and almonds, sacks of lentils, chickpeas, and beans lined the walls. Never have I seen such plenty! A city of five thousand could live their entire lives on such stores and never know the gnaw of hunger.

I led the mule to graze at a basket of cucumbers. I had grown fond of him on the journey from Mari. In his ignorance, he reminded me of another incurious beast: the man Adam, who loved Progress over Wisdom.

We crept through pathways amid the mountains of food to a door on the other side. Flaming torches lit a warren of low corridors, tunnelling far below ground. "She insists I use the servants' entrance," Samael said with a wink. "I quite like it."

The corridor levelled, then rose past forks branching into wider, more brightly-lit halls. It twisted and turned like a labyrinth. Soon, the plain walls gave way to painted plaster, adorned with frescoes. At a thick cedar door, Samael knocked. The door swung back on silent hinges and he led me into a room thick with sandalwood incense.

☽

She walked towards us, solidifying out of the smoke. Tall, and seeming taller still for the hair piled upon her head in great coils fastened with ivory combs. At her back, it tumbled to her waist in oiled and perfumed locks. Her eyes were startling, painted in pigment of lapis lazuli, her lashes lined with kohl. Her gown dazzled, overlaid with thousands of tiny pearls. I faded before her. She was magnificent.

"Sam—ael." A low voice, like a rolling ocean wave. She stroked his cheek. "Storm of my heart, how I've missed you. What are you wearing? You look like a beggar. And what have you brought me—a pretty slave?" She looked me up and down with disinterest.

"Priestess!" He kissed her full on the lips, squeezing her close. "Have you wine? It's been a thirsty journey."

She clapped for an attendant and led us to a divan laid with silk cushions, pulling Samael to sit beside her. A boy bearing an ostrich-feathered fan rushed to her shoulder. As she embraced Samael, kissing his forehead and cheeks, I stifled a laugh. He looked like a lapdog.

"The slave may sit." She waved a hand in my direction. "Where have you been, my angel?"

He coughed. "She's no slave." He lifted her hand from his inner thigh. "This is Lilith. Formerly consort to the man, Adam. Child of the Lady Asherah and Lord Yahweh."

A young girl in saffron robes set a jug of wine and honeyed cakes on a table. She retreated backwards, eyes down.

The priestess poured libation and muttered a blessing. She broke a cake. "How many times, Samael? Your Asherah and Yahweh are but blasphemies to me."

I ventured to sit at the edge of a couch. I plunged my fingers into the sun-bleached fleece to take strength. I dared to say: "We believe, my lady, that the Holy Mother Asherah was once a goddess of Uruk."

She laughed. "You are mistaken. Our gods do not leave this fairest and foremost of cities. Here, they receive the richest tribute, prayers from every tongue. Incense is burned for their pleasure every hour of day and night. The purest white bull-calf sacrificed at the new moon, his blood poured for their honour."

"Gods go where they are called, Priestess." Samael knocked back a second goblet of wine. "If some citizens of Uruk travelled away from here—well, might She not have gone with them?"

I stood and walked around the cavernous chamber. A row of yellow-robed girls awaited her bidding, lined like spring crocuses beside the door. Rolls of linen, pots, and slim-necked vases surrounded a sunken bath in the centre of the room. I picked up an exquisite alabaster jar and smelled the fragrance. Precious nard oil, borne by camel unfathomable leagues from the east. I slipped it into a fold in my robe.

"The thing is," I said, "She's gone. She's missing."

"What's that to me?" The priestess had lost interest in Samael, and lay back, wine in her hand, against a plump cushion.

"Those that took Her said She is with Her sister," he said. "I thought—perhaps, you know where Her sister might be?"

The priestess finished her wine. "I told you I do not know this Asherah!" She dashed the dainty cup across the chamber, where it smashed into a thousand pieces. A girl scuttled forward to sweep the shards.

"Forgive my ignorance, Lady," I bowed my head, "I am but a foreigner. Tell me, whom do you worship?"

"Can you really not know where you are, child? This is the Moon Temple at Uruk. Sacred to the moon god Nanna and the moon goddess Ningal. I am the high priestess."

At a low table in the corner of the room, a carved tablet box lay open. Styluses spilled from an ivory case. One lay across a half-marked tablet as if she'd just set it aside when we entered.

"Tell me of your mistress Ningal."

The priestess sighed. "She is the Great Lady. Daughter of Ningikuga and Enki, the god of water. Mother of Utu, the sun god." She toyed with a blood-red carnelian necklace she wore like a slash at her throat. "She lives in the space between water and land. She sends me dreams that I might cast my prophecies."

"Has she a sister?"

She returned a withering gaze. "No."

"And Ningikuga?"

"Goddess of the reeds, Daughter of An, lord of the sky and Nammu, mother of all gods." She looked me in the eye. "Many sisters."

"You write?" I gestured to the table.

She gathered herself and advanced, coming to stand beside me at the table. "I write prayers. Hymns to the gods, to be sung throughout the kingdom of Sumer."

"Who's this?" I pointed to a stone carving set into the wall above the low table. A naked woman, with wings at her back, a regal countenance. She stood in front of a tree, flanked by she-leopards. The evening star shone at her crown.

The priestess flushed. She gathered her scattered tablets and returned the styluses to their case. She turned to Samael. "How dare you! You cannot bring your lovers here to question me as if I were a common harlot! A curse upon you! May you dwell only in shadows!"

He stood and wrapped her in his arms. "Dear heart. I would not ask were it not important."

I did not care to see him kissing her. They made a handsome couple. "Come Samael," I urged. "This was a mistake, she will not help."

He broke away with a kiss to her forehead and cast his begging eyes to the stone carving.

She softened. "Inanna," she said. "Eldest child of Nanna and Ningal. Queen of Heaven. Lady of the four quarters of the world."

Queen of Heaven? My heart skipped a beat.

"My Lady," she breathed, staring beyond Samael to the carved relief. Her voice rippled through me like wind through wheat.

"Daughter of the moon,
Nursed in heaven,
    ripened on earth."

Was this then our Asherah? Had she really sprung into being here in Uruk?

"You circle the sky,
You encompass the earth.

You raise the waters
You unleash the winds.
Hail, Great Lady, shining, supreme!
You wield the powers of the old, old gods."

An image came to me. Of divinities dissembling throughout aeons, taking on different forms and guises, ever new manifestations of that original, ancient Spirit of Creation. Inanna was Asherah. Both were the Creatrix that hovered over the waters at the dawn of time.

Samael and I looked at each other. The priestess was lost, utterly, in her rapture.

"And has she—" I started, but she did not let me finish.

"Yes, yes!" she snapped. "She has a sister. Ereshkigal, Queen of the Underworld."

The Divine Garden

The mule was waiting where we left him, happily quartered in the temple's vast storehouse. We loaded him with supplies, exchanging the wine in his packs for goatskins, cheese, fruit, and olive oil. We led him back into the thronging city.

Turbaned merchants astride overloaded donkeys headed for the marketplace. A flock of thin goats scuttled past, led by a boy holding aloft a crook. We pressed ourselves into the wall to allow a cart to pass, a rickety, angry thing, leaving in its wake the yeasty scent of beer.

At the eastern gates, as vast and high as those through which we'd entered in the west, we waited for a lull in the waves of incomers.

"Take me to Asherah's garden," I begged Samael. "I want to see it. If your priestess is right, it's on the way."

"She's not my priestess! And her directions weren't precise. We must find the mountain that marks the path to the Underworld."

A fight kindled in the crowd outside; the sound of hard blows and bellows reached us within. As they turned on one another, the flow of travellers jamming the gates stemmed and we surged through.

"She said it's in the east." But looking that way, there was no sign of mountains. Only marsh and unending brown plain. Even now, in the late afternoon haze, a steady stream of wayfarers flowed relentlessly towards Uruk.

He stared, as if willing the mountains to appear. His shoulders sagged. He yielded. "But we can't stay long. "When those goons find out I was lying about Asherah escaping, they'll be after us."

☽

65

We set off on a trail alongside reed-strewn marshes, leading the reluctant mule, Adam, as we both now called him. His packs bulged with gifts from the priestess to gain entry to Ereshkigal's grim palace.

Two hours after the marbled ziggurats of Uruk had retreated behind us, we came to a high-walled fortress rising from the plain. Unlike the towns we had seen from the river on our journey south, it was unguarded. No archers nor swordsmen paraded its parapets. There was but one entrance: a solid maple door with a great bronze handle set into the mouth of a lion. Two stone channels brought water from east and west, trickling into the garden through narrow gaps in the wall. The door was locked. We tethered Adam to the great door-ring, unfurled our wings, and flew over the wall.

It pains me to relate what we found inside. Trunks of figs, date-palms, and olive trees lay where they were felled, stumps hacked, as if in a frenzy. Every rose plucked and trampled underfoot. A carved fountain in the image of a bull's head was smashed, its ivory horns ground to dust. Apricots and dates, golden apples, lay rotting on the ground. Not even the jewels had escaped the violence: carnelian fruits, leaves of lapis were smashed and trodden into the dirt, a solitary dove-grey feather mangled in their shards. A grapevine, trained and pruned with care over centuries, lay slashed to shreds, the fruit crushed, glistening purple like innards on the ground.

"They know." Samael gazed at the devastation. "Which means they're ahead of us. We have to leave, Lilith—now!"

I picked an unblemished rose from the ground. Palest pink. I inhaled its intoxicating aroma. The same powerful scent, the same delicate yellow stamens of the roses I had tended in Eden.

"But why, Samael? Why do they hate Her so?"

"They don't hate Her." He looked nervously over his shoulder. "They just want to erase Her. They'll destroy everything She made, kill all that She nurtured. They will lie, cover up Her works, carve Her name from all records. It will be as if She were never here at all."

"This is His doing. How could He? She was—is still—His wife!"

Samael dipped his finger into what was left of a beehive, clinging to the bough of a young oak. "Not any more. He's gone solo."

He licked the honey from his finger and offered it to me. It tasted of thyme and lavender, nectar of the gods. There were hips on the slashed rose bush before me. I picked them, hoping to salvage something from this place to plant again.

As we passed a severed olive tree, I saw the vandals had carved their initials into the trunk: three interlocking samechs, cut like wounds in flesh.

A New Paradise

Where were they now, those vengeful angels? As we travelled east, across the ploughlands between the mighty rivers, we watched for them amid the cornstalks growing high and golden in the fields. When the land gave way to marsh, we searched for their grey wings and furious countenances among the cranes' nests in the reeds.

And where was He—the author of my misfortunes, the unloving Father who had spurned me, turned me over for refusing my own subjection?

I'd seen nothing of Him since leaving Eden. Had it not been for the desecrated garden, I could imagine Him alone and powerless in weed-ruined Eden, rueing the day He betrayed His wife and cursed His own children.

Was it my fault? Had I never offered Eve the fruit, would she and Adam have lived on—unspoilt, unbanished, undamned?

No, Samael consoled me. The crime was already in motion. Asherah usurped. I—the equal woman—ousted. All harmony and balance lost. The plot to deny humankind their Mother's gifts of Wisdom and free will, already unspooling like a loosed mooring rope.

We travelled through the marsh by slender-prowed mashoof, Adam perched obediently at the rear. As we poled our way through feathery, brushing reeds, I began to understand what else was denied in Eden: glorious reality. For I was falling in love with this world—this real paradise that improved in every way on that place of artifice and illusion. The seed that had been planted in the soil of my desires that first spring in Alashiya, now sprouted and thrived. We glided through the placid water to the music of croaking herons, chirping otters; to the sound of children laughing as they fished and swam from their own narrowboats.

Oftentimes, their parents saw us resting on our travels and called us to their dwellings, which rose like floating towers on the marsh, to share their meals. We broke bread with them, cross-legged, the breeze wafting through the airy reed-woven walls. Once, our bellies filled with stewed water-buffalo, I cradled a newborn as her mother tended the fire. She was the first baby I ever held: I, once destined to be the mother of all. My quest now replaced that destiny. I would not rest until I was revenged on the Father who had cursed all Womankind; until I'd restored the rightful world—for her, and all her daughters to come—that they would not be damned to a life of servitude.

The night before we returned to solid ground, as the dying sun lit a shining orange path at our backs, we saw a vast flock of flamingo. Ungainly in flight, like a badly-trained army on the move, they landed before us, transforming the wetlands to a vista of flaming pink. Basking, preening, squawking, they parted as one for the slim prow of our boat, their beaks held aloft on snaking neck.

Now I saw that Garden of my birth, not as it had started—the hoped-for pinnacle of Creation—but as it became after She was gone. Without Her divine protection, with all female power banished, it was a place of subjection and tyranny. Of perpetual stasis, not regeneration. Of Shalts and Shalt Nots issued by male authority. A place of masculine hierarchy, domination, and progress, unbalanced by the female urge to nurture, sustain, and renew.

It drove me onwards. This was why She must be found.

"What will happen to this world?" I raged at Samael. "What of Wisdom, curiosity—these qualities She prized. Are they now to be punished? What of our role in this world—as part of nature, not set above it? Will all be lost without Her?

He tolerated my fury. He shared it on my behalf, gently nodding his assent. He never tried to calm my rage.

It made me love him all the more.

☽

Eventually, the marsh gave way to the rushing, swirling Tigris. We struggled in the roiling eddies, carried far downstream, barely making it to the far bank. We saw the mountains for the first time. Beyond a poppy-field, oak and pine forests rose like storm-lashed waves into shimmering snow-capped peaks.

We camped that night on firm ground for the first time in weeks. The marsh-dwellers had given us flintstones, bows, and arrows in exchange for oil, and we ate well on the meat of the skittish, spotted deer of these parts. We still had wine in plenty, dates and nuts, dried apricots and the salty, crumbling cheese of Uruk.

"We might have flown," said Samael, as I stretched beside him, warming my toes at the crackling fire.

His words touched a nerve, for I'd considered it myself. But without the mule, we couldn't carry the packs. "Your priestess said we must bring offerings to enter the Underworld," I reminded him.

"Stop calling her my priestess!" He took his arm from my waist.

It was a clear night. The crescent moon was waning, soon to sink into the silvery, glinting marsh. Thousands of stars dazzled and danced, as if for us alone. From the river came the chorus of frogs that greeted every nightfall.

And here was something else that was better than Eden: a partnership. With a man who was my equal, who showed me love in myriad ways. Who never ordered or directed me, who admired the sure flight of my arrows. Who *never* forced me under him. Who delighted me in all ways, as I delighted him.

I had known this joy before Adam turned from me. Before his nonsense talk of the evils of the body. What fool denies carnal pleasures? Who would part from this world and all its rich delights?

No—*this* was Asherah's plan. Harmony. Man and woman as equals. Enjoying our bodies, not despising them. Sex as an act of pleasure and connection, not domination and control.

"In any case," I kissed Samael's honey-sweet lips, and he responded, kissing me back. "The journey will purify us for the task ahead."

"I'll purify you." He pulled me onto him, pushing my robe above my hips. "I shall ordain you with my mighty sceptre and anoint you with my sacred waters."

I laughed, as we sported on the lambskin, sending our own joyous night-chorus back to the frogs.

☽

The next morning, I woke to find a she-leopard at the embers of our fire. She was wounded, with a freshly-slashed ear. She raised her eyes to mine, blinked, then padded away towards the mountains.

I left Samael hair-tousled in sleep and went to the water's edge to bathe. In the still beauty of the rosy dawn, I considered his suggestion. Perhaps we could fly. Between us, could we not bear the weight of the gifts we brought for Ereshkigal?

I rippled my shoulders and summoned my wings. Nothing.

I tried again, eyes fixed on a crane swooping low among the reeds. I focused on her graceful wing, recalling that feeling of rushing air, the powerful sensation of muscled flight. Still, they would not come.

I submerged and cleansed myself. My wings, Asherah's blessing, had deserted me. Her gift, vanished with Her fading power.

Cakes for the Queen of Heaven

We set off without eating, following the route taken by the she-leopard I'd seen at first light. Leaving the watery realm of the marshland behind us, we took stock of the journey ahead.

According to the priestess, the entrance to the Underworld lay on the far side of the mountains. We must ascend the foothills where the sun rises on the autumnal equinox. There, we would find a path leading to the mountain pass. Descending from the summit, aiming true east, a shepherd's hut marked the cave from which a staircase led down to Ereshkigal's dark palace.

By my reckoning, the equinox was two days past. Scouring the hills, I saw a jagged cleft, a dip in the treeline: undoubtedly the path.

By mid-morning, we reached the poppy-filled valley we'd seen from the water's edge. My fears about our slow progress had not subsided. I saw ill omens everywhere. To my mind, the crimson blooms resembled a vast lake of blood. Worse was to come.

A dark cloud buzzed and hummed, swarming above the waving petals. Adam refused to move. It took all our strength, Samael pulling at his leash, I, pushing at his rear, to lead him on. Not until we were upon it, did we see the cloud was made of flies: millions of them. In our eyes, on our lips, evil-tasting on our tongues. We tore strips from my hem to wrap around our faces and stumbled blindly on the path.

Beyond the swarm, on the lowest slopes of the foothills, wheat had been planted. It should have been ripe for harvest, but the sheaves were ragged, the grain turned to sand. Dead locusts littered the ground. We crunched their desiccated bodies with every step. Among the stalks and stems lay orange eggs, the sign of further devastation to come. Ravens cawed from an outcrop of rock.

We climbed higher, through forests of oak and almond. At noon, the sky darkened as if it were night. A soft rain fell, then turned to hail. Stones as big as walnuts assaulted us, bruising our skin, sending Adam into a braying frenzy. Stumbling against the icy onslaught, we lost the path. Samael made an arbour of saplings to protect Adam and we crept inside our goats-hair tent.

"Is this His work?" I asked as ice hammered the hide above our heads.

Samael nodded grimly. "Plagues of locusts. Hailstones, flies. It's His style, alright."

"But we're so far from His domain. How has He this power here?"

Samael peered out of the tent to see if the storm was relenting and looked back with a grimace. "Perhaps He's getting stronger."

It came to me then: "As She weakens."

The wind howled through the trees. The hide snapped. Hailstones clattered from all sides.

"What will happen to this world, if we cannot restore Her?"

"We must hurry. We can fly above the storm, take what we can of the offerings. I'll charm my way in, Lilith. You know I'm irresistible."

"I've lost them, Samael. My wings. I can't fly."

He reached for me in the darkness, and we listened to the violence of the gale, to His fury hurled against us.

It was night when I woke, dark but silent. No howling wind nor hammering hailstones. The far-off cry of a tawny owl lured me outside. Where the forest canopy thinned, I searched for the great constellations: the Bull of Heaven, the curving tail of the Scorpion. I looked for Asherah's star, the evening star. But it was nowhere to be seen. I could feel Her shrinking, diminishing into the void like the waning moon.

☽

At first light, we found the path again. It wove through a grove of walnut trees before emerging to overlook a lush plateau. Grey mountains rose sharply on the far side.

The day bloomed bright with none of the ill omens that had dogged our journey from the marsh. At this early hour, the birds were in full song. A pair of rock thrushes darted, blue breasts dazzling in the sun. They trilled like reed-flutes till even Adam, that incurious beast, looked for the source of the tune. In the field before us, women worked, bent double, baskets at their backs. Brightly-dyed scarves kept the beating sun from their heads.

"It's the saffron harvest." Samael pointed to the tiny purple flowers that covered the plateau. "You should see the fuss when they bring it to the temple at Uruk. They sing and dance for days." He plucked a bloom at our feet and picked one of the bright yellow strands reaching from the petals, like a serpent towards the sun. "It's sacred." He placed it on my tongue, where it fizzed with a mild woody tang.

As we crossed the crocus fields, I looked for signs of His wrath, for I dreaded bringing it into this tranquil valley. A cyclone, perhaps, a thunderstorm of hail and ice. But there was nothing. No dark clouds threatened, no wolves howled from the mountain passes.

Beneath the spreading shade of a terebinth, we came to a dozen women separating the flowers and stigmas. For all the great mounds of purple petals they produced, scant piles of the deep yellow strands covered the silver platters at their feet.

"Hail matrons, well met," Samael called. "What have you, saffron for sale?"

"Be gone!" said a thick-browed woman. "Men cannot tarry here, you'll spoil the harvest."

Samael grinned. "There is nothing in heaven nor earth that I spoil."

She looked up then, as they all did.

"Anyway." Samael crouched to their level. "I am not a man."

"Is that right?" asked their leader, without pausing her work. "Then what, may I ask, are you?"

"An angel," he said, scooping a handful of the petals and inhaling deeply. "Of the heavenly host."

She shooed him away. "Come," she beckoned me. "She can join us. Such a beauty will only bless the crop."

Samael led Adam away, to beat the dust from his travel-grimed flank. I sat and a woman emptied a basket of freshly-picked crocuses into my lap. I followed their lead, plucking the stigmas, setting the petals aside.

"What are you doing here, missy?" asked the leader. "You're not from these parts."

"We journey over the mountains." I pointed to the peaks beyond.

"To the Underworld, no doubt. To Ereshkigal's dark palace. You seek the Queen of Heaven there."

"How—how do you know?"

"Because She's gone."

"You've noticed too?"

"Of course we've noticed," she frowned. "Do you think we're simple, we mountain folk? The wheat and barley are failing. The goats do not breed, our women are barren. It can mean only one thing: Our Lady is stuck in the Underworld. Even the saffron harvest is tainted." She gestured to the pitiful pile on the platter before her. "And we need it to make Her saffron-cakes."

"To make what?"

"Cakes for the Queen of Heaven. To tempt Her back."

I didn't know what to say, so I stayed silent. My fingers lacked nimbleness, I lagged behind the other women. "I'm not sure She can be tempted," I said after a while. "We think She is kept there against Her will. Imprisoned."

"Indeed. By Her jealous sister. It wouldn't be the first time."

"Will you take the cakes to Her—to the Underworld?"

The woman dropped her petals and laughed. "We cannot go there! No mortal can enter the shadow-world and return. But you can, Daughter of Heaven." She winked. "We've been waiting for you."

She called to one of her women, who laid a basket on the ground in front of me. Inside: a batch of crescent-moon shaped cakes. Yellow-hued, from the saffron. They smelt of dough and musky sandalwood.

"Offer the cakes to Ereshkigal as tribute. But eat nothing she gives you in return. If she offers you water, do not drink it. If she offers you a stool, do not sit. Take nothing, touch nothing, or you must stay there forever."

"Will she release her sister?"

"The cakes will flatter her. No one bakes for Ereshkigal. But they won't be enough. You must offer her something else."

"Where will I find a worthy replacement for the Queen of Heaven?"

She coughed, looked away. "It will come to you." She patted my arm. "Now," she said briskly. "Can you see the stone eagle?"

I stood and looked to where she pointed, towards the mountains rising out of the green plateau. The image of a fierce bird—its head thrown back, beak thrust into the sky—emerged as clear as day from the rock.

"That's the only pass. The path will lead you to the cave, and from there, down to the shadow-world."

Samael loaded the cakes into Adam's packs.

I embraced the woman. She held me to her ample breast, then grasped me firmly by the shoulders. "Go well, Daughter of Heaven."

She whispered: "And know that you are followed." She raised her brows towards the dark outline of the forest behind us. A flash of white stirred the leaves of the canopy, just above the path we had travelled. She tucked a crocus behind my ear.

How Do You Kill a Goddess?

"She said we need an offering," I told Samael as we reached the edge of the plateau. The mountains reared above us like a furious wave.

"We have gifts. From the priestess."

"Those are to bribe the gatekeepers. We must offer Ereshkigal something to replace Asherah."

He grimaced.

I should have understood. But my eyes were drawn to the path, searching for a break in the solid wall of rock. I looked back to see if there was any sign of the angels, for it was surely they who pursued us. But the sky was clear, save for the playful, spiralling flight of starlings, their whistles cutting sharp across the sun-scorched silence of the valley.

We examined the wall of limestone rising from the plain. Above us, nimble goats clung to the narrow ledges and crevices. But there was no break to admit a path. Samael walked north and I south, each with a hand to the rock to test if its solidity were mere illusion.

My mind turned over what lay ahead. The Underworld, where the dead eat clay and drink dust. Where grooms are torn from their brides, and babies cry piteously for eternity, never knowing their mother's touch.

Was this Asherah's plan? Had She devised such horrors for Her children? Worse—I shuddered at the thought—had I unwittingly brought it into being? For they said there was no Death before Eve, and I'd brought Eve to her Fall. But it made no sense. All creatures die. Crops wither and fade, even trees reach the end of their lives. Death is part of this world—of the real world, not the unreal Paradise

I had known. I alone had evaded it—why? Not because He willed it, surely—nor because I'd dodged His curse, as Samael believed. I saw Her hand in it. I had been preserved. For something She would have me do.

A shout from Samael disturbed my thoughts. His beaming face emerged from the rock ahead, beckoning me into a crevice that widened onto a worn cobbled path. From here, the route was clear, snaking up the sheer cliff, and disappearing far above us.

☽

The midday heat played tricks with our minds. Strange noises echoed from the rocks. The clatter of goat-hooves rebounded from all directions. The distant call of a mountain lion threatened.

Above the treeline, the landscape was stark and unforgiving. The merciless sun reflected blindingly from the white path that led through narrow clefts, over huge boulders. There was little vegetation: only moss and stubborn nightshades grew from the cracks.

As evening fell, there was relief from the heat, but with it came a mist that descended suddenly, obscuring the way. The call of the eagles we'd seen wheeling above us in the bright day took on a new and forbidding sound. The thick veil of cloud forced us to rest for the night and we finished the provisions we'd brought from Uruk.

"Samael," I asked, savouring the last of the cheese. "How do you kill a goddess?"

He drained a wineskin and laid his head on the pillow of my belly. An eagle returned from the broad plateau to her well–built eyrie, perched on an outcrop of rock, high above us.

"A goddess's power comes from those who adore her," he said at last. "To kill her, you deny her worship. Gods cannot live without prayers, sacrifice, incense—these things are their air and sustenance."

"So if no one worships Asherah, She will die?"

"Have you heard of Amunet or Kišar? Of any of the bird-headed or snake-haired goddesses even I've forgotten? They all once created, nurtured, and destroyed. Who utters their names now? Who burns incense for their delight? No one pours libation for them. No blood of an unblemished heifer is spilled on their altars. So they decline and fade away. Gods are made by belief and undone by disbelief."

"Is She dead already then? It's been a thousand years. Is she worshipped still?

"Undoubtedly—somewhere. She's known by different names and honoured in different ways: She's Inanna in Uruk, Hathor in Kemet, Anassa in Alashiya. Astarte, Isis, Anath—they're all the same goddess, the Queen of Heaven. Asherah may have been gone a thousand mortal years, but those women collecting saffron worship Her still. As long as She is known, She lives."

This mystified me. How did they know Her if they hadn't met Her, as I had? Who had taught them? It had been my task to pass on Her Wisdom and I had failed. I had shunned the world, keeping to my desert valley, as the offspring of Adam and Eve thrived.

The stars emerged from their slumber, blinking into life. They hovered around the glowing moon like bees to a hive. As Samael slept, I replayed his refrain over and again in my mind: *They are made by belief and undone by disbelief.*

How much longer did She have?

Get Thee to Sheol

At the snow-covered summit we shivered in our meagre garb, shoulders bared, feet exposed in open sandals. Far behind us, to the west, lay the crocus-blooming plateau. Eastwards, the mountains fell away to a patchwork of fields: lush green, ripe yellow, fallow brown. Dwellings were cut into an escarpment, huts sprouted like mushrooms beside a sparkling stream. But we would never reach that far: our path lay below, to the dank, dripping chambers deep within the mountain.

Towards the highest peak, the path led by way of a swinging rope-bridge across a deep chasm. Timber boards hung down in shards. Splinters of rock thrust upwards like spears. Within the abyss, a gloomy mist shrouded the lowest pits. It boiled in the darkness, churning out the unmistakeable smell of brimstone.

Samael stepped gingerly onto the bridge. It swayed madly but held. He sped, with growing confidence, leaping two or three timbers at a time, bounding easily over the gaps, his whoops and hollers echoing back to me. His shoulders twitched with readiness but he didn't need his wings.

He was within the last few steps when they arrived, swooping from the sky on beating wing, mightily wroth in countenance, like three angry, spitting doves.

Samael turned to see the angels. "Quick!" he yelled. "It will hold."

I took one look at their brutish faces and led Adam onto the bridge.

"I might have known!" Senoy jeered, hovering beside me. "Two poisonous outcasts in unholy union!"

"Pathetic!" spat Sansenoy. "Foul demons of iniquity! Depraved evildoers!"

"How far you have fallen!" screamed Semangelof. "The first woman, a virgin bride. Now you fornicate with this devil in wanton desire, your lips to his anus, he sucks on your teats."

My lips to his *what*? They were deranged. A millennium and more of safeguarding a tree had enfeebled their minds.

"Barren Lilith, shrivelled Lilith! Artificer of fraud!" scorned Senoy.

The boards creaked and groaned, the rope swayed in fury. Adam bore down the bridge behind me so every step was a huge effort to climb.

"And what do you hope to achieve?" continued Semangelof. "You won't release Her! She is restrained by adamantine chains, kept in a pit of livid flames. Do you think you are a match for dark Ereshkigal?"

Ahead, Samael had reached safety. He bristled with anger, hopped from one foot to the other.

"You turned your backs on Paradise and its eternal splendours. You spurned holy light for darkness! Now, you will perish in the realm of the dead, in the depths of the fiery pit, just as you deserve!"

A board cracked behind me. Adam stumbled and brayed in fear. Senoy and Sansenoy descended to either side of the bridge and shook it, viciously. I fell against the rope-netted sides.

"Where are your wings now, false Lilith?" Semangelof taunted.

Samael took a running leap and soared into the air. He dived onto Senoy, sending him spinning into the chasm. He soared upwards to knock Sansenoy, limbs flailing, into the sky. Adam sat, parked firmly on the boards. I dropped the leash and ran for solid ground.

Locked in airborne struggle, Sansenoy and Samael tumbled as one into the void. Senoy was nowhere to be seen. Adam, senseless to the commotion around him, perched rigid on the bridge.

"Come!" I beckoned. But he would not move.

Semangelof saw I wanted the mule. He understood why I needed him. He rose and dived into the bridge like a falcon at his prey. With a great splintering crack, he broke through the boards. The ropes snapped. Severed, the bridge fell to each side of the chasm.

Adam fell through the rushing air. He accepted his fate as he bore all life's events, issuing but a mild whinny of amazement as he dropped into the void. He was gone. With all the gifts and offerings we'd brought: the crown of pure gold, the pearl-woven robes, the coral bracelets, the carnelian necklace, the lapis-inlaid dagger, the brooch-pins and clasps—even the saffron-scented cakes. All we needed to bribe our way into the Underworld and flatter its Queen.

Senoy emerged from the sulphurous mist, bleeding and bruised. Sansenoy rose alone from the gloom, his garment rent and torn. I waited, I watched, but Samael did not come.

They arrayed themselves: arms folded, chins lifted, they lorded it over me.

"Be gone, foolish Lilith," seethed spineless Senoy. "Get thee to Sheol. See how you are greeted now in the realm of the dead, without your odious offerings."

"Join your whore of a mother and your worm of a lover in its bottomless depths," taunted pitiless Sansenoy.

"Remain forever in that seat of desolation in ignominy and shame!" bellowed Semangelof.

They soared into the sky as one, clapped hands to each other in glee, and flew west.

I sank to my knees and wept for Samael. My love, my life, my breath. Gone in the blink of an eye, along with any hope I had of rescuing Asherah.

Humbled

I went on only because there was no turning back. The bridge was broken, the only pass across the mountains closed to me. Nor did I have anyone or anything to return for. I would go east, descend to the lush valley I had seen from the heights.

The path continued on rough cobbles. As it descended, the air warmed. The snow thinned, then vanished. Vegetation returned: scrubby vetch and yellow-flowering fennel. Grey spikes of asphodel broke through the stony ground. From the valley, a dog barked, a shepherd answered. Ordinary lives unfolded there.

I walked, heedless to that world, one foot after the other on the worn and ancient cobbles.

It is a wonder then I even saw the shepherd's hut, standing ten paces beyond the path. Low and lonely, barely more than a heap of stones. But I was drawn to this unlooked-for sign of habitation, and stooped to cross the threshold into the dank, windowless room. A rough, uneven table and three-legged stool furnished the straw covered floor. On the table, cheese and dried figs were laid on a wooden platter. I ate ravenously. The water in a clay jug was stale. I ventured outside to search for the mountain spring from which it had surely been filled.

I found it behind the hut: a mere trickle falling from the sheer cliff and drank my fill of the sweet, cool water.

It was not until I sat back, sated, that I saw I wasn't alone. A sleek she-leopard drank, a stone's throw away, her eyes on me all the while; a cut in her ear, just like the one by our marsh-side fire. She paused, licked the droplets from her lips, and padded silently away, along the course of the stream. I followed her.

Tufted grass covered the ground as it inclined up a gentle slope. The leopardess waited for me to catch up, then turned and loped into the yawning mouth of a cave that overlooked the hillside.

So this was it, just as the priestess told us: the cave marked by a shepherd's hut; the entrance to Ereshkigal's abode. I'd given up all aim of finding it and still it found me.

Inside, the cavern was vast and high. The floor was littered with the ashes of hearths and small bones, the remains of sheltering shepherds' meals. The leopardess ran out into the blossoming day.

☽

Was there any question I would venture below? I had nothing to offer. No jewels, no finery, no gifts to placate a dark goddess. Only a fool would dare enter empty-handed. So be it.

I felt my way, one hand to the dank and dripping wall. The entrance receded behind me; onwards, nothing but an impenetrable void. I crouched as I disturbed a colony of bats. They flocked from their roost, screeching as they soared towards daylight. I walked towards the distant sound of running water until I felt a step carved into the rock. Sulphurous clouds coiled up the stairwell from the bowels of the earth.

How long did I descend? Until my thighs and buttocks ached. Until my fingers bled from feeling the stony wall. Until I could barely breathe from the smoke that writhed and thickened, embracing me tighter the deeper I descended. But eventually I turned the final spiral and felt flat ground. A thin light pierced the gloom, revealing a wide chamber lit by flickering torches. A narrow walkway flanked a churning black river: the Abzu, the deep waters at the centre of the earth. The river roiled and tumbled, a swift current sweeping onwards, until it disappeared further underground and the path ended in a passage no wider than my shoulders.

What would I say when I met the gatekeeper, as I surely must? Even a simpleton would prepare a story. But I could muster no deceit. I felt naked, utterly diminished. How lowly and insignificant I had become.

Once, I walked the leafy groves of Paradise that were made for my delight. I loved and was loved. I tended the first garden, as I would nurture children. But I refused the condition of servility and was expelled.

In my winged days, I soared above the earth. The entire world was my domain. Nowhere was forbidden to me. My joys and pleasures were undimmed. Still, that was not enough: I must meddle and bring Eve out of subjection with me.

With Samael I knew true contentment and happiness. A future of joy and partnership was mine, an eternity of conjugal bliss. Instead, I led him to his death, and now I walked alone.

Here, in the depths of hell, I saw myself in my true form. Empty-handed and unadorned. Bereft of all my former gifts and blessings.

I was nothing but a mistake. A prototype cast out for malfunction. How arrogant I was, thinking I could save a goddess—the Queen of Heaven, no less. As I walked through the dark tunnel towards Eresh-kigal on the path of no return, my humility was complete. It was sincere and all-consuming. My will and my ego had deserted me.

Truly, I was nothing.

My Teeth Could Crush Flint

Through the crack of the tunnel, I saw the glint of bronze armour. The gatekeeper held an iron-topped spear casually in one hand. He faced away, revealing a lion's head engraved on the back of his helmet; such a negligent guard, unworthy of his mistress. I looked about me for a rock to dash out his brains, but there was nothing. The passage was empty, the floor swept clear. I loosened the folds of my robe around my breasts and pinched my lips. Seduction would have to do in place of violence.

I emerged from the tunnel just as he turned in surprise. But my astonishment far outweighed his, for he was expecting me—and his was the last face I thought to see again. His eyes lit up, his lips broke into a welcoming smile. I wept as I threw myself on Samael's shoulder, in delight and unrestrained relief.

☽

"I thought you were dead," I sobbed.

"Naturally."

"Where is the gatekeeper?"

Samael turned to a dark corner where two leather-shod feet emerged from a large boulder.

"Are there others?"

"Seven gates, seven gatekeepers. But I know my way around now. We can bypass the others." He pulled the body further behind the rock and led me into a side-chamber.

As we walked through a succession of passageways and caverns, he told me how he had fought with Sansenoy when they fell into the chasm at the mountain peak. How they had wrestled in the sulphurous mist until Samael found himself beside a cleft from which the thick fog issued. He threw himself, as if pierced on the rocks, and mimicked death pangs until Sansenoy ("He's really not the brightest, Lilith") returned to the summit in triumph. Descending into the crevice, Samael had found a network of tunnels leading into the Underworld.

I pummelled his breastplate. "You left me to face the angels alone!"

He brushed my fists away. "I knew you'd be fine. And here you are, without a scratch on you." He kissed me. "Loveliest of women."

"They killed Adam! Lost all our gifts."

"I saw that." He showed remorse at least, for the poor beast. "But I did rescue this from the depths." He reached for a battered leather bag from his back; one of the mule's packs, lost as he fell into the void. Samael opened it to reveal the basket of saffron-cakes and one solitary carnelian necklace, gift of the priestess of Uruk.

"Aren't you glad I'm alive, dear Lil? And here I am, saving your skin again, guiding you through the Underworld." He pulled me sharply to a gap in the wall of the walkway, overlooking a vast chamber. Flames cracked and licked. Shadowy figures drifted. They sat in melancholy by the banks of murky, boiling waters. They wove garlands from phantom-flowers, wilting in the oppressive heat beneath a shadowy elm.

"Behold the dead!" Samael whispered theatrically. My heart leapt. He was more alive amid such misery and death, shining brighter than ever on this grim and fearful stage.

"Is Adam here?" I asked, scanning the shades. I meant the man, of course, not the mule.

"I haven't seen him. But I've seen his son: jealous, murderous Cain. He is kept in particular torment," Samael grinned. "Forced to watch others eat the finest morsels and drink the sweetest wine, while he is parched and starved for eternity."

"Have you seen *Her?*"

"No. But I know where She is. Come."

☽

Samael, still wearing the gatekeeper's armour and helmet, grasped me by the wrist like a guard with his prisoner. He was ushered instantly through the waiting chamber, pulling me in his wake.

We stood before the high, carved doors to the throne room. The air was thick and still. No breeze, not a waft of air, moved in that frightful, buried place.

He turned to me. "Ready?"

I shivered.

A guard pushed back wailing petitioners. He beat his ebony mace three times on the echoing floor. Slowly, creaking mightily, the great doors opened.

She sat resplendent on a throne of human bones. Her hair, shining like obsidian, tumbled to her waist. Her dark robe shimmered in the torchlight, as if fashioned from feathers. To see her was to shudder with fear. Her eyes screamed terror. Her lips dripped blood. She looked upon us as worms beneath her feet—and truly, I felt like one. We fell to our bellies, kissing the floor.

"You are not Neti, my gatekeeper." She pointed a pearl-inlaid sceptre at Samael's bowed head.

"No, madam. You are astute."

"Who are you? How did you bypass my guards?"

Her voice could wither flowers, blunt knives, and curdle milk.

"I am the Angel of Death," Samael dared to say. "This is my domain. I come and go as I please."

I stole a glance and wished I hadn't.

"You are not *my* Angel of Death. I did not appoint you to that role."

"Nay. I belong to your divine sister."

"My siss—ter!" She hissed the word and stood. She was impossibly tall, fantastically slender. From the floor, I could no longer see her face. I did not need to, to discern her shrivelling contempt. "Why must She meddle in my affairs? We each have our spheres. Death is mine!"

She passed, her opal-glittering sandals inches from my face.

"We bring gifts."

Samael manoeuvred awkwardly, to set out the offerings without lifting his head. "These cakes were made to honour you. This necklace sent by your sister's high priestess to adorn your sublime throat."

She made a gesture with her long forefinger, and an attendant whisked the basket to her elbow. Ereshkigal broke and ate a cake in silence, never taking her terrible gaze from Samael. She assessed him from every angle, before returning to her throne.

"You may rise," she said at last. She barked to an attendant: "Bring stools."

I flashed a warning glance to Samael as they were placed before us. We stood, conspicuously, behind them.

"Indeed, it is your sister we are here to see," Samael went on. "We beg an audience."

"Who is she?" Ereshkigal pointed the sceptre in my direction. The attendants lining the hall turned heads as one.

"Lilith," said Samael. "Your sister's child. A Daughter of Heaven."

"Lil–ith." She dragged the name out slowly as if she tasted it and found it bitter. She came towards me and appraised me like a heifer at market, sweeping my hair from my shoulders, pulling down my lips to see my teeth. She stepped back, eyes flashing.

"And you are here for my sister?"

"I am." My voice wavered like an aspen leaf.

"What if—" She brought her fingertips together and summoned a cold, fleeting smile. "I offered you something better?"

She cupped my chin. Her fingers were both cold and burned like fire.

"Something—better?" My witlessness shamed me. But I was nothing beside her. A trembling child, a mewling infant.

She cast her eyes towards the throne beside hers. Lesser and lower. Forged in a dull, dark metal, wreathed in periwinkles. It was empty.

"Niece, I have no daughter. Stay and rule by my side."

Niece! I stared in amazement. It had not occurred to me this goddess was my *kin!*

"Child." Her voice lowered and softened, rumbling like a she-lion. "You say you are a Daughter of Heaven, but you stand before me in rags, your hem is torn and filthy. No brooch-pin to fasten your garment, no bangles at your wrist. You bring me a pauper's gift." She gestured to the cakes. "My sister has not provided for you and it shames me."

I remembered then. How Asherah *had* provided for me. What She had given me was more precious than jewels and robes. She had gifted me knowledge. Nurtured my curiosity. Bequeathed to *me* the protection of justice and the natural world. I felt a surge of power in my feet planted in this living tomb within the earth. It jolted through me, electrifying every nerve and sinew in my body. My fingers bristled. My head was thrown back as it soared, tingling delightfully, deliciously, into my brain.

My righteous rage would not be cooled. My teeth could crush flint.

"She was taken to *prevent* my provision! And *you* enabled the crime!" I lifted my chin. "It is not worthy of you. Doing Her husband's bidding as if you were His running-boy!"

Ereshkigal sat straight-backed. Her courtiers dropped to the floor, as if to withstand the earthquake that was surely coming. A joyless smile curled her lips. "You are fiery, niece. Like a bushfire raging. A dark storm charging. You would rule well here."

But the winds of my fury had been released and there was no containing them. I advanced towards her throne. "Do you think I come here for power? For mirth? I come not for my sake—nor even for Hers. I come to return Her to the living world. Else Her husband will rule alone. Against nature. Against reason. Against all justice."

Her eyes burned like coals.

As did mine.

"What of harmony—of the balance of opposites? What is day without night? Light without darkness? How can there be flow without ebb, birth without death? Your realm is worth nothing if the world above is diminished."

Ereshkigal glared. The courtiers on their bellies held their breaths.

I leaned closer and whispered, "Do you think you can keep your position, if women in the living world are stripped of all power? For they surely will, if His diabolical plan succeeds."

She eyed me, gripping the thighbone armrests of her throne.

"I did tell Her," she said at last. "I warned Her not to take a husband. It never ends well. But I regret She's not fit to return to the living world now." She signalled to an attendant, who came rushing with ewers of wine.

"I will take nothing," I said, loftily, "until I have seen Her."

Ereshkigal drummed her fingers on her grisly throne. She stared at the shadows in the mournful heights.

"You may see Her," she conceded. "Though the sight is unlikely to please you. But he," she pointed her icy forefinger towards Samael, "stays here."

I Am Here So You Can Die

I was led down stone stairs, each one hotter than the last. What did I expect to find in that clammy dungeon at the very depths? A comfortable bed, a mattress of soft feathers dressed with fragrant linen, lambs-fleeces, cushions of silk? Did I think to find Her clothed in soft robes, adorned with shining jewels?

I imagined none of these things but nor did I expect to see Her kept so ill. There were no adamantine chains, as Semangelof had boasted. Instead, She hung from a meat-hook in the wall. Her hands and feet wept with sores. Blood dripped into a dark puddle. The heat stoked the scents of the room: the diseased and rotting flesh, the smothering, sulphurous odour of brimstone.

I dragged a stool to bring Her down from the hook and laid Her broken body upon the burning flagstones. I dipped the hem of my robe into a pail of ashen water to wash Her face and body. Her eyes were clouded; a slow, rattling breath issued from Her lips. Her cheeks ran with sweat. I turned Her to clean the bloody wound between her shoulders. It cut deep, revealing white bone, the gore of slashed muscle and severed tendon.

When I turned Her back, Her eyes were locked on mine. They leaped like flames, shining with a mother's love. "'My Lilith, my joy." She put a weak hand to my wrist. Her voice was cracked and wavered, all sparkling melody gone.

I tried to lift Her head, but She cried in pain. She seemed to remember something. "But how? What are you doing here?" She tried to move. Her mouth worked in effort to sound the words. "You can't be here! All this for nothing if you are here!"

It was a horror to see Her reduced like this, She who once strode in divinity through Eden; glorious, luminous, a fountain of light.

"Go! Go at once! Do not look back." She coughed, a great hacking sound, spat blood and yellow phlegm.

"Not without You."

"I don't belong there anymore! I am here so you can die. We made a deal."

So I can *die*? She was confused. Did She mean so I could *live*?

"What has He done?" She cried over and again. "What has He *done?*"

She shook Her head as if to dismiss the horrible image unfolding there. I knew, of course, whose doing this was. But what deal could She have made with Him? Surely She hadn't consented to this imprisonment? For *my* sake?

She was raving. It was not enough to break Her body, Her mind must be destroyed too, its keen sharpness blunted. The source of all understanding. Her wisdom, finer than rubies. Her fruit, better than gold. She was counsel and resourcefulness, prudence and shrewdness. She taught me to uphold truth; to enquire to attain knowledge and foresight.

I stooped to pick her up. She was fragile as a child, her once-lithe limbs that leapt chasms now wasted and brittle. Her mouth moved but made no sound, Her weak hands flapped against my chest. I remembered their strength, their suppleness, as She plucked Her lyre, so fast Her fingers barely seemed to move. Her hair, once raven-black, shining like the surface of the dark sea, now white like a crone's.

I carried Her out of the dungeon. The guard stood meekly by as I passed. I ascended the stone steps taking care not to bruise Her lolling head against the rock. It was all I could do to place one foot in front of another, to rise out of that fiery and desolate place. The fury drove me upwards. What a crime! A bestial, infernal crime! Who would stoop so low as to imprison the Queen of Heaven here? Stripped of all divinity and power. *Hung upon a meat hook!*

☽

As the vast oak door to Ereshkigal's throne room slammed behind me, I saw immediately something was wrong. The throng of attendants turned. None looked surprised. No one rushed forward to take Asherah from me.

Ereshkigal watched me coolly from her bony throne. Samael sat beside her, a stiff, unwelcome smile on his lips.

"Samael!" I cried. "You must not sit!"

"It's far too late for that!" Ereshkigal snapped. "You cannot expect to take what is mine without leaving something in return."

He sat. Said nothing.

"You dared refuse me. But he is better suited, in any case. He has . . . many qualities you lack." She put her hand on his, where it rested on the throne. He flinched and recovered himself. "A prince will suit me very well."

He lifted her hand to his lips and kissed it. Horror dripped like ice down my back. He turned to her and uttered words that did not reach me. She nodded and he rose.

"Lilith, once dear Lilith," he started as he approached. "I elect to remain. I stay here freely. Darkness is, after all, my natural domain." He spoke to his audience, to the courtiers lining the hall. He turned, so they could see his piercing gaze, his strong jaw, his sweeping arm. But his words said one thing, his eyes another. They looked upon broken Asherah in my arms and upwards to the living earth. Ice hardened around my heart. It gripped me in a frozen embrace.

Ereshkigal strode towards us. "You cannot beg for him now. He sat in my chair. He drank my wine, ate morsels of food from my own hand. He cannot leave."

He kissed me, his lips brushed my ear. I felt the blood pulsing in his throat. "It's the only way," he whispered. "Everything, for you." He rested there at my cheek until he was pulled sharply back.

I could not hold him, I could not speak.

He knew this from the very first, I realised with a sickening jolt. He hadn't stumbled, never blinked an eye, when I told him the saffron-gatherer said something—*someone*—must be left in Asherah's place. He had not warned me. He did not confer. I was unprepared.

"Go, niece! You have what you came for. Go with my blessing." She did not look upon her sister in my arms, whose back dripped blood, whose breath came ragged.

I could not look upon Samael. I turned and walked through the great doors to the antechamber.

☽

An attendant led me through the caverns of that place. She beat a drum to mark my path. Phantoms drifted, doomed to mope in melancholy for all eternity. There was no repose. They sat, then immediately stood. They lay, turning endlessly. There was no comfort, no rest. What purpose did it serve, this grotesque afterlife, this unavoidable fate?

As I walked, Asherah raved. She'd been silent in the throne room but now could not hold Her peace.

"Adam," She groaned. "My child too. Never listened. Wouldn't learn. Stubborn, like you. But vain and reckless. All my children. Would that I had saved them." Tears welled in her eyes.

The attendant marched swiftly ahead. Holding my burden, I could not keep to her drumbeat. I paused, overlooking a vast, grey field. No breeze lifted the stalks of the colourless crop. No sound of rustling leaves or calling cuckoo broke the silence. The wraiths laboured, as they did everywhere in that grim entombed world, starting in one direction, before turning for somewhere else, which brought as little satisfaction.

In the midst of this ceaseless motion, one was still. A woman, wearing faded garments. Her dull hair was braided in a long plait over one shoulder. She watched me intently. She opened her mouth, but nothing came out. She waved as if she were drowning. Though pallid, she was returned to her youth, as she was when I knew her. Not aged and bent, as she must have grown.

"That one." Asherah lifted Her head. "She was not mine." She looked upon Eve with sorrow. "But she must be saved too." She beat Her wasted hands at my breast. "They must all be saved!

Beside Eve stood the man for whom she had sacrificed freedom. Adam's head was bowed; he stared at the limp reeds of the barren field. Eve held him up by the crook of his arm. He saw no more clearly in the land of the dead than he had in the living world.

The beat of the drum faded into the distance. I couldn't stay here. I nodded to Eve. What could I say? She chose that place. She chose that man. This is where her love for him had led. My rage at her betrayal dimmed.

"What has He done?" Asherah returned to the same endless refrain. "We had a deal! Curse Him for eternity, we had a deal!"

I shifted my hands to get a better hold of my burden as I followed the echoing drumbeat ahead.

My Fruit is Better Than Gold

I walked towards the light and out of the cave. It was early evening, the time of swallows darting. Goat bells rang from the mountainsides. A boy whistled to his flock. How glorious was the living world, how rich in sound and colours and change. How grim and desolate, how static the place I left behind.

The air was chill. Was it winter already? While I was gone, the world had continued as before.

But Asherah was fading from it fast.

Her breath slowed. It came in stops and starts. Her laments ceased. No word had passed Her lips since we left the vaults of Hell. Returning to the world did not restore Her, as I'd hoped; it had the opposite effect. Eyes closed against the light, She frowned when the dying sun fell upon them. The breeze could not lift Her colourless hair. Her cheek was lifeless, like chalk.

I laid Her on a flat rock beside the stream. I wet Her lips but She wouldn't swallow. I went to the shepherd's hut to see if any food remained there, wading in the icy water to wash the thick clay and red dust of the Underworld from my sandals.

My sorrow and fury over losing Samael were so tightly knit, I could not pull one strand free from another. How quick he was to choose Ereshkigal. He could have found another way. And now what? We were too late, that was plain to see. Asherah would not live. No longer was She divine. She was empty. A shell, a husk.

Inside the hut, I found the remnants of a meal. How long had I been away? A day, a century? But someone had been here in my absence. A crook leaned in the corner, a goatskin furnished a chair.

There was a rusk of dried bread and a wooden pot of honey on the table. I lifted a waterskin to my nose: watered wine.

At the rock beside the stream, I folded the goatskin beneath her head. I crumbled the rusk, sweetened it with honey, and coaxed Her to eat. I dribbled wine on Her lips and begged Her to drink. I rested my head on the stone, feeling the warmth of the winter sun that had embraced it all day.

This is not how it should have been! I was the child, not the mother. Once I was mortal, She divine. Transcendent, eternal, the source of all life. How could this happen? Her holiness had vanished; taking with it all my dues and birthrights. I had hoped to return triumphant to Eden with Samael by my side. To triumph over the Father who had exiled and replaced me; who cursed all women to inferiority. To set things right, to start again for all womankind.

All that was gone, forever.

As my forehead drank in the warmth of the rock I felt a vibration, tiny at first but growing ever stronger. A dark mass shifted at the yawning mouth of the cave. It strained and stretched at its edges, expanding and contracting as if bursting to get out. It hovered there, a deafening buzz, then shot from the cave. I jumped back, startled, expecting the full desolation of Sheol to explode into the world.

As it swarmed towards me, rearing, redoubling, I saw it was a great mass of bees. They lingered above us, pulsing and drumming. I felt a great calm; pure serenity, infinite grace and heavenly peace. It rang through me, tingling, pulsating, throbbing; it was a kind of bliss.

Asherah opened Her eyes and was radiant again. Her skin glowed like sunlight on honey. Her hair shone raven-black once more, splayed in abundant tresses on the rock. I saw Her, in the eye of my mind, walking resplendent through the balmy groves and blooming watersides of Eden, lyre at Her hip.

"Courage, Lilith. My fruit is better than gold." Her voice was melodic, no longer wavering. She reached for my hand. "You will find me in those who are to come, for they shall be their own gods. My end is your beginning: you shall finish what was started."

In a blinding flash of light, She was gone. The bees dispersed in all directions at once, their hum spreading out, rippling into the tree-tops, swarming over the thyme and the lavender, hovering above the wildflowers and the rustling grasses, before speeding off into the great beyond.

☽

Her body remained. I buried it at the mouth of the cave, using water to soften the hard earth and sharp flint to dig a grave. I wove a wreath of aspen leaves to mark its place. I poured libation from the shepherd's wineskin. She did not need the sacrifice of blood, nor burnt offerings, those things He demanded. No threats to worship Her alone, on pain of death or damnation. No shows of power or domination. She was above all that.

Part Three

FLOOD

2347BC

When Noah awoke from his wine and knew what his youngest son had done to him, he said, "Cursed be Canaan! Lowest of slaves shall he be to his brothers."

Genesis 9:24–25

Judgement and Salvation

By Asherah's grave, the valley fell away in wintry tones towards the east. Somewhere out there lay Harappa and the mighty Indus. Beneath my feet: the desolate caverns of Sheol, where Samael now played prince and consort to Ereshkigal. Above: the soaring peaks, where we'd fought Senoy, Sansenoy, and Semangelof.

I turned my back on Harappa, on Samael, and started to climb.

How do you live when your god is dead? The thought consumed me. There was only one person I wanted to ask—the saffron-gatherer. I would take her this news—of Asherah's death, of my failure—and seek her counsel. She would advise me. But how long had I been gone from the mortal world? Did she live still? And how would I reach her? What awaited me at the mountain peak but a broken bridge, ropes and boards clattering above the sulphurous, misty chasm? Perhaps there was a new bridge. Another navigable pass. Anything was possible.

The weak sun warmed my back. An eagle rode the current. Stubborn winter flowers bloomed amid the snow on the stony path. I drew the goatskin I had taken from the shepherd's hut tightly around my shoulders. With Her death, was I mortal again? Certainly, I suffered the cold. My feet sank into the snow with each step, my toes were blue with ice. If I died here of cold and want, it was no more than I deserved. I had descended to the deepest pits of Sheol, faced the Queen of the Underworld and brought Asherah out of imprisonment, only to lose Her—and Samael too, into the bargain—as well as all my hopes for restoration in Eden. There was nothing I could not lose.

The higher I climbed, the sharper the icy wind blew. Snow fell; fat soft flakes that dusted my hair. They swirled and danced, masking the path, drawing a veil of solitude and silence around me.

☽

At the mountain ridge, I gasped. The bridge was gone. No sign of it remained, no ropes nor broken boards to show it once was here. But nor did the chasm yawn and gape beneath. The void through which Samael had fallen into the Underworld was gone, filled by a huge rockfall. The south side of the mountain peak—the eagle's back that had towered over the ridge—was freshly exposed, like bone shining through a wound. Scree littered the face, where the rock had blasted and fallen away. Huge boulders had tumbled into the chasm forging a land bridge to the far side. I tested my weight; the rocks held. I proceeded across, peering over the edges to see if any gaps remained. I told myself I was not looking for Samael. But if he'd hoped to make use of his secret entrance to escape Ereshkigal, it was gone.

Even more astonishing was the sight that greeted me in the valley when I arrived at the foot of the mountain path, many hours later. The once-vibrant fields were now barren and brown—and on fire.

In the centre of the plateau, exactly where the saffron-gatherers had sat beneath the spreading terebinth tree, a colossal timber structure blazed out of all control. Flames leapt as high as oaks, feeding the thick black cloud above it. Flakes of burning ash fell upon me where I watched in horror, crouching behind an outcrop of rock at the foot of the cliff.

Four men came, carrying buckets of water. The eldest, white-bearded and haggard, directed the younger men, but it was as raindrops against the raging inferno.

Beyond the blaze, three women stood before a cluster of huts. One of the women worked the wheel of a well. Another readied buckets. The third stood apart, hands to her head, watching the devastating scene unfold, the only still figure in all the valley. No grass nor flowers remained of the verdant crocus fields. The forest that fringed the valley had been hacked away. Felled trunks piled amid stumps of once-mighty oaks and graceful cedars. The swallows that had swooped and spiralled here in delight were gone, so too the soaring eagles.

As I crouched, wondering at the sight, a hand touched my arm. I jumped. A woman, finger to her lips, crept into my hiding place beside me. She was of middling age, dark hair braided and coiled above her ears. Her breath was hot on my cheek, one hand rested on my shoulder. Her body shook with laughter, her hand clamped to her mouth to muffle the sound.

"What—what is it?"

She could not speak for some moments. Once she had controlled her mirth, she took a handful of walnuts from a bag slung across her chest. She cracked one under her heel and tossed it to me.

"It is our judgement," she said darkly. "And our salvation."

She turned her back to the rock and leaned against it, taking me in. I savoured the nut. It was bitter, but I was hungry.

She jerked her head towards the mountain pass. "You came from the top, eh?"

Her sharp, knowing countenance unnerved me. I looked at my feet. She shrugged and started to walk away.

"Wait!" I called. "Whose judgement? What salvation?"

She was beyond the rock now and in full sight of the men, who had given up firefighting and sat upon the ground, shoulders drooping as they watched the fire burn. She threw a walnut shell onto the ground.

"Come," she said. "I'll show you."

Like a Zephyr

She led me along the edge of the rising cliff and slipped into a crack in the rock. Within, the passage opened to a grove of oaks, still green in the midst of winter, surrounded by the mountain on all sides.

It was a glorious sight after the barren, burning valley. The leaves rustled in soft wind; the late afternoon light dappled the moss beneath the boughs. A bull and a cow eyed us meekly from fenced pasture. A boar and a sow grazed on acorns beneath a tree. Honeybees buzzed in and out of an apiary.

At a stone altar before the trunk of the widest oak, she struck a flintstone and summoned a fire, sprinkling dried rosemary into it and muttering words of prayer. She threw in dried leaves that sparked and cracked, issuing a pine-scented smoke that danced before my eyes. It tickled my nostrils and made me light-headed, like wine.

She held my waist. "Do you see it?"

"See what?"

But all of a sudden, I did.

I saw rain, endless rain, falling on plains and ploughlands. I saw dried fields drink every drop, blooming lush and green, before sinking beneath a watery deluge. I saw a cyclone spiralling, rivers rising, marshes swelling. The towers of Uruk, Mari, and Babel fell beneath the waves. Mountains submerged, their peaks became as islands rising from a vast, unending sea.

I saw the narrowboat in which Samael and I had traversed the marshlands buffeted in the swirling river. People drowning. Animals flailing. Black water roiling, a mighty storm wheeling. I saw fury manifest in flood. Righteous anger swelling.

I staggered, fell backwards. I coughed at the smoke and blinked to rid myself of the terrible vision.

"I knew it," the woman said. "You are a seer too."

☽

"Call me Norea," she said.

"What was it? What did I see?" The sage tea Norea had steeped at the fire washed through me. My fear and agitation drained away. The cow lowed, a comforting sound; an echo of Eden.

"You saw Her rage. A storm is coming. The Holy Mother's fury. There will be a great flood to punish us all."

"You mean Asherah?" I crept closer to the fire. "She's gone. She can't raise a flood."

Norea shrugged. "You buried one manifestation of the Great Mother. There are many more."

"How do you know I buried Her?"

"I'm a seer, Lilith. Like you."

I didn't feel like one. Nor did I think Norea's claims possible. I had seen Asherah weak and impotent, hung from a meat hook in a dungeon. I had seen Her die.

"She wouldn't drown Her own children."

"Oh, but She would," Norea said cheerfully. "She is night as well as day. Cruel as well as tender. She who creates can also destroy. Nor can we blame Her. Her children have forgotten Her—betrayed Her, worshipping instead a false god." She spat into the fire.

Could it be it true? The possibility thrilled me. That Her power hadn't died with the body I buried. That She still had the means to punish and be revenged.

"What has that to do with it?" I gestured to the valley beyond the grove, where the crackle of the flames was only now abating.

"His god." She made a sign with her fingers at her breast. "Told him to build an ark. To save himself and his sons. There were daughters too," she scowled. "Not that you'd know."

The boar grunted and she threw him a handful of acorns.

"But why is it burning?"

"Because I set fire to it!" she laughed. "That was his third. I wait until they're nearly finished. Then—boom!" She mimed the explosion, the fiery end to his endeavour. "He doesn't know it's me." Her shoulders started to shake again. "He thinks,"—she could barely get the words out for laughing—"his god is testing him."

"And who is he—the old man?"

Norea scattered the sodden sage leaves in the ashes of the fire. She poked them with a stick, rearranging them to her satisfaction as they steamed a mild, herby vapour.

"My husband." She pronounced the word with distaste. "A drunk and a fool. His name is Noah. Don't feel sorry for him. Now you're here, he can keep the next one."

☽

Norea made me a shelter of skins in the evergreen grove. I slept there, under the silvery moonlight.

Every day, more animals arrived. Rabbits. A ram and a ewe. Two mules, a pair of geese. A mountain lion and lioness, who paced up and down their fenced strip of the grove, teeth bared in fury. All in pairs, all waiting to be taken aboard the ark and saved from destruction. Norea marshalled a network of agents—turbaned men, kilted soldiers, wildwomen, and goatherds—who brought them from across the land between the two rivers. Shinar, she called it, a name I'd not heard before. It would be entirely flooded, she said with glee.

By day, I fed the animals, watered them. I collected honey and hunted for partridges. As Norea predicted, Noah and their sons set to building a new ark. I watched it rise from the ashes of its predecessor, every day another plank, another beam towards completion. Seven stories high, it was now. They painted the hull black with pitch. Propped up on its blocks, it shone like ebony in the sun.

From the shadows of what remained of the forest, I studied the women—the scraping, bowing wives, as Norea called her daughters-in-law. They fetched and carried food and water to the men. They hovered at their husbands' sides, ready to dart forward at the flick of a wrist, the nod of a head, a barked summons.

I never questioned whether I would board with them. From the day I met Norea, it was assumed. The agreement was unspoken. I belonged.

〉

After sundown, I ate with Norea beside the fire amid the cacophony of her oak-grove zoo. I was curious that she lingered here, apart from her family and the homely fires beside the growing ark.

"Your husband—your sons—do they not await you?" I asked.

She bit into a golden apricot, passing another to me. "I keep from them, as much as I can. I have my work to do." She gestured to the animals crowding the grove, pressed against each other in makeshift cages and restraints. "I can't leave it to them. They'd collect two bulls and wonder why they do not calve."

I coughed. Ventured to ask, "Why did you burn his former arks?"

"Have you never been married?" She sucked the last of the flesh from her apricot stone and threw it into the fire. She watched the flames surge and recoil before continuing. "He said the ark was for the pure and faithful. That I am unwelcome because I worship a false god. Not that I wanted to board. I thought we should take the Holy Mother's punishment, not defy it. I wanted to see the world scoured clean."

"But still, you collected the animals?"

She rose to feed the goats, stroking their silken ears as they ate. "Why should they suffer for our mistakes?"

"And he will admit you to his ark now?"

"Admit me?" She laughed. "The man can't boil an egg. I will board or he will starve."

Norea proceeded to the chicken run. She scattered grain for the hen. The cockerel looked on from his perch, his scarlet comb resplendent in the firelight.

"So why change your mind? Why join him now?"

"It's not him I'm joining, you fool! It's you."

"Me! How can that be?"

Norea dragged a bale of hay for the donkeys, stopping to scratch their velvet noses. "I had a vision. I saw the world that will be remade. Only a thousand or so years in, mind you—already Creation needs a restart."

"What did you see? Will the new world be scoured clean?"

Norea looked up. The new moon slipped above the silhouette of the mountain, to be greeted by an owl from the netted aviary.

"Far from it. It will become filthier than ever. I can scarce understand what I saw. Green fields and lofty forests will shrivel and die. The seas will froth with waste, rivers will run dry, skies will be poisoned with black smoke. I saw people everywhere, like locusts, who do not cherish the earth from which we came. Who think they possess it. Taking from it, never replenishing."

"Then why save humankind? Let them drown!"

"Because I saw something else." Norea said softly. "I saw the Truth that will be carried in the ark and into the new world."

"And you think I carry it?"

"I saw you in my dreams. A woman, descending from the mountains, bereft and in despair. But in possession of Wisdom that must be shared. I am sent to shepherd you—as well as these animals. I will bring you to safety. Until one day a prophet will come, who will take on your Truth. Like a zephyr it will sweep the earth, blowing under doorways and through windows. It will whisper in every ear and tug at every heart."

As the moonlight silvered Norea's lined face, I felt the rising of something new. "My end is your beginning," Asherah told me on Her deathbed. "You will finish what was started." This was how I would avenge the crime done to Her—I would thwart the Father who had failed me and usurped my Mother! I would broadcast Her Truths—bring the Wisdom She had bequeathed me in the Tree of Knowledge—into the new world.

"What prophet?"

Norea shrugged. "Man or woman, I don't know. I didn't hear a voice. I saw a bright light. I felt Truth like balm of aloe on salt-rash. Water to a parched throat, breeze on a stifling day. There was a tree."

Her vision revived me. I saw the bright light, felt the balm of aloe, I tasted the water. This was surely what Asherah intended for me. This was the task for which She had preserved me from mortal death.

Two By Two

Soon, the rain came. For forty days and nights it pounded the goatskin of my shelter. Poured in rivulets down the mountainside, swamping the pasture in the grove. The animals sank in the mire. The bees, unable to fly, hummed with restiveness in the clay pipes of the apiary.

I rejoiced in every drop. Danced and wheeled in the quagmire. I revelled in the cleansing rage of Her righteous flood. My own Lady of the Sea! It was as if She'd gathered up the vastness of Her watery domain and hurled it to the land in fury.

Noah and his sons redoubled their efforts. They heaved felled trees from the boggy ground. Hammered in the final roof planks; the sound carried to me blunted in the sodden air. And still the animals came. A sleek-necked leopardess and her mate. Two cackling, bushy-tailed jackals. Grasshoppers and lizards carried in a wooden box. At the last minute, a pair of elephants arrived from the mangrove forests of the delta. I had never seen one before. I marvelled at their trunks, the gentle intelligence in their eyes.

☽

"It's time," said Norea when she next came to the grove. She was draped in a drenched wool cloak, leaning on a staff. "Wear this." She handed me a billowing garment, as dark and vast as a thundercloud.

She smoked the apiary to pacify the bees and sealed the pipes. They alone merited salvation in greater numbers than one solitary pair: the entire colony would be saved. "For they will pollinate the new world!" Norea said with glee.

In my garb, I looked like any of the other agents, tugging on a bridle, leading carts loaded with caged birds and snakes, squirrels and frogs. The sky loomed low and black. Clouds churned and rumbled. The land was swollen, half submerged. We waded in thick mud to our shins. Hooves sank. Cartwheels stuck. The rain never ceased, so thick I barely saw an arm's length ahead.

At the boarding ramp, Noah stood guard, grasping an olivewood staff. So aged, he was practically bent double. His eyes were clouded, his hand shook. Norea, dragging a cart stacked high with the pipes of her apiary, ignored him as she ushered us aboard. We slipped and slid on the steep incline, slick with mud from the animals who had gone before.

I hurried inside to be free from the rain. Within, ramps descended to six lower floors. I made myself at home on the fifth, among the goats and sheep, the black-tailed gazelles, the curve-horned ibex. The wolves howled in the deepest deck below, alongside the bears and jackals, leopards and lions. The elephants were housed there too, in the reinforced hull.

Norea's agents departed as a huge thunderclap cracked the sky. I comforted the animals, going from cage to pen to aviary to rub a nose, or scratch an ear. I laid straw, refreshed water bowls, until a great creak resounded as the ramp was pulled up. The ark lurched as the rising waters lifted it from its blocks. The bitter smell of bitumen seeped into the lower decks as Noah sealed the hatches. We were all closed in now, like wine corked in a jar.

I settled into the straw and breathed in the comforting scent of the animals. Here I lay, a hidden passenger in the belly of the vessel intended for man's deliverance. The very last person He had intended to save. The trick would have pleased Samael immensely. I imagined him striding through the caverns of his princedom in Sheol, his natural mirth undimmed, his humour untested. I found, for the first time, I was no longer angry with him.

☽

The days settled into a rhythm, as predictable and reassuring as the rocking of the ark. In the morning, Norea and her sons' wives came below to feed the animals. I retreated to the lowest deck, where the girls refused to go, on account of the lions. I never saw them, but I knew them from their chatter above me.

Aradka was young and whimsical, wife to Japheth. She sang as she worked; old songs, of harvest moons and unrequited love. Norea was cruel to her, this girl of fifteen or thereabouts. She told her to cork her godawful racket, that there was no such thing as love in this world, only strife and duty.

Nahalath, the wife of Ham, was petulant and irritable. She hated the animals, could not contain her fury at her new vocation as zoo-keeper. She complained she could not sweep away another mound of dung, that the screeching of the macaques, the howling of the jackals, was an affront to her senses.

Shem's wife, Sambethe, worked in a daze. She talked of walking to the mountain heights to collect a certain herb, to the depths of the forest to gather bark and moss, as if she'd forgotten these things were no longer possible. The solid world around her: the timbers of the ark that marked the new limits of her life—three hundred cubits long, fifty cubits wide and thirty cubits high—held no meaning.

When they had finished tending to the domestic beasts—the goats and the cattle, the mules and the deer—I heard three pairs of feet ascend to the deck where the fowl of every kind and the birds of every wing lodged. Up again, to where the rodents, lizards, and insects dwelt. Beyond the storerooms, pantries, and beehives, and up once more, into the realm of men.

Noah, Shem, Ham, and Japheth never came below. What they did all day I could not guess. There was no navigation or ship-craft to occupy them: the ark was left entirely to its own devices, tossed wherever it was carried. From the afternoons onwards, they drank. Jars clanked. There was unmelodious singing. But no instruments, no harp or lyre lifted their voices, no woman's voice joined them to sweeten the air.

Only when the girls had returned to the family quarters would Norea descend. She brought me bread, cheese, water—oil, if I needed it for my lamp. It took several trips to bring down the meat—she bred rabbits and sheep on board for this purpose—for the bears, wolves, lions, and leopards, for the tigers, vultures, and other raptor birds.

On one of these visits, I summoned the courage to ask her what had been gnawing at me since the day we met. "Tell me, Norea—" I lit my lamp. A multitude of heads, bowed at their meat, flickered in the oily flame. "What happened to your girls? You said you had daughters as well as sons."

She passed me a broom and set to sweeping the cages.

"Gone," she barked. "Sold as chattel brides beyond the mountains. Bright as a sunrise, each one. I'll not see them again."

She tapped the deck above with her broom. "Instead, I am sent those donkeys, dull as mud and twice as thick."

For a moment, I thought she was talking about the mules.

"Such are the ways of the false god!" she thundered. "This is why She is angry! The Holy Mother cannot tolerate such profanities. Her daughters to be traded like sacks of salt for the power of their wombs."

This, I realised, was the consequence of the lost goddess. The degradation, demotion, the subjugation of all women.

"And those girls," she pointed a shaking finger upwards. "They know nothing of Her! Naught of the Queen of Heaven! They are ignorant. Unthinking and unquestioning, like animals at the trough."

She leaned on her broom. At her feet, the lions tore at a sheep carcass, crunching rib bones as if they were pea-pods. Two decks above us, the desert larks sang sadly in the dark.

"How do you know of Her?" I asked. How could she know, so long after Asherah had been stolen from Eden, wiped from all human memory?

Norea scratched the bull-elephant's trunk as he bundled dried grass into his mouth.

"From our mothers, of course. My daughters took their knowledge with them, over the mountains. There, at least, they will be preserved from the flood. I learned from my mother and she from hers. All the way back, twenty generations and more, unto the first mother."

Twenty generations! Had it really been that long?

The lioness finished her meal and yawned. She stretched at the very limit of her cage, as if to remind us she did not comply with her imprisonment.

"Wait—the first mother?"

Norea looked at me as if I were as stupid as her sons' wives.

"The first mother, yes. She who drilled the love of Her into her daughters. Who trained them in ritual and divinity. Who passed on Her knowledge. She taught them whose Wisdom is finer than rubies, whose fruit is better than gold. All flows from her."

Norea scattered fresh straw for the elephants. She went to check on the leopardess, who was pregnant. Soon there would be cubs down here in the bottommost depths of the ark.

I followed. "Do you know her name?" I barely dared hope.

"Of course. She is venerated by all her daughters. She is the first mother. Eve."

Eve! I had not failed her. Nor had she failed me! My heart leapt to think she had, after all, profited from the Wisdom of the fruit. That she'd nurtured Asherah's truths, cultivated them in her children, even as Adam continued on the blindness of his path. Samael had told me of her three sons: the murderer, the shepherd, and the patriarch. He had not mentioned her daughters.

I remembered Eve as I'd seen her in the depths of Sheol. Pale and miserable. Holding up her worthless husband, as she had chosen to do in life.

I would not abandon her again. I would not leave her in that desolate place for eternity.

Nor would I turn my back on Samael, who had chosen to stay with Ereshkigal to save Asherah, all for my sake.

The Corked Jar

More and more, I kept to the lowest deck where the wildest animals lay, incubating their wrath. They were free from the knowledge that they bore responsibility for the continuance of their kind. They did not think, they did not brood.

Alone on this craft, I was spared the burden of reproduction. All others were paired male with female, two by two. I completed myself. I didn't need to produce new life. Instead, I carried an idea; a Truth to be gestated in the belly of the ark. To be birthed, as Norea had prophesied, in the coming world.

And truly, it felt like the idea, the Truth, was growing. As the ark rolled and pitched, buffeted like driftwood on the waves, I examined it from all sides. In Eden, Asherah's fruit had gifted me the knowledge that life and death are but a cycle. Neither are eternal. One leads inexorably to the other. That we are of this world, not set above it. So why were those poor souls tortured so in Sheol? Deprived of living bodies, condemned to an eternity of want and longing. Conscious they would never again eat, laugh, run, or dance. Why should humans, among all the creatures of this world, endure after their bodies were gone?

It made no sense. It defied everything Asherah had taught me.

Death itself was surely natural. Not Eve—nor I—had brought it into the world. But what purpose was served by this afterlife, by the misery and punishment I'd seen in Sheol? That was surely His plan, not Hers. How could humans be free of it? I yearned for the prophet who would bring these answers.

☽

Above me, the girls moved about the creaking ark, unaware of the unlikely passenger stowed below. Aradka was often in tears. I wondered at Norea's lack of compassion for her; this girl, like her own daughters, taken from her mother, to be given to a man twice her age. Her sisters-in-law were no kinder. Nahalath mocked her barrenness, for she was still not pregnant, despite the frequent bouts of intercourse Japheth forced on her—overheard, night after night, by the whole family, berthed alongside each other in the narrow confines of the upper deck.

"You're supposed to enjoy it!" said Nahalath. "All that squealing and protest. That's why you can't conceive."

"It hurts!" Aradka cried. "I can't bear his stinking breath in my face. And you're no better. Your womb may open, but you can't bring forth a living child. How many more times must we mop up your butchered creations?"

There was the sound of a sharp blow at that, howls of anguish, more tears.

Sambethe's attempts to pacify the other girls only heightened their fury. "The babies will come," she'd say. "Did not the Almighty preserve us to bring forth the children of men?"

I had counted ninety days of seclusion. A quarter-year fermenting in this corked jar. I was not sure the three of them would survive each other's company to populate the remade world.

☽

Outside, the seasons were passing. As the ark grew hot and clammy, I remembered with longing the almond blossom and budding hillsides of Alashiya in spring. At night, I'd creep up, past the birds of every wing, past Norea's sleeping family, and climb the ladder to the only unsealed exit onto the ark's roof.

There, under the watchful eye of the moon, I looked upon the watery new world. It was endless; nothing but a vast ocean. The waves peaked and fell away, the white foam gathering and dissembling like fragile mortal lives. The southern breeze carried red desert grains that rasped my cheek. The stars wheeled across the heavens.

When the first signs of dawn spangled in the east, I'd replace the hatch and descend below.

Often, I'd pause to watch Aradka sleep. A pretty thing, she looked younger even than her tender years. She slept at the very edge of the bed she shared with Japheth, her long tresses streaming back towards him, as if tethered by the rope of her hair. How easy it would have been to drive a knife into his heart and end her misery.

☽

The leopardess birthed her cubs. Three of them. I heard her whimpering in the night and ran, so I was there when they slid, blind and hairless, onto the straw. She rejected the smallest.

I brought him to my berth and fed him goats-milk from a cup. When his eyes finally opened, I was the first thing he saw. His soft, downy fur grew in; he tripped about the ark with me: my tiny, spotted shadow. I called him Malakbel, for the golden backdrop to his pelt shone like the sun.

The shapeless days passed. I brooded and planned. Asherah had lit the spark of knowledge in me. I had passed it to Eve, who handed it to her own children, down unto Norea.

Now, Norea had found me, given me hope again; stoked the fire of my purpose.

Unbreakable

When did I first notice it? The days all ran into one in the sweltering heat and the swaying, never-still darkness. I marked them by the daily descent of the girls and Norea's morning visits. But each day was indistinguishable from the next. Time became one molten lump and I was trapped within it, like an ant in resin.

All I recall is that Malakbel was quite grown by the time I felt the first flutter. It was night, judging by the stillness and silence from above. The sounds of Noah and his sons at their cups, Aradka's howls of pain as Japheth took his conjugal pleasures, had ceased.

It felt like a fall down a step. A flip of the stomach. The beating of wings from inside. I was half asleep—perhaps it was a dream?

But the following day, it returned. Like the rippling I used to feel when summoning my wings. What now? Some new transformation?

But it was nothing so extraordinary. For soon, my belly grew, in the usual way of women, rounded and firm. The fluttering strengthened. Little humps bulged across my taut skin, a foot, a tiny fist.

I felt horror at this creature growing inside me—unbidden, unwanted, unsought. How was it possible? I counted the months since I'd known Samael in that way. Five, maybe six, by my reckoning. Do angels procreate in the manner of men? How could I—immortal, inhuman—conceive? It scarcely mattered, for there was no denying it.

Norea noted it with raised brow. "How have you managed that, my girl? Don't tell me the old goat has been down here."

I barely disguised my disgust.

"Well, it can't be Japheth. We all know he's entirely sated in that quarter. Not my Shem: too lazy. Nor my Ham: too gentle."

I left her to her wonder and paced the deck, shadowed by my skittering leopard cub. I was driven mad by hunger, wracked by sickness in the airless, rocking chamber. When it became harder to hobble between the decks, I moved permanently below, nestled between the elephants and the lions, a lying-in serenaded by deep-throated roars and rumbling trumpets.

I prepared as best I could—I who had held a baby but once in my life. Norea brought me squares of linen and showed me how to swaddle an infant. I practised on Malakbel, who enjoyed the game, holding his soft paws in the air as I wrapped him. How Samael would have relished this. How he'd have spoiled and loved his own child. Perhaps he'd have found another way to leave the Underworld, had he known.

I mused on the possibility of my own mortality. For if Asherah could die, then surely I could too. A fitting end for the first woman. To expire giving birth, like so many.

☽

The day came. My waters broke. A gushing out of me, the herald of new life. The pain struck like a thunderbolt, coming at intervals, then faster, each torturous wave crashing on top of another with no time to catch my breath.

"I shall make your pains in childbirth most severe!" God had threatened Eve. But I was not of her line, untainted by the curse, and still it was an agony.

It was long before dawn, many torturous hours until Norea would come. But somehow she knew and was beside me, bringing cloths and warmed water. She burned tiny, black seeds, had me inhale the smoke to dull the pain. She mopped my brow, made me walk to keep in motion. "There, there, my girl. Nine times I've done this, only two born dead."

That was not comforting.

I had never seen a human birth before. Had no conception of the horror, the bursting forth, the violence of it all. No mother to warn me what birthing life truly means. What a joke it was—an affront to all women—to parody life's creation as one easeful puff of His breath.

Only a man would imagine such a thing. This is what it truly entails: the blinding light of pain. A sacrifice of flesh. Disfigurement to create anew. How could it not be torment, to bring forth what is most precious: new life?

After all the moaning and the arching and the searing, white-hot pangs, the end was quick. Norea wiped the blood from his face and placed him warm and slippery on my still-heaving chest.

She cut the cord between us, but, as the link was severed, I felt my horror vanish, and the unbreakable bond of my love for him begin. He had his father's black eyes, the same prominent bow of his lips. A thick head of hair. As I marvelled at his tiny feet, I noticed a defect that made me love him all the more: the second and third toes on each foot were joined together. It made him perfect. Unique.

I must be immortal, I reckoned, to have withstood such an ordeal. But was he mortal or divine? Each brought its own curse. The former, and I would watch him age and die. Finally, he would go to Sheol, where I could not visit him. If he were heaven-born, he would be condemned, like his parents, to an eternity despised by a vengeful god. I examined his shoulders, but there was no sign of sprouting wings.

The she-elephant unrolled her trunk through the bars and caressed us both. Malakbel retreated to my feet, patrolling the end of my bed, a furry, spotted guard.

Among my few possessions, I still had the nard oil I had taken from Uruk. I anointed him with drops on his crown. I blessed him as a child of Asherah. After all this time, my destiny as the first mother was fulfilled. I had felt free from the burden of motherhood, but still it came. The greatest and most ordinary of Her gifts.

And so, my child was the first to be born in the remade world. It was all worth it. The death and the watery destruction, the sacrifice, the starting over. I was glad the world was scoured clean, just for him.

The Promise

I called him Asmodai.

My child's infancy was spent much like his months in my womb: cradled in the darkness, buffeted in the rocking ark. As for me, I was glad of the seclusion. For weeks, we remained cocooned together. I sang and rocked him. I relished the grip of his tiny hand in mine, his feet kicking idly at my ribs as he suckled. My mind was cleared of the fury and the fears that had consumed me for so long. I revelled in the satisfaction of his needs and desires, in his contentment, in my joy in his perfection. But it would not last forever.

When he was eight weeks old, Norea reported the flood was retreating. I'd almost forgotten what lay beyond the ark. It jolted me from my ease, reminded me of our inevitable return to solid ground.

Noah had released a dove, Norea said. It had returned with the budding stem of an olive tree in its beak.

"So there's land?"

Norea clicked her tongue. "Open your eyes, Lilith! It means there was always land—elsewhere. Can a tree survive months submerged in the briny sea? His god—" she rolled her eyes, "told him the whole world was flooded. Lies! It was only the land of Shinar."

I thought of the desert sand on the southern wind, those nights I sat on the roof of the ark, and knew she was right.

"So what now? Will Noah steer a course towards land?"

"Po! The old fool has no stomach for steering. He has no will of his own. We shall come to rest wherever the waves leave us."

"And us—" My baby watched Norea solemnly as he suckled. "How will you explain your secret passengers when we emerge?"

Her eyes sparkled as she stroked the rosy bloom of Asmodai's cheek. "Ha, my girl! That's the beauty of God's will. It explains everything!"

$$\smallint$$

Norea was right. She was always right. For after the ark came to rest with a stomach-turning crunch, after the waters had retreated so the peaks and sodden valleys reappeared from beneath the waves, I walked out of the ark, cradling my infant son in my arms.

Finding themselves at last released, the animals lumbered into the emerging undergrowth. The lions prowled, the elephants thundered, the sheep meandered. The birds flew joyfully into the wide, free skies. Off they all went, with never a glance behind them. Except for Malakbel, who cowered, hiding behind my skirt, when I froze at the foot of the ramp under the unrelenting gaze of the righteous family.

There was total silence. Then Norea sank to her knees. "God be praised, it's a miracle! Witness how the Almighty has preserved this mother and child in the very belly of His ark!"

Noah looked from his wife to me with astonishment. His sons gaped.

Norea beat at her breast. "What can this be but a sign of Your forgiveness?" she called unto the heavens. "You have sent us a promise that Your new world will be fruitful and abundant! We thank you for this child, this pledge to us, Your servants!"

The sons stood, awkward and silent, watching their breast-beating, raving mother. I knew Japheth from my night-time sentries over his marital bed. His jaw clenched and released. Aradka never took her eyes off him—not from love, but watchfulness. Shem had a paunch and a reddening beard. Ham's face was soft and childlike, framed by dark, curling hair.

Sambethe broke the silence. A willowy girl, she seemed to float as she came to embrace me. "Thank the Lord you were saved!" She took Asmodai from my arms and held him up in the bright morning sun. "It is clear you are righteous, or He would not have blessed you with this fine, healthy boy."

Nahalath eyed my child with envy. Her hand flew unbid to her belly. Aradka allowed herself a brief glimpse of me, before returning to watch her husband's every move.

Noah rapped his staff on the ground in grudging assent. He built an altar at the foot of the ramp and made sacrifice. "The Almighty has granted my prayers! Never again will He bring his vengeance on this polluted world, and we for our part must keep ourselves pure. This is our covenant, for Man is lord of all those that walk on the land, all that swim in the water and all that fly in the air."

I swallowed my distaste. Lord of all, indeed. A true heir of Adam. The new world would start with the errors of the first.

As the sky cleared, a rainbow appeared, vast and resplendent in the sky. A sign of His forgiveness and love, Noah proclaimed.

Or the ordinary effect of rain in a sunlit sky. I kept that to myself.

We prayed. As the incense curled around us, caressed by the warm embrace of Norea's mind-softening herbs, we sent forth grateful thanks for our deliverance. Perhaps not all in the same direction.

Mount Ararat

So I found myself in the bosom of this warring family. My son was dandled on their knees. It was to them he crawled, their smiles he craved, their hands that held him when he learned to walk. I spun and wove with the women. I tended to the bees and goats. I wandered the hills and valleys of the ever-widening world with Malakbel at my side.

We had landed in a mountainous country, high and exposed. As the summer sun burned away the floodwater, a lush valley emerged. We descended, cut birch trees and raised barns and dwellings. A separate house for each couple and one for me and my child. Was it decent, asked Noah and his sons, was it godly, for a woman to live alone, unsupervised by any man?

"Po!" Norea scoffed. "In former times, a woman could not live alone for risk of defilement. But has our Lord not drowned the evildoers? Only the righteous remain, just four good men in all the world. What danger can there be for her now? Which of you would dare lay a hand on she who bore His sacred child, who wears His protection as her mantle?"

She didn't need to mention the full-grown leopard that followed me at all times, my guard and protector. Malakbel snarled to make his presence known.

Shem, Ham, and Japheth looked at the floor. Noah stared wearily into the fire. Perhaps he saw there the embers of his former arks, all burned to ashes by his wife.

☽

The first winter was hard and long. We had no harvest to put aside. We survived on the last of the grain from the ark, on the plentiful salted fish taken before the waters retreated, the dried apricots, plums and figs stored from the first autumn. There was at least no lack of water, thanks to the thick snow that quilted the mountain and dusted the valley.

Asmodai, Malakbel, and I slept huddled together for warmth, the ever-burning fire barely keeping the ice from the bedcovers. Through the sharp winds and howling storms of winter, we watched as the ark on the mountainside broke and fell apart. By the time spring arrived, it was gone, entirely.

As the snow melted and the days warmed, we found the waves had chosen well indeed to leave us in this place. The mountain had once been a volcano; the black soil was rich and fertile. An icy stream brought fresh water, teeming with green chub and rainbow-hued trout. The valley bloomed with flowers: purple lilies, blue lupins; orange tulips that drooped like weeping brides.

We cultivated a wild grain like barley. We planted orchards of apricot and plum. Norea grew her mind-altering herbs on the mountainside where the altitude increased their strength. Noah cultivated a grapevine, the first, he claimed, in existence. He did not answer when I asked him from where he had taken the seeds, nor the source of the wine, which had been plentiful before the flood. Until the vine fruited, he brewed beer and drank it to great excess. It was commonplace to find him sleeping naked in the goat-pen in the mornings, his long beard matted with dung and straw, after Norea had barred him from their hut for drunkenness.

And so we lived, we ten who had survived the flood. Ten in the entire world, according to Noah. Ten in the land of Shinar, according to Norea. It was all the same to me. I planned to leave when my baby was weaned, when he could walk beside me into the unknown.

I had not forgotten my mission. I would find the prophet Norea had prophesied. Together we would spread Asherah's Truths into the new world.

But somehow, I found my horizons shortened. My world had shrunk to the size of my child. The fears I had conceived for humanity—for womankind; diminished and humbled by an intractable, usurping god—were transferred entirely to his care.

I found myself preoccupied with the everyday concerns of an ordinary mother. I was filled with dread for every danger. He crawled and I worried for his tender knees against the stony ground. He walked, and I watched for every unguarded ledge. When he ate, I hovered over him, fearing he would choke. My mind played over and again the possibilities of his imminent demise, while he acted as if he were unbreakable. Fearless, he was drawn to the fire. Curious, he ran from my arms to the forest, heedless of the wolves and scorpions that dwelled there. He was transfixed by flowing water and would try to catch it in his hands as I washed clothes at the riverbank. Many times, I plucked him from the swirling eddies just in time. The fragile skein of his life was only ever kept spinning by my unceasing watchfulness.

My terrors grew as his world expanded. In time, he rode horses, wildly, climbed cliffs and crags recklessly, swam in the raging torrents of the icy mountain streams.

He wandered far from our valley, his slingshot little protection against the mountain lions and bears that had thrived since leaving the ark.

These were merely the natural dangers. I have said nothing of the threat from the people we lived among. Not all of them believed he was sacred. Not all of them wished him well.

The Lines of Noah

We had gone forth and now we multiplied. As my son grew into a fine youth, we ten doubled, then trebled. We were now a village of thirty-two souls.

Sambethe bore five sons: Elam, Asshur, Arpachshad, Lud, and Aram. Our land of milk and honey put an end to Nahalath's repeated miscarriages, but her misery was replaced with the life-draining menace of continual pregnancy. She birthed Cush, Mizraim, Put, and Canaan. Aradka, whose body barely seemed up to the task, brought forth Gomer, Magog, Madai, Javan, Tubal, Meshech, and Tiras.

These were the boys, whose names passed into the records. From them issued the tribes of men: the Ludim, the Anamim, the Lehabim, the Naphtuhim, the Pathrusim, the Casluhim, the Caphtorim (and whence the Philistines). The Jebusites, the Amorites, the Girgashites, the Hivites, and the Hamathites.

The girls, from whom also issued these tribes, were not recorded. I give them here. Sambethe's daughters were Elisheba and Bademath. Nahalath's three girls, Serah, Timna, and Mehetabel. Aradka, whose fresh face and tiny body had been ravaged by her seven sons, finally produced a girl: the youngest of our clan, sweet, doe-eyed Anah.

Twenty-three children in all, including my Asmodai, now a young man of seventeen years. Born among animals in the ark, he had grown to cherish all the creatures of the world. The sight of Japheth's dogs chained to a post in the midday sun reduced him to tears. He hunted, but never killed a female deer, for fear her fawns would go hungry. Our hut was full of the animals he rescued. The lambs who would not suckle. The puppies, those runts of every litter, that Japheth would have drowned for their weakness. Wherever Asmodai went, they followed him, as did the children. He led a bounding rabble, a human and canine pack.

I, however, was never entirely welcome. I was an interloper, an unaccompanied woman. "Where did you come from?" Japheth asked me once. "Go on, you can tell me." He laughed, the sound of a crow calling. "Who's the father of the lad?"

I lived close to the valley of Noah, I told him. Heard a Voice one day that spoke directly to my mind. It told me I was with child and must hide myself within the ark. It was a miraculous birth, a virginal conception. There was no father.

"Come on, Lilith. You know I don't believe that. And why," he changed tack, thinking to catch me off guard, "don't you age? You're as fresh as the day we stepped off the ark."

I smiled as if it were a compliment. "Ah," I returned. "It is husbands that age women. I stay young because I am free."

Ham alone among the men was different. Norea's favourite; she lavished affections on him that were never shown to Shem or Japheth. She cooked lamb and barley broth just for him. She made his garments, for she said Nahalath's weaving was unskilled. It was no mystery why she favoured him: he was gentle and kind-hearted. He never raised his voice, like his brash and querulous brothers. Never embarrassed himself in drunkenness like his father. He had a fine, clear voice, which he raised in song at the altar. He preferred his own company to that of his family, and when Asmodai was old enough, he took to him too. He gave him a sparrowhawk he had reared from a chick. Together they would take off, hawking in the woods and the vast, empty valleys beyond.

Shem and Japheth's only interest in my son was to make of him a fighter. Like Adam before them, they prepared for war with imaginary enemies. Shem, the metalsmith, fashioned a sword for Asmodai and engaged him in combat. I watched, heart in my throat, as my nimble son side-stepped and parried. He had not the stomach for attack, never landed so much as a scratch.

The women took their lead from Norea and accepted me in their way. Indeed, we had little choice but to get along. Even Nahalath and Aradka's feud settled over time, as snow levels a furrowed field.

Together, we delivered each baby, made compresses to heal the mother's torn flesh. As Norea had for me in the ark, I burned azallu seeds to ease each mother's torment in childbirth. I blessed and anointed every child with nard oil. I dedicated them all to Asherah.

Together, we grieved for the infants that were lost: four before, or at the moment of their birth, another six before they could walk. We buried them on the mountain within a small cave, to protect them from the howling winds and winter snows. Ten little burial mounds, ever heaped with fresh flowers and keepsakes: baby's rattles, feeding cups, cloth-bound dolls. The men did not come to these funerals. They concerned themselves only with the boys after they came of age. Often, I'd look up from the beehives or the dairy churns to see a lonely figure on the mountainside path and know it was Sambethe, Nahalath, or Aradka going to weep over her dead children.

Watching them, I understood the fullness of Eve's double curse: the agony of childbed was not enough. She must be subject to her husband too to deny her the power to escape it. "He shall rule over thee!" God had thundered. It made women little more than animals, labouring for a master at the cost of their own health and happiness— at the expense even of motherhood, for they could not care fully for the children that lived, so many of them there were, so reduced were the women by the relentless pregnancies and loss.

I alone was free from this never-ending cycle: the forced and joyless intercourse, the pains and sicknesses of pregnancy, the dangers of birth and grief for the dead babies. I had time to love and care for Asmodai, protect him and relish his company. I learned to live with my fears as the price of his life. What choice did I have? At night, as he slept peacefully beside me, I raged that his death would come before mine. But I was lucky. At least my child would *live* before he died— unlike so many of Sambethe, Nahalath, and Aradka's lost infants.

And we did live, we two, very happily. At the end of each day, we retreated into our hut and shut the door on the righteous. Asmodai, would return to his latest project: whittling a wheeled horse for one of the younger children, perfecting the design of a slingshot. Malakbel would stretch before the fire. I took to carving too: a naked woman, full-breasted, a triangle for her sex. Her long, coiled hair, crowned with a crescent moon, like bull horns. Over and again, I made my idols, from stone, from wood and clay. I lined them on the hearth-stone: a very army of Asherahs. When my work was done, I took a cup of wine to the rose garden I had planted from the seeds I took from Uruk.

Sambethe, Nahalath, and Aradka were denied all this. Condemned to spend their youth in the repeated agonies of childbirth, watching their children die. They had no time for roses, warming hearths, or wine. They were forbidden to deny their husbands their conjugal right though the act led only to pain and misery for them.

God had commanded: *Be fruitful and multiply!*

It costs men nothing and women everything.

Yoked to the appetite of a man for whom procreation posed no pain, no risk at all, but only pleasure, the women had no choice but to keep walking the path that led to the burial cave again and again.

☽

"Can nothing be done for them?" I asked Norea. Nahalath had just lost another boy. He survived the birth only to die in his crib three weeks later. He looked too perfect to bury, as if he were merely sleeping. Nahalath had screamed and raved. She would not be carried up the mountain. She did not see him laid to rest.

It was a beautiful early summer morning. We ground grain, the river singing beside us, as Malakbel, lazy in his old age, basked in the sun at my feet. Norea had given me the keys to the grainstore. It was my job to keep it full, down to me alone to banish the howling wolves of hunger. Norea poured grain into the quern and set to it with vigour. She was in her mid-sixties now, still strong, still angry. "It is their lot. We must have children, and who but those three can birth them?"

"But so many of them? And so frequently—without relent?"

"The babies die," she shrugged. "They must be replaced."

"Perhaps they wouldn't die if their mothers weren't so exhausted!"

Norea rolled her eyes. "They can't stop yet. There aren't enough girls. We need them—or have you forgotten your task?"

"*My* task?"

She wiped the sweat from her brow. We had been at the quern since dawn. "Who do you think you will pass the flame of your Wisdom to, if not these girls? There are only six of them. Six alone, in all the world!"

"In Shinar."

"That *is* our world."

"So you will condemn Sambethe, Nahalath, and Aradka to continual agony just to produce girls to preach for you?" I gestured to Shem and Japheth, who were carving new altar posts in the village. "You are no better than they—who treat their wives as breeding mares."

She watched Shem, polishing the horns carved from acacia wood that crowned the altar. "Lilith," she sighed. "I want to remake the coming world. If those foolish women must be sacrificed, so be it. Anyway, I don't know what you think I can do about it."

I emptied the milled flour from the quern and poured in fresh grain. "I've watched you." My voice wavered. "You know the properties of every herb, root and leaf in this country. You grind, you boil, you dissolve. You devise salves for every ailment we suffer. You have cultivated your medicines so they are twice as strong as before. There is no pain you do not know how to treat. You keep the bulls from the cows when you do not want them to calve, you keep the rams from the ewes. Do not tell me you don't know how to stop a pregnancy!"

I heaved the grindstone into the river. A petulant act, it would be hard to find another that served so well. Malakbel sensed the discord. He padded after me, leaving Norea sitting back on her heels, open-mouthed.

I climbed to the burial cave and looked down upon our settlement. Nahalath had been here. A hank of her hair, tied in a leather cord, lay on her child's fresh grave. Where were they now, these babies? Among the howling, never-comforted infants of Sheol. And what, I brooded among the dead, is the purpose of Wisdom if not to free women from this tyranny—to escape a fate producing children like farmed animals?

Norea was right—I had forgotten my task. I had furnished the grainstore instead of minds. In my preoccupation with Asmodai I had retreated inside myself, forgotten Her plan. Endowed with Her Wisdom, all women could avoid an earthly hell.

Far below in the valley, I saw my son. A tumbling pack of children and dogs followed him, as usual. They ran into the forest, to check the snares and practice with their slings. They hung on his every word, reached for him, like flowers towards the sun. Elisheba, the eldest girl, was at his side, as always, barely a barley stalk between them.

There was Norea, bent double, feeling for the grindstone in the river. Shem was still at work on the shrine. Under a fig tree, Noah cradled a jar of wine. Ham was in the far distance with his flock. And there was Japheth. He had wandered from the altar towards the edge of the village. He watched Asmodai and Elisheba as I did, saw their hands reach for each other far too soon, before they gained the safety of the forest. An icy jolt of dread ran down my spine.

I never was a true seer. It was Norea's herbs and sorcery that gave me foresight of the flood. Not before nor since was I gifted prophecy again.

And yet, I knew in that instant. I saw exactly how it would all end.

The Grove

I returned to my task with the resolve of a spider at a broken web. I started with the three women and six girls. I lost the boys at the tender age of seven, when they were taken, hands still reaching for their mothers, to be taught the ways of men.

Every afternoon, as Noah drank, and Shem, Ham and Japheth dozed after their morning's work, we left the village for a grove in the forest. Sambethe drifted slowly, arm-in-arm with her daughters Elisheba, who had the same willowy gait and vacant, dreamy expression, and loud, funny Bademath. Nahalath had to be dragged by her girls: clever Serah, harp-playing Timna, and Mehetabel, the mimic. Aradka, keen to escape Japheth for a precious few moments, ran, carrying little Anah, always laughing, on her shoulders. The youngest boys, Canaan, Aram, and Tiras, raced ahead, fighting with sticks, ambushing each other from the undergrowth.

Among the silvery birches and ancient oaks, as red-winged finches darted above our heads and squirrels watched beady-eyed from the boughs, I talked of the Holy Mother. Of the role She had intended for them, of Her natural law. I told them what it meant. That they were equal to their husbands, not their subjects—nor that word that still sent my ire raging like a furnace—their *helpmeet.*

I told them of their ancestors, naked and unsullied, in the Garden of Eden. How Asherah had chosen woman to receive the gift of Wisdom. That their foremother Eve brought reason into the world, not sin. That they must use their hard-won Wisdom to question, to improve and advance; not accept and endure. That men would have them believe disobedience was Eve's vice, when it was her greatest virtue.

In time we came to the point that most closely concerned them: that all life is precious, but Creation is a power to be used sparingly, not relentlessly, without care or concern for their health. That Wisdom demands they choose when and how often they bring new life into the world: the power to give life comes with the right to deny it. That as they nurtured and cherished their young, so they were bound to protect this living world that sustains us, not dominate and exploit it. I told them their bodies are not foul nor sinful; these are bold calumnies advanced to deny the power of our wombs. The blood we shed is the source of all life: it is holy, not unclean.

There was more, so much more. I had barely got started.

They listened, readily. But they did not respond. They seemed as pebbles at the bottom of the river, the current coursing above their heads, while they languished immobile and unstirred beneath.

I was beginning to grudgingly admit Norea was right. Her daughters-in-law were dull as donkeys. Perhaps I should send them home to their spinning; my time would be better spent on the girls.

Then, one day, at last, Aradka came unstuck.

She was pregnant again. For the twelfth time in seventeen years. Her hand rested on the bulge of her belly, her legs astride so it fell forward from the log on which she sat. She was thirty-two by now and worn out, utterly.

"Then where is She?" she demanded. "How can you tell me I have a Protectress, when we have seen nothing of Her all the days of our lives? Why is She silent? What power can She truly wield?"

I fell at the first fox-hole. What could I say? That She was dead? That I, with my sloth and self-indulgence, had killed Her?

"You will not hear from Her. She has been laid low by Her enemies. But in the act of honouring Her laws, you will remember your own worth."

"What use is that?" yelled Aradka, seeing my own doubt and disappointment. "No! It is as I thought. We are alone. It's fine for you. No one masters you—and it shows. You have kept your youth and beauty." They all looked at me then, seeing it for the first time. "But look at me! Who is there to hear me? Who can punish my tormentor?

How can I refuse he who is bigger and stronger than me? He has a living god to bolster his rights, his brothers to stand beside him. And I have none to protect me—no one!"

☾

Aradka did not return to the grove for a while. Instead, she wandered to the burial cave, or sat throwing stones into the rushing river. We took Meshech and Tiras with us, but Anah would never consent to be separated from her mother.

My lessons continued and the older girls became more voluble.

"It seems to me," said Elisheba one day, as we sat on felled logs in the grove, "that a woman's lot is decided by her choice of husband. Aradka is unlucky." Sitting behind her, Sambethe and Nahalath both looked down. "But her torments shan't be mine, for *I* shall marry someone who loves me."

She smirked, in that self-regarding way that comes easily to the young, congratulating herself on seeing what she supposed Aradka had not.

"You stupid girl!" Sambethe threw a pinecone at her head. "Do you think you—or I for that matter—will have any choice over who you marry?"

Elisheba's smirk vanished. Her cheeks reddened to burning crimson. She could hardly be blamed. The eldest of the girls, she had not guessed what was waiting for her. Sambethe knew, Nahalath too, judging by her anxious glances towards her own daughters, the hands that turned relentlessly in her lap, picking at the skin of her fingers.

I watched, helpless, as Asmodai and Elisheba's attachment grew. They were discreet, but I saw it in all things. How they were both often missing from the altar when the offerings were burned. How Elisheba arrived, dishevelled and rosy-cheeked to the goat-pen for morning milking, dried leaves and moss still clinging to the back of her tunic. How Asmodai's eyes were drawn to her when she passed, carrying milk into the dairy. How he would slip there when he thought no one was watching, and their two heads, one dark, one fair, would sink below the churns.

But I was not the only one watching. Where Elisheba walked, brooding Japheth followed. Her happy, shining countenance only ever one step ahead of his grim shadow. The young lovers continued on their merry path, heedless to the dark cloud gathering behind them.

☽

One afternoon, as we set out from the village, Aradka looked up from the bench beside her hut, grabbed Anah's hand, and rose to join us.

Japheth hulked, filling the doorway. "Where are you going?"

Aradka froze. Looked from us to her husband.

I answered for her. "To the forest."

"I didn't ask you." His eyes were fixed on his wife. She shrank under his gaze.

"We must prepare the girls for their marital duties," Sambethe said brightly.

"Then she'll be of no use to you. She is a failure as a wife. What man's rod would not lose its vigour faced with such a wretched, haggard creature. Stay!" He clicked his fingers and pointed to the bench, as if she were a dog.

Elisheba marched over and took Aradka's hand. "I need her. She is my aunt."

"And our sister," said Nahalath, as she took Anah from Aradka, who was struggling to hold the squirming child. Elisheba led Aradka briskly away, as fast as her heavy belly would allow.

Japheth's hands balled into fists.

Norea and I had spoken little since our argument by the river. She rose now from beneath the fig tree, put aside her spindle and spoke to her son. We didn't dally to hear what she said. We hurried away, before he turned his wrathful gaze back to his wife.

In the grove, Sambethe told us of her childhood, far to the west, in a land of olive trees and resined wine (she, too, laughed at Noah's claim to have invented viticulture), where girls swam, ran, and wrestled, like the boys. I had forgotten these women, like me, were exiles. Brought from elsewhere for their fresh blood and fruitful wombs. It worked very well for the men. How much easier it was to bully their wives, separated from all those who loved them. Stripped from their families, were they even human? Mere vessels, bearing babies for their masters.

As we gathered our belongings—the linen in which we wrapped saffron-cakes, the tambour we beat in worship, the jars of water and wine—little Serah spoke up. Nahalath's eldest daughter, twelve years of age, sharp-eyed and serious. "If women once were gods," she asked, "can they be prophets—priestesses too?"

At last! The first bud on my vine! I pulled her to me. "Of course! And you shall be the first. These—" I put her hand to a strong oak, to the furrows and ridges of its bark, "shall be your altars. In the woods, the hills and high places. Wherever there are trees, for they are all sacred to Asherah. Like Her and like you, they give life. Bear fruit and sustain."

Next time, I thought. Next time, I would tell her of the mighty priestess in the moon temple of Uruk. Of the snake-wielding celebrant by the sparkling sea in Alashiya. Of those women in the very valley of her ancestors, who harvested saffron for the missing Queen of Heaven.

Aradka

When I look back, my grief is like a mountain, eclipsing the path that led there. For there was no next time. No more secret meetings in the grove. That first bud, Serah's awakening, was also the last.

It started on the day I was woken before dawn by a child screaming. In my half-sleeping panic, I looked to see if Asmodai were safe, before remembering he was no longer a child; that he'd gone to bathe in the river and check his rabbit-traps on the way home.

No, the sound was coming from outside my hut, near the olive press. From Japheth's dwelling. It was close to Aradka's time. I expected to be called at any moment, awaited the mewl of a newborn. But this was the shriek of an older child, bereft and inconsolable.

When I got there, Norea was on her knees. Aradka lay in a pool of blood, eyes open, staring. Her legs were twisted, her swollen belly bulged on the cold floor. My breath came fast and jagged.

"What happened?" Norea asked.

"Nothing!" Japheth protested. "She fell."

Anah crouched in the dark corner, her face shining with tears.

Shem, Sambethe, Ham, and Nahalath arrived. In the room beyond, Aradka's little sons stood silent. They flinched when their father came to comfort them. Sambethe stepped forward to embrace Anah.

"Get out!" Norea waved her blood-stained arm behind her back. "The lot of you! Not you, Lilith. We must save the baby."

She sliced Aradka open like a calf for sacrifice. I mopped the blood with straw. I closed Aradka's unseeing eyes. I held her still-warm hand, a grotesque parody of a commonplace birth.

Norea peeled back her belly like a flayed hide. The viscera glistened. She wrestled inside the corpse and lifted out the baby, thin and grey, the cord wrapped around its neck like a noose.

☽

We buried them in the cave, the baby cradled in Aradka's arms. I laid a wreath of roses. The burial mound seemed obscene, outsized among the infant graves. Asmodai squeezed my hand as Norea led the prayers. What was there to say? A miserable life, filled with suffering. At least it was over. At least she didn't bury this baby. He, alone among his lost brothers and sisters, would have his mother to console him amid the desolation of Sheol.

Never was there a sadder funeral procession. Eight motherless children stumbled down the mountainside. Japheth walked alone. His brothers held back, his mother refused his touch. As we reached the village, she picked up Anah, who'd not said a word since her mother's death. "She'll live with me now. She needs a woman's care." There was no argument from Japheth.

☽

I was expecting it, like the first drops of rain after thunder. After two weeks of mourning, at the close of the morning offering, Japheth spoke up: "I need a wife and a mother for my sons."

I felt a rising tide of panic. Coils of smoke from the altar clouded my nose and throat.

"Elisheba is of age. I choose her."

I breathed again. But Elisheba let out an anguished cry. Sambethe trembled and swayed. Asmodai stiffened and looked to me.

Noah struck his staff against the ground and embraced his grand-daughter. "Our first wedding. What joy! Great blessings will surely follow from this union."

"But he's my uncle!" Elisheba cried. "It's not right—it's forbidden, surely!"

"All the men in the world are your uncles and cousins. "Who did you think you would marry?"

She betrayed herself by glancing at Asmodai.

Japheth exploded. "A fatherless boy! The son of a whore! He carries the mark of the devil in his four-toed feet!"

Norea slapped him hard across the cheek. Japheth put a hand to the reddening weal. "What say you, brother?" he demanded of Shem. "Will you give me your daughter?"

Sambethe seized this glimmer of hope. "He says no! Don't you, husband?"

Shem shuffled and coughed.

"Do not dare speak for him! Brother, answer me!"

"Elisheba is ripe for marrying," Shem muttered. "She must have a husband. Japheth must have a wife."

"Coward!" raged Sambethe. "We all saw what he did to Aradka!" She dragged her trembling daughter away.

Asmodai cast a furious glance at me for my silence and raised his palms to speak. "Why not me? I am of age. I have vigour in me. Has he not enough children?"

"He is my son!" Noah's aged voice shook. "I am the patriarch. I alone was found righteous. My seed shall found the tribes of men. My descendants shall be as numerous as the stars of heaven, as the sands on the seashore!"

Norea gestured to departing Elisheba. "She's your seed too, you great oaf! Her children are your line whomsoever she marries. Or does she not count—like your daughters, when you were called upon to save your offspring?"

"You forget," I addressed Noah. "Asmodai was saved too. Did not the Almighty command me to the ark, that he might live? That his seed would prosper as well as yours?"

Japheth spat at my feet. "Do you think we believe that nonsense? Who are you to speak to my father? An unmarried woman, disputatious and perverse!"

"Enough!" Noah cried. I will ask the Almighty for a sign. To choose Japheth or Asmodai as husband to Elisheba."

You don't need me to tell you how that went. I barely attended to the revelation when it was announced. A dove alighting on Japheth's hut, perhaps. The smoke curling towards him from the burnt offerings. The accusatory whinny of a mule as Asmodai passed.

Strange how the signs always fall in the favour of he who reads them.

Cursed Be Canaan

So they were married, Japheth and Elisheba.

How unseemly for a bride to weep throughout her wedding. For her mother to sob, her father to look away. Her grandmother to curse under her breath. The groom wore no garland, for his mother refused to make him one.

Bademath's joy in life vanished as she realised she was next in line. Happy girl, whose laughter had filled our village. Now, she looked furtively at the men around the bridal table. Into whose arms would she be thrust?

Asmodai could not bear to watch and was gone the full three days of the wedding feast, Malakbel following at his heels. Together, they tracked the river downstream to the pastures and lowlands.

At the close of the third day, Elisheba moved into her husband's house. She crossed the village behind her parents, head bowed and veiled. She may as well have been yoked and bridled too.

It was the season of the olive harvest, and I was glad of the excuse to linger by the great stone press beside their dwelling. A full red moon rose, illuminating the baskets of freshly-gathered fruit laid at my feet. Above the grating of the donkey turning the grindstone, I listened for his fists bruising her skin.

But the truly awful comes without warning. It creeps when we look the other way. So while I attended the bridal home, the seeds of my own tragedy were sprouting elsewhere. Spreading their tender roots under the fig tree, where Noah sprawled in his drunkenness.

And so it was that on the day after the conclusion of that miserable wedding, the second calamity befell our settlement.

☽

For three days Noah had drunk his fill. He'd barely moved from the long table beside his vines. Only at night, he withdrew to recline on the ground like a helpless infant. We ignored him. We were used to it. But the morning after Elisheba moved into Japheth's house, I was woken by shouts and jeers.

Ham strode away from the vines, towards his dwelling. His face was crimson, dark curls flying over his shoulder. Behind him, his father stood, dishevelled and unsteady. His robe was torn and gaping, his shrivelled nakedness on display for all to see. He pointed at his retreating son. "For shame! He has defiled me!"

Doors opened, faces appeared, still heavy with sleep. The boys returning from the river stopped in their tracks, hair dripping. Norea emerged from her dwelling, carrying Anah on her hip. "What folly is this now, old man?"

"He came upon me," Noah whined. "He knew me naked. He has desecrated the holy covenant between father and son. Foul iniquity! Unrighteous Ham!"

"We can all see you naked!" Norea yelled. "Cover yourself, you indecent ass."

"I mean he *knew* me," Noah shrieked. "He tried to lie with me as a man with a woman!"

"I was trying to carry you to your bed," Ham wailed. "To stop you shaming your sons, embarrassing your grandchildren with your drunkenness. But you must make it worse, you witless old goat!"

Noah would not be silenced. "My son has unnatural desires! We all know it! We all remember his crime before the flood! He's an abomination!"

Shem and Japheth came out of their huts. Averting their eyes, they covered their father in a blanket and led him away, even as he continued shouting, gesticulating wildly at Ham. Norea refused him when they reached her door, so they took him to Shem's house.

Ham disappeared inside his hut. The boys continued to their own houses to eat. Except for Shem's sons, who wavered at their threshold, unwilling to face their shameful grandfather. I beckoned them and fed all five, cross-legged and silent, on my floor.

☽

Was Noah not ashamed? Did he not want to run from the settlement, never to meet our eyes again? Retreat to a dark cave and forever regret his drunken ignominy?

Later that day, at the twilight burning of the offering, he exited Shem's hut, sober and dressed. He proceeded to the altar as usual. We were all there: Ham, the furious son, biting his tongue, Norea, the scornful wife, tapping her foot, Elisheba, the new bride, eyes red from weeping. Asmodai had returned from roaming the valleys. He kept his distance, his moping, miserable countenance painful to behold.

Shem fetched an unblemished yearling lamb. Noah slaughtered it, dashed its blood on the altar, and placed it whole to burn. He poured libation before the stone.

Ham awaited his apology. Contrition for his father's absurd claim. He was to be sorely disappointed. For at the conclusion of the ritual, Noah extended his finger towards Canaan, Ham's youngest son, a little boy of five years of age. "Cursed be Canaan!" Noah roared. "The lowest of slaves shall he be to his brothers."

Nahalath drew the child to her. The boy, aware of all eyes on him, dropped the pinecone he was playing with and started to cry.

Noah continued. "Blessed be Yahweh, god of Shem. Let Canaan be a slave to him. May God enlarge Japheth. Let Canaan be a slave to him."

"Say something!" Nahalath shrieked at her husband. "You cannot stand by while he curses our son!"

"What can I say?" Ham raised his eyes to the heavens. "He's mad! His words are as the bleatings of a goat, the heehaws of a donkey!"

"Then you must say something!" Nahalath beseeched Shem. "Say you do not accept this curse! That you will not have your brother's son as your slave!"

"I cannot argue with my father," said Shem, the coward.

Nahalath knew better than to beg Japheth, who was enjoying the uproar. She asked nothing of Norea. She picked up her wailing, cursed son, summoned his brothers and sisters from the floor and returned to her hut. Ham followed. Loud crashes, raised voices and children crying were heard from their dwelling late into the night.

☽

"I think," I said to Asmodai, as we sat at our warming hearth, listening to smashing bowls and plaintive cries next door, "it might be time for us to move on."

He laid down his spoon, rested his bowl of broth on his knees. "Move on? Where would we go? We've lived here all my life!"

I had never given any hint of where—or how—I'd lived before he was born. It had never occurred to him to ask. Was he not curious that we alone in the settlement were not Noah's kin?

"There are . . . other places," I said carefully. "Other villages. Cities even—far away. We needn't be lonely."

Samael had wanted to travel to Harappa or Caphtor—to the shining palace at Knossos. Had they, too, been lost in the flood? Had life survived there, or in those places further afield I'd seen when I was blessed with wings? The northern steppes, the steaming jungles, the vast red continent in the south. Surely, they were preserved. I'd been stuck in Shinar far too long. There was a whole world I had neglected; my prophet to find.

Asmodai looked out the window towards Japheth's hut, where fifteen-year-old Elisheba now played wife to her uncle, mother to her own cousins. "What do I care of other places? Please, Mama. I can't leave her."

"You'll not be able to bear it. She will be abused and ground down. It will get worse—not better."

He stirred his cooling soup. Fished about in it for the final scraps of fatty meat.

"And you can forget about marrying any of the other girls." I laid my bowl on the hearthstone for Malakbel to lick the dregs. "They'll never permit it. We will always be outsiders."

"I don't want another girl!" His face glowed golden in the firelight. My beautiful child. Despite my past blessings, the powers I'd lost, he was the greatest glory of my life.

Malakbel licked the bowl clean. He rested his chin on my lap for his head to be stroked.

"What if—" Asmodai started. "She came too?" He leaned forward, his eyes sparkled.

"You cannot mean Elisheba?"

But of course he did.

And so the roots of my tragedy gained purchase in the ground. Sour shoots broke free of the soil. Bitter leaves unfurled, poisoned fruits made ready to fall.

Was I Not Merciful?

The knock came before dawn. I opened the door to a crack to see Nahalath shrouded in a dark cloak. "Can I come in?" She looked over her shoulder at the slumbering village. No candle burned at any window, no light shone under any door.

"We're leaving." She drew her hood and sat at my table.

Asmodai was still sleeping. I lowered my voice. "Ham too?"

She clicked her tongue with fury. "Can he stay, with a father like that? With those brothers? They've always hated him. They think he's soft, unmanly. Because he's different."

I raked the embers of the fire and set fresh kindling to revive it.

"What was the crime Noah spoke of? Before the flood."

Nahalath snorted. "There was no crime! He had a friend outside the righteous family. A man he loved. That was it!"

"Where will you go?"

"West—to my homeland. We wandered, lived in tents. In winter we descended to the valleys, in summer we travelled to the shore. The land is fine, there's good pasture for a herd. Figs and pomegranates, olives and vines in plenty. I'll not stay here to watch my son enslaved by his cousins."

The kindling crackled. I watched the flames dance. "What do you want from me?"

Nahalath, of all the women, liked me least. She was suspicious and self-serving, but she was at least direct. "Give me the key to the grain store. Now, before they wake."

I pretended to be occupied with my poker in the fire. Norea would be furious if she found out I'd given away our stores. "Winter is coming. We cannot spare it."

"I sowed it!" Nahalath whispered angrily. "I harvested it, as well as any of you. I demand my share."

In his sleep, Asmodai threw an arm above his head. We had no intention of remaining ourselves. We'd soon be gone, and I would take my portion of the grain, too.

"Please," she begged. "You have shared my sorrows these seventeen years—and my joys. You held my hand when I gave birth. You caught my children when they stumbled, wiped their tears when they cried. Would you deny me—them!—food for our journey?"

Nahalath was right, she had earned this, at least, for all her striving. But it was Serah I was thinking of as I unhooked the key from my girdle. It was her inquisitive mind I wanted to nourish. "Five households, five shares," I cautioned. "Take only what is yours."

She ran out without a further word.

☽

I watched in the low dawn light as Ham carried sacks of grain across the sleeping village and loaded them onto a donkey. They had little to show for nearly two decades here. Some pots and plates, Nahalath's unskilled weaving. The new season's wine.

The children were brought out at the last moment. They looked like fattened calves, wearing every piece of clothing they possessed to save the carrying. Serah peered everywhere for one last sight of the place of her birth. Timna grasped her precious lyre. Cush, the eldest boy, carried sleepy Canaan to his mother on the donkey's back.

I grabbed an idol from my mantel and ran to Serah. I closed her hands around it. "Do not forget the goddess who chose you to have Wisdom." I gave her the tambour we beat in the grove. "Take this and dance. It's your Mother's heartbeat, always with you."

Nahalath returned the key.

Ham grasped my hand in farewell. "Take him away." He gestured to sleeping Asmodai behind me. "He's not safe here."

We should have packed up there and then.

☽

When Ham's family failed to emerge for the morning offering, Shem hammered on their door. It swung back to reveal the unswept hearth, the barren room. Not a plate nor spoon remained. Only Canaan's treasured collection of pinecones piled in the corner.

"They've gone," I said. "They did not care to stay."

"You knew of this?" Japheth barked.

"Only this morning at first light. I saw them leave."

Norea launched herself at her husband, raining blows on his feeble chest. "May your precious god damn you! You cursed his son! Your own grandson! Did you think they'd stay to see what more devilry you had up your sleeve?"

Shem pulled his mother away.

Noah coughed. "Ham was perverse. Foul-minded. He had not the vigour of a man. Do not be wroth with me, woman—was I not merciful to curse his youngest son, not his heir?"

He shifted uneasily from one foot to another as if the ground was scorching. Norea crumpled to the floor, skirts spreading like a dark pool. "What is left to me, but drunkards and fools! And still, you don't see it. Three of them we've lost! Three girls. How can we prosper now?"

The realisation dawned on all the men at once. I confess, unconcerned as I was with the future of the settlement, it hadn't occurred to me until that moment. Bademath saw it at the same time and shrank as everyone turned to her.

"She's the only one left!" Japheth cried.

One girl, fourteen years of age. Twelve sons between Shem and Japheth. And none of them—not her brothers nor her sister's stepsons—permitted to marry her. There was Anah as well, of course, but she was barely walking.

I made no attempt to stifle my laugh. "What an unholy knot! Oh, Japheth, what a shame you married Elisheba. For now, your line will end, for your sons cannot marry their stepmother's sister." The proscription applied only to aunts, you understand. There was no such ban against uncles, as Elisheba had discovered to her lasting misery.

"This is your fault!" Japheth snarled. "No doubt it was you who incited Ham to his perversion and caused them all to leave. God knows you've poisoned the minds of all the women here, teaching them sorceries and dark arts in the forest. There's no act too base for you! You lie with animals—share your bed with a leopard! You seduce our sons! I saw you bring Shem's boys into your dwelling the morning of Ham's crime!"

"I fed them, you fool!"

"Suckled them, no doubt, with the poison-milk of your teats."

Embarrassed, the boys stared at their feet. Japheth's language, the bestial nature of his claims, troubled me. Similar words had been hurled at me—a long time ago.

"And tell me, tell us all—why, of all the women, you never aged?" He strode towards me, all fists and menace. "They soured." He gestured, cruelly, to Sambethe, to the burial cave where Aradka lay, to the valley into which Nahalath had fled. "Their hair turned grey, they grew stout and ugly. But not you. You're as ripe as that day you walked into our lives, like a viper in our midst. Why is that? What kind of demon are you?"

Sambethe's eyes widened. Norea cradled Anah, her eyes closed.

Japheth turned to his kin. "She comes to me, you know. At night."

"I do not! Nor could anything compel me to!"

"She visits me when I sleep. Her hair unbound, lascivious, wanton. She has made a spell that my manhood cannot thicken in the face of my wife. But it swells when she comes near. She coaxes my seed from me so it's wasted, spilled on the bedsheets!"

I laughed at that—unwisely. Elisheba looked set to burst with shame. Shem looked away.

"Japheth!" Norea scolded. "This is unseemly."

But he was not to be stopped. "She could still breed. But she holds herself apart, looking down on us. She is the reason we've fallen into argument and strife. She is the poison in our well."

"My son and I will leave," I said. "No longer will I feed your children. No more shall I visit you in your dreams to swell your manhood and steal your precious seed. We want only our portion of the grain and we'll be gone."

"No!" Japheth's face twisted with rage. He grabbed my wrist. "The grain belongs to us. You will not have it. Nor will you leave. You stayed here all these years when we did not want you. Now that we need you, you cannot go."

Now that they *need* me?

I had plenty of time to think over the sinister intent of those words. For Japheth took the key to the grain store from the chain at my waist and shut me there, behind the only lockable door in the village. I sat among the provisions I'd husbanded with such diligence and care. I kicked at the solid walls I built myself with stones brought down, one by one, from the mountain.

I rued the day I joined this miserable family. The labour, care, joy, and grief I had shared with them. The mission I had neglected!

How had I stayed so long in this den of bullies and fools?

Exodus

It was black as pitch in the grainstore. Beyond my prison walls I heard the hoot of an owl, a wolf howling on the mountainside. I was grateful for the raised floor that kept the rats from my toes, but it was cold and airless and my fears were rising.

My first thought was for Asmodai. What would they do to him? Japheth said they needed me, but he was only a threat to Noah's kin, obsessed as they were with the line of their seed. Would that he had the sense to take himself away.

Of all the treacherous, evil-doing men I had known, Japheth was the worst. A wife-beater, a killer too, I had no doubt. Men were not born bad. I saw that in my son—in all the gentle, loving boys I'd helped rear from birth. Their nature was corrupted by power: by their god-given dominion over women and the living world.

I idled. Threw dried beans across the floor and counted where they fell. Where was Norea? I expected her at any time to release me, having wrestled back the key from her son. But when the soft rap against the door came, it wasn't her voice I heard, but Asmodai's. The key turned, the lock clicked. His beloved face greeted me in the moonlit doorway. Pale Elisheba stood beside him, peering backwards in watchful fear. Malakbel too, the tip of his tail quivering.

"Come, Mama," Asmodai beckoned. "We leave now. Come quickly!"

We took no grain, there was no time. We would survive on what we foraged. No donkey, mule, nor goat. We would go on foot to defy followers, on the lonely paths that Asmodai, who had tracked the valley further than anyone, knew best. He left his dogs behind, for they'd bark and give us away, but he couldn't abandon his beloved sparrowhawk, Naamah. She perched on his shoulder, cold eyes darting, white breast shining.

So we hastened onwards to my grief. To the inevitable conclusion of this first settlement in the remade world, which had improved so little on the first.

$$\mathbb{)}$$

The journey is a distant memory. It was dark, the moon hidden beyond the forest canopy that shielded us. The stream ran black and cold. Occasionally we waded through it to mask our scent.

It wasn't just my row with Japheth that had hastened our flight: I learned that Elisheba was pregnant. And as her husband had broadcast to us all, he was incapable of begetting a child on her. So the father was Asmodai—I would be a grandmother!

It spurred me, immeasurably, gave me something to run towards.

I knew exactly where to go.

"There is a garden west from here. Unknown and neglected. No one will find us there."

I had observed the stars. At Ararat, the constellations rose to the same height in the night sky as they had in Eden. No one else had travelled as I had. No one had studied the stars from more places in this world than I. So I knew Eden lay at the same distance from the midpoint of the earth. We had only to travel westwards, to where the four rivers met. The wheatfields could be weeded, the orchards pruned. My roses would be reborn. The Paradise it had been before it was ruined by Adam's greed and powerlust could be restored. My son, a far better man, who understood his place in the world, who loved and cared for the creatures within it—he would remake it with me.

Once, I'd dreamed of returning there with Samael, outcasts no more, having returned Asherah to her rightful place. It was not to be. Instead, I would return with my son, his wife and my grandchild. We would start again in the place of my birth, and right the great wrong that had been done there. Dig out that which had taken root and spread its bitter curse across the world, the poison ivy that had smothered all life ever since: the lie that man was fit to rule over woman and nature, that he was set above them both.

"Is it true, Mama?" Asmodai asked. "Japheth said you do not age. Were you there—at Eden? At the beginning?"

I'd never meant to hide this from him. I had almost forgotten it myself. Concerned only with the daily troubles of my life, focussed entirely on my son, I had become human once more.

"I was."

"Then what are you?" demanded wide-eyed Elisheba. "A demon?"

I could not answer that. I still can't. What am I? All I know is what I was: a woman, possessed of dignity and Wisdom, as Asherah intended. An equal woman. The only woman untainted by the curse God laid upon Eve. Thus I had my role: I would reverse it.

Elisheba was not satisfied but she had little choice. She could go on with us or return to the husband who would kill her.

I had another reason to return to Eden. I had accepted Asmodai would die before me, but now his life was in danger long before his rightful time, something else had occurred to me.

"Send them forth!" Yahweh ordered of Adam and Eve, so long ago, "lest they take also of the Tree of Life and live forever!" His booming words still rang in my ears. The memory of the angels guarding the true prize in the Garden of Eden.

The fruit of the Tree of Knowledge granted Wisdom. The fruit of the Tree of Life granted life eternal.

If my son was not yet immortal, I would make him so.

My Foes Return

We travelled throughout that night, never stopping. We slept, briefly, in the middle of the day, then sped onwards, through thick forest, mountain ridge and dell. We crossed a boulder-strewn plateau and slipped into the safety of a dense oak and juniper wood.

The close-grown branches slowed us down. Hunger forced us to stop and eat: stale bread, some nuts and fruit. Malakbel downed a young deer and we roasted its meat.

Perhaps it was the flames that drew them to us, for they came that night. Boughs snapped, shrieks and curses echoed. Wings snagged and a flurry of autumn leaves cascaded, as my bitter enemies Senoy, Sansenoy, and Semangelof descended.

Only then did I remember where I'd heard Japheth's taunts before. How similar his words were to Semangelof's when we fought on the mountain bridge. They were in league. In communication. Seventeen years I had lived openly among the elect. Did I think I could evade their notice for so long?

"Well, well, well," said Senoy. "We have found you at last."

Asmodai leapt to his feet, drew his sword from his side.

"And here is the son." Sansenoy held his arms in mocking welcome. Asmodai slashed helplessly at the air before him. "The heir of Samael, no less. He looks like him. But is he as vain, I wonder, as fat-headed?"

"Who's Samael?" Asmodai brandished his sword, first at one demonic angel, and then another.

"So you have not told him?" asked Senoy with mock surprise. "He knows not his birthright. What sort of mother are you?"

"*I* am his birthright! His father is dead."

"Not strictly true, is it, Lilith?"

"He abandoned you," Semangelof screeched. "Passed you over for a better offer. Not that it was hard to find."

"Does he live?" Asmodai pleaded. "Where is he?"

Malakbel prowled before the angels. He leaped to scratch Senoy, tore the hem of his trailing garment. Senoy kicked at him feebly, scrambled higher in the air.

"He does not live. He is not dead," I sighed. "He lingers between the worlds. He cannot leave."

"Oh, but he can," cried Semangelof, teeth bared. "As we, daily, leave the heavenly realm. He chooses not to."

I knew their aim was to sow discord, but still I raged inwardly. It was what I'd always feared. Samael could have tricked Ereshkigal and got away. He should have raised Asmodai by my side. He had not wanted to.

Distracted, I soon discovered the real danger was behind me. Japheth and Shem crashed through the undergrowth, arrows drawn on ashwood bows.

"Elisheba!" Shem dragged his eyes, wide with awe, from the angels. "Come, daughter. You have no part in this. You have been beguiled by these demons. All is forgiven."

"Not by me," screamed Japheth. "She's an adulteress! A whore!"

Asmodai stepped in front of her. "I took her against her will. Sired a child on her, while she protested. Let her be, and let the baby live. I will come with you."

"He thinks he's a hero!" laughed Senoy.

"He thinks he can make demands!" Sansenoy tittered.

Japheth retrained his arrow on Elisheba's belly. His eye narrowed, his drawing-finger twitched. Shem leapt towards his brother. He nudged the bow just as Japheth loosed the arrow. It flew in slowed motion. It travelled against the laws of nature, in violation of gravity, in defiance of my love. It drew a perfect arc above the heads of the angels; its feathered vane brushed a perfect orange leaf, which spiralled gracefully to the ground. The arrow seemed to hover there, at the apex of its flight, all possibilities suspended. Until it descended, with sickening violence, and plunged into the breast of my boy.

He slumped. Dark blood filled his tunic. I screamed his name. I kissed his adored face, the pox mark on his forehead, the scar on his chin. I did not look up as Malakbel leapt upon Japheth. I welcomed his screams, the ripping of his throat, the lifeblood pumping out of him. I rejoiced in his slashed belly, the spilling of his innards, exposed to all.

Elisheba knelt and wept. The angels watched the tragedy they had wrought. Naamah perched on Asmodai's shoulder, pecking gently at his cheek.

Out of nowhere, from the dark shadows of the forest, Norea was there, as she'd come on the night of his birth. She tore off his garment, extracted the arrow's barb, packed the wound with a salve. The scent of honey and yarrow masked the drear stench of blood. Bright green rupturewort mingled with the dark stain spreading across his chest. She lit a fire, fanned the smoke for him to inhale.

Live, my darling boy. Live, I willed with every nerve in my body.

But I knew he could not be saved. I'd known since he was born. Had waited for it. Listened for it in his breathing at night. Looked for it in every grasping weed reaching out to entangle him in the river.

All the grief of Sambethe, Nahalath, and Aradka for their dead babies was nothing to the loss of my only son. They would be reunited with their children in Sheol as I never would. He was lost to me, utterly and forever.

Naamah saw her master was dead. She soared beyond the dark outline of the branches into the endlessly-starred sky.

I kicked Japheth's corpse, stamped on his bloodied, slashed face. I rued those nights I stood over him as he slept beside Aradka on the ark. How I wished I had killed him when I had the chance.

All Must Be Saved

We buried my son in the forest.

Norea put a hand to my quivering arm. "Come back with us. It will be different now. You'll have a grandchild to care for soon."

Shem comforted his grieving daughter. He listened to Norea, obeyed her commands. But I would not go back to that place. I couldn't live in the hut where Asmodai took his first steps; sleep in the bed we had shared when he was a loving, wriggling infant; sit by the hearth where he'd played with wooden toys at my feet. I couldn't watch his own child grow. I had done it once—sacrificed everything to raise him. But I'd forgotten myself and my mission. I would not do it again.

"The prophet will come," Norea said. "You must be ready."

I sniffed, looked at my feet. "How will I know him?"

She laughed. "There is no *him*!"

I was in no mood for her riddles. "You talk nonsense, Norea."

"The prophet is a woman!" Her eyes sparkled. "I saw her in the coils of my incense. I felt her power and fury. She is the one you must find."

"How will I know her?"

Norea traced a line on the skin below my collarbone. "She bears the mark of the goddess here. A snake, no less."

"How will I find it?"

"Oh, Lilith," she sighed. "Still so impatient. Yet you have so much time."

She embraced me and was gone. Shem too, and Elisheba, with my grandchild growing in her belly.

☽

For three nights I didn't leave my son. Day and night, I remained in vigil over Asmodai's burial mound, loyal Malakbel by my side.

I wept and prayed. I had told Aradka once not to expect to be heard, but I hoped She still had that power—somewhere, somehow. Like mothers at gravesides everywhere, I begged my son might be returned. Just this once, let a man cheat death. If he couldn't be returned, I begged, spare him the miseries of Sheol. Let him rest in the ground at peace. I could not bear the thought of my child, life and joy incarnate, as a mournful spirit. Not in that place. Not without me.

As I prayed, I wondered. Where was *He*? I hadn't heard His voice since leaving Eden. I'd lived among His chosen few, for seventeen full years. It had taken all that time for Senoy, Sansenoy, and Semangelof to find me. Even then, He did not arrive to boom my name, curse my descendants, expel me once more. Was His power waning, as Asherah's had?

On the third night of my vigil, a phantom did come. Malakbel snarled. I felt a hand on my shoulder, arms around my waist, tears on my neck. Surely it was Asmodai. I dared not open my eyes in case he vanished.

But it was not my son.

Instead, I heard the tender words of his father—come after all this time, when it was far too late.

"Lilith, dearest one." Samael nuzzled my neck.

I threw him from me. "Where have you been? Why didn't you come?"

"My love. You know I couldn't!"

I struck him. "You can do anything—charm your way anywhere. And here you are *now*—too late to save your only son!"

Samael recoiled from the blow and reached for my hands. "My dear heart, I am only permitted here *because* he is dead."

"What? Why? Who permits you?"

"You *know* who. She allows this so I can bring him away—back to Sheol with me. Better that I shield him than he go there alone."

"No! Anywhere but Sheol!

He threw my hands down. "You were happy to leave me there!"

"You chose to stay! You left *me*!"

Samael sat beside me, his back to the grave. "I stayed *for* you—so you could leave with Asherah. And you turned from me without a second glance. Nor did you ever return to tell me we had a child."

"How could I? By the time I knew, the world was under water." I looked aside. "So how did you know?"

Samael rubbed his neck. The moon shone through the canopy onto his angelic face. From the gloom of the forest came the eerie call of an eagle owl.

"It's been quiet down there—very quiet. We were busy at first, with the flood. So many drowned corpses. Grey and bloated, tongues lolling. The place stank of seaweed for years. And then—nothing. For a long time. Ereshkigal was furious. Said she'd been cheated of her dues, deprived of her rightful subjects by her sister."

"And then?"

"After a while, it started again. The unborn. An infant here and there. A couple of toddlers. Then, not three weeks ago, the first adult in many years. A woman carrying a stillborn. A bitterly angry woman, struck by her brute of a husband. She told me where she lived and whom she lived among. She told me of a woman who emerged from an ark that withstood the flood." He raised his brows. "A great beauty called Lilith, who preached the Queen of Heaven. Who had a baby, but no husband. Nor did she ever take one thereafter, for she never forgot the lost love of her life."

"She didn't say that."

"No, I made the last bit up."

"And still you did not come?"

"For the last time, Lilith, I couldn't!"

I lay my head on his shoulder. He smelled of that place. Of dust and clay, melancholy and loss. Of yearning and the end of hope.

"I'm here to take him, Lil. Sometimes, when they're reluctant, they need to be fetched. You must let him go."

I howled at that. Great wracking sobs that left me fighting to breathe.

"You have to say goodbye, then I can take him. I'll look after him. I promise."

"I'll never see him again."

"No." He stroked my hair. "But you will see me."

"When? How?"

"Are we not immortal, Lilith, you and I? We shall outlive death. Outlast the Underworld. I cannot be tied there forever."

"I thought Asherah was immortal—but She died, when I brought Her out."

"I know," he sighed. "The celebrations were intolerable. Ereshkigal feasted for forty days."

"And yet—*She* did not arrive in Sheol?"

"Of course not. Gods have no afterlife."

I am here so you can die, She said. I thought She meant so I could *live*. But now I understood. The deal She raved about: had She willingly gone to Sheol, offered to stay out of human affairs if He would put an end to that place of His devising, that eternity of misery and despair? But He tricked Her. Set up Her own sister as jailer and reneged on the agreement.

We sat at our son's grave, enfolded in each other's arms, Malakbel curled at my feet.

"That's when you'll be freed," I said. "When the Underworld crumbles. When humans have become their own gods, as She intended. When worship of He who demands obedience, enforced with the threat of eternal punishment—a god of hierarchy and domination—fades away."

He lifted my chin. "Well, that shouldn't take long." He kissed me. "I've waited for you since the dawn of time, Lilith. I can wait again."

I held him as if I could stop him leaving. As if it could save Asmodai from his hellish fate. Samael unhooked my fingers.

I didn't see them go. I didn't see Asmodai as a wraith. I whispered my blessing, buried my face in Malakbel's warm neck, and felt an icy kiss on my cheek.

All my children, She'd murmured as we walked out of the depths of Sheol. *They must all be saved.* At last, I understood. My task was so much bigger than I'd imagined. There will be no damnation for humans who are their own gods. Only I could finish what Asherah had started—and end Hell itself. The prophet foretold by Norea would help me. All must be saved. My son and Samael too. Eve, Aradka. Even the wretch, Adam. All of them.

Part Four

SAMARIA

870BC

Now therefore have all Israel assemble for me at Mount Carmel, with the four hundred and fifty prophets of Baal and the four hundred prophets of Asherah, who eat at Jezebel's table.

1 Kings, 18:19

My Babies

Time held no meaning for me. When I lived among humans, I was as a loaded donkey, slowed by his burden. My years in Ararat had passed as seventeen human years. But after Malakbel died and was buried beside my son, I was alone again. Time sped. It stretched like mastic resin, looped like a knotted cord. The world of men and women spun at dizzying speed, far beyond my horizon in that lonely forest in Shinar.

But one thing tethered me to their puny lifespans. Every full moon, I swept aside the drooping holly-oak boughs and ventured to the slopes of Mount Ararat, where I'd lived among them. I crept to my old hut, where Elisheba now lived alone with her child. I'd stand over my granddaughter in her crib, watching the curl of her smile in sleep. Naamah, she was called, after Asmodai's beloved hawk. She had the same curve of my son's brow, the full lips of her angelic grandfather. When she frowned, I tickled her toes to make her laugh. Sometimes I'd hold her. The weight of her little body, her heartbeat against mine, her downy cheek soft against my lips, sent me breathless with longing to hold my own child again.

My visits continued throughout her life and beyond—for in time, I visited her own babies, and their children, their children's children, and so forth. Before long, I had some thirty-two thousand living descendants. I watched over them in their sleep. Tickled their feet. Watched their smiles. I delighted in those that bore traces of my lost son. Some had his conjoined toes and these infants pleased me best. I poured all my love for Asmodai, my undying need to protect and keep him from harm, into those babies. And each girl-child I examined for the mark of the snake on her breast. I would know my prophet from her earliest days.

By then, I had little time for skulking in the forest. Visiting them took me far and wide, from the lush valley of Jezreel to the bitter waters of Marah. From the snowy heights of Mount Hermon to the mighty-walled, gleaming city of Jericho.

Against all probability and despite what they deserved, the sons of Shem, Ham, and Japheth must have found wives to marry, for the land was by now thickly populated. Perhaps more people had survived the flood high in the mountains, across the sparkling western sea, beyond the arid deserts of the east.

In time my many descendants flourished, mingled irretrievably with Noah's seed, in every part of the known world. In Egypt, Edom, Moab, and Negeb. Throughout the land named Canaan—which meant, I hoped, that Ham's cursed child had thrived. They peopled Judah and Israel, Galatia, and Assyria. They were Philistines, Amorites, and Hebrews. They built Damascus, Haran, and Ninevah. Birthed the Iberian, Thracian, Phrygian nations; they were Ethiopians, Armenians, Scythians too. Truly, they were everywhere.

And everywhere, they told tales of Lilith. A night-demon who took babies from their cribs. A succubus who stole seed from sleeping men. Stories that had grown from Japheth's wild accusations, from Elisheba's fears. Embellished perhaps, by those mothers who saw me fleetingly, a moonlit shadow at their babies' sides.

They cursed me. Wrote charms and spells on tablets and incantation bowls, exhorting me to leave their infants alone. But words have never scared me. Still, I visited. Still, I watched my babies.

Another story spread: that only the angels Senoy, Sansenoy, and Semangelof could ward me from sleeping children. Amulets bearing their entwined initials, the loop of each samech imprisoning the next, were hung over every cot. As if those goons could scare me away! They never did in life. Their written names had no power over me.

They couldn't drive me from the cribs. I loved those babies. I delighted in them. But as they grew, my interest waned. They turned brutal and ugly. My kin was also the kin of Noah, Shem, and Japheth—and Adam before them. Like their forefathers, they were obsessed with the line of their offspring. It turned them brother against brother, fuelled endless war and violence.

My descendants dug wells and fought over the water. They tore down cities and slaughtered the inhabitants. They sold each other into slavery, cheated each other of birthrights. They stoned infants for the sins of their fathers. They had the same poison running through their veins as Adam: the unrestrained urge to dominate and command.

These were just the men, you understand. For by now, as I'd once warned Ereshkigal, women were stripped of all power. As worship of the Holy Mother declined, the position of Her daughters fell even lower. Reduced to little more than livestock, they were listed in holy books as a man's possessions, alongside oxen and donkeys. They lived at the mercy and disposal of their fathers, husbands, and brothers— their rape and murder punished as the spoiling of a man's property. Men even stole from them the power of procreation. Generation, they taught, was solely the gift of man—his seed alone creates the child, the mother nothing but an empty vessel in which it grows. Even the children she knits together with her own flesh and blood were not her own.

It made me hungrier than ever for the prophet.

Would she right these wrongs? Restore women to the role Asherah had intended? Could she succeed where I, at the dawn of time, had failed—help me bring harmony and Wisdom to all humankind? Only then would Samael and Asmodai, my grand-daughter Naamah and her progeny—all my children!—be free from an eternity of suffering in Sheol.

The Dancing Girls of Shiloh

How long do you think it takes to beget a multitude of nations? Less time than you might suppose. For a mere millennium after the death of my son, from Damascus in the north, to the Red Sea in the south; from the sparkling shores of Ashkelon to mighty Babylon in the east, barely a baby was born that was not of my line.

Noah had boasted that his seed alone would found the tribes of men. But they were my kin too. They were Norea's, Elisheba's—and Eve's. No longer could I watch over all my babies—it was an impossible task. I set to searching for my prophet with vigour.

☽

Festivals drew me. I hoped to find her among multitudes of people. So it was I turned my face to Shiloh, for the feast of the Lord. I walked through the rolling hills of Ephraim in midsummer. The wooded vales were parched. The land still smoked from war, for the Israelites had returned from bondage in Egypt and taken much of Canaan with bloodshed. The people of Jericho, Ai, of Makkedah, Libnah, Eglon, Lachish, and Hebron were put to the sword. All were slaughtered. Men, women, the young and old, ox, sheep, and ass: none was spared. Proud cities were burned to desolation, made a mound of ruins for all time. Their kings were impaled on stakes. The victors settled amidst the ruins of destruction and enjoyed vineyards and olive groves they had not planted.

They were all my children: the invaders and those who perished.

They were His children too. But of all these nations, only one worshipped Him alone. And for that, He commanded the annihilation of all others.

She would not have countenanced such horrors. She would not have set Her children, brother against sister, nation against nation.

The road from Bethel took me through wide plains and deep valleys, between hillsides scoured with rock-hewn tombs. Eventually, I heard the babble of the life-bringing spring of Shiloh. Black tents rose among terraced vines. On the hilltop, a low, windswept building of rough stone housed the Ark of the Covenant—the source, it was said, of the Israelites' unparalleled victory in war.

I lost myself among the crowd. Was she young or old, the prophet I sought? How would I glimpse her breastbone? When the feast was served, I sat among the women, and no one wondered what I did there, alone. The woman beside me introduced herself: "Milcah, wife of Phinehas."

I had learned, of course, not to go by my own name, feared and degraded as it now was. "Hannah," I said, taking the dish of lentils she proffered. "Wife of no man."

Milcah laughed and served me meat. "Then you should be up there," she gestured to the hillside. "Preparing. A beauty like you would do well here today."

"Preparing—for what?"

"For the dance of the maidens, of course." She frowned. "Where are you from?"

"I've been away." I gestured vaguely beyond the hills. "Tell me, who dances?"

"The unwed girls," said Milcah. "They will dance in the vineyards to win a husband."

Milcah babbled on. She talked of her husband, who would soon take over from his father, the high priest; of the coming harvest, which would be lean. She chattered of the iniquity of the Benjamites at Gibeah and the treachery of Philistines everywhere. And I ate ravenously and drank my fill of unwatered Shilonite wine, awaiting the dancing girls who would soon appear, arms and necks uncovered, any marks upon their breastbone clear to see.

☽

Perhaps you have guessed I was to be profoundly disappointed. For there was no prophet. Instead, the Feast of the Lord at Shiloh was recorded in the annals for far grimmer reasons.

You will know perhaps, how the girls came out, wearing thin linen shifts, their hair unbound. Their eyes sparkled, their laughter resounded. With graceful arms and trim ankles, they snaked in undulating coils, each girl dancing to the rhythm of her timbrel.

The women watched with pride for their lovely sisters and daughters. The unwed boys, and I suppose, the married men too, looked on in lust. And I, with eager eye, searched each dancer for the mark of Asherah. The beat of the drums and the pace of the tapping feet sped, hastening to the dance's conclusion. But before the boys of Shiloh could come forward, men burst from hidden places. They fired arrows that kept us at bay. Each took a maiden at her waist; they carried them off, their screams rending the night air.

Milcah, whose eldest child had been among the dancing girls, screamed for the high priest to act. He stood in silence. An ancient man, eyes glazed milky white. He made no judgement. Ordered no response.

"The Benjamites," Milcah spat. "They were denied wives for their savagery in Gibeah, so they've taken our girls. And he," she pointed at her father-in-law, the high priest, "has allowed it."

The crowd wept. Women screamed at their husbands to make chase. But it was forbidden. The laws, written by men, upheld the divine right to wives, however they are got.

Later I heard the full story. How a travelling Levite, staying overnight at Benjamite Gibeah, had been besieged by a lustful mob. Surrounding the house, they demanded the host put out the traveller to satisfy their desires. Instead, the Levite forced out his concubine to be raped and abused. She died in agony. In response, the other Israelite tribes cursed the Benjamites and swore never to give them their daughters in marriage. Not for the sake of the murdered woman, but for the wrong done to the Levite, the wanton destruction of his property. Later, regretting their curse, and unwilling to see a tribe of Israel extinguished, they told them to lie in wait for the girls of Shiloh, and take them as their rightful prize.

I raged at these men who treated their kindred women as spoils of war. Chattels to be won and abused. Such are the consequences of the want of the Queen of Heaven to uphold the rights and dignity of Her sex. I resolved to leave this troubled land and seek counsel elsewhere.

Oracles

From the hilltop of Shiloh, I walked on dusty paths and sandy by-ways. I joined the mountain highway that journeyed from Beersheba in the south to the ruins of Hazor in the north. Travellers walked in groups for safety. I fell in and out of these pedestrian caravans as their company sustained, or more frequently, bored me. I barely stopped for food, or to wash in the baths that lined the way.

At the Waters of Merom, I took the cedar-lined road to the coast. Iron-wheeled carts and fleet chariots flew by, spitting out stones that bit my calves, as they raced westward to the sea.

I arrived at Tyre in the middle of the sea-snail harvest, the source of the city's famed purple dye and all its wealth. The stench of the creatures rotting in piles in the midday sun followed me everywhere. I was glad to take passage on a roundship heading west. As the oarsmen heaved us out of the harbour, I watched the land of my birth retreat, with all its injustices, insults, and miseries; swallowed up by the calming waters of the Western Sea.

☽

The Hellenes had not abandoned their goddesses. Their women still held counsel, issued prophecies, and commanded respect; so that was where I sailed. I disembarked at rocky Krissa and walked the sun-bright, silent hills to the sanctuary at Delphi. There, I would consult the Pythia, who voiced the wisdom of Themis, daughter of the Great Mother Gaia, patron of justice and natural law.

Themis had chosen well. The sanctuary dwelt high in the mountains, surrounded by soaring peaks on all sides. I bathed in the

Kastalian spring, refreshed and cleansed myself, and walked the passage of laurels to enter the shrine.

The Pythia sat on a high stool. Her gauzy robe rippled. It shot high above her head, carried by the intoxicating fumes rising from the cavern beneath her feet.

She laughed when she saw me, a croaking sound, hoarse and low.

"Welcome, Daughter of Heaven! But do I pronounce you mortal or divine?" Saliva dripped from the corner of her mouth.

I laid the ritual payment at her feet: a tri-cornered pie baked with cheese and herbs.

"Why do you visit my temple, deathless one? What would you learn from the Lady of Good Counsel?"

"I seek a prophet, Pythia. Where will I find her? How will I know her?"

She closed her eyes. Her body shuddered with violent convulsions. The twigs of oleander she grasped fluttered in her hand. A leaf spiralled into the smoking fissure in the rock floor.

When she spoke again, her voice was changed and terrible. Her breast heaved as if it were a great effort to speak. Her hair blew wild with the current of the fumes from below.

"I count the grains of sand on the shore and measure the sea," she juddered. "I understand the speech of the dumb and hear the voiceless. A smell comes to me. Of fish drying; salt, preserving. In the shadow of a tower, you must wait."

Had I not waited enough? "For how long?" I demanded.

"Hush, daughter." Her arm shook, sent the oleander flying. "Between the seedtime and the harvest of the grain, she will come. She will appear when you are hidden and hide when you appear."

☽

I could make no sense of the Pythia's words, so I travelled on to Dodona, in the land of the Epirots, where the cult of Dione, another of Gaia's divine daughters, held sway. On the slopes of snow-topped Mount Tomaros, in a valley of a hundred springs, I found the sacred oak. As I approached, through chill vapours that misted the air, a dole of doves was startled into flight. Three barefoot priestesses rang the bronze cauldrons that encircled the oak's vast trunk. I wrote my question on a lead tablet and they listened for the answer in the rustling leaves and the peal of the cauldrons.

The tallest priestess held her sisters' hands and intoned:

"Goddess-born
She you must find,
Grants Wisdom with
Her perfect mind."

In the twilight lands of the far west, I sought the Sibyl at Cumae. I passed through a stone passage into a cavern hewn from a cliff overlooking the sea. There she raved, possessed by divine forces. Foaming-mouthed, jerking, she wrote her reply to my question on dried oak leaves. I ran, hastened to catch them before they were cast onto the rolling ocean.

"Await," she wrote: "the one who is scorned. She who is despised. She shall be the discoverer of those who seek her."

On another leaf: "You will find her in the sordid places, with those who are disgraced. She is the silence that is incomprehensible. The voice whose sounds are many."

And the last: "The second and the third shall be as one. They who find her will live. And they will not die again."

I returned through the cold, stone passage to the rocky shores of the sea.

What was I to make of these baffling oracles? That she I awaited was hidden, but would find me. A silence and a voice. Scorned and a saviour. How could she encompass all these opposing qualities at once?

Mystifying as they were, what pleasure it gave me that these prophetic women were descended, like all Hellenes, from Japheth's line. How he'd have hated to see his daughters deferred to, their counsel heeded by kings and emperors. How he would have denied the proud goddesses who bestowed their powers!

Though I felt no more enlightened, the oracles invigorated me. Gave me strength to return with their divine Wisdom to the land I called home.

Sidon

I returned by way of countless diversions, as the Sidonian ship I sailed in called at the colonies and trading posts of the Phoenician empire. When I embarked at Cumae, the hull was already stocked with tin from Baratanac, wine from vine-rich Gadir and beaten silver from Tarshish. At Maleth, they bartered for white-wool cloth, at Kythera, for iron. Cargo was stacked high upon the open deck.

We put in at Caphtor—too late for me to wonder at the palace of Knossos, for it was gone, destroyed by earthquake and fire, centuries since. At Tarsus we took on horses, at Adana, sad-eyed slaves. Our final stop was for copper at Kition, on the island of Alashiya where I'd first tasted spring so long ago. As the galley glided through the crystal waters of a wide bay, a faint drumbeat called to me, carried on the jasmine and pine-scented breeze. I felt it again: that sense of renewal, the pulse of life I'd felt here so long ago.

Before long, we spied the welcoming flame of the lighthouse at Sidon. This was Phoenicia—Canaan of old—the land to which Nahalath and Ham had fled when they left Ararat, more than a thousand years ago. The city was named after Canaan's first-born son. Spared during the invasion of the Israelites, it had kept its old ways, growing rich from its swift ships, from trade in every commodity that passed through its quayside warehouses; from its purple dye, its peerless glass-making, from the famed craftsmen and the weaving-women renowned from Ilium to Iberia.

I stepped off the ship, swaying with sea-legs, and found myself in the midst of a festival. Sidonians thronged the streets, dressed in bright tunics and oiled hair, gold glinting at their necks and waists. From every quarter came the lilt of flutes and the strumming of harps.

They headed in one direction: towards the gleaming white columns of the royal palace on the far side of the harbour.

I wove though the crowd, past the vendors of spiced meats, the conjurors performing magic tricks, a chained monkey walking on its hands. I marvelled at the jewel-coloured silks for sale, the perfumes that had travelled half the world, the intricate sculptures carved from elephants' tusks.

At a glassmaker's workshop, I paused. His exquisite creations were arrayed on boards open to the busy quayside. Among the glass bowls, the tiny amphorae for perfumed oil, the mosaic-patterned platters, were scores of dazzling blue pendants in the shape of a naked woman. I picked one up. Her breasts were full, a triangle marked her sex. Her hair fell in coils to her waist. She was crowned with a diadem, gold etched into the glass. A silver crescent moon shone above her head like bulls' horns.

They were exact replicas: the very same idols I had carved in my contented days in Ararat.

The glassmaker looked up from his bench. "Are you buying?"

"What are they?"

He put aside his work. "Commemorative figures. To mark the coronation."

"What coronation?"

He scowled. "You must be fresh from across the water. What are you—Egyptian?"

I shook my head, speechless.

"The high priestess is crowned today." He pointed to the palace, where the exultant crowd was headed. "The king's daughter is of age. She'll be anointed at dusk."

"Whom does she serve?" I could barely mask my passion.

He muttered a curse on all foreigners before answering. "Elat, of course. The Lady of Sidon."

I suppose he saw my disappointment because he added: "She Who Walks on Water. Mistress of the Beasts. She's Athirah in the north, or to the Hebrews in the south—"

"Asherah?" I almost crushed the pendant.

"The same." He took it from me. "Do you want it or not?"

I scrabbled in my pouch and brought out some old, tarnished shekels. He rubbed one. "Israelite, then." He raised his brows. "I suppose I must call you my countrywoman now."

"How so?"

"Our nations will be allied when our princess marries your king."

I looked to the palace. "You mean the new priestess?"

He nodded.

Could this be true? I struggled to master my leaping heart. A high priestess of Asherah—set to become the Queen of Israel?

The glassworker threaded a leather cord and tied the pendant around my neck. He admired his handiwork adorning my breastbone.

"It becomes you."

I caressed the glassy smoothness, the rounded contours of the divine body. Never did I dream this day! Was I really to see Her honoured, this very evening, in public, by thousands?

She Who Walks on Water

There were still several hours before dusk, so I wandered the city. I pounded the airy squares and narrow alleys. I marched to the forested hills beyond the city walls. North to the citrus groves lining the river. South to the orchards of cherry trees, plums and almonds. Everywhere, from the rocky promontory of the harbour to the loftiest hill, I found shrines to the goddess: great cedar posts embellished with silver and gold beside stone altars. They burned azallu there, the same mind-altering leaves that Norea had brought onto the ark and cultivated in Ararat. Through the windows of the neat, white-plastered houses, Her idols ruled domestic shrines.

They worshipped other goddesses too. Anath, the warrior, Nikkal, patron of orchards, Ishat, the source of fire. Not to mention the gods: bull-like El, raging Baal of the storm, fiery Moloch. But none inspired the same love and devotion as Elat, the Queen of Heaven, my Asherah. Her image enlivened walls. She was cast as a tree, Her branches spread wide, sheltering people and animals. As Mistress of the Beasts, She stood on horses or beside leopards or lions.

Her gleaming, colonnaded temple crowned the city's highest hill. I sat there, among the olive groves. Looking down upon the harbour, I noticed what I'd not seen before: the very ships, the source of Sidon's power and wealth, honoured Her. At every helm, stood a gold statue of a naked woman in the same pose as my idols of old. She guided the vessels, divining the way, calming the raging seas.

All this, the legacy of Serah, the first, and only, bud on the vine of my ministry. The Canaanites, named for her brother, were her line. She had founded this worship. She had set up these altars in the hills and high places, as I had taught her, so long ago in the oak-grove of

Ararat. She had brought my idol here. She had planted her own vine and it had fruited—magnificently.

I whispered a blessing to the solemn little girl I'd known; the first high priestess of Sidon. To Nahalath, who brought her to the land of her own birth. To Serah's brother, the cursed child Canaan, and the nation that bore his name.

I sat among the olive blossom, watching the sun drop behind the watery horizon. The hoopoes and cicadas serenaded me as I set out for the palace in joy, with the certainty that at last, I had found my prophet.

☽

The ceremony was a blur to me. Amid the jostling, jubilant crowd, I could barely see what was happening. But it was impossible to miss the procession of hundreds of women, each beating a tambour or rattling a sistrum to a rhythmic beat. They descended from the inner sanctum of the palace, down wide steps, to form a circle around a dais strewn with hyacinths and anemones.

A slight girl, dressed in a fringed robe the colour of blood, followed. They melted aside to admit her to the platform. The flounces of her dress fluttered—with the evening breeze, or from nerves, I could not tell. She wore so much gold, I wondered how she stood. Charms dangled from her ankles, wrists, neck, and waist. They sang as she moved like a thousand tiny bells.

An older woman, wearing a high cap and queenly robes, ascended the dais. She anointed the girl with oil so strong, the scent of onycha and frankincense reached me in the crowd. She furnished her with the implements of her office: a hip dagger, a knotted girdle, a jewelled brooch. She placed a towering golden diadem on her head.

The young priestess took her dagger and slit the throat of the white bull-calf, who had calmly awaited his fate. The sistrums sped to frenzied pace. Blood poured from the dais. The crowd ran forward to dip cloths in it, dotted it on the foreheads of their children, smeared it on their own wrists and necks. They snatched and tore at the yew-leaves that had garlanded his neck. The girl sacrificed the calf's entrails on the altar and the carcass was carried away for the feast.

"Who are the women?" I asked a child pressing at my side.

"The doves." She saw my confusion. "The priestesses of Elat. That's what they're called." There must have been four hundred of them. They lay now on their bellies before their mistress, like rays emanating from the sun. Polished brass mirrors reflected the girl's magnificence: each sparkling jewel multiplied beyond measure.

The queen mother who had anointed the girl kissed her hand. The king honoured her. The crowd chanted a three-note musical refrain. At first, I thought it meaningless, the ai-lai-ai of a celebratory song. A pleasing sound, like the sea rolling onto the shore. The tinkle of shells, as the waves retreat. Then I realised the chorus was her name.

She followed the priestesses, her doves, out of the palace and up the path to the temple on the hill. The royal party followed by torchlight. Still the crowd sang. Her name was on the lips of every man, woman, and child in the city, as they shadowed the bobbing flames to see her invested in her new domain.

Over and again, they sang, long into the night.

"Jezebel, Jezebel, Jezebel!"

Give Me a Sign

I watched and waited. I learned the habits and customs of the Sidonians. As Norea once told me, I had plenty of time.

Jezebel had a predictable routine, presiding over the city's most important rituals. Not long after I arrived, after the last of the spring rains, the barley was gathered. She rode to the fields in a shining chariot, cut and bound the first sheaf with a moon-shaped sickle and brought it to the temple's threshing-floor, where she brandished the golden flail herself.

The wheat harvest followed, then the summer fruits, the figs, peaches, pomegranates, and dates. At the blessing of the winepress, her doves led the dancing in the vineyards, signalling the time for the girls to choose husbands from the beardless boys. On the seventh day of every month, she sacrificed a ewe to Baal. On the seventeenth, she burned a ram for Elat. She bathed at a public lustration ceremony every new moon and hosted a banquet of prodigious merrymaking.

In the hot and barren midsummer, she led the women in mourning for the death of the corn god Tammuz. She was the first to weep, she beat and tore at her breast with the loudest, most violent wails. At his rebirth in spring, she impersonated the goddess in the ceremony to bring him back to life.

Alongside King Ethbaal, her father, she oversaw the purification rites for the new year, when children leapt over images of the god Moloch in a fire.

She blessed every ship that sailed from the harbour. She welcomed each returning captain home, and relieved him, for the good of her temple, of a ninth of his profits. She provided for the childless women, the widows, and the orphans. She was the patron of the midwives, the craftswomen, wet-nurses, ale-wives and prostitutes, hearing their complaints and acting on their behalf.

I watched her fulfil these duties and grow from the girl who had shivered at her coronation into a commanding woman, the pride of her wealthy, powerful city.

And never was she more forbidding than the day she welcomed the Israelites, sent by King Ahab, to escort his bride to her new home at his capital in Samaria.

☽

They arrived in a fleet of six hundred chariots. Sidon-made, of course, for none were finer. Two hundred horsemen followed.

She met them at the steps of her temple. Dressed in red, surrounded by her white-clad doves, she bloomed like a rose in the snow. From my hidden place in the olive grove, I watched the commander jump from his chariot, sweeping his scarlet, brimless cap in a flourish. He approached the steps and knelt. But he would not climb them.

She called to him in the stilted Hebrew of a newly-acquired tongue: "Approach, revered envoy of my lord, King Ahab. Come rest in my temple and be refreshed."

Still, he would not move. The armed men grew restive. The horses pounded the dusty ground.

Jezebel lifted a finger and a priestess flew from her side. She spoke in the commander's ear. He answered without looking at her. The girl looked at her mistress, distraught. Whatever she meant to convey, Jezebel understood it perfectly. She turned her back and withdrew into her temple. Her women followed. The great doors closed with a thunderclap.

The commander returned to his chariot, his face shining with fury. His men parted for him, and he led them, down the hill, towards the palace.

Amid the dustclouds thrown by the rearing horses, I saw a flash of white—the lone priestess, running. I reached her before she gained the steps.

"What happened? Why wouldn't he meet her?"

The girl shook. "He said—" she took a deep breath. "He said he wouldn't set foot in the house of a false god. That *she* must come to him. He called our temple—" her eyes drifted to the cedar doors, carved with entwining foliage and gentle animals, "*an abomination!*"

☾

It was cool inside the temple. Fountains echoed from unseen court-yards. Light filtered through gaps in the ashlar blocks so not a torch was needed, whatever the angle of the sun. Vast frescoes of the goddess decorated every wall. Her animals, Her trees, Her bounty celebrated at every turn.

I had convinced the girl to take me to her mistress. She led me to a chamber in the private quarters and ushered me in.

Four or five white-clad doves melted into the background, leaving Jezebel alone in the centre of the room. She was still in her finery, gold glinting at her neck, wrists, ankles, and waist. Her eyes were lined black with stibium, shadowed green with powdered malachite; her lips stained red with ochre.

"Who are you?" she demanded. "Why are you here?"

Gone were the days when I could unfurl my wings and impress humans with my divinity. All I had now was my tongue. But prophets had bent kings to their will with less.

"I am sent to you."

"Who sends you?"

"You call Her Elat, I call Her Asherah. She is one and the same: the Queen of Heaven."

She lifted her chin. The jewelled earrings that brushed her shoulders rang as she moved. "He besmirched my Lady as well as me. I will not meet with such a man."

"Indeed, you have been gravely insulted. But I come to tell you that you must meet him."

She circled me. "You—a stranger—think to give me orders? In my own temple?"

"Princess Jezebel—" I could not help but sing her name, as her people had the night of her coronation. "I have waited for you for countless ages. I have conversed with your foremothers and walked with gods. I have fought with angels and descended to the fiery pits of the Underworld. These are not my orders, but Hers. You alone can bring Her light into the world. Would you keep it hidden? Remain idling in comfort in the house where She already reigns? Or will you take Her word to the places from which it has been banished? A burning lamp cannot hide under a basket. It must shine where it is needed."

She stopped prowling. Cocked her chin in haughty disdain. "How can I know She sent you? Give me a sign."

"Signs are for unbelievers!" I roared. "Does She talk to you? Do you feel Her presence?"

She fixed her black eyes on mine and nodded.

"Then you know what I say is true. There will be no sign."

I poured wine and mixed it with herbs and honey in a silver bowl. She drank like a child at her evening milk. I told her what she knew already: that the Israelites had gone from here to her father's palace for the welcome feast. "And you, Well-beloved of Heaven, you must go too, wearing your richest garments, your finest ornaments, your hair combed and coiled, your eyes lined and lips painted."

I wiped the wine from her mouth with a cloth and threw it to the floor. "This rude and vain man, the stiff-necked servant who insulted you—he is but dirt. It is not him you must charm and please, it is his lord, your husband-to-be, King Ahab. By him, you will be the Queen of Israel. You will mother nations and found an empire. Take your priestesses—all four hundred of them!—into the heart of Ahab's city. Build a temple to the Queen of Heaven there—in the very place She is denied. Win their minds with love, not by the sword, and your name will be blessed for eternity!"

Your Fame Will Last for Generations

She did it all—everything I asked and more besides.

I cast aside the prophecies. I had no need to see the mark of the serpent on her. I gave no credence to the signs. I believed in her—utterly.

She swept into the banquet at the palace, dazzling in a gown of Tyrian purple. Strings of jewels—red carnelian, milky pearls, glowing amber—adorned her throat. Her rich black hair, crowned with a band of myrtle wrought in gold, tumbled to her waist in perfumed locks.

When she walked into the feasting hall, all heads turned. Goblets stopped halfway to mouths. Meat was left untasted, harpists' strings unplucked. She didn't need them. She had music of her own: the charms at her ankles rang as she walked. Her beauty sang.

She spoke only to her father, the king. She ignored the man sitting at his right hand, the commander of the chariots, Ahab's steward; the pig-headed man I would come to know as Obadiah.

Instead, she passed her greetings to the Israelites through King Ethbaal. He indulged such eccentricity, his eye fixed only on the peace and prosperity this alliance would bring him: trade beyond Israel's borders to the east, the power of a strong-armed ally.

A week later, when we left Sidon on the long road to Ahab's new capital at Samaria, she took four hundred and fifty priests of Baal as well as her four hundred doves. She brought warriors and guards, cooks and craftsmen. Her father refused her nothing. Her retinue was a thousand strong.

And she took me. Indeed, she would not suffer me to leave her side. She called me her prophet, never suspecting she was mine.

I had left Israel alone, shunning all company, rage-filled and hopeless. I returned by camel, wearing the finest Egyptian linen, adorned with gold in my ears and silver at my wrists, in the procession of a queen.

A zephyr, Norea had promised me. A soft wind that would sweep around the world, blowing truth and wisdom under every doorway, through every window. To whisper at every ear and tug at every heart. If there was anyone who could achieve these things, it was Jezebel.

☽

The journey took three nights. She had never left the lush Phoenician lands that clung between the mountains and the sea. She had never seen the desert. As we left behind the ripe vineyards, the thick cedar forests and fruitful orchards of her homeland, she looked with dismay upon the parched and stony ground, the dried riverbeds, the grey hills. She looked down from her saddle. "This is the land you would have me rule?"

I answered as a prophet. "You will be its rain. You will bring it sustenance."

We rode on swaying camels for twelve hours every day. We rested in tents at night and as respite from the midday sun. Jezebel lived as luxuriously on the road as she did at home; her doves saw to it. They prepared her meals, baked flatbreads daily, warmed the water to fill her silver bath.

Jezebel did not trust the Israelites to keep her safe. She stationed her own guard outside her tent at night. She refused to converse with or let her eyes fall upon Obadiah. He seemed, for his part, content with the arrangement.

On the fourth day, as we prepared to leave our resting place in the looming shadow of Mount Ebal, King Ahab himself arrived. Amid a fanfare of trumpets, he leapt from his chariot and called for Jezebel to show herself. He could not wait for her to arrive at his royal city, he must set eyes on his new bride immediately.

He was said to have fathered seventy sons already. I didn't doubt it when I saw his lusty countenance. His eyes sparkled with vigour, his thick thighs quivered, his spear arm bulged. And though she was caught unawares, with the veil of sleep still on her as she emerged from her tent, still she shone with unrivalled beauty and he was far from disappointed with his prize.

She entered Samaria on his stallion, cradled by his loins, his arms around her. People crowded the streets to glimpse their new queen. They bowed as she passed, laying palm fronds at the horse's feet.

That night, at the wedding feast, wine flowed from glinting silver ewers. She sang to her husband. Her voice was low and tender.

Praise be to your god
Who set you on the throne of Israel.
You are fairer than all men.
Your speech is endowed with grace.
You are glorious, victorious.
Let your right hand lead you to awesome deeds.

He gazed with delight at his beautiful bride and commanded his musicians to sing to her.

O royal princess,
The greatest people will court your favour.
Your fame will last for generations.
People will praise you forever.
Forget your people and your homeland.
The king is your lord now.
Bow to him.

From the women's benches, where I sat among the merry, laughing doves, I watched grim-faced, unhappy Obadiah. This marriage had been his plan, I'd learned from the Israelites on the road. He had suggested it to Ahab, for the sake of peace and an alliance with powerful Sidon. He had promoted it, argued for it against the wishes of the prophets of Yahweh who despised foreign wives. But he had not reckoned on such a woman. A queen who worshipped her own goddess. Who brought hundreds of priests and priestesses into the heart of Israel. Who would—he was beginning to suspect, as he watched her dazzle and disarm the court—bow to no-one.

The Golden Age

The years that followed were a golden age. I could scarcely have dreamed what we would achieve together.

She built not one but two temples in Samaria. The Temple of Baal was in the east of the city. There, she lodged the four hundred and fifty priests she'd brought from Sidon. The second temple, surmounting a high western hill, she dedicated to Asherah.

Though the name was reviled by Israel's prophets, Hebrew women had never forgotten it. She was still their Queen of Heaven. And how little was required to reignite the flame of Her worship. Kept alight in domestic shrines, on wild and lonely hilltops, in the cakes they baked to honour Her, and the rituals of feminine life they kept from men, it roared into life with the arrival of Jezebel, fanned by the bellows of her devotion.

I lived there, in Asherah's golden house, very happily among the doves. Never have you seen such splendour. Sixty cubits long, forty cubits wide and thirty cubits high, an airy, pillared portico caught the first rays of morning sun. Winding staircases led to upper stories, overlooking the open court within. The floors were laid with cypress planks, the walls painted vermilion and studded with gold. Sidonion craftsmen fashioned the bronze doors and gilded the altar. In the holiest recess of the cloistered court stood a towering black basalt stone, an abstract image of the goddess. It was anointed every holy day; at first, and until it ran out, from the very flask of nard oil I'd taken from Uruk so long ago. A fire lit before it was kept ever burning.

The temple was surrounded by trees of every kind. Cedars and oaks, cypresses and tamarisks, date-palms and olives. Fragrant and welcoming, arriving there from the arid and dusty city below was always the sweetest homecoming.

I took on the role of high priestess. The doves made of me a kind of mother; I gained four hundred daughters in place of my lost son. They served me as they had served Jezebel, asking for my counsel, bringing me their troubles and protests. Not that they had much to complain about. These firstborn daughters of the noblest families of Sidon, and now Samaria, were pledged to the temple as soon as they were weaned. They were rewarded with enviable lives. Freed from the burden of caring for families, they tended the hearth fires, wrote prayers and hymns, led worship. They pronounced oracles and divined prophecies. They performed sacrifices, rites and rituals to celebrate the land's fertility and remind the people of their responsibilities to the earth that sustained them. They administered the offerings and tithes that enriched the temple, farmed the fields of flax, wheat and barley, pruned the vineyards, managed the orchards, olive groves, and wine-presses. As the priestesses aged, and if they so wished, they retired from the temple and lived as ordinary citizens.

In short, the doves wanted for nothing. They had comfort and security, power and respect. They were honoured as wise-women and leaders, the equals of their counterparts at the Temple of Baal. In them, and in Jezebel, a queen who was to her fingertips the equal of the king, I saw the fulfilment of Asherah's plan for womankind.

But who was displeased with this state of paradise? Not the women of Israel, who regained their dignity with the restoration of the goddess they had never forgotten. Not the men, who saw no good reason to deny their wives and daughters. Not the king, who was beloved for allowing his people freedom of worship. This, he had learned at his mother's knee, for while Ahab worshipped Yahweh, the god of his fathers, his mother was a Pharaoh's daughter who bowed to Isis.

No. Those it displeased were not many, but they had foresight and power. Most of all, they had patience. Jezebel's feud with Obadiah, begun with his obduracy and her pride on the day they met, would bear its fruit in his own good time.

☽

It had been sixteen years since we had come to Samaria. Sixteen years of contentment, as I had known in those far-off days with my beloved son in Ararat. I rose before dawn, as I always did, for I loved to watch the first rays of sunlight reflect from the bronze city gates to dance and dazzle on the temple's marble columns. One day, I was certain, as sure as the sun chased night's gloom away, I would chase the shadows of Sheol from my son's cheek. I had found my prophet. It was only a matter of time before I fulfilled my destiny.

It was the seventh day of the Festival of Ingathering. I descended the hillside to speak to Jezebel about the feast that evening, passing the dwellings of palm fronds and willow branches built for the celebration on every flat roof. As I hastened towards the palace, the cobbled streets grew busier, the hubbub ever louder. A pack of thin dogs followed me, hoping for scraps.

I was ushered immediately into Jezebel's chamber, where her maids were dressing her. The two leopards she kept as pets curled on her bed, watching her every move, as loyal Malakbel had once attended me. She leaned back on her elbows between them, as a girl laced red-leather boots around her calves. Another laid a pair of riding gloves by her side. I raised a brow. "You hunt today?"

"What of it?" She yawned. "I have done my duty, made sacrifice every day for a week, and tonight you will have me dining with colossal bores. Today, I am free. I have a fancy to feel the wind in my hair and catch one of my own."

I dismissed the maids and finished lacing the boot. "Catch what?"

"A colossal boar!"

"Very witty, Queen."

"Come with me, Litu." It's what she called me. A joke, a play on the eastern demoness Lilitu, which, had she known it, truly was named for me. "We haven't sported together in such an age."

"Someone must arrange the feast or you will dine tonight on yesterday's bread and pickled walnuts."

"Leave it to Damaris. She's perfectly capable. In any case, I adore pickled walnuts."

She stood at the galleried window, looking upon the city. The latticework was elaborate, carved from ivory, like much of the palace. She could sit there for hours, watching unseen behind the ivory screen. Still a fine figure of a woman, despite bearing three children. But her childbearing days were over now—I saw to that. Old Jerusha, who lived by the Lamb's Gate, prepared her a daily draught of silphium. Jezebel was too precious for me to lose now.

"Come, Litu." She beckoned me to the window. "My eyes are not what they were. Who's that?" She pointed to two figures in the vineyard beyond the palace wall. One tall, clad in purple, instantly recognisable; the other short, dressed in a farmer's shift. The shorter man gesticulated wildly, his hands flying as he talked.

"It's the king." I squinted against the early sun. "He's with . . . I think it's Naboth the Pious. That's his land, isn't it, the vineyard?"

"I wish he wouldn't do that." She scowled at her husband.

"Do what?"

"Talk to commoners. It is not kingly."

"They love him."

"That one doesn't."

I fetched her golden quiver. She slung it across her back and pulled on her gloves. Ahab and Naboth parted. Only then I noticed a third figure, almost hidden by the vines. He waited until they were gone, then crept towards the palace gates. His striking red cap was impossible to mistake. But what was Obadiah doing there, skulking in the shadows?

☽

I sent word to my deputy, Damaris, and dressed for the hunt. Jezebel always got her way. But when we were away from the dusty city, racing in the verdant hills outside Samaria, I was glad to be at her side in the speeding chariot. The rushing winds, the triumphant call of the hunting horn, the bark of the hounds thrilled me.

Of course, she caught her boar, she always did. She was an unrivalled shot, even at great speed. Exhausted, the giant beast slowed his pace. She loosed a gilded arrow and he staggered, before falling to the ground with a bloodcurdling squeal. She petted his bristling back, wiped the slaver from his mouth as he lay dying. She sent the bloodied creature back to the palace, slumped in her chariot, and kept two fine stallions, the pride of Ahab's stables, to bring us home.

It was only mid-afternoon. It would be hot and airless in the city, and many hours before the feast, so we rode instead to the slopes of Mount Gerizim, where the fresh springs fed a bathing pool.

We scoured the grime of the hunt from our weary limbs. With a handful of sage leaves, I scrubbed the boar's blood from her hands.

She grasped my fingers in hers. "How blessed I was the day you walked into my life, Litu."

But it was I who was blessed. I kissed her shoulder, and noticed, for the first time, that her breast was unblemished. I'd seen her naked many times. I'd watched her nurse three children. I had stayed with her day and night when her first baby burst into the world in a haze of blood and pain. I brought her the infant when she was too melancholy to move. I showed her how to hold him, how to pinch the breast to coax the flow of milk. I slept alongside her, comforted the screaming infant when his cries unmoved her. I sponge-washed her and rubbed oil into her skin when she cared nothing for her cleanliness. I knew every inch of her body. Yet it struck me only now for the first time: there was no mark. No serpent etched upon her skin.

The waters babbled, the sun warmed our backs. Blue hyssop rippled in the breeze. I pulled a tall, bowing stalk to me, and breathed in the fragrance. The same herb would dress the lamb's-meat at the feast tonight.

"Do you regret coming to Israel?" I asked.

"Never!" she answered in her usual forthright way. "Someone once told me a burning lamp cannot be hidden under a basket. It must shine where it is needed." She smiled. "I have served my Lady a thousandfold more here than I ever could in Sidon."

She was right. What did it signify whether she was the prophet foretold by long-dead Norea? What mattered was what she'd achieved. She had brought the goddess back to this parched land. She had filled the hearts of women and raised them to their rightful place. She had restored harmony, reintroduced the rites that instilled gratitude for the earth that nurtures and sustains us all.

In time, the end of Hell. Samael and Asmodai would be freed from torment. She would fulfil all that was promised. Her name would be sung for all time.

The Feast of the Ingathering

The peacocks were in full cry as I arrived at the palace. Or rather, one of them was. For all the cacophony, sounding like a flock of vexed crows, the noise came from one solitary male parading the lawns.

Damaris had done me proud. Low trestle tables lined the Great Court so the guests could gaze upon the dancing and celebrations following the meal. Jezebel had brought her own traditions to Israel as well as her gods. Over the years this festival celebrating the harvest and welcoming the new year had combined the rituals of the Jews, the Phoenicians, Moabites, Aramites, Edomites, and Ammonites—in short, of every people in this blended city.

She and Ahab reclined on embroidered couches under awnings of fine-spun gold. A thousand lamps burned. They lit a path to my place between Shaharu, the high priest of Baal, and Kemash, a priest of Moloch. We were kept apart from the priests of Yahweh, for they did not share Ahab's desire to honour all the gods.

It was a feast like any other. As the stars shimmered into life, the food was served. Pages from Shaharu's temple brought water to clean our hands and linen napkins to dry them. Then came baskets of barley bread, lamb dressed with bitter herbs, lentils and beans, salted greens, endives and salads. The first barrels of young wine were tapped, sampled first by Jezebel and Ahab. An early harvest after a hot, dry year, it was a fine, aromatic vintage. The dishes were replenished, empty cups refilled. I passed pleasantries with Kemash, an elderly, white-haired man, who ate little and smiled much. Shaharu was my sparring partner, a vigorous, handsome man in his forties. Had I any lust for men remaining, he would have sparked it. But I was weary of them,

peacocks all, just like the one still screeching from the lawns. I mocked
the high priest's blue-black beard and pointed out the patch under
his chin he had missed with his dye. He challenged me to a game of
Hounds and Jackals to see if my mind was as sharp as my tongue.

The commotion started after the pickled walnuts were served. I
was much occupied with the delicacy, savouring the honeyed spices,
but I gathered someone had praised Naboth's wine, for it was his vineyard that supplied the barrels. Jezebel had drunk too much, as she
often did on these occasions.

"Truly," her strident voice rang out. "It is too fine a wine to be
savoured by wretches with no taste. We shall accept the vineyard as
your gift to the palace."

I didn't hear Naboth's response. I saw him rise, the wisps of his
long beard trembling as he spoke. Presumably, he objected. The land
belonged to his forefathers, thus could not be sold.

"I do not propose to buy it!" she thundered. "You should be honoured to give it to your king."

Ahab held out his palms, one towards Naboth, the Famously
Pious, one towards his wife. This, then, was what was discussed when
we saw them from Jezebel's window: Ahab had attempted to purchase
the vineyard and failed.

The priests of Yahweh stumbled to their feet, pressed the legal con-
straints and obligations of hereditary land. It belonged not to Naboth
but to his descendants; he could not dispose of it under Moses' law.
But Obadiah, who sat among them, held his scarlet cap to his chest
and argued—astonishingly—for the queen. The king must have the
right to acquire any plot surrounding the palace grounds, he reasoned,
for the sake of defence and privacy.

Jezebel's face marked her confusion as well as mine. What was he
up to? But I barely had time to consider it, for the fuss disappeared as
quickly as it started.

The celebrations began. Frail, stooping Kemash lit the bonfires in
honour of his god, fiery Moloch. The Moabite children leapt over the
flames to purify themselves, and the city by proxy, for the new year.
The first of the season's grapes were presented to Shaharu, to offer to

Baal. The priests of Yahweh intoned their prayers, poured sacred water on the burnt offerings, beat branches of willow and laid them before the altar. My doves came out, bearing palm leaves, myrtle, olive and willow branches bound together, hanging with lemons, pomegranates, and dates. They laid these symbols of the goddess's fruitfulness before a wooden post and sang prayers to thank Asherah for the earth's bounty. Then they danced beneath the full moon, with ever increasing revelry, drawing out those at the tables to join them, until the party was a riot of drunken joyfulness and abandon—save for the prophets of Yahweh who disdained the female rites and whom the doves knew better than to drag from their couches.

They looked on with disgust, reserving their sourest grimaces for Jezebel, who wheeled among the burning fires, black eyes sparkling. Her unbridled joy, her grace and litheness, the undisguised pleasure she took from her own body, was repugnant to them.

☽

That night I dreamt I was walking in the palace rose garden. Bees buzzed, birds swooped and sang. But a peacock's screech disturbed the idyll. Searching for him, I found myself in the orchards under a blossoming peach tree. At its roots lay a carcass. A dead lamb, a yearling of purest unblemished white. But a hole gaped in its belly, a rotting mass of writhing maggots and flies. The ribcage bulged and rippled, before a great cloud of wasps emerged. From something pure, out poured a deadly swarm.

I woke dripping with sweat, the sheets twisted and drenched, my breast heaving with dread. Something festered at the heart of the palace. A nest of unspeakable malice, growing in strength, hidden, unseen. I went to her at once.

The Persecution of Naboth

The court was in session when I arrived. I battled my way through the petitioners at the palace gates to find the Hall of Judgement packed with courtiers. Guards fronted the platform on which Ahab and Jezebel sat upon ivory thrones. Before them, a man lay prostrate, his lips to the ground. Naboth had been summoned to pay for his obstinacy the night before.

Obadiah paced up and down before him. "So you deny the charge? That you wilfully, and with great dishonour and public insult, denied your king that which he is due."

"I do deny it," the wretch answered, his voice muffled against the ground. "For I cannot do that which my god has forbidden."

"Has your god not placed the king on this throne?" Obadiah gestured to Ahab, who looked uneasy. "Has He not commanded you to obey your king?"

Jezebel tapped her sandalled foot. I knew her mind. In Sidon, royalty did not submit to lowly officials to sanction their desires. Across the expanse of the hall, I sensed her growing fury.

"Do you even have children?" she barked. "You talk of your ancestral land. But you are as limp and impotent as an ass ready to be boiled down for glue. No right-thinking woman would take you to her bed! What descendants can you hope to pass it onto?"

Naboth did not answer. I cared nothing for him, but Obadiah's prosecution worried me. He despised Jezebel. What did he hope to gain?

Obadiah stopped pacing. "Your silence says it all. Your land is forfeit to the crown. Exile beyond the city walls for ten years," he pronounced to the recorder.

A murmur of approval rippled through the hall. Naboth gathered himself slowly, his aged joints inflamed by the cold stone. He had only raised one foot to the ground when Jezebel rose from her throne.

"Wait!" she called. Ahab looked at her in alarm. Even I, who knew her better than anyone, could not fathom her purpose.

"I am a compassionate woman." She flashed a dangerous smile. "You may stay and care for the vineyard of your fathers. You may prune and gather the grapes on behalf of your king. All I ask is that you consecrate the wine to the goddess." She held out a hand to help Naboth to his feet. "Your wine is excellent," she said, almost kindly. "The first fruits should go to the Temple of Asherah, to honour the Great Lady."

"I regret, my queen," Naboth bowed. "I cannot do that. For I serve none but Yahweh, the god of my fathers. I cannot honour a false god."

They were the same height, had he stood straight. Stooped as he was, she towered over him. The blow she unleashed on his temple floored him. Blood streaked the flagstones. She stormed from the hall, calling over her shoulder, "Take him to the cells. Charge him with blasphemy."

There is only one punishment for the crime of dishonouring a god. Naboth was taken to the place of execution beyond the city walls and there the gleeful crowd rained upon him weighty boulders and pebbles ground to a point until he stirred no more. His bloody corpse was thrown in an unmarked pit, where the jackals and ravens feasted on his flesh and innards.

As a convicted criminal, his property passed to the crown. So Ahab won his vineyard after all, and the Temple of Asherah took the first pressing of wine in every season. Jezebel considered it a great victory.

I wasn't so sure. What god would demand such retribution? A jealous, cruel creator. A narcissist and psychopath. A weak god, who rules by fear. Not Asherah, I was certain.

☽

Was She then behind the drought? I can't remember when it started, whether it befell us straight away, or months after the demise of unfortunate Naboth. But the autumn rains never came. The ploughing was delayed, for a week, two weeks, then indefinitely. No barley could be planted, nor wheat, when the time came. Winter was cold and dry. The peaks of Mount Gerizim and Ebal remained undusted with snow. Spring came, but the quails never arrived. There were no first fruits, no harvest to reap nor threshing to be done.

Rain charms were offered. The priests of Baal snaked through the streets, rattling gourds to entice the thunder. Criminals were impaled on stakes, blood dripping into fields to restore their fertility. Sacrifices were made to all the gods, the major and the minor deities of every faith. Daily, for months on end, flesh burned on every altar in the city. But the animals were withering for lack of food. It became foolish to kill them to please the gods, who needed no sustenance.

Around the same time, the prophets of Yahweh disappeared. One by one, the faces that had glowered at my doves at every rite and ritual throughout the year vanished. Their numbers depleted so slowly it was hard to tell when they went. But by the following Feast of the Ingathering, there were no priests to pour water on the burnt offerings or beat the willows; they had all departed.

Obadiah, who might have been troubled by this development, seemed unconcerned. He walked lighter around the palace, the hint of a smile playing on his lips.

☽

On the day that would have marked the Feast of the Gracious Gods, had the gods been gracious enough to bless the land with rain and food sufficient for a feast, a stranger arrived at the palace.

Jezebel's leopards startled as he entered. His appearance warranted it. He was vast as a bear and just as hairy. He wore skins of wild beasts, but so overgrown and bushy was his beard, his untrimmed locks, his eyebrows—even the back of his hands—it was hard to tell what was borrowed fur and what was his own.

"Elijah the Tishbite," proclaimed Obadiah. "He craves an audience with the king."

The creature approached Ahab. As he neared the ivory thrones, he did not fall to his belly as the occasion demanded. Instead, he raised his finger and pointed at Jezebel. "Is that you, troubler of Israel?" His voice rumbled between the pillars. "Thou painted woman. Desolate whore with braided hair and adornments of gold!"

She froze. Ahab gestured with one finger to his guards.

"And you, vexer of the Lord!" the hairy Tishbite addressed the king. His voice rose unsteadily, like an eagle taking flight. "She is but a foreigner and a woman. But you have forsaken the god of your fathers! He made you a ruler, but you have broken His commandments. You stole the land of Naboth, protected by His law! You sacrifice your children to Moloch, the abomination of the Ammonites, and worship the posts of Asherah! You allow your women to weep for Tammuz at our holy temples! You bow low to Baal of the Phoenicians and Chemosh of the Moabites! You permit whoredom at your festivals and feed the prophets of false gods at your table!"

The guards seized Elijah. It took four of them, a giant limb each, to carry him off, still raving. "I bring you God's Word, King Ahab! He will strike at Israel until it sways like a reed in water! He will uproot and forsake you! Your people will be scattered on the wind. There will be no rain in this land, except at my bidding! The jackals will feast on your bones and blood as they ate of murdered Naboth!"

Ahab ordered his musicians to strike up, but the curses continued, resounding from the hall beyond the throne room, a booming dirge deafening the sweet melody of flute and harp.

"And the dogs shall devour the flesh of Jezebel," the Tishbite thundered, "and her carcass shall be like dung on the ground!"

Hounds and Jackals

What to do with such a troublemaker?

I'd have left him to rot in the dungeons, subsisting on bread and stale water for the rest of his miserable life. But Ahab, for all his strength, despite his sturdy thighs and broad spear arm, had one weakness. He longed to be loved by all his people. It was why he encouraged the worship of all gods, why there were no fewer than seventeen temples and a thousand sanctuaries and shrines throughout his capital. He must have everyone's gratitude and adoration.

He did not relish this hairy prophet's words. He could not bear to be forsaken by anyone, let alone the god of his fathers—nor did he wish to become meat for the jackals. So when Obadiah brought word from Elijah in the cells carved from the bedrock beneath the palace, there he went, like a servant to his master.

Ahab returned proclaiming he would take up Elijah's challenge; that the question of worshipping one god or many—the rival claims that divinity was manifest in one solitary being (male, naturally, to the men of the Yahwist party) or in a variety of forms representing all humanity—this great matter would be settled once and for all. The prophets of Yahweh who had abandoned Samaria, whose whereabouts Elijah alone could reveal, would return to battle the prophets of Baal and Asherah, of Chemosh and Moloch. The slopes of Mount Carmel would witness a contest to determine which god was the greatest, which deity alone should command the love and devotion of the people of Israel.

I would never have agreed to such a plan. Who allows their enemy to propose the terms of a trial? Elijah would cheat, or he would never have suggested it—that much was obvious.

"We cannot take part in this folly," I told Shaharu, as we played our weekly game of Hounds and Jackals in the spreading shade of the fig tree at the Temple of Baal.

He scratched his beard and separated the playing sticks. I played hounds, as always. Shaharu liked to think his personal qualities recommended him as a jackal. He threw the counting sticks, judged his score and moved his first piece accordingly.

"What do you suggest, Priestess? That we do not go?"

I cast the sticks. A poor score. I advanced my first hound.

"Of course we should not go! Can we dignify such a crass spectacle? What is a god, but an ideal—a guide towards a better life. A model to strive towards. Gods are not wrestlers in an arena, fighting for plaudits and victory!"

He moved his second jackal. I followed his eyes around the board to deduce his strategy.

"It sounds to me," he observed drily, "as if you don't expect to win."

"Of course I don't expect to win! Can Baal be commanded by your will? I do not issue orders to my lady Asherah. She is my inspiration and guide, not my servant."

He stared at the ankh symbol on the second row. "But if we do not go, the Yahwists will say we have no faith in the power of our gods."

I knocked his first jackal from the board. His face fell. "It is a trap, Shaharu. Elijah will cheat. His god is no more responsive to human demands than ours. What will happen to the losers? Ahab has not revealed the stakes."

He took a sip of sage tea and surveyed the state of play, rocking slightly. "Do you think we have a choice?" Landing on the ankh sign, the symbol of life—a pleasing omen—he permitted himself a brief smile. "If the king commands it, we must go. Unless you can use your . . . influence," he raised his brows, "elsewhere."

He meant Jezebel. He imagined I had more sway with her than I did. She was stubborn as an ox. Unpredictable as the southern wind.

I cast the sticks. Shaharu always made the same mistake: all response and no attack. I would win in three moves. Another victory to add to my tally, marked in chalk on the trunk of the fig tree.

⟩

I found Jezebel at the ivory window in her chamber, staring at that wretched vineyard. Her fingers worked a spindle, though she hadn't the patience for spinning. The shadow of the latticed screen fell onto her face like a dragnet.

"It's cursed." She gestured to the withered vines. "The old goat cast a spell before he died. That's why there's no rain. It's why that deranged prophet came here, bringing strife and foul threats."

I took the spindle and distaff from her and set them aside. "It is not cursed. There was no spell. Droughts are not uncommon. We have survived them before and will again."

Freed from spinning, her fingers drummed at her thighs. Beyond the vineyard, a pack of dogs ran through the empty streets, ribs visible through balding hides.

"Well, we will show them, eh, Litu?" She bit her lip. "At Mount Carmel."

"No, we will not!"

"What? Why not?" Her black eyes flashed.

"Because we must not agree to this contest. The outcome is already decided. You must tell Ahab to call it off."

She gripped my robe, her face inches from mine. "This is our chance! We will call upon Asherah to reveal Her power. We can be rid of this prophet—all of them—their sour faces and disdain, once and for all!"

"She will not come. She will not reveal Her power. She cannot."

She gasped. "You have no faith?"

"We cannot wager our beliefs—our lives!—on the actions of a goddess who may not hear us."

"Do not speak like this! You are the high priestess! If you don't believe in Her, who will?"

"Of course I believe in Her! You cannot know the depths of my devotion. That's how I know She would scorn such a contest, deny the claim of one god to replace all others. She does not demand the destruction of those who do not worship Her! Yet these intolerant prophets would see Her destroyed. Why can Elijah's god alone not abide others? This god who despises His own children! I will never bow to Him! But if we lose, we will be forced to worship Him—and worse, cower to the men whose purpose He serves."

She paced the narrow balcony, her eyes on the quiet city. Few ventured abroad in those dusty, baking days. They conserved energy, abstained from any activity that would drive them to the last jars of brackish water and the vanishing grain.

I loved her defiance. The tilt of her jaw. Her furious, flashing eyes. But her arrogance, her belief in her own powers, which had never failed her yet, blinded her to reality.

She put a delicate, jewel-studded hand to my wrist. "Courage, Litu. We will not lose."

Fool's Errand

Oh, what did she have in mind? Did she realise what we would face amid the canyons and crags of Mount Carmel? That was another thing that preyed on my mind. Why there? It was two days' journey from Samaria, at the border of Israel and Phoenicia. Why must we travel so far? I asked Jezebel and she inquired of Ahab. No answers were forthcoming.

The day came when we departed on this fool's errand; Shaharu and the four hundred and fifty priests of Baal, Kemash with two hundred priests of Moloch, Balak, the high priest of Chemosh, Hazael, the leader of the Aramite temple of Rimmon—and I, with four hundred doves. The lesser deities' temples were excused, but we five leaders must up and away across the entire country to prove the power of our gods to this upstart, Elijah. Witnesses were required, so the heads of the noble families of Israel, representatives of the merchants, the artisans, farmers, and winemakers all came too. Two thousand people, one-third of all Samaria on the move.

We travelled through a land devastated by famine. Past barren fields, where golden barley once swayed. Across dried riverbeds, littered with the carcases of scrawny goats and bleached oxen ribs. Abandoned villages and withered vines lay in every direction. At night, the ground was too parched to hammer in tent pegs, so we slept beneath the stars.

I watched my sleeping doves shimmering in the moonlight; my daughters in reality, as well as sentiment, for many of them bore the mark of Asmodai's descendants in their toes. What would become of them if we lost this contest? I'd left the youngest, uninitiated, girls at the temple in Samaria. But they too would be in danger if we lost. I could not bear the consequences if we lost our temple and our goddess again. Women's power—all control over our bodies and fates—would be there for the taking, like the girls of Shiloh, snatched in the night by men with men's laws and a male god on their side.

How precarious all our success had been. How relentless was man's drive to destroy our independence. Elijah was merely the latest in a long line of men who denied female authority. Fear gripped me. Men want too much from women. They desire our bodies, for pleasure and begetting children. Like Adam, they cannot tolerate refusal. If one sole male god prevailed, He would bolster their claims to us. Women would never know peace or freedom again.

I knew what I must do. I searched among the women for Damaris. She slept at the edge of the sleeping doves, along with the other senior priestesses, to protect the younger girls from the groping hands that would otherwise assail them in their sleep, even—perhaps especially— here, among the righteous.

"Damaris! Wake up!"

She sat up sleepily. "What is it, sister?"

"You must go. Immediately." I gave her a bag of gold. "Return to Samaria. Fetch the girls from the temple and take them to Sidon. Do not rest a moment until you are safe within the city walls. Beg sanctuary from King Ethbaal. Tell him you follow the orders of his daughter, Queen Jezebel. Wait there for news from me."

She looked about the sleeping camp, calm in the soft moonlight, no sign at all of looming peril. "What's wrong?" She gripped my arm. "Are you in danger?"

"There's no time. You must leave now."

She fastened her sandals and arranged her cloak. She secreted the gold inside her robe and kissed me.

"And Damaris—" I hissed. "Take the stone." The symbol of the goddess. I would not have it unprotected, open to attack.

She ran for the cover of a solitary acacia tree that had withstood the drought, then on towards the grey outline of hills. We were only a day's journey from Samaria, I reasoned, to quell my rising alarm. She would reach them before the contest began.

I slept and woke calmer. Perhaps I'd over-reacted in the gloom of night. In the centre of the Baalists' camp, Shaharu smiled warmly at the endless procession of priests bringing his hearty breakfast. The stores at the Temple of Baal, it seemed, were undiminished by the famine. Among the Moabites, kindly Kemash nibbled at olives and cheese, surrounded by his bare-chested, bald-headed acolytes.

I could not get close to the royal party to converse with Jezebel. I saw the tips of the ostrich-feather fans that cooled her as she ate, the glint of the guards' spears. Where did their loyalty lie?

Obadiah's scarlet cap flashed as he scurried to and from the royal table, unstopped, unchecked. My fears returned instantly. He was the enemy at the very heart of the palace. The wasps' nest in the bowels of the sacrificial lamb.

☽

We travelled downhill, into the once verdant Jezreel Valley. Far ahead, the purple plumes of the stallions on which Jezebel and Ahab rode glistened. Beyond, leading the convoy, was the vast figure of the Tishbite, gnarled olivewood staff in his hand.

I stumbled on the parched earth. No grass remained to bind the soil and it crumbled on the steepest descent. Naomi, the newly-invested daughter of a noble Jewish family of Samaria, put out her arm to help.

When she had righted me, she pointed out the swans above us. Five of them, in arrowed flight. We marvelled at their sleek beauty, the way they flapped their wings as one, their unity maintained effortlessly. Then we watched in horror as an eagle, flying from the north, attacked the leading bird, downing it, so it thudded to the ground a mere stone's throw away. The remaining swans scattered, screeching in distress and confusion, as the eagle alighted on its helpless prey and sank its ravening beak into her soft white breast.

Am I Not an Israelite?

Mount Carmel was the haunt of outlaws and rogues. Shadows shifted in caverns as we passed, leaves rustled in the rocky outcrops. No wonder Elijah felt at home here. After the final climb through forests of oak and pine, boxthorn and laurel, he led us towards the table-topped peak. Below, the mighty Kishon River had dwindled to a trickle. To the west, the bright sea shimmered.

"Here!" he proclaimed, when the final stragglers arrived. Barely was there room for us all in the hollow beneath the overshadowing ridge. Priests and prophets, guards, my doves, the nobles and merchants of Israel; we all perched on boulders, clung to low boughs, to hear the Tishbite speak.

"Here we will set up two altars! Two oxen shall we sacrifice. But we will not light the fires by ordinary means!" He waved his staff to emphasise this important detail. "Each god shall be called upon by his prophets. He that answers shall be the victor!"

So King Ahab had allowed Elijah to devise the terms of the contest. Elijah alone decided which gods would take part, determined the order of play. Asherah was beneath his consideration, so I was exempt from the ludicrous spectacle. Since Baal was deemed the worthiest opponent, Shaharu would represent all opposition.

"Why then have you dragged us all this way?" I asked.

Ahab opened his mouth to speak but Elijah talked over him. "That you false prophets may witness the power of the Lord God of Israel! So you will shake and cower on the ground in regret of your offences that disgust Him!"

"Am I not an Israelite?" came a voice from the crowd. My heart sank, even as it pounded with pride. Naomi stood on a boulder with her back to the valley. Her chin was raised in defiance, the white sash at her neck streamed in the wind. "Asherah is beloved by Israel as much as Yahweh!"

Elijah pointed his staff at her. "He is the Rock! There is no alien god at His side. You have vexed Him with your abominations! Did He not say: 'There is no god beside Me! I deal death and give life. Vengeance will I wreak on my foes. I will deal with those who reject Me. I will make My arrows drunk with blood as My sword devours flesh.'"

I shuddered. Night was already gathering above the black hills. Elijah decided we would rest overnight and set the deities to their task in the morning.

The gods could battle any time they wished, of course. How illuminating that their timetable must run to mortal demands.

☽

In the grotto where my doves camped, I paced and thundered. Foolish Ahab! How had he allowed this? Why had Jezebel not prevented it? Beyond our cave, the other factions dispersed to find space to light a fire, a mossy patch to lay their heads. I found Shaharu in a dell further along the ridge, in a tent his servants had raised despite the rocky ground. He preened himself before a bronze mirror.

"What now, Priestess?" He laid his comb on the table. I sat on a heavy sandalwood chair. The Baalists had certainly come well equipped, though I pitied the underlings that had borne this furniture, the fleeces and awnings, the lamps and bronzeware, up the mountain on their backs.

"I tried and failed with Jezebel," I started angrily, "and here we find ourselves. Tell me: what is your plan?"

He leaned back in an extraordinary ivory throne. "I have no plan!"

"Then you—and all of us—are doomed!"

"Calm yourself, Priestess. What will happen? I will call upon Baal. Elijah will call upon Yahweh. There will be no fires, no divine pyrotechnics. We will go home. Ahab will cast this enormous lunatic aside, and we will go on as before. Rematch?"

He bought out his gameboard and separated the houndsticks from the jackals. I swept them aside and slammed my fist into the table.

"You do not listen! This prophet will cheat. His fire will be lit. You must find some way to see yours does the same!"

He scrabbled about the floor to pick up his precious gamesticks. "How can I do that? You've seen the arena. It's overlooked on all sides. I am no magician, I have no mastery of illusion!" He held a broken jackalstick to my face in reproach.

His servants brought a light supper. Bread and vinegar. Figs dipped in honey, radishes, and stuffed cabbage leaves. I ate my fill and packed a cloth to take to Naomi. My hunger satisfied, the vague outline of an idea suggested itself.

"See that your altar is filled with driest kindling, Priest. I will do the rest."

☽

The guards at the royal tent stepped aside when I arrived. They were used to me visiting Jezebel every morning, bringing her daily contraceptive draught to the palace. She ushered Ahab away, into the outer chamber. "Women's talk, my darling; not for your ears!"

She turned to me. "Well, my Litu! Are you ready to see this scoundrel shamed?"

"Indeed I am. And I bring word from Our Lady. She has shown me how it is to be done."

Jezebel's eyes widened. "Asherah has spoken to you?"

"Did you bring your bow?"

She tapped her chin as she held me in a haughty glare. "I never travel without it. I will hunt at Jezreel when this nonsense is over."

I breathed again. "Then excuse yourself for the contest. Say you will retire to watch alongside the women and come with me."

☽

From our vantage point on a steep limestone crag, we had a clear view of the two altars, piled high with cut branches. Elijah, Shaharu, and

Ahab stood between them, beside two white bulls, tails shaking in quiet fear.

Everyone else had their backs to us, facing the arena and the mountain ridge rising sharp beyond it. Obadiah's peaked scarlet cap shone like a beacon amid the wisps of fog that floated above the crowd. Around him were the prophets of Yahweh, emerged from hiding. I had told my doves to distance themselves and run fast should proceedings go against us.

They sacrificed the bulls at the same time. Shaharu twisted his knife, looking away. Elijah relished the act, almost to decapitation. Priests from each side removed the entrails and jointed the carcases for burning.

Elijah turned to the expectant crowd and raged. "How long will you waver and hop between two opinions? If the Lord is God, follow Him! If Baal and these other deities," he waved his staff at the priests of Moloch, of Chemosh, appearing not to notice my doves, thirty cubits distant, "then follow them!" His blank face suggested it was all the same to him.

"Can I shoot him now?" Jezebel's arrow was poised, aimed directly at his heart.

"No," I said, though her suggestion had merit. "To win is not enough. It must be a spectacle."

Ahab raised a myrtle branch and dropped it. "Let the contest commence!"

Shaharu stood behind his altar. He prayed ostentatiously, raising his arms to the heavens. His low voice sang the sacred words of his faith. He convulsed, as if filled with divine essence. His priests circled the altar in a low, hopping dance.

"Devils take them!" Jezebel lowered her bow. "They're in the way."

I could not fathom what Elijah was up to. He stood with his back to his own altar, watching the Baalists.

"O Baal, answer us!" they called.

"Shout louder!" mocked Elijah. "Perhaps he's asleep and will wake up!"

The Baalists cut themselves with knives. Blood streamed down their bare arms.

"Cut harder!" Elijah yelled. "He will smell the blood and come to your aid!"

Jezebel tensed her drawing arm. I dipped a cloth in palm oil and wrapped it around the arrow's shaft. I lit it. "Now!"

She released the blazing arrow high into the air. It must seem as if it descended from the heavens. And it would have done; I told you, she was an expert shot. She judged the arc perfectly. It was on course to land at the back of Shaharu's altar, behind the heaped willow branches, hidden by the ox carcass. It would have lit the tinder: the birch bark, the thistle seeds, the thrush-nests. It would have ignited a fire to damn Elijah and save us all. The flames would have killed forever that ardour for a sole, male god. Preserved the notion of many gods for different people. Upheld the right of women to worship a goddess who cherished their sex and bolstered their independence and power.

But none of this happened.

As the arrow reached the peak of its parabola, I saw a blur of movement, white and grey. There were wings. The blazing tip stopped and changed direction. It descended, but no longer to Shaharu's altar.

Elijah watched the falling arrow blaze. He raised his palms. "O Lord, God!" he cried. "You are God in Israel and I am Your servant. Answer me O Lord, that these people may know that You are God!"

The arrow fell upon his altar. The fire ignited and the flames took hold.

"The Lord alone is God!" yelled Elijah.

The Yahwist priests fell to their bellies and cried out, "The Lord alone is God!"

The nobles and the witnesses of Israel, the merchants and artisans, the farmers and winemakers, ground their faces in the dirt and called, "The Lord alone is God!"

The Baalists, the Molochites, and the Chemoshites heckled and roared. They banged staffs against the rocks, threw stones at Elijah's altar. My doves saw the lie of the land and ran.

"Seize them!" screamed Obadiah. "Let none escape!"

Jezebel and I watched in horror from our hidden place. No longer did I wonder about the loyalty of the palace guards. Pledged to Obadiah's command, they brought down each priestess, every priest, all the prophets who tried to escape.

The clouds pulsed thick with smoke from the fire. I searched in vain for any sign of what I suspected.

I saw none, but had no doubt this was the work of those malignant angels I had thought long departed from this world.

Elijah's Victory

They were slaughtered. All of them. The priests that is; the fate of my doves was far worse.

By the time Jezebel and I caught up with Ahab and Elijah in the valley below Mount Carmel, it was done. The dried-up Kishon River flowed again, but with torrents of blood.

The bodies of the murdered priests were flung into a pit. Among the twisted limbs and eviscerated bellies, I saw the unmistakeable brush of Shaharu's dyed beard. Robes, sandals, and adornments lay in a pile beside the mass grave. A guard, searching through the clothing, came across Kemash's walking stick and threw it aside.

But where men are killed in the throes of war, women are enslaved. Why waste a valuable resource? I counted three hundred and twenty-three of my doves, Naomi among them, hands bound, ankles roped together, to be marched back to Samaria. So seventy-seven had escaped. I hoped they had the sense to cross the mountain and head to Tyre, only a day's walk from Mount Carmel—or on to Sidon, where the youngest doves would be safe if they had reached sanctuary in time. I would go to them, I resolved, when I was sure Jezebel was not in danger. She appeared bent upon thwarting such an outcome.

"What have you done?" she screamed at her husband. "What power does this—" she looked Elijah up and down, recoiling at his blood-soaked tunic, "this *lunatic* have over you? You provoke the gods with your murderous spree! What will become of us?"

Ahab could not meet her eye. "Return to the tent, Jezebel! This is not for you."

"You dare to tell me the slaughter of my priests is not my concern? My own prophets?"

"False prophets!" boomed Elijah. "As is she!" His staff pointed squarely at my breast. The palace guards stepped forward. Jezebel put out a protective arm.

"If they touch one hair of her head, Ahab, I will leave you and return to Sidon. I will tell my father what you have done to the priests of Baal and you will meet my brothers on the battlefield."

The king moved his head imperceptibly. It was enough. I led Jezebel away.

As the much-reduced camp was packed away, the tents rolled up, the mulepacks loaded, the first rumble of thunder broke across the valley. Elijah triumphed. "There, King. Can you hear it? You have done His work. The drought is over."

Ahab looked up, but even the longed-for rain could not banish his misery.

We had brought little from the temple in the way of comforts and finery, so there wasn't much to bring away. I packed my own pouch and left the wine-bowls, tinder boxes and cast-off travelling cloaks for the palace guards, who would be here soon. There would be no temple to take them back to.

Beyond the grotto, raindrops started to fall, fat as berries. I raised my hood and stole across the dell to Shaharu's tent. I wanted a memento of my friend. There it was, on the rosewood table, just where he left it. His ivory gameboard—the jackalstick I had broken in my fury still laid across it: a rebuke from beyond the grave.

☽

Elijah did not taste victory for long. During the sad, diminished progress to Samaria, Jezebel visited him where he slept, at the head of the procession. She took no one with her, not me, not Ahab, no guard. I did not hear what she said. I saw only his face, lit by the flickering flames, in an attitude of unparalleled fear. By dawn he was gone. Fled into the south, to the wilderness, where he cowered in a cave, so I later learned, never to be seen again.

My doves were given to the notable men of Samaria as concubines. Rarely were they permitted to leave their houses, so I was spared the sight of them degraded and humiliated in public. Naomi's father was rich enough to petition Ahab for her return. She was married off to a linen merchant thrice her age from Judah. She was at least a wife, a step above concubine in status.

Jezebel insisted I move into the palace. Her last prophet, she called me. From the rose garden I watched the gleaming white columns on the hill welcome the pink-hued dawn every day. I could almost smell the jasmine on the west wall when the evening sun fell upon it. Forbidden to the citizens of Samaria, it fell into ruin and disrepair. The Temple of Baal was burned to dust, the site desecrated, used as a public latrine.

Jezebel withdrew from her husband's company. She refused to attend the Yahwist festivals by his side. She spent her days with her children: the boys Ahaziah and Jehoram, now coming of age, and her daughter Athaliah, who was ripe for betrothal. She hunted more and more, going further afield, staying beyond the city walls overnight.

When war broke out with Aram over disputed lands in Gilead, she didn't see her husband off to battle. At the last moment, before he passed through the palace gates, Ahab turned to the overhanging balcony of her chamber, his eyes full of longing. A shadow stirred behind the ivory screen. He left without her kiss, with no tears of lament nor prayers for his safe return.

He was killed on the first day of the battle. Struck by an arrow between the plates of his armour, he remained propped up at his chariot, a figurehead for his men, even as the life drained from him. When his blood was rinsed from his chariot, dogs lapped at the crimson water, and it was said Elijah's prophecy had come to pass. *The jackals will feast on your blood as they ate of murdered Naboth!*

A poor return for Ahab's loyalty at Mount Carmel.

As for Obadiah, Jezebel seized him the minute Ahab went to war. She did to him what she could not do to unreachable Elijah. By sundown, he was impaled on a stake outside the city walls. I did not take my eyes from him, missed not a moment of his agonising death, until I was certain he could suffer no more.

She Shall Mother Nations

The end came, as night follows day.

Ahaziah, Jezebel's seventeen-year-old son, was crowned king of Israel. Her daughter, Athaliah, married the king of Judah. But Jezebel, the queen mother, took no public role, for she was plunged into misery. Despite the turmoil of their last months, she had truly loved Ahab. The melancholy that had struck with the birth of her first baby, and which returned with every pregnancy thereafter, took her again. She retreated to the divan in her shuttered chamber. She caged the peacocks to stop their shrill crying across the lawns. She stirred only to cross the room and sit behind the ivory screen of her window, glaring at Naboth's vineyard. She saw enemies everywhere: Obadiah lurking in the shadows; the murdered priests haunted her dreams.

Her grief mirrored mine for I had lost everything: the temple, my doves, the return of Asherah to the heart of Israel. All that was left was the future: Damaris and the young priestesses in her care.

I set out for Sidon, determined to bring them home. They would heal this broken, joyless city; banish the cloud of paranoia and dread that hung over the court like the stench from a tannery. With their return, we would rebuild the temple on the hill and restore the rituals and festivals that had brightened life in this once-happy nation.

☽

I arrived at dusk, just as the maidens of Sidon returned with the evening water jars from the wells. Jezebel's father had died that winter.

Her brother, the new king, Baal-Eser, greeted me. I would see Damaris that evening at the welcome feast, he said, as he led me to the rooftop of his palace.

Darkness gathered in the maze of narrow alleys below. Beyond the swaying masts of the harbour, the sun disrobed a succession of veils, pink-hued, then orange, magenta, purple, before sinking into the sea.

"How is my sister?"

He had seen her in a fragile state at the coronation of his nephew. I could not lie.

"Still . . . troubled. But she plans to see Ahaziah married. The return of her priestesses will revive her."

He coughed politely. "I am aware, as you know, of the shameful events at Mount Carmel. The priestesses sought sanctuary here. I cannot allow them to return to Israel if they are in danger there."

"It's perfectly safe. Ahab is dead, his prophet is gone. Those troubles are over."

He sipped his wine. He was as strikingly beautiful as his sister. The same full lips, the same unhidden contempt for fools.

"I have an alternative suggestion." He stared out to sea, where the memory of the departed sun streaked the sky a dazzling pink. "There," he pointed squarely. "At Kition."

"In Alashiya?"

"My colony there. I am building a new temple. It is a quiet, remote island, which enjoys our protection." He bowed his head as if accepting thanks. "They would be safe there from those who cannot tolerate other gods."

I considered his plan. How I longed to be at Alashiya again! The place drew me, it always had. But I couldn't bear to see Jezebel engulfed by melancholy. She must have a purpose. My own words came back to haunt me: a lamp must shine where it is needed.

Damaris would express no opinion when I asked her later that night. Since I'd saved her life, sending her from the slaughter of Mount Carmel in the dead of night, she trusted entirely in my foresight. I was

Asherah's earthly representative in her eyes. Where I led, she would follow, unquestioningly.

The decision, it turned out, was taken from my hands.

I'd been at Sidon only days when a messenger bade me to the palace. From the Temple of Elat, the very place I had met Jezebel eighteen years before, I descended the winding path to the city. I revelled in the warmth of the early sun and the scent of thyme between the cobbles. Beyond the roofs, a mere two days' sail across the white-crested sea, Alashiya called to my heart. But my mind turned inland, and to the dusty road to Samaria.

At the palace, I found a fleet of chariots abandoned on the forecourt. The stables overflowed with steaming horses. I hastened to the throne room where I found Jezebel's personal guard kneeling before Baal-Eser. A ball of dread pulsed in my breast.

The king dismissed the Samaritans and drew me into his quarters.

"What is it?" I demanded. "Has something happened to her?"

He sank into a purple divan. "It's not Jezebel."

"Then why are they here?"

"King Ahaziah is dead."

"Ahaziah? He's not yet twenty! Is it war?"

Baal-Eser pinched the bridge of his nose. "There was no attack. He fell from the balcony of his upper chamber."

"He *fell*?" Impossible. An ivory lattice screened the king's chamber, just like Jezebel's. It wasn't possible to fall unless the screen were broken.

Baal-Eser shrugged. "Jehoram will be king now. I will go to the coronation." He opened his palms. "You will return with my retinue?"

"Yes."

"And the priestesses?"

I needed no further prompting. "Send them to Kition."

Once again, I took my leave of Damaris. I invested her as high priestess of the new temple and bade her take the basalt stone of the goddess to that safe, placid island. We set off the following morning.

On the third day, Samaria's thick defensive walls rose up before us. I dreaded what I would find within.

〉

So Jehoram, Jezebel's youngest son, was crowned king of Israel. Her paranoia blossomed. Ahaziah was pushed, she whispered. The ghost of impaled Obadiah was everywhere. He was relentless, would pursue her until every member of her family was dead. Why did his god hate her so? She paced the shady corridors of the palace. Why should she not worship her own gods? Such loyalty was prized among the Yahwists, why did they despise it in others? But even Asherah had abandoned her in her misery, she howled. Had she not observed the rituals? Shown reverence when others had abandoned Her? Why was she punished so?

I told her these troubles were not the cause of gods but men. That Israel had tolerated foreign queens before. Solomon himself had sacrificed to Asherah. It was her voice, her power they could not endure. But it was impossible to reason with her.

War came again. Jehoram fought the Aramites in Gilead, as his father had before him. Injured, he retired to his second palace at Jezreel to recover. Elisha, the vexatious prophet who had succeeded Elijah, slipped to the battlefield in darkness and anointed the commander Jehu as king of Israel in Jehoram's stead. They met, the king and the pretender, on the road out of Jezreel, amid the swaying ears of wheat.

"Is all well, Jehu?" Jehoram asked.

Elisha had coached Jehu well. "How can all be well," he replied, "so long as your mother pollutes Israel with her harlotries and witchcraft?"

Jehu lifted his bow. The arrow plunged into Jehoram's heart.

〉

At the palace in Samaria, by Jezebel's side, I watched Jehu approach. As soon as she saw him, she knew her second son was dead.

"Come with me," I begged. The stallions were saddled at the rear gates. No chariot could equal them. We could have ridden to Sidon and safety before they even changed horses at Meggido.

But at the very last, her vigour, her stubbornness returned.

"Nay, Litu. I will not run."

She painted her face, lined her eyes with kohl, adorned her hair with silver. She smashed the lattice of her window to face him at her finest. At the jagged edge, she looked down upon him in fury.

"Well met, Jehu," she cried. "Usurper! Murderer of your king!"

He stilled his chariot and raised his spear. "Who is with me in the palace?" he cried. Attendants emerged from the shadows of her chamber.

I reached to pull her back. She stared at me, her black eyes wide and fearless. I felt the fleeting graze of her fingertips. Her lips moved, wordlessly. She smiled, caressed my cheek. Then, with a ululating war-cry, she jumped. There was a blur, a sickening thud. My own voice, screaming. Her blood spilled like wine on the stony ground below.

☽

My beautiful, brazen, darling Jezebel.

How I loved her. She was pig-headed and vain. She was cruel and disdainful. She was not my prophet. But still she was a whirlwind, a tidal wave. She was the spring rains and the autumn harvest. Was her passion for her goddess any different to the men who loved Yahweh? How different would the world have been had she won her war against Elijah; had her memory, as I once hoped, resounded through the ages, her name sung for generations; if men had tolerated many gods, instead of one; had the Hebrews permitted women's reverence for their goddess alongside men's devotion to their god.

But the coming world was built otherwise. No deviation from a solitary truth was allowed. Divinity, and consequently, full humanity, was invested solely in men and denied to women. I had poured everything—all my hopes to overturn God's curse—to give women power and security with the authority of their goddess. It had come to naught, for nothing changed the truth that She was gone. Men's earthly power flowed from their sole male god who endured, still.

Nothing would change until this god, too, was defeated. Until we became our own gods, as Asherah intended.

The seventy sons Ahab had fathered before his marriage were tracked down and beheaded. All his line was destroyed. Jehu left Jezebel's body to be eaten by dogs, just as Elijah foretold.

But my prophecy that she would mother nations also stood. For through Athaliah, her daughter, the queen of Judah, every king at Jerusalem thereafter was descended from Jezebel, up to the last of the line. Yes—even he, the king of the Jews, who was crowned with thorns—was her kin.

Part Five

THE PROPHET

37AD

I am the woman crying out, cast upon the face of the earth.
Thunder: Perfect Mind, The Nag Hammadi Scriptures

Magdala

After Jezebel's death, I fled north. I had no desire to see what would become of Israel. I knew what was coming with Jehu's rule. A land where only men dispensed orders, wrote holy books and defined laws. A world ordered solely in their image, to their convenience and benefit. Where women were men's property once more; vessels for carrying their children. Invisible, erasable, subhuman.

Already, Jezebel was demonised. Painted as a harlot: she, who was so faithful to her husband. Damned for her carnality, her beauty, the delight she took in her own body. Her very name was altered, the final syllable pronounced *gel*; that is, in Hebrew: *dung*.

Where would I go? Perhaps I'd see Damascus again. Nurse my furies among the shady colonnades. Travel on to the fragrant oasis of Palmyra.

I did not hurry. Time is the one thing I was never short of.

I lingered at Jezreel. I crossed the Jordan to the disputatious land of Gilead. But the vultures were gone from the carrion-fields by then and flown further afield, for now the whole of Israel was at war. Empires in the north, east, and west rose and fell. All of them, it seemed, must come and march across this land. Egyptians, Assyrians, Persians, and Greeks. The Israelites were plucked from their land and scattered beyond the Euphrates. Their cities were burned, crops trampled to dust, livestock slaughtered.

In the blink of an eye, or so it seemed, they returned. Towers rose once more in Jerusalem and Samaria. Vines were replanted. Temples rebuilt.

New invaders came, this time from the west. Battle-hardy Romans, descendants of those ancient fugitives from Troy. Marching under figureheads of eagles, they choked the highways. They brought new laws, new gods. The same evils.

Drawn to water, I followed the sparkling Jordan north. Travelling against the current, it felt as if I journeyed backwards in time. I came to a place I thought I knew. Maybe I *had* been there before. I have wandered these lands for so long, it is not unlikely. The village was unremarkable. A cluster of white-plastered houses nestled beside the Sea of Galilee. I cannot say whether I chose to stay or if it was merely where I came to a halt, like a boulder coming to rest at the bottom of a hill. Only later did I notice the chief industry was salting fish. There was a tower—a crumbling shepherd's watching-post. The town was named for it—Magdala.

I took an empty hut at the outskirts of the village, far enough from the stench of gutted fish, but close to the shore so I could watch the ever-changing sea from my doorstep. In winter, blue-curled mists sat stubbornly on the water. Pale hills loomed over the flat roofs of the town of Hippos on the far shore. Every morning the sunrise lit a path across the placid sea to my gate.

Rarely did I think of my wings these days, but when the swifts swooped down from Mount Arbel, darting through the windows of the watchtower to speed low across the water, how I longed to join them. I kept goats and roamed through the western hills, among the rock-rose and wild caper bushes. I made balms from Norea's old recipes, selling them in the market at Capernaum. I tended olive trees and pressed the oil, as I had long ago, on the slopes of Ararat.

In summer, seeking relief from the heat, I climbed with my flock. From the cliffs overlooking Magdala, I watched the full-bellied sails of fishing boats returning to harbour in the fresh dawn; women drying fish on the great wooden frames lining the shore. Every month, the melancholy sound of the shofar welcomed the new moon from the synagogue at the water's edge.

They were simple folk, and superstitious. I took a common name, Salome, to fit in. But they did not like me. I lived alone, unsupervised. I did not hire a boy to herd my goats. I drove my own cart to market. I refused to cover my hair, for Asherah's lustrous coils were her glory, as were mine. Yet, after dark, the men who scorned me in daylight sought my door, for since I lived so scandalously apart, beyond all oversight of the elders and scribes, they assumed my body was for hire.

Occasionally, for the company, rather than the coin, I let them in.

☽

One stormy night, one of these late-night calls brought me something other than a fisherman seeking the pleasures of my flesh.

Dark clouds rolled in. Boats were tossed like wooden toys on the roiling waves. In the lamplit comfort of my hearthside, I fancied it was only my oversight that kept them safe.

The rain hammering my roof was so loud I scarcely heard the knock.

"Sister," the man at my door begged. "Let me in! The innkeeper has put me out. I will sicken in such foul weather before I reach Capernaum."

I observed the wet curls slicked to his forehead, the tender hollow of his neck. I closed my fingers around the iron blade I carried everywhere and let him in.

He was a tax-collector, I saw from the sack he embraced tightly. The clink as he set it down told of rich takings from the fishermen who could ill afford the governor's toll, nor the cut he no doubt added for himself. He peeled off his sodden robe to reveal a fine body, strong from walking the hills of Galilee, lean from being turned away from every door.

I warmed him some broth. "Did she tell you to seek me?" I meant Judith, who kept the inn. A wild, foul-mouthed creature, who was nonetheless more acceptable to the people of Magdala than me.

"She said I'd find welcome with you. Since you are, like me, possessed by demons." He rolled his eyes. "I'm Levi," he smiled.

I was about to tell him my name, but he stopped me. "I know you. You're renowned from here to Tiberias. A perverse and rebellious woman!" He winked. "Well met, sister Salome."

When he'd supped, I asked news of the world beyond Galilee. I didn't care, but I liked the sound of his voice. It tripped with a rising lilt, like a goat on the hillside.

"What news," he murmured, "what news? The usual tumults, the same calamities." His right leg jerked as he spoke. "Pilate brought graven images into Jerusalem. Antipas has taken custody of the High Priest's vestments. You can imagine the disorder and chaos."

I mixed wine and handed him a cup. "Who is Pilate? Antipas?" I was ignorant of events at Jerusalem. I hadn't been there since Solomon's time.

"Pilate, the governor! Herod Antipas, the tetrarch! Where've you been?"

There was little point telling him.

"Then you know nothing of the king of the Jews?"

I did not. Nor did he concern me—or so I thought.

He whistled. "Then it's true, you really do prefer the company of goats to men. Truly, you have heard nothing of the Messiah?"

I reclined on a sheepskin before the fire. "Tell me all. You say there is a king again. At Jerusalem?"

He took a long draught of his wine and put a hand on his knee to still his unquiet leg. "There *was* a king. Though they only called him that in mockery. In truth, he was a prophet."

Levi was a fine storyteller. Emotions fluttered across his face. His hands told the tale as much as his words. He talked of miracles, resurrections and weddings. Until one part of his tale stopped my ease. "And so, he was crucified, this Yeshua they called Christos, the Messiah foretold by Moses. He ended on a cross at Golgotha. But it's said he didn't die, for after he was buried, he rose and walked again."

"Who said it? Who said he defied death?"

"His followers. Surely you've heard them preach? They are Galileans, after all. Kephas Peter returned to Capernaum, after Yeshua was killed. Or not killed. Depending on whom you believe."

I sniffed. "I do not listen to rabble-raisers in the market."

"But you must have seen them here in Magdala. It's the place of *her* birth, after all. It's said she returned and haunts the lonely cliffs yonder." He looked towards the towering rock through my window.

"*She*, you say?"

"His . . . I don't know what you'd call her. His lover, his muse. His first disciple."

"His first disciple was a *woman*?"

"He was a strange man. He never said he was the Messiah. He called himself Chrestos, the good man, not Christos, the anointed one. He mistrusted the righteous, hated the sanctimonious; he loathed priests. He preferred our sort, Salome. Tax collectors, lepers and the sick. Sinners. Even women."

His eye ran up and down my body as if appraising my membership of that sex. "And they loved him. They followed him everywhere. They gave their last coin to fund his mission. But none loved him more than she. Now, she lives on in squalidness and filth, alone with her grief."

The wine-fog dispersed in an instant.

You will find her in the sordid places, the Sibyl wrote.

I saw the watchtower of Magdala in new light. *In the shadow of a tower, you must wait.*

"Is—is she a prophet too?"

He polished off his wine and joined me on the floor. "Don't be ridiculous, she's a woman! But she was his well-beloved. It was unseemly, the way they were together." He pulled me to him and kissed me.

Levi's news enlivened me. I found him delightful, he who was so unwelcome everywhere else; his need for me as urgent as mine for him. Afterwards, we listened to the rain hammering at the leaky roof, and the furious sea beyond my gate. I realised I had taken my protective eye from the storm-tossed boats.

"What's her name?" I asked Levi. "Yeshua's beloved."

"Maryam," he said. "Of Magdala. They call her the Magdalene."

She Will Hide When You Appear

In the morning, as soon as I'd put Levi onto the northern road with a husk of dried bread in his hand, I turned towards the cliff path.

The storm had passed. Below me, the sparkling bay was strewn with wreckage. Gulls rode the current above the calm water. The white columns of Capernaum soared skyward from the north shore. From the jetty at Magdala, children dived into the sea; their shrieks of joy reached me on the hillside.

As I climbed, I pondered: how had I missed the coming and going of this prophet Yeshua? For decades—centuries, even—the Israelites had awaited the Messiah. A saviour, foretold by Moses, who would free them from the tyranny of foreign overlords. There was no shortage of applicants for the role. Conjurors toured the land, with daring philosophies and magic tricks to satisfy the thirsting crowds. They healed the lame, opened the eyes of the blind and the ears of the deaf. There was The Magus. The Standing One. The Living One. The Teacher of Righteousness. Now—this Yeshua. But I was searching for a woman. None intrigued me so much as this rare disciple, Maryam.

Was she the one I awaited? She, who would take Asherah's truths into the world at last? But could she even know of Her? For the dead goddess was barely remembered now. No one baked cakes for the Queen of Heaven any longer. No incense was burned at shrines to honour Her. No statues in Her image guided ships' helms. No idols at every hearth, in pendants at every neck, as in Jezebel's days.

It had gone entirely as Samael had once predicted.

No one pours libation for them. No blood of an unblemished heifer is spilled on their altars. Gods are made by belief and undone by disbelief.

The crime committed in the Garden of Eden—the expulsion of the goddess, my banishment that mirrored Hers, God's outrageous command that woman is inferior!—I had watched as it had come to full fruition. For millennia I had observed as if from a ringside seat the total degradation of women; their subjection, entirely, to men.

What should have been balanced was unequal. The half mistaken for the whole. Humanity meant men alone. Women were an afterthought. Lesser, inferior. The servants. Often, slaves.

My hopes had been dashed before. Yet, the longer I searched, the less I could abandon them. My heart pounded for the prophet who would avenge these wrongs, who would restore the dignity of women, and all that was lost, thousands of years ago in Eden.

☽

My own goats wandered these cliffs, unherded. I spied them now, in the dizzying heights. They gathered by the gaping mouth of a cave where I often sat, looking down upon sleepy Magdala. All bore the triangle painted in ochre that marked my ownership.

Levi had disclosed no further clues. Where would I find this hovel where Maryam lived? I had seen no such dwelling, no shelter, no shepherd's hut, among these lonely gullies and crags I knew so well.

As I reached my errant flock, the scent of rockrose overpowered me. The sticky stems clung to their coats. It would not be wasted: I'd make a balm for cuts and grazes from the resin. I'd need olive oil too, fresh thyme and golden yarrow. Moss, too, for wound dressing; all could be sold together for a tidy sum in Capernaum. I wandered inside the cave where the sphagnum grew, cloaking the boulders and damp ground there a luminous green.

From deep within, something stirred.

A crackling from unseen depths. A shift in the indiscernible gloom. *She will hide when you appear,* the Pythia said. *And appear when you are hidden.*

I scraped the boulders to fill my pockets with moss and retreated to a rocky outcrop, unseen from the cave. One of my goats, a mother seeking her kid, bleated piteously. I combed and collected the rockrose resin from her fleece, soothing her.

Whether I recall it rightly, I cannot say. But in the image lodged in the vaults of my mind, it was her foot I saw first. Unsandalled, black-grimed. A beggar's foot, cut and bruised from weathering the sharp rocks without protection. A gold chain encircled a narrow ankle, decorated with rusted charms that must once have rung gaily as she walked. Her toes were conjoined, *the second and third as one.* Like Asmodai's, and just as the Sibyl foretold.

So she was my kin. I had waited two thousand years for my own offspring. One hundred generations at least, my blood flowing through each child. The unforgettable features of my lost son, of Samael, my own, combining and recombining throughout the millennia. Each one, a link in the chain that led inexorably to the extraordinary woman standing before me.

She was unspeakably beautiful, though she approached her middle years. Dark, wide eyes. Sun-beaten cheeks, the same pronounced bow of the lips as my son. Her black hair was matted, and she wore rags. Once-fine linen fell in tatters from her shoulders, revealing a coiling, serpent-like scar on her breastbone.

In the crook of her arm, she carried the lost kid, now kicking to be freed at the sight of his mother. Reunited, they skipped joyfully away together. She stared at me sharply, full of reproach.

"Finally!" she scoffed. "You took your own sweet time!"

Perfect Mind

"What have they told you about me?" she asked, between mouthfuls of the food I brought: bread and cheese, stewed peaches and wine.

I fought the urge to look away. She tore at the crust like an animal. Peach juice dripped from her chin.

"I heard you were a . . . follower," I started. "Of the prophet Yeshua, who defied death. His lover—" I ventured, when she did not reply. "That you live up here in solitude with your grief."

That roused her. "Pah!" she spat. "Not grief, but fury."

She chewed, clutching her knees with one arm, looking down upon the marjoram-flecked hillside that unrolled into the glistening sea. The wind had risen again. White crests peaked. A gull hovered, unmoving, in perfect resistance to the wind.

"Nor was I his *lover*!" She glowered. "Such meagre imagination. A *follower*! I thought *you*, at least, would be different." She drained the wineskin.

"How—what can you know of me?"

"Everything!" She laughed. "For I am born of you, and all the generations between. I possess the memories of us all. Of you, naked and perfect in a blooming garden. Later, humbled and insignificant, carrying a dying goddess. I remember you hovering at countless cribs. Do you think I could forget your lullabies?"

"But I never sang to you. I stopped that long before you were born!"

"I *told* you: I have the memories of us all. You sang to multitudes of infants. How could I forget you, the mother to all my mothers, the angel at their side?"

She licked the sticky peach juice from her fingers, following its path from her forearms to elbows.

The signs were unmistakeable. Undoubtedly, she was my long-awaited prophet. She, who would bring Asherah's truths to power. A zephyr, to whisper in every ear and tug at every heart. But who would listen to this wild and ragged woman?

As if she read my thoughts, she stood and leaned into the wind. It held her on the very edge of the crag, as if she were flying. Her filthy robe flew behind her, her hair snapped and streamed in the eddying gusts. My hand flew to steady her, but I needn't have worried. Instead of falling, she yelled into the void:

> *"I am the first and the last!*
> *I am the honoured and the mocked!*
> *I am the whore and the holy one;*
>   *the wife and the virgin; the mother and the daughter!*
> *I am a barren woman with many children!*
> *I am the silence that is incomprehensible*
>   *and the voice whose sounds are many!*
> *I am Wisdom and ignorance; I am shy and proud!*
> *I am disgraced and I am great!*
> *I am compassionate and cruel; I am witless and wise!*
> *You who deny me, know me!*
> *I am the one they call Life and you call me Death!*
> *I am the one they call Law and you call me Lawless!*
> *I am the one you seized and I am She you scattered!*
> *I am She you despise, and yet you profess me!*
> *I am peace, yet war has come because of me!*
> *I am Perfect Mind!"*

Her voice washed over me in soothing waves. Each quality matched by its opposite. The polarity that drives all life. Harmony and balance; completeness. I felt the presence of the lost goddess; of the Wisdom I had first tasted in Eden. A goddess of strength and power, but also frailty. The cry of a deity who had been slandered, ridiculed, and abused, just like Her daughters. A divinity born not of judgement and control, but of understanding and compassion.

My disbelief was chased into the wind, my doubts upended.

Who would *not* listen to this wild and ragged woman!

It felt like a closing of what should not have been opened. The tightened string of a discordant lyre. Two halves rejoined. I remembered the vision Norea had described to me: *Like balm of aloe on a salt-rash. Water to a parched throat, a breeze on a stifling day.* It was a healing.

And then she shrieked. Impossibly high-pitched, it penetrated to the core of me. It echoed from the cliffs behind us. The boughs of the acacia trees shivered as the sound travelled across the bowl of the valley towards the sea. The sky answered. Thunder rumbled. Lightning flashed, forks danced over the water, which roiled and tumbled in turn.

"Come!" Her cheeks were rosy pink, revived by her joyful prayer. "We don't have much time. They will come for me soon."

Two Parts Sundered

"Who?" I stumbled after her. "Who is coming for you?"

"It doesn't matter," she laughed. "Do not ask who or why, for it will always be the same people and for the same reason. All that matters is *when*—whether we have enough time."

"Enough time for what?"

She turned to me at the entrance of the cave. "We are lost," she said solemnly. "But now we will find the way."

She lit a lamp and led me deep within, through a winding, narrow tunnel, which emerged into a glittering cavern. Above us, roosting swifts chirped from hidden nests. Oil lamps in recesses of the dank walls lit up blue-salt columns and orange-tinged stalactites. A pool at our feet reflected the whole sparkling spectacle.

"Come." She entered an unremarkable grotto beside the main chamber.

It was bare, save for a wooden box, from which rolls of parchment spilled onto the floor. A reed-pen and horn of ink were set upon a flat boulder. A hearth, embers still glowing, filled a cavity at the rear.

Maryam revived the fire with bark and twigs she took from inner pockets of her robe. A bird's nest followed, lined with tufts of goat-fleece, moss, and black feathers. "Two halves," she uttered earnestly, as she broke the nest in two. "Two parts have been sundered that should have been joined. Without one, both shall die."

She dropped the broken nest into the fire and a flame leapt into life. Grease from the goat-hair smouldered.

"There is no freedom without harmony. No life without balance. Both halves needed for creation. Equality between them to nurture and sustain. This is the Wisdom of our Holy Mother."

"Tell me!" I begged. "I brought Wisdom into this world against the wishes of a punishing god! I have laboured for millennia to revive it. I waited and sought you for untold centuries! Tell me what to do, for I am not enough!"

"You are enough," Maryam returned. "Indeed, you are the only. Through you, Wisdom should have flowed to all mankind. But it was thwarted by those who set themselves above nature, who know nothing of balance and harmony and care even less. Womankind was crushed to stop these truths from spreading—but still, they remain. Her laws govern this earth and all living things in it. They govern reality, whether we believe in them or not."

"But how can we revive them?"

For only then would the misery of Sheol end and my son be rescued from eternal torment. Only then, might Samael return to me.

A thump reverberated from the main chamber. The water in the pool rippled, dappling the reflection of the flickering lamps. She dragged my face from the source of the sound and held my eyes.

"Listen carefully, Lilith. Everything is in the box. All the answers you seek. My words, my teaching, my message. Her Wisdom, which is finer than rubies. Her fruit which is better than gold. You must reveal it when it is time."

"Time for what?"

"When the world is ready to hear. The people of this age don't comprehend. The world must grow in understanding. You alone are deathless. You alone have time to wait. You must bring my words to those who are to come, that they will find Her, through me, through you, and truly *live*. That is how Her Wisdom will prevail."

"Who is coming for you?"

"Take it *now*." She thrust the spilled parchments inside the box and lifted it into my arms. "Follow that ledge above the pool and hide in the crack. Do not come out until they are gone."

"Until *who* is gone?"

"May Her abiding love bless and keep you." Maryam kissed my forehead. "May Wisdom guide you."

The echo of feet in the narrow passage got closer, but she would not be rushed. She waited until I was hidden, squeezed between the slabs of cool rock.

She sat and arranged her skirts around her folded knees. Her face was radiant in the soft lamplight, a vision of serenity and perfect peace. The only sounds, the timeless dripping of water through rock and the footsteps of the men who came to seize her.

The Inferno

Too many times in my long and pitiful life, I have stood back as evil prevailed. I watched when God ousted Eve from Eden, forced inferiority upon her, and all women to come. I idled in the desert of Edom when I should have raced to save Asherah. I stood by as the women of Ararat were bullied, as Aradka was beaten to death. I failed my beloved Jezebel.

No longer.

I knew not who pursued Maryam or why, but it was clear what they would do to her when they came. I'd waited too long to lose her now. She would lay down her life to save her message. She desired martyrdom. So be it.

But not yet.

Torchlight flickered in the tunnel from the cave's entrance. Heavy footfalls echoed. I leaped from the ledge and crossed the cavern in two strides. I clamped a hand over her mouth to stifle her cries and pulled her into the dark recesses of the cave. There, the pool emptied into a rivulet which flowed beneath the black rock to unseen inner depths. Crouching in the icy water, hidden by a huge honeycomb of rock, we watched as six men poured into the chamber.

They arrived in a bubble of light like a halo around them. All were bearded, dressed in the garb of shepherds or farming folk. They carried knives and adzes, one had a pruning-hook for a weapon. I recognised a fisherman of Magdala, one of those who jeered at me in the marketplace but who darkened my doorstep at nightfall.

"The bitch is gone," said one, in Aramaic.

"She can't be far," said another. He wore a fringed mantle in the Galilean style.

"There was another with her," said the Magdalan. "A harlot of the town."

"Come!" The ringleader, a stocky, stern-looking man, waited by the tunnel, barely entering the chamber. He raised his torch, peering into the heights, as if we might cling there, like bats. "We will find them on the hillside." He spoke with a distinct Judean lilt.

They grumbled over the loss of their prey. Searched for clues to Maryam's disappearance. Then they upturned the lamps, set torches to the spilled oil, and left as a blaze took hold behind them.

We watched in horror as fire filled the cavern. It soared from the oil-drenched ground to the rocky ceiling. The grotto where Maryam wrote at her stony bench was engulfed by the inferno. Stalactites glittered like diamonds through the thick smoke. A tremendous screeching filled the air as the swifts left their burning nests and swept towards the tunnel, before thudding, wings singed, to the floor.

Oil spilled into the pool so even the water burned. Flames danced across the surface. They licked at the ledge where the chest of parchments was hidden.

"My scrolls!" Maryam cried.

"They can be written again. They are not worth your life."

"I was ready to die!"

I bit my tongue and did not say what I thought: *You still might.*

"What have you done?" The raging flames reflected in her tears. "I would have died, but my words would have lived. Now, I die for nothing! You have killed me twice as much as they!"

She was right. There was no exit. No path through the blaze to the tunnel. The chamber was black with smoke and filling rapidly. It burned my throat, scorched my lungs. Soon, there would be no air to breathe at all. I ducked beneath the water.

As I emerged, a cool draught of air swept my cheek. Fresh oxygen to feed the flames. Sucked along the water's surface, it came from the very back of the cavern, where the stream flowed under the rock. I stooped and looked again. The narrowest of gaps—barely an inch or two—between the water and the rock. But there must be air beyond, for it rushed like the southern wind in its haste to join the fire.

I never did believe in luck. Nor, for reasons I am sure you understand, in the guiding hand of angels or an Almighty who wished me well. I have learned well enough there is no justice, no reward for the deserving. But you must know, since I am here to tell the tale, that there was an exit.

Together, we drew great lungfuls of the poisonous, burning air, and submerged. We swam through the water-filled tunnel beneath the rock, blindly holding on to each other, never knowing when or if we would find the other side. We scrabbled along, fingertips scraping the rough tunnel wall, until around a bend, a hazy light appeared. We emerged, spluttering, throats burning with acrid smoke, into a chamber that opened onto a green valley, flooded with daylight. It dazzled with life, abounded in fresh, sweet, soothing air.

Speak of Paradise, Think of Damascus

It was days before Maryam would speak to me again. We hurried north, keeping to the donkey-tracks that crossed the wild ridges and gullies of the Galilean hills. Under cover of night, we descended into the plain of Gennesaret and skirted Capernaum, its pillars of ivory marble shimmering in the moonlight. Maryam spat at the sleeping city and beckoned me onwards.

Though silent, she directed our route. She knew the countryside to the last cubit: every grove of shady poplars, every secret hollow in which to shelter from the noontime heat. She led me to the ancient caravan path to Damascus, far from the bustle of the paved Roman highway.

"Why Damascus?

She had been silent for three days. Finally, she spoke.

"I have kin there. We will need a place to hide while I write again."

"Who pursues you?"

Still, she would not tell me. She lifted her chin. "Damascus is at a crossroads. We have a choice to make."

I tolerated her sullenness. She was, thanks to me, still alive.

☽

We arrived at the outskirts of Damascus in the hot forenoon. Before us lay fields of apricots and almonds in full spring blossom, a dazzling display of pink. In the west, the peak of mighty Mount Hermon was still cloaked in thick snow. The triple-streamed Chrysorrhoas, the golden river, flowed through the city; gleaming temples and towers of rosy marble soared from its banks. Tributaries irrigated the plateau, a patchwork

246

of orchards, vineyards, and ripening grain. What was said of the city was assuredly true: when you speak of Paradise, think of Damascus.

We entered by the new Roman gate to the southeast. It was quiet: no crowd jostling to enter, no carts of grain brought to market or animals led to slaughter. The streets were empty, dust thrown up, still settling on the air, as if a crowd had just passed through. As we neared the centre, we saw that stalls were deserted, spices, cheese, and fruit abandoned on the planks.

Maryam observed it all and bit her lip. She led me off the wide main road into a tangle of alleys. We passed beneath towering arches, by walls daubed with fresh graffiti, towards a dark lane.

Maryam rapped at a drab, unpolished door. There was no answer. Five, six, seven times she knocked, but no one came. She ran to the next house, where the door swung back on a creaking hinge. She looked both ways down the lane, dragged me inside, raced up steps and tore through three bare rooms that led to a terrace overlooking a verdant courtyard of palms and figs.

"Come!" She straddled the balcony and dropped into the neighbouring garden.

I fell into fragrant balsam bushes. "What are you doing? Whose house is this?"

But Maryam had no time to answer before the figure of a matron emerged from the house. She stared in consternation and fury at the bedraggled interlopers she found in her garden.

☽

"Yohanah." Maryam held out her palms as if to calm a rabid jackal. "Do not be wroth. I had nowhere else to go."

"And who is this?" Yohanah gestured to me. "Another of your troublemakers? What does this one do? Walk upon the clouds? Turn figs into lamb chops?"

"Sister, do not be childish."

"You are the child! With your nonsense talk of goddesses. Of an angel who would come for you and help you change the world! You sent our poor sweet mother to the grave grieving over your fantasies."

"That's not fair! Sister, please. I need your help."

"Of course, you do!" Yohanah raged. "When have I not seen your face and been asked for a thousand favours? To keep you from the soldiers! For silver for your missions! To hide your latest protégé! For food and drink!"

"And did you not do these things for me, every time I asked?" Maryam smiled disarmingly. It seemed to stoke Yohanah to even greater fury, but she continued, "And now you come to mention it, we are rather hungry. We ate nothing on the road but carobs and mulberries. Darling, bring us water to wash and your excellent pistachio cakes. I know you've been baking."

"How—through one of your visions?"

"No. Because you have flour on your cheek." Maryam wiped it away and embraced her unyielding sister.

☽

Yohanah did bring cakes, as well as wine, mutton stewed with okra, vine leaves stuffed with meat and herbs, cheese pies drizzled with honey and apricots in cream. She brought water, fresh towels. She even bowed to convention and washed her guests' feet herself, slowly thawing in her rage as she fulfilled the obligations of hospitality.

I have seen enough of other people's families to know such disputes are never all they seem. So it appeared with Maryam and her sister. Having seen the sorry state of Maryam's feet, she brought balm to heal them. A tub, for us to wash. Yohanah fussed over Maryam's hair, washing it with lotus oil and combing the tangles with great care. She fetched clean Egyptian linen to clothe us.

I saw Yohanah's fury was, more truly, fear. For a sister who lived far beyond the bounds of common custom. Who disappeared for months on end, only to return in a cloud of passion and urgency, bringing danger to her door, yet again.

This occasion, it seemed, would be no different.

For when we were fed—as well as I ever was in all my life—and reclining in Yohanah's fragrant, shady garden, Maryam asked, "What occurs in the city, sister? Why is it so quiet?"

Yohanah snorted. "One of your lot has arrived."

Maryam was unsurprised. "Which one?" She looked at the novelty of her spotless feet, nails cleaned and pared, enfolded in soft kid-leather sandals.

"Not one I ever saw with you, before. A new one, with the zeal of a convert. A tentmaker, no less. He speaks today in the marketplace. We must be the only bodies in Damascus who bide at home."

Maryam groaned.

"I thought you'd be pleased," Yohanah said. "Your faith is growing."

Maryam kicked over the wicker table. Empty plates clattered to the floor. The sparrows that had been picking at the crumbs scattered into the sky. "It's not *my* faith!" She strode furiously into the house. "Not anymore!"

I Am the Woman Crying Out

When news came that the zealous new convert, Pavlos, had fled Damascus, having agitated the city so much he had to be smuggled away in a washing basket, Maryam's fears faded. She stopped veiling herself in the front rooms of the house. Looked less anxiously towards the door at any sudden sound. But she was driven to even greater urgency in rewriting the texts she had lost (that I had lost, as she reminded me, repeatedly) in the fire at Magdala.

"We have so little time!" she raged. "You must write faster!"

For it was my task to put to parchment all the hymns, sermons, and prayers she recalled; each word plucked from her perfect memory as she pounded the neat paths through thyme, rosemary, and balsam in Yohanah's garden.

"If you would only tell me," I said, through gritted teeth, "who pursues you and why we must rush, I could help you. I am not without uses."

"Oh, I know how useful you are! It is because you are so useful that my life's work is now in ashes!"

And so we went on. She, enraged. I, with aching fingers and ink-stained thumbs. And Yohanah doing the donkey work. Out to the marketplace every day to buy food, barter for the expensive parchments Maryam demanded. Grinding and mixing the inks of different colours. Cooking and clearing away.

Why did I stay? you rightly ask, when I had such little joy of my spiky, long-awaited prophet.

Simply—for her words. For the delight of inscribing them for lasting record. For the joy of seeing the enduring urges of my heart voiced at last, and so beautifully. Because, in contrast to the scorn she poured on me and the orders she barked to her sister, the prayers that fell from Maryam's lips were powerful and sublime. She spoke in parables, prayer and song, rich in imagery of the natural world and all its blessings. Of love in all its forms, the glories of life and never the fear of death. Through them all coursed a rallying cry for the undying Wisdom of the goddess:

I am the First Thought
and the last.
She who exists before All.
I dwell in those who came before
and those who are yet to be.
I am numberless,
immeasurable, ineffable.
Through me comes Wisdom,
The Wisdom of everlasting things.
I am the First Thought
and will be the last.

She expanded on the prayer she had yelled from the cliffs of Magdala, her exultation of opposites, the hymn to balance and completeness, the celebration of female divinity and Wisdom she dubbed Perfect Mind. She added to it a new voice of fury and defiance. The cry of a goddess who would not be banished. This text, I bound separately, as one codex of nine papyrus leaves, for it was my favourite.

Do not abandon me if you see me on the dung heap, she sang.
Do not mock me or cast me aside with those who are condemned.
Draw near to me.
For I am speech that cannot be silenced.
I am the knowledge of the search and the discoverer of those
who seek me.

I am the one who cries out and the one who listens.
Be alert: for I am Truth.
I alone exist, and I will have no one judge me!

Her message was simple, yet appealing:

We were born of this world. There is but one. One world, one life given to each of us. No god is set above nature. No man above woman. As we are not above, nor apart from, this world that nurtures us.

Women bring life into the world. To denigrate women is to degrade life itself. There must be equality, not domination. Harmony, not hierarchy. Compassion, not violence. Women must be cherished as we cherish this world that sustains us.

We had a Mother once, but She is gone. Returned to the earth that birthed Her. But Her eternal Wisdom lives on. Nourished by it, we too shall bud and bear fruit. In death, we shall return to the earth and live on only in our children. We possess no soul to be redeemed, or judged, or measured. There can be no afterlife, no heavenly authority. We are enough. In our opposites, we are complete.

We must keep our eyes on this world, the source of all life. On its blessings and charms. Not be careless with it in hope of something better to come. No paradise in heaven, but it can be made here, on earth, if only we nurture and respect it, the Mother from whom we sprang.

In so doing, we shall be free of tyranny, free of brutal, dominating authority. We shall be our own gods.

She condemned the sufferings of women in this world ruled by men. There was a line she returned to again and again, that sang like a chorus throughout:

I am the woman crying out, cast upon the face of the earth.

It moved me to silent tears every time. For it was me. I *was* that woman. I had cried out for what I had lost. I was cast aside. I walked the face of the earth for millennia.

This was, as she put it, her life's work. For me, it was so much more than that. It was everything I had striven for. The overturning of all that had happened in Eden so long ago, when female divinity and Wisdom were banished, so too all balance and harmony, and a new and horrifying creed was born: of male supremacy; hierarchy, domination of women and the earth; judgment and control.

It was the correction and repudiation of Adam's course, sanctioned by his god. This was the work of countless lifetimes.

The Empty Jar

We worked that whole summer. We slept late, until the beating sun had passed over the tall palms and cast Yohanah's garden into blessed shade. Late into the night, we continued, as the stars blinked upon us.

We charted our progress by the waxing and waning moon. When three full cycles were completed, Maryam finally started to slow. She smiled more, stopped pulling at her hair, which was thinning in patches. She showed concern for her sister's life, in which she had hitherto expressed no interest.

"What news of Shimon, of Yakov, of Joses?" And Yohanah talked of her sons, scattered across Judea, Samaria, and Galatia, of whom she had never spoken, unprompted by Maryam, before now.

In unguarded moments, if I were careful to approach the subject indirectly, Maryam would talk of Yeshua—of the early days, never the last. How they had met, beside the sea at Magdala, when he worked as a carpenter on the new synagogue there. How he, alone among the workmen, paused to listen to Maryam preaching beneath a palm-tree, an oddity tolerated in the village for the sake of her dying mother. How he returned after his shift one day, to ask her a singular question.

Inseparable thereafter, they had walked out alone together into the hills of Galilee, sailed in fishing boats into the choppy waves, where judging eyes could not follow. Snuck into caves among the clifftops, where they loved and laughed and plotted. And eventually, after Maryam's mother finally expired, and her sister had departed for Damascus with her new husband, took off together, scandalously unwed, to Egypt. There, in the shadows of ancient temples, beside the mystics of Lake Mareotis and the goddess-worshipping rabbis of

Aswan, among the great Jewish, Egyptian, and Greek thinkers in the melting pot of Alexandria, their philosophical project took shape. Together, they would preach the lost Wisdom of the goddess; Sophia, as She was known there. A message of love, compassion, nonviolence, of respect for this world, of equality.

"What did he ask you?" I ventured one day, as we paused at our work.

"Hmm?" She stopped in the middle of the garden, eyes shut, basking in the dying rays of the sun.

"The day you met," I said, as casually as I could muster. "What did he return to ask?"

She smiled. "That was the funny thing, given what came after. He asked: *Who am I?*"

"And?"

"And what?"

"What did you reply?"

"As he spoke, I saw him transformed. A blinding light descended. A fruitful tree grew and sheltered him. A dove roosted in its branches. I told him what I saw: that he was a child of the Holy Mother. That he had been sent to me. That we had great work to do."

☽

As summer died and the ibises took flight, we went into the dusty streets of Damascus. Maryam was heavily veiled. At the market, she chose a strongbox of sturdy oak with a weighty iron lock. Back in Yohanah's garden, she carved patterns in the wood: interweaving vines and leaves, boughs heavy with pomegranates, a soft-eyed calf nibbling at the foliage.

"This, you shall fill with my scrolls and codices." She didn't take her eyes from the chisel. "You will preserve them. Keep my words safe until they can be heard."

"And what of you?"

"The end is coming. I shall return to Jerusalem."

I remembered the bold features of the Judean ringleader, lit by the blaze in the cave. "But the men who seek you—won't they be there?"

"Let them have me! Death lends flight to some ideas." She arched a brow. "I have seen it happen."

I don't know where the notion came from. Dropped from the sky, perhaps, a gift of the ibises flying to Egypt for winter.

I grasped her thin wrist. "No. Come with me. These men you fear, who follow you, who preach in the marketplaces. Why should you— we?—not do that? Your words are sublime. Let them be heard across nations—now!"

"Do you think I haven't tried that?" she scowled. "What do you think I was doing with Yeshua? We preached together. Very success- fully, I might add. Until—" She traced her finger along the vine she had carved along the edge of the box.

"Until what?"

"Last night, I dreamt I bought a jar of grain at the market. As I walked home, the handle broke and the grain spilled behind me. I didn't notice until I returned home and found my jar was empty."

"Your jar is not empty!"

"Perhaps. But it is no longer full. I have seen what happens when women dare to assume authority. It is why he was sent to me. His voice was like honey. He could talk a man into walking through fire."

"You, too, have that power."

"No. These people do not want what I offer—what Yeshua and I showed them. They chose the appealing lie over our truth."

"What lie?"

"All of it! Forgiveness. Redemption. I cannot offer that for there is naught to forgive, no sin to redeem. Good and evil are not exter- nal, both reside in all of us. I cannot offer everlasting life. These new followers, who speak in Yeshua's name—they say a world is coming in which we will have no need of our mortal bodies. That they are prisons that constrain us. No! That is a man's fantasy. A woman's body tethers her to this earth. We are wedded to this life, to its pleasures and its sorrows. Our bodies cycle like the seasons, we bleed with the moon. We yield children, as the earth yields its fruits. We cannot live forever! It is not natural. It is not right. But that is all people want."

"Is it? Do they not want freedom? From judgement, from tyranny? Do they not want the comfort of knowing we are here in Paradise already? That we are part of this earth, will return to it one day, but our children will live on."

"That is why you must wait," she snapped. "You must preserve my words until the world is ready to hear them. When women may be heard. When freedom, the contentment of belonging to this earth—all that you describe—becomes desirable. Necessary, even."

From the upper storey window, Yohanah watched us. Her usual aspect of barely concealed contempt was gone. She raised a hand to the lintel. How much older and worn she suddenly seemed than Maryam. Overhead, the last of the ibises croaked a farewell.

"Indulge me, Maryam. I will deliver you to Jerusalem before the spring rains. But first—a diversion. Do not waste your one life. What have you to lose?"

Never was there a woman as stubborn as Maryam. She did not answer. She returned to her work. She chose a slim file from her leather roll of tools, and refined the curve of a heavy, fruited bough. But she didn't say no. I knew her well enough by now to take that as assent.

☽

We took our leave of Yohanah the next morning. The sisters embraced; Yohanah alone blinked back a tear. We left the strongbox, filled with the scrolls and codices of all our labours, in her care. I promised I would return for it.

"And you, sister?" Yohanah's voice cracked. "Will you return?"

"A prophet can have no sister, no mother nor brother, too," Maryam replied. "Think of me no more, I am dead to you now."

Maryam reeled, as if surprised, as the door was slammed in her face.

Ordinary Deceits

"What was that about?" I asked as soon when we were beyond the walls of Damascus. We walked north, beside the feathery tamarisks and giant reeds that lined the swift river.

"What was what about?"

"That nonsense about having no sister."

"I have no sister."

"She has taken care of you for three months and more! Fed you, clothed you, sheltered you from harm. Why do you deny her?"

"I was being kind."

"*Kind?* You don't know the meaning of the word!"

I side-stepped the yellow crabs scuttling at the water's edge. A turtle raised his head from the water, then returned to the depths.

"I shall soon be dead." Maryam devoured a pistachio cake Yohanah had packed for her. "Far better for her to forget me now. It will save her grief." She licked the crumbs from her fingers. "Anyway, you misunderstand. I said it because she is not my sister."

"Don't start that again."

"She's my mother." She smiled to see my dismay. "I told you once. I have the memories of all my forebears. That's how I knew you: from the countless times you lingered at my mothers' cribs. And that's how I know Yohanah is not my sister." Maryam winked. "She claimed it was a miraculous conception. A gift from God. But there was nothing miraculous about it at all. It was perfectly ordinary, for I was conceived in violence when she was but a child herself."

The weight of all Yohanah's sorrow and love for this infuriating woman fell upon me. "Then that is worse! Could you not have left her with some words of comfort?"

"What use is comfort?" Maryam shrugged.

The reeds beside us bowed low as the wind sighed through them. I saw the child, Yohanah, violated and scared. If Maryam was of my line, then Yohanah too was among my daughters. She would have been killed for the sin of bearing a baby out of wedlock, had her parents not covered the crime and raised the infant as their own.

Maryam walked on, in blissful contemplation of the whispering tamarisk leaves.

"You had that in common then," I called to her, ahead.

She looked over her shoulder at me. "Hmm?"

"You and Yeshua. Both miraculous births."

She laughed. "There are no miraculous births! Only ordinary deceits."

☽

We skirted majestic Antioch and headed west through Tarsus, Lystra, and Perga.

Maryam's fears were proved right. The crowds we addressed in the marketplaces, at the harboursides, in the courts of the synagogues, were not eager to hear from women. They hissed, they mocked, they threw eggs and rotten fruit. But where it was possible to disregard the heckling of the men, the women were attentive. They put down baskets of fish to listen, hushed children and soothed laden donkeys.

"Consider a tree," said Maryam, her rich voice halting in the unpractised Greek. "Its foliage is beautiful, its fruit abundant. All the beasts of the field find shade beneath it. The birds of the sky dwell in its branches and all living creatures feed from it. What is that tree but our Holy Mother? She is a tree of life to those who take hold of her. Happy are all who embrace Her. Planted by a stream, She yields fruit in season. Her leaf can never wither. She is Wisdom, more precious than rubies, Her knowledge better than gold. She is the circling of years and the guiding light of the stars. The hum of bees and the raging of wild beasts. The gentle breeze and the violence of waves."

The men mocked, the women listened.

On we went.

260   Nikki Marmery

At each town or settlement, she went directly to the public spaces. If other preachers were in residence—often those espousing the new religion, the multiplying followers of her own Yeshua—she turned heel and left. Many times we arrived someplace dusty and road-sore, only to leave immediately without a bite to eat or a gulp of water to revive us.

That all changed at Myra, a city of Lykia.

We arrived at the harbour when the distant mountains were already dusted with the first winter snows. Tombs hewn from the cliff-face cast a sombre shadow over the town. Pigeons swooped down from the hollows like avenging spirits.

As we climbed towards the acropolis, we saw a crowd on the hillside. Elevated on a rocky hillock, a preacher loomed above his audience. He wore plain brown robes and carried a staff, for his legs were bowed. He was bald, with a full beard in the Jewish style.

Until now, Maryam had never strayed so close, but this time she asked a passer-by the name of this preacher.

"Pavlos," she was told. He who had preached in Damascus when we first arrived.

She marched to the side of the crowd, where the scrubby kerm-oak bushes marked the women's space—away from the ground reserved for men at the front.

It was the usual sort of speech.

"O foolish Lykians!" the preacher cried. "I marvel that you are turning away so soon from Him who called you to a different gospel. The gospel I preach is not according to man. For I neither received it from man, nor was I taught it, but it came through revelation from Christ. Who has bewitched you that you should not obey the truth?"

Maryam drew down her berry-red veil and crossed her arms.

"The law was our tutor to bring us to Christ. But now we have faith, we no longer need a teacher. For you are all sons of God through faith. There is neither Jew nor Greek, neither slave nor free, neither male nor female. You are all one in Christos."

"No male or female?" Maryam called, in scornful voice. "We are all the *sons* of God?"

The preacher turned. Maryam's hair streamed behind her, catching on the oak twigs. Her proud chin was lifted, her black eyes flashed.

"No female!" Pavlos repeated. The crowd hummed approval.

"Then we are equal, you and I?" asked Maryam.

The crowd surged, as ocean waves teased by a rising wind.

"Not equal," the preacher cried. "For man was not made for the woman, but woman was made for the man. Was not Adam formed first, and then Eve? Nor was Adam deceived, it was the woman who became a sinner."

The rumbling of the mob grew. Women's voices rose high in uproar above the men's.

"Nonetheless!" The preacher lifted his staff to silence them. "Woman shall be saved through childbearing, if she continues perfectly in faith and love, holiness, and soberness."

"You mean," Maryam returned, "if she *serves* man and is *quiet*?"

I scoured the landscape to prepare for a sudden departure. Behind us, beyond the patchy bushes and the thinning crowd, there was a path, too narrow for many to follow at once, which led through scrub towards the harbour.

"Yes!" The preacher pounded his staff against the stony ground. "A woman must dwell in silence and submission! I do not—shall never!—permit a woman to teach or have authority over a man!"

The women around us exploded in fury. "What of the priestesses of our own goddess of Myra?" they demanded. "Must the holy women of Artemis Eleutheria bow to men too?"

"Yes, yes and thrice yes!" he roared. "For what is she but an idol? You sacrifice to demons, not the living God!"

Fury rippled through the crowd. Men turned to wade through the multitudes to reach this obstreperous woman. The women linked arms, keeping the men enclosed, tightly contained against the rocky hillock where Pavlos stood.

Maryam cast one last furious glance upon the speaker, lifted her voice and yelled into the deep blue sky, "Chrestos! Chrestos! Chrestos! He was Chrestos, the good man, never Christos, the Messiah! *He* never silenced women! He spoke with us and of us. He spoke for Sophia, of the Wisdom of the goddess! Thou art a false prophet! You would turn the world upside down! Tis your gospel, not his, you preach!"

Her words passed, like the eye of a storm, over the mob. A tense heartbeat, as their meaning soaked into the thirsty ground. Then chaos reigned. The enclosed men jostled harder to escape. The women held the line, hemmed them in, all the tighter.

Someone grasped my shoulder. A tall woman, dressed in the brightly-coloured robes of a priestess, beckoned us. I grabbed Maryam's wrist as the crowd opened from behind to let us pass.

Our benefactress led us through briar and thicket, stumbling on loose rocks and shingle, all the way to the lower town. We did not stop, not for mule nor cart, not for the Rhodian ship that had brought us here, still riding at anchor in the broad bay. Bidding the woman goodbye, we slipped into the dark forest towards the west, never stopping to catch our breath until we were sure we were not followed.

Mathetriai

After Myra, Maryam grew in volubility and rage. We crept through the dark forests that hugged the rocky shores of Lykia, pursued by jackals that howled on every moonlit night.

"This is how it happened before!" she raged. "These new followers. They never knew him! They do not understand. This is the work of Kephas!"

I held aside a juniper branch for her to pass. "Kephas?"

"Once Shimon. Then Peter. Always Kephas to Yeshua. His *rock*," she said, bitterly. The bough swung back into place. "He liked to give followers new names. As if they were born anew."

We emerged from the forest into a wide bay. Boats bobbed in the water, tied to stakes in the sand. Women gutted fish in the shade of salt-stunted cedars.

"But he!" Maryam raised her arms to the blackening sky. "Kephas *was* like a newborn. As angry as a baby denied milk, spiteful as a child who will not share his toys. He turned Yeshua from me. *Me!* Who understood his worth. Who loved him best."

I drew her into the lee of an overhanging cliff to shelter from the coming storm. I lit a fire and cooked a fish bartered from the women on the beach. As the smoky, briny air coiled around us and the sky sank to swallow the sea, I entreated her to continue.

"From Egypt, we travelled," she sighed. "For years. To India, to the mouth of the Indus. We returned through Parthia, Arabia, Idumea. We taught and we listened. We started to attract crowds. In the places that remembered the goddess, we were triumphant. The trouble started in Capernaum."

I remembered how she had spat at the place as we passed it on our journey northward to Damascus.

"That's where we met Kephas." She stared darkly out to sea, where the waves reared ever higher. Spray hissed on the spluttering fire. "Shimon, as he was then. A fisherman, not that you would know from the excess of his self-importance. A man who slipped between names and faces, like an eel among weeds. A hanger-on, an empty shell, a house-snake in the bed." She smashed embers with a stick.

"It was my idea to court the fishermen. It's a good story, no? To make of them fishers of men. But Kephas had no interest in what we said. He did not care for Wisdom. He had no understanding of harmony or compassion. He saw only the power Yeshua could command. It was Kephas who told him he was the long-awaited Messiah. He, who put it about that he was born in Bethlehem, fulfilling the ancient prophecy, not Nazareth, where Yeshua was bred. 'He is *not* the son of that angry Father,' I told Kephas. 'He is the child of a loving Mother.'

"'Who is to say,' Kephas said, 'and what does it matter, if it brings people to listen? *This god, his Father*, he can say, once he has won them. *He has a new message. He offers a new covenant.*'

"'It is not a *new* message! It is Her eternal message! We tell people to love thy enemy. The Father desired enemies to be massacred and impaled on spears! We tell women they are holy. That they must be honoured for bringing life into this world. He condemned them to be won as chattels in war and to be enslaved by men! We say that heaven shall be made on earth when we pursue peace, not war. Harmony, not domination. This is the Wisdom of the Holy Mother!'

"He smiled as if placating a child. 'You will not reach people with such radical, outlandish ideas. It must be done slowly. We must build on what came before.'

"'This *is* what came before,' I told him. 'These are old truths. Older than your angry Father. They will never die.'"

She drummed the stick against the ground. I turned the fish.

"And with Kephas came others. His brother, Andreas. Yakov and Jochanan, so filled with fury they were like the north wind. Sons of Thunder, Yeshua called them—in the days when he still laughed. Tauma, who looked so much like Yeshua they called him the Twin. Another Shimon, the jealous one. Philip, Mattityahu the tax-collector, Yakov, the son of Alphaeus, Bar Tolmey, Thaddeus." She looked skyward, through the slanting rain. "And he, the betrayer. Yehuda of Kerioth." She closed her eyes, allowing the rain to wet her face.

"A man bleeding raw with need. A pebble in orbit around the sun. So desperate for meaning in his life he betrayed the love that was before his eyes for an idea that was not real. But he was not the only one who killed him. They all led him to his death. They were all the same, a brood of vipers! They didn't listen. They never understood. Yeshua was nothing to them. An unblemished lamb to be sacrificed for their own ends."

I took the fish from the fire, scorching my fingertips on the charred skin, and opened it to take out the bones. I handed her a portion. She picked little flakes, barely tasting them, staring into the fire.

"What was he to you?" I asked.

I hardly expected her to reply, but the cloud had burst. The silence she had kept until now, entirely banished.

"He was . . . my teacher and also my child. He was sent to me, and I to him. Together we were whole."

☽

We passed into Karia. Here, as in Lykia, the new religion appealed to men. It offered them everlasting life, release from bodily toil and pain. It bestowed glory through humility. The last shall be the first, they said. But not for women.

Those who had shared in its early days, the women who had joined Maryam, those who'd been equal to the men, who had funded the mission—afterwards, the first female apostles and deacons—were now denied a role. At its root, the same argument I had heard for all time: that woman was cursed for Eve's disobedience in Eden. She was weak, inferior, the source of all sin. She must never lead men.

But this land worshipped women. It always had. A different goddess pre-eminent in each city, though all the same; variations on the Mother of All: Artemis, Astarte, Asherah. Sophia, incarnation of

Wisdom. Queens here had ruled empires, waged war, and won. These women did not warm to the notion of submission, of silence; salvation through agonising childbirth.

As Maryam's rage reignited her preaching, they started to follow us. Just one or two at first, in each town we passed through. The trickle swelled into a stream, a river, a flood. Young women left their families, their betrothed. Older women too. Widows, the heartsick, the lonely. Averse, for obvious reasons, to the word *disciple*, she called them *mathetriai*.

They were drawn to her confidence, her simplicity; the wildly appealing sight of a woman unafraid to say *no*. She performed no miracles, no healing; she raised no dead, cast out no demons. Instead, Maryam dazzled her followers with words, with her wonder and delight with this world, her love for this life, and no other.

Wherever we travelled, we camped beneath the bright stars and danced long into the night to the beat of a drum. "It is the heartbeat of your Mother," Maryam said, echoing my own words to Serah so long ago. "She is always with you."

At beautiful, pine-scented Pinara, at the foot of mighty Mount Cragus, she invited her followers: "Ask me anything." The questions flowed like an icy mountain stream.

"How shall we overcome death?" asked Phoebe, a bright-eyed girl, who had joined us when we crossed the turbulent river by Xanthos.

"We shall never overcome death," said Maryam. "It is futile to try. Keep your eyes on this world, for there is no other. If you love life, you must accept death and never fear it."

Artemisia, who had joined us near Sidyma, asked: "Must we fast and scourge ourselves to please the Almighty?"

"These bodies are Her gift," said Maryam. "Why deny your body what it needs? Why harm what is most precious?"

Tabitha, a young widow from Patara, raised her hand. "I have heard the Christians say—"

Maryam corrected her. "Chrestians."

"Just so, sister. I have heard them say we are all one in God, but that one is male. They say women, through sexual abstinence, can become male and be loved by God. Is that so?"

"No," said Maryam. "For opposites are necessary. Without male and female, there is no new life. A god who requires the female to become male to be loved is no god of this world."

Tabitha's friend Vereniki spoke up. "But we are told the female is malformed, her body foul and unclean. There are women who cut their hair and fast until their monthly bleeding stops, whose breasts and bellies wither. Should we not do this to become holy?"

"You are a woman. You are already holy," said Maryam. "What is holiness but the magic of Creation? Men will tell you they are the source of life, that they implant it in you, an empty vessel, as a seed is planted in the soil. But both the womb and the earth are where sacredness reside, for they create the child and the tree from nothing but a seed. A woman's body is the source of all life. You must wear it with pride."

They murmured her words to commit them to memory. They slurred them in their sleep. No wonder, for no other prophet had holy words for women like this.

"Are we born into sin?" asked Demetria, a matron of later years.

"No!" thundered Maryam. "For there is no such thing. Sin is a crime that offends a god. What fool can imagine an infant offends his mother? Do not seek to be judged or punished; She wants you to rule yourselves."

"Is it ungodly to have relations with a man?" asked Pelagia, holding the hand of her husband, who had joined her in Maryam's following.

"Never. Indeed, it is divine," said Maryam. "For through such intimacies come pleasure and love and new life. Our bodies desire each other. Trust your body. It is right and good."

"What of the end of the world?" asked Chrysame, a pretty Pamphylian. "How must we prepare for it? My husband left me. The Chrestians told him he must be chaste, since there will be no begetting children in the life to come."

"They are mistaken," said Maryam. "There is no life to come. You should enjoy this one—without your husband, since he was so easily led away."

Lydia, who bore the mark of the branding iron from the slave market in Tarsus, spoke haltingly. "Is it . . . wrong to have relations with a woman?"

It was a question close to many in the camp. The girls had found fellowship here, and love. Couples walked into the hills at dusk, curled in each other's arms at night. The fire crackled. The young women leaned in, blankets clasped around their shoulders, to hear the answer.

"No," Maryam smiled. "Love is never wrong. It is always good."

Great is Artemis of the Ephesians!

By the time we arrived at Ephesus, we had three hundred followers. We had money, the gift of Apphia and Eryxo, two rich widows among our following. They paid for the road taxes, bread and meat, blankets for all. We had protection: Laodiki, who claimed descent from the Amazonian warriors who once ruled these lands, taught the young women to fight. She showed them how to use the weight of a male attacker against him, the ways in which nimbleness and guile can be used as weapons. Her infantry took the front line wherever there was trouble—which was often. The shock of their skill, not to mention the knives strapped to strong thighs beneath their tunics, made them surprisingly unassailable.

We arrived at the holy city on a glorious midwinter day. The sky was of deepest blue. Above the agora, as if marking it for our attention, floated a solitary wisp of cloud. But it was the Temple of Artemis that drew every eye. Magnificent and vast—four times longer and three times wider than the Temple of Asherah at Samaria. Each of the 127 shining marble columns measured two cubits across and forty cubits high. Scenes of the goddess, as Mistress of the Animals, protectress of the forest, champion of childbirth and fertility, covered every pediment and façade.

Within the innermost sanctum of the temple sat the goddess herself, on a throne of pure gold. Carved in cedarwood, she wore a robe decorated with lions, leopards, goats, and bulls. Her chest was festooned with eggs, for fertility; a crescent-moon diadem crowned her head, just like Asherah of old.

As we descended into the lanes leading to the public places, we found the temple's priestesses everywhere, like bees in a hive. Every fourth woman wore the intricate woven headdress that signified the office. Indeed, all industry in the city, the work of every man, woman, and child, was directed towards to the temple. Here, a silversmith sold idols of the beloved Artemis Ephesia. There, a stall of votive offerings. Cages of doves for sacrifice lined the marketplace. Cakes to offer at the shrine, lamps to be lit, then crushed underfoot at the altar. The city was utterly devoted to the goddess. Even ordinary women dressed to honour her, wearing the same flounced dress, hair coiled and adorned with pearls and golden diadems, just like the statue at the temple.

At the agora, a speaker was already mid-flow. He was young, barely had his beard grown in, clothed in the simple robes of the Chrestians. Unlike Pavlos at Myra, this man did not have the love of the crowd. Angry hands pointed towards him.

"For there is one god and one mediator between God and man, the Christ Jesus."

The preacher was met with howls of fury. "There is not one god! Do not deny our goddess!"

"The king everlasting, immortal invisible, the only god. The living god who is saviour of all . . ."

"Artemis Ephesia is our saviour! She alone saves those who take refuge in her!"

The preacher battled on. "For men will be lovers of themselves, lovers of money, boasters, proud, blasphemers, disobedient to parents, unthankful, unholy, unloving, unforgiving, slanderers, without self-control, brutal, despisers of good, traitors, headstrong, haughty, lovers of pleasure rather than lovers of God. From such people turn away! For this sort creep into households and make captives of gullible women loaded down with sins, led by lusts."

"We are not led by lusts!" cried the women of Ephesus.

"Look at you!" the preacher returned. "Arraying yourselves in riches, without shame. Your hair braided, adorned with gold and pearls. Women who fear God dress soberly, without decoration! You are idle prattlers and busybodies, filled with curiosity. She who lives in pleasure is dead while she lives!"

This proved a step too far. One woman climbed onto the preacher's block, pulling at his feet, which sent him flailing backwards, a great crack resounding as his head met the ground.

"Let us be gone from here," I urged Maryam. "Walk on to Levedos."

"Stay." She pressed my arm. "This is about to get interesting."

She was right. In a moment, the dazed preacher was hoisted onto the shoulders of six men. The crowd progressed down the hill towards the amphitheatre, their prize held aloft like a beetle carried by ants. "Great is Artemis of the Ephesians!" they chanted without relent.

Pulled along by the crowd, we too were dragged to the amphitheatre. The preacher, a hand to his bleeding head, was set upon the stage beside two others seized from their houses along the way. Ephesians filled every inch, standing in every seat. Still, they chanted the name of their goddess, so none could speak above the great resounding din of her name.

A man took the stage alongside the three captives. He called for silence and waited for the chanting, the jeering and taunting to fade. One of the older Chrestians put his hand to the beardless boy's shoulder to fortify him. He was not unlike many of the men from here to Jerusalem—stocky, full-bearded, dark-haired—yet something in his manner seemed familiar to me. The third man was fair-haired, like barbarians in the north.

"Friends!" the spokesman cried. From where Maryam and I stood in the highest tier of seats, every word rang clear. "In Myra, in Xanthos and Halikarnassus—across nations!—these men have turned followers away from the Great Goddess. They say that our gods are no gods at all!" He paused, waiting for the crowd's immense fury to abate. "What will happen if they succeed here too? Our great temple will fall. Our goddess will be deposed, her majesty ground into ashes!"

From the front, a man called, "How will we, the idol-makers, make our living then?"

"And we, the dove-sellers?"

"And we, the votive-makers!"

The theatre erupted as representatives of every profession in Ephesus, all dependent on the goddess, aired their grievances.

"Indeed!" the spokesman cried. "Our livelihoods and the prosperity of our city are at stake!"

As if summoned, a grey cloud rolled above the theatre. A rumble of thunder sounded in the far distance. From beside me, Maryam's clear voice rang out in mocking tone. "Your livelihoods? Is that what concerns you? Do you not have more care for your *lives*? For these men would press you to give them up, to abandon your children, and those you love."

"Yes!" the preacher cried from the stage. He raised one hand into the gathering clouds above him. "We do ask this. Did the Christ Yeshua not say: 'I am not here to bring peace, but the sword! I am come to set a man against his father and the daughter against her mother! He that loves his son or daughter more than me is not worthy of me!" He asks this so you will follow him and win life everlasting in the kingdom of heaven!"

His companion, the stocky, bearded man, raised his hands in prayer. "For while we are at home in the body, we are absent from the Lord. Rather we must be absent from the body to be present in the Lord. Soon, the end days will come. This is the news the Christ brought us."

"He said no such thing!" spat Maryam. "He wanted to make a kingdom of heaven here on earth! He wanted you to rule yourselves. Did you not listen? Did you not understand when he said: *The kingdom is inside you?* But it is no surprise you misunderstood him, for none of you were beside him—beside *us*!"

The bearded man leaned forward in the gathering gloom. He turned, said inaudible words to his fair-haired companion.

"Leave these people to their goddess!" Maryam cried. "Take your god and go from here. Do not press Him upon those who have no need of a new Master."

The crowd roared their approval. "Great is Artemis of the Ephesians! Great is Artemis of the Ephesians!"

"You who hate this world!" she cried. "Who hate your own bodies, who hate pleasure, life and love! Who condemn your sisters to subservience—go from this place! You sell a cult of death, not life."

The cloud broke and a solitary ray of sunlight fell upon her shining face. How joyful to see her mastery of this crowd of thousands. Every head turned towards her. She was invincible, triumphant, glorious in the power of her words. Even the sun saw it, bathing her and only her in its light.

The stocky, bearded man saw it also. He extended his finger towards her.

"It is she!" he cried. "The fornicator, the whore of Magdala!"

His words skimmed like a stone over the crowd. Whoredom was no sin to the Ephesians. What was fornication but pleasure and desire? They were untroubled by his baffling pronouncement.

But it reached his mark with Maryam. She had seen, moments before I, who this man was—the ringleader of those arsonists at Magdala. She knew, better than I, where it would lead.

Take Up Your Bed and Walk

Time was running out. I had promised to return Maryam to Judea by spring. Already, the first crocuses tested the thawing hillsides.

The incident at Ephesus unnerved me. We were conspicuous, both by Maryam's loud and public opposition to the Chrestians, and by her following, which only grew after the turmoil in the amphitheatre. Five hundred women on the road were hard to miss.

"Send them away," I urged. "The mathetriai know your teaching. Bid them leave and carry it far and wide."

She shrugged. "It is no matter where they go. My time is coming. One will betray me. It will happen again."

But she did as I asked and sent them into the corners of the world. Phoebe and Artemisia travelled to Thessalonika, Tabitha, and Vereniki sailed for Crete. Chrysame returned to her home in Pamphylia, while Pelagia and her husband Demas walked north, to Bithynia. Demetria and Lydia sailed to Syracuse. Apphia and Eryxo funded missions from their splendid villas in Miletus and Mylasa. As for Laodiki, I insisted she remain with us, with a small corps of her elite fighters.

So Maryam and I, accompanied by Laodiki's discreet, unlikely guard, sailed to Athens. There, in the shadow of the shining temple on the hill, Maryam wrote to her women. Long, loving letters, in which she encouraged them in their ministry, bolstered their hearts, lifted their spirits, and reminded them of their purpose. "Beloved daughter," they all started. "Grace to you and peace from the Holy Mother." They were beautiful epistles, generous of heart, full of love and joy.

She was never short of fresh acolytes to transport her letters across continents. An endless supply of young women followed her home from the agora, from the baths, from the riverside—wherever she preached. They collected like stray cats outside our door. Laodiki stood at our second-floor window, hand on her sharpened blade, glowering darkly upon them.

"Write to Yohanah," I begged Maryam. "Give her something to cherish in the days ahead."

Sulkily, grudgingly, she sat at a table in our simple, bare room. The words did not come easily. She stared out of the window, at the winter rain falling heavily on the acropolis. Fat, fast drops obscured the glorious marbles, blurred the graceful, stoic faces of the pillar-sculpted women who bore the roof of Athena's ancient house.

She handed me a small, folded parchment, sealed with wax. "Take this to her when it is over."

☽

Those last days are a blur. After Athens, Corinth. She was a hit there too, in the city that had always welcomed new ideas; unloaded with the spices and treasures of the east into the dusty, crowded harbour.

From Corinth to Argos. We passed the great Lion Gate of Agamemnon's ruined city, then onwards to the healing sanctuary at Epidavros. Everywhere, we found gatherings, ekklesiai, they called themselves—churches, of this strange new sect, the Chrestians. Each one slightly different, with varying, often contradictory, memories and interpretations of their founder, Yeshua. One group said he was sent from divine Sophia. Another that he was the son of God. A third contended he was merely a man. Some prayed to his Father; others to the Mother. Yeshua advocated peace, or he came to wage war. He performed miracles, they said, or merely showed the path to knowledge. He rose again, some said. But others said that was a faith of fools, for it was not possible. The resurrection was symbolic, representing the eternal presence of the Wisdom that he brought.

"Why can no one agree on what he did and what he meant?" I asked Maryam.

"I will tell you a story," she said, "and you will understand."

She paused to gather her breath.

We were on the road to Ermioni, climbing between the twin mountains of Didyma. It was a pine-fresh early morning, one of those spring days scented with promise. Laodiki and her girls strode purposefully ahead.

"One day, at Capernaum," she said, "we were at the house of Kephas. An ordinary meal, such as we ate together a thousand times. After the platters were cleared and fresh wine was poured, there came a hammering at the door. We froze. Some dived under the tables. But it was not the soldiers, who often came to arrest the men and assault the women. It was a cripple, carried by his friends. Andreas sent them away for the bier would not fit through the door. 'Call him back,' said Kephas. 'We will lower him through the roof.'

"It was a simple Galilean house. Rough, unplastered walls, roofed only with branches packed with mud and straw. So they took down the branches and the dirt spattered onto us below. A man lying on a bier was lowered with ropes onto the table.

"'What do you expect him to do?' I asked Kephas, who was enjoying the spectacle.

"'Heal him, of course.'

"'I cannot heal him,' Yeshua whispered.

"'Of course you can,' said Kephas. 'You are the Messiah.'

"We had already argued about this, Kephas and I. I bit my tongue, for this was not the time, when a man lay on the table, groaning and gnashing his teeth.

"Yeshua could hardly walk away, for they had taken down the roof to bring this man to him. So he approached the bier. He stroked the man's brow, he held his hands and he perceived the man suffered inner turmoil. 'Brother,' he said, with love and compassion. 'Your sins are forgiven.'

"'Who are you to forgive him?' called one of his friends from the rafters. 'We brought him here so you could heal him!'

"Yeshua burned with fury. 'What do you want me to say? *Take up your bed and walk?*'

"As he said it, the crippled man rose from the bier. He put his feet unsteadily on the ground. He rolled up his mat and walked away. All was in commotion. His friends scrambled down from the roof, and we heard them joyfully proclaiming Yeshua the Messiah as they caroused down the street. Andreas fell to his knees. Yakov and Jochanan bowed their heads in reverence. 'A great miracle has been done here today,' intoned Kephas. 'Not just the healing, but the forgiving of sins, too, which, as we know, can only be done by God.'

"Yeshua would not speak to any of us. He walked into the hills, not returning until the next morning. He did not meet my eye for days."

We had reached the zenith of our climb. From the heights, we glimpsed the sea. A white sail flickered against the shimmering blue. Soon we would sail for Judea.

"What did you do?" I asked.

"I started following Kephas around Capernaum," Maryam said. "To see with whom he spoke. Into whose palms he pressed coins. So I could recognise those faces later arriving at his house, or whom we passed in the street. Those who saw again, or heard again, or walked again, those lepers who were cleansed, the possessed who were exorcised, the dead who breathed again, after their unforeseen encounters with the Messiah, Yeshua."

I had eked out our mission as long as I could. But the winter hellebores soon gave way to the spring blooms, to the riot of lime-green euphorbia, the dazzling cyclamen. Sunny narcissi and blood-red poppies dressed the hillsides. Maryam insisted we return.

We took a Nafpliot ship, for it made the most stops. Still, I was dragging my heels. Embarking at Ermioni, I was glad to have Laodiki with us. The place was riddled with pirates and other nefarious men.

It was an uneventful journey, marked only by Maryam's strange behaviour. She paced the deck. Refused to speak to me, or the other women, preferring instead the company of the sailors. She barely ate. On the morning we sighted the high cliff of Joppa, signalling the end of our voyage, she turned to me.

"When we arrive in Jerusalem, there is something you must do."

"What is it?" I asked, with due foreboding and dread.

"I want you to betray me."

"Betray you? How?"

"You will give me up to the men who seek me."

The breeze gathered; the famous black winds of Joppa, which rose from nowhere and could splinter a boat in full sight of shore. A flock of cormorants, buffeted by the gusts, headed inland. I eyed the rocks and hoped the pilot knew these waters. "I won't do it."

"But you must. I will die so my words may live. You have always known it."

The Anointed One

The road to Jerusalem was busy, filled with pilgrims for the Feast of Weeks. We travelled through undulating fields of wildflowers and wheat, orchards resplendent in peach blossom. We passed the pious town of Lydda, walked in the shadow of the stronghold of Emmaus. At our first sight of the city, of its shining towers and wooded hills, of Herod's golden palace, the grim hill of Golgotha, Maryam wept.

Laodiki found us rooms in the lower quarter. Maryam and I washed at the Pools of Siloam among the other travellers. The bleating of yearling lambs as they were taken to the Temple for sacrifice filled me with agitation for how little time we had left.

"You must finish your tale," I urged, as we dried on the steps beside the women's pool. "What happened after Capernaum?"

She wrung out her shift and stretched her delicate ankles in the sun. "Why do you want my story?" she asked. "It is not as pleasing as the histories that will be written. It is not as convenient."

"What do I care for convenience? Tell me the truth."

"The truth?" she muttered, as if she had never considered it before. "Very well. You shall have the truth to whisper into the thunder of lies." She hugged her knees to her chest and went on. "In short, the miracles continued. Yeshua started to doubt himself. I think he truly believed in them. *Who am I?* he would ask me, over and again, when we were alone in the dead of night. The disciples bickered. They argued over who would sit beside him in the kingdom of heaven. When they should fast. Was circumcision still necessary? Kephas drew ever closer as I was pushed aside. We had sat together at meals, but soon it was decreed that women must sit far removed from the men, where we ate inferior cuts of meat and drank sour wine. Kephas took the seat that had been mine, at Yeshua's right hand.

"Then Kephas decided I must teach only women, and after a while, not at all, for the women too must learn only from men. Rumours started that I was possessed by demons. Seven of them, one for every day of the week."

She blinked against the sun. "One day, I overhead Kephas urging Yeshua that I must leave, for women, he said, were not worthy of life, they pollute all whom they touch. Yeshua said nothing.

"Not long after that, he started saying strange things. He spoke the language of war. Of coming tribulation and a great judgement. Of eagles gathering for the carcasses of men. The kingdom of heaven became a place *beyond* this world, not in it, inside us all, as we had preached before.

"I resolved myself to go. What we had started, Yeshua and I, was gone. It was ruined. Unrecognisable. He would not listen, even as I begged him to flee, to start again, elsewhere, with me.

"I tried one final time to remind him of who he was—who we were, together—of the plan we had made those long years before in Egypt."

The sun had passed beyond the city wall. We both shivered in our damp clothes, but I did not want to interrupt Maryam's tale. "It was in Bethany," she continued. "The men were eating in the house of a follower. The women and I dallied outside, for there was no room for all to sit, and Kephas said it is obscene for women to sit while a man must stand. I bought a jar of nard oil at the market and forced my foot inside the door. Yeshua was at the table, all eyes upon him.

"I anointed him. I poured every last drop of oil onto his head. It soaked his hair and beard. When it dripped onto his garments, I unbound my hair and wiped his face with it. I caressed him, before them all; I kissed his eyes, his lips, his neck, his chest, his feet. I pressed my body into his to embrace every fingerbreadth of him. He knew what it meant. I anointed him in the name of the Holy Mother. I reminded him Who had selected him. Who had elevated him. By Whose grace he spoke. I reminded him of our carnal love that bound him to me and me to him, and both of us to this physical world. I reminded him what he owed me."

The scene sprang into life before me. I heard the stunned silence. Saw the horrified disciples, forced to witness this intimate and erotic act, performed upon the body of their own Messiah. The shock of a mere woman daring to act as priestess, a female with power and authority.

"No one spoke for a long time," Maryam said. "He remained perfectly still, his eyes closed. The scent of spikenard overpowered the small room. Every drop that fell from his soaked shift, from the ends of his hair, hit the floor like a clap of thunder. There was an eternity of silence. When he opened his eyes and looked at me, my heart broke. I knew then it was too late and what would come. I left Bethany. The sun had already set, but I walked anyway, through the dark, past bands of thieves and cut-throats, here to Jerusalem."

She wiped a tear from her eye.

The pool was emptying, and we gathered our belongings to return to our lodgings. As we descended into the lower city, a cripple caught her ankle.

"I know you," he said. "You were the woman with *him*. He made the blind see, the deaf hear and the lame walk. You can heal me."

She shook him off. "I cannot," she said. "You are mistaken."

But they crowded around her: the sightless, the afflicted, the limbless, dragging themselves by calloused hands, carried in friends' arms. They pulled at her robe, clamouring for her touch. "'Why am I punished?' How did I offend the Almighty? When shall I be forgiven?"

"You did nothing wrong," she said. "You have not sinned. There is nothing to forgive."

I saw it then, what a bitter pill her message was to swallow—above all, to those suffering injustice and pain. Why even the rage of a punishing god, the false hope of a miracle-worker, the fiction of another life, might be preferable to the void.

At Gethsemane

The next morning, we rose early and walked to the Temple. It took an hour to walk the short distance, so crowded was the way with pilgrims bringing their offerings: the loaves of bread, the young bulls, the pure white lambs. Multitudes of foreigners also filled the streets, the tongues of Parthians, Medes, Elamites, Phrygians, Pamphylians, Egyptians, Cretans, and Arabs mingled as one resounding din. Vast numbers of Roman soldiers had been drafted in to patrol the festival crowd.

At the Shushan Gate, the Chrestians were instantly recognizable by their simple robes, their unshod feet, the beggars who followed them like gulls to a trawler. There he was among them: the man who had led the arsonists at Magdala. He who had suffered, and evidently escaped, the wrath of the rioters at Ephesus. He joined his palms in contemplation as the man beside him spoke.

"Seek those things that are above, where Christ sits at God's right hand, not on things of the earth. For you are dead now, and your life is only with Christ. Put to death in you what belongs to the earth: to fornication, lechery, desire, and idolatry. Mortify these passions in which you walked, for the wrath of God is coming for them."

Once, Maryam had avoided these men and evaded their notice. Now, she sought it. She took up position a short distance away, in the lee of the great walls of the Temple, and she preached.

"Good people of Jerusalem," she cried. "I am here to tell you to beware those offering eternal life. Shun those who sell endless light and abundance. Ask yourselves: is it right to live forever? Can a tree live eternally, or does it live on only in its fruit? Why do you seek to escape this world, the gift of your Holy Mother, for another place? Why forsake Her gift, your bodies, in favour of a spirit you cannot see? A heavenly, bodiless eternity is no better than eternal hell. Why do you not cherish what you have been given?"

The unceasing river of pilgrims flowed past her to the Temple steps. They were used to the Chrestians by now, a familiar sight in Jerusalem. Not so a preaching woman. They slowed to hear, stopped to listen, slack-jawed, to this strange teaching, this undoubted blasphemy. Who would talk of a Holy Mother here, at the very gates of the Father's Temple? A bottleneck grew, the way jammed. Barely could she be heard above the frightened animals pulling at their ropes, over the Chrestian preacher who raised his voice to drown hers: "Wives, submit to your husbands, as is fitting to the Lord. Slaves, obey your masters in everything, with sincerity of heart."

"Why do you seek to be led? Lead yourselves!" cried Maryam. "You were given Wisdom and you shunned it. You were given the world, and you spurned it. You were given companions and you dominated and destroyed them!"

The captain of the Temple came out to see the cause of the commotion. He took no notice of Maryam, but, recognising the Chrestians, called to a Roman patrol. He pointed, gesticulating in fury. The patrol started, with great difficulty, to cross the crowded street, as the Chrestians, alert to such disruptions, scattered in all directions.

Maryam continued regardless. "You have heard prophets talk about the end of the world. I am here to tell you they are right! For I have seen it. I have seen the trees and grass burned to ashes. I have seen the ice melt and the seas rise to cover the land! I have seen poisoned skies and suffocating smoke. I have seen the waste laid by weapons that annihilate all living creatures in the work of a moment; that poison the earth for millennia. This world will burn! All because you have turned your back on the Holy Mother. You thirst for what is unnatural. You hunger for the impossible. I have seen what happens when you do not love each other, when you do not love this world!"

The patrol, finding the way impassable, resorted to violence. At the points of their spears, with piercing screams and the cries of children taken underarm and carried to safety, amid the cacophony of the petrified lambs crushed underfoot, the crowd ran.

"But there is still time!" Maryam cried above the melee. "We can still return to what was lost. If we remember Her Wisdom, we can still follow Her guiding hand. We shall be our own gods!"

I grabbed her tunic. We slipped among the pilgrims fleeing back the way they had come, through the Shushan Gate, into the crowd of bewildered newcomers flooding into the city. We descended into the valley, crossed the Kidron Brook in full springtime flow, then parted from the packed Jericho road, onto the narrow path, screened from the city by a line of cypress trees, leading up the slope of the Mount of Olives.

We waited all day among the ancient olive groves in the garden of Gethsemane, until the flow of pilgrims into the city resumed, a sign that the Romans had abandoned their search.

"Are you set upon this path?" I demanded. "Is it truly necessary?"

"Without question. It is required to fulfil Her plan for humankind."

I had waited for this woman for two thousand years. She was all I had hoped for and more. I'd known from the first she was determined to die, but now the end was so close, I could not bear her loss too.

Everyone I ever loved left me. Samael, Asmodai, Jezebel. And I did love Maryam, despite her obstinacy, her infuriating ways. Since losing Samael, I had forged my way alone. At last, I had someone beside me. I loved her certainty, her resolve, her pride. Was it too much to ask not to lose her, too?

Maryam, lying against the gnarled trunk of an ancient olive tree scorned my hesitation. "Don't you want to overturn this world built on a lie? A world undirected by Her nurturing hand? A world for only half of the whole? Such a world is set on a path to destruction! She wanted us to rule ourselves, not cower in deference all our lives. Isn't that what you want, too? An end to needless domination, an end to judgement—to save your son? To save us all!"

It was all I had ever wanted! Perhaps I believed in her more than she did herself. For I truly had faith that her words could end Hell. I needed her to *live*.

A dove cooed from above. Maryam looked through the twisted branches as he took to wing into the darkening sky. "This was where I last saw him."

I was lost in my own thoughts. "Saw whom?"

"I knew they would bring Yeshua to Jerusalem. I watched them and I waited. I saw the traitor Yehuda enter the house of Caiaphas the high priest. I saw he was not alone. I came here to warn Yeshua what his friends planned. That he was to be sacrificed for the movement they had made. He would not listen. It was the night he was taken."

"Is that why you are set on this course? To follow him into martyrdom?"

Below us, flames flickered as the travellers camped beside the Jericho road lit lamps and cooking fires.

She reached for my hand. "Lilith," she sighed. "I must die, but you will live. You will take my words and fulfil Her plan." She kissed my knuckles entwined in hers. "May you finish what was started."

We waited for the shadows to lengthen, then disappear altogether into the night sky, before returning to the city. The smoke from the sacrificial fires that had burned all day lingered in the air.

"Who was with him?" I asked, as we made our way through the silent streets to the lower quarter. "You said Yehuda was not alone when he betrayed Yeshua."

"Who do you think?" She fretted at one wrist with the other. "Who assumed all authority at his death? Who denied him to save himself? Whose vision prevailed? Of a judging Father, not a loving Mother. Of inequality and hierarchy, not harmony and balance. Who ousted the women, who hated me? Kephas, of course! He guided Yehuda there. He turned his face back to the task when he faltered."

She was determined to relive this tragedy. For love of Yeshua, or to correct the perversion of their faith, I would never know. But it was clear she would never be silenced. Of all the places in the world, the Holy Mother, the end of God the Father; these things could not be preached here. Her blasphemy would provoke the Temple. Her talent for disorder would rouse the Romans. If I did not deliver her to the Chrestians, there were plenty more who would come to claim her.

Last Supper

We ate a simple meal that night in the upper room of the tanner's house where we lodged. Lamb cooked with bitter herbs; beans, bread, and wine, a basket of fruit; all fetched from a tavern by one of Laodiki's girls. The talk was light, inconsequential, until Maryam, mopping the remnants from her bowl with a crust, said, "I wish you had not sent the mathetriai away. Would that they were with us now, for this last meal."

The girls exchanged anxious glances.

Laodiki chewed her mouthful thoughtfully. "Why do you call this the last meal?"

"Because they will come for me tonight."

"Not while I have my strength—and my knife." Laodiki pierced a hunk of meat from the platter and devoured it from her blade.

"Dear Laodiki," said Maryam. "You have been a comfort and a shield to me. But the time has come, and I must go out alone. It cannot be helped."

It was the third hour of the night.

She held up a pomegranate from the table. "Remember me," she said, "when you eat the fruit of this tree. For this is the symbol of Wisdom, the gift of our Holy Mother. She is the tree of life. In perfect communion with this world. Rooted in the earth, yearning for the sun. Watered by rain, caressed by wind. Her fruits sustain the creatures that carry away the seeds that the tree might grow again. We are like the fruit of that tree."

She held up her cup. "Remember me," she said, "when you drink this wine: the fruit of the vine, the blood of our Mother. May Grace flow into all who drink of Her."

She stood. "I am going to the garden." She kissed my cheek and whispered: "Send them to me there."

I did not ask which garden. She meant Gethsemane. She would go to the last place she had been with *him*.

The door closed softly behind her.

"And you will let her—" Laodiki pointed her knife at the door— "go like that?"

I finished my wine. "If you think I—or anyone else for that matter—has any power over her, you are greatly mistaken." I poured and knocked back another cup for good measure, and went out into the cold, clear night.

A thin, waning moon rose above the city walls as I trudged the dark streets. It did not take long to find them. They prayed every night at the hill of Golgotha, beyond the Gennath Gate. I wrapped myself tighter in my cloak. I told myself nothing would come of it. She was just one woman. A solitary thorn in the side of their rapidly expanding movement. What threat was she to them?

Nonetheless. I did what Maryam asked. I took her pursuer aside, he from the cave at Magdala. I told him where she was. That she was alone, without protection. That I betrayed her, not for a bag of coin or any reward, but in the name of the Christ, for his glory and remembrance, for the good of all mankind.

☽

I arrived at Gethsemane at the deepest hour of night. Norea's vision was right: there was a tree. The last rays of the evening star shone upon Maryam as she swung from the bough of an ancient terebinth. Her feet barely cleared the ground. Had she been but an inch taller, they would have been obliged to find a higher branch. The rope creaked as it bore her little weight, cutting a welt into her delicate neck. Her hair lay scattered in matted clumps about the rocky ground. They had stripped her naked and made free with her body. Purpling bruises told where she had been struck and restrained. A deep cut marked her temple, the blood congealing into darkening rust.

I cut her down, loosed the rope from her neck.

My child and also my teacher. Born of my very body, and countless other mothers between us.

I buried her there in the garden and piled a cairn of stones above the grave. I lit a lamp to banish the gloom from her resting place.

I had acted against my better judgement. Against all that was right, or just. Such is the curse of Wisdom. We are free to make our choices. We pursue our own will. But we must live with the consequences.

Some of us have lived longer with our regrets than others.

The Gospel of Maryam

At Damascus, I stood at the same drab, unpolished door. The streets were quiet, the alleys dim, though it was hours before nightfall. All was unchanged. Save, this time, the knock was answered.

Yohanah looked a decade older than the last time I'd seen her here, just eight months before. "Is she gone?"

I nodded. "I've come for the box."

She stood aside, gestured to the stairwell. "Up there."

The upper rooms of the house were in disarray. Sheets lay twisted and filthy on the bed, a chamber pot unemptied in the corner. I found the strongbox and carried it downstairs. I searched for Yohanah. In the back room, the bench where she prepared her abundant meals was empty. No jars of flour, amphorae of oil, no baskets overflowing with figs, pistachios, peaches, plums. The hearth was unlit. The water jug empty.

I found her in the garden, where Maryam and I had worked throughout that summer, not even a year since. Where she had brought us an endless supply of delicious pies and exquisite delicacies, limitless wine and honeyed tea.

"She asked me to give you this." I held out the letter.

Yohanah stared blankly. "I cannot read. She knew that. Else she forgot."

I broke the seal and read it to her.

"Greetings to my mother. In body and also in mind, for you showed me how to live and how to love. Do not be grieved that I leave you for how glorious it was to have lived. You were the roots of my

tree. You anchored me and kept me steadfast as I reached into the light and air. You watered and nourished me that I might blossom. What am I but your fruit? I regret I leave you with nothing of myself but my words, which I plant, as you planted me, in the fertile earth of all our mothers. You will find me in those who are to come. Blessings to you, dear mother, go well with love, from your child, Maryam."

I left her in the garden among her balsam bushes, a solitary tear unwiped from her cheek. I hauled the strongbox to the cart outside and closed the door.

I grieved for Yohanah. I still do. I know what it is to lose a child.

☽

I did not open the box until I returned to my old hut at the water's edge at Magdala. When I did, I found that Maryam—that endlessly astounding and confounding woman—had left me one final surprise. Alongside the scrolls and codices that I had written with great care, at her dictation and direction, were other texts in a different hand. The letters were uneven, as if written in haste, at slants and in unequal sizes; often obscured with blots of ink, yet mostly legible. Written on loose papyrus sheafs, in incoherent order. Finally, laboriously, I re-assembled them.

On the first page, in the red ink I had mixed myself from ochre, crushed red anemone and goat's blood, in clumsy, untutored letters, she had scrawled:

The Gospel according to Maryam

I took a deep breath and read on.

In her easy style, so familiar to me now, I read Maryam's account of her life with Yeshua. It differed in every way from those other testaments, which in the years to come would be bound together, the words of men become heavenly gospel. But I never read a more loving report of this man than I did in these pages. Of her love for him, and his for her. My bridegroom, she called him. My heart's delight.

She told of the message they had hoped to bring to humankind: of equality, not domination; of harmony, not hierarchy, compassion, not barbarity, of Wisdom, not tyranny. Of their hopes to make *this* world a better place, and not the hereafter. She described how they had grown together, like two twisting vines, in their formative days in Egypt. How, as they travelled and preached throughout Parthia, Judea, and Galilee, they complemented and improved each other's discourse, as beans planted beside corn find a strong frame to climb. How they argued, and in their difference, found greater strength. Two halves of one whole.

I understood at last why they hated her so much, those followers. They saw the potential of such a man, the power that might be wielded in his name, cut loose from the woman who completed him. They would never accept her. Never tolerate his love for a living woman, with a female's carnal, alluring body, which tied her to this world, to physicality and reality. They would never acknowledge this woman with whom he spoke and argued, and walked out with, alone, before their very eyes. With whom he sailed, unaccompanied, in little boats upon the sea; their laughter and impassioned voices carried to those left behind, watching jealously from the shore. Whose company he preferred above all others. Whom he kissed, and who kissed him, uncaring of the eyes upon them. A woman who had once dared anoint him before them all, as if she had power and divinity of her own.

But that was not why she had to die.

The threat she posed was much greater than all this. For, as with her account of his life, so too, did she have a differing report of his death.

For Maryam had been at the tomb on that bright morning, the day that founded a faith. How inconvenient it must have been when they discovered this particular woman could not be threatened. How enraged they must have been to learn she paid no heed to warnings, had no regard for the entreaties, and later the threats. That she ignored the demands to stop telling of what she had seen—or not seen, more accurately—and what she had done, which she repeated here in her gospel with unmistakeable clarity.

That she had taken his body from the tomb in the dead of night and buried it. As was her right. For she was his well-beloved.

Buried Treasure

There, in Magdala, I made copy after copy of her writings. The prayers which sang of opposites, the two halves of every whole that together describe the totality of life. The conversations she had with Yeshua, the man she loved, who loved her back. I learned other tongues to translate them for wider reach, from Maryam's Aramaic into Hebrew, Coptic, and Greek.

I loved her words, her intellect, her Wisdom. Her infinite understanding of the vastness of the cosmos, and the smallness, and yet the interconnectedness, of our place within it.

I learned them, but it seemed as if I re-learned them; that they had always been known, always been a part of me.

And when I was ready, I travelled. For centuries I wandered.

As Maryam had before me, I preached in marketplaces, at harboursides and synagogues. In the churches that came in time. In the old shrines, on hillsides, in the high places, in forests and caves. I took the flame of her teaching to those places where the spark was lit by Phoebe, by Lydia, Tabitha, Vereniki, and the other mathetriai. Often, I found evidence of their ministry: in tombstones of the long dead, proclaiming a Magdalene faith; in the sheltering and nourishing tree that stood for her sign, carved into lintels and gateposts, above storehouses and barns. I found communities of Magdalenes who preached the Holy Mother, who ate pomegranate seeds as their sacrament and drank wine as Her blood in their eucharist rites.

I was shipwrecked in Crete, chased in Egypt, imprisoned in Sicily, stranded in Malta. Abused and harassed in Antioch, Salamis, Paphos, and Rhodes. As empires rose and fell, as the centres of power shifted and changed, I found myself in Rome, Constantinople, at Nicaea, Aachen, and Avignon.

But I was never enough. Her memory was despoiled. She was too well known to be entirely effaced from Yeshua's story, so she was traduced instead. That lie, first hurled at Ephesus, took root: she was nothing but a whore. Her only significance was *his* forgiveness of *her* sin. How easy it is to destroy a woman of ideas. No need to refute her arguments, expose the faults in her philosophy. Merely remind listeners she possesses a woman's body: inferior, the source of all sin. A woman's mind, weak, and malformed, the devil's gateway. What is she but a vessel, both the cause and the receptacle for man's sinful sexual desires.

That one word, *whore*, was all that was needed to degrade Maryam in the millennia to come. Nothing else was required. How stubborn was the legacy of Eve, how unalterable.

I understood at last, why Maryam's testimony of Yeshua's resurrection persisted in their gospels, when all else she had said—as a teacher, a prophet, a consort—was expunged. It was the final victory over her: to put into her mouth the words she denied.

"We shall never overcome death," she told her followers that frosty night at Pinara. "It is futile to try. Keep your eyes on this world, for there is no other."

I understood too, far too late, what was at stake in her conflict with Kephas. For it was the same conflict that had raged since the dawn of time. When he ousted Maryam, hierarchy won over equality. Male supremacy won over harmony and balance. Tyranny succeeded over Wisdom. Sophia, and female divinity rejected, a godhead reimposed that was entirely male. One half of the whole. Separate from the beauty of this world, not in it, of it. As a consequence, men were once again afforded all power—and none more so than those successors of Kephas, the rock on which the church was built: the papacy, which inherited unimaginable earthly power for two thousand years to follow! A tyrannous, judging power that required a tyrannous, judging god to uphold it. In time, these churchmen would enact and enforce cruelties so far removed from the ideals Yeshua and Maryam espoused together, as to be utterly unrecognisable. They laid the blame—again!—at women's feet. Those inheritresses of Eve's supposed sin responsible for all the evils of the world. Barred women for millennia from power and influence, demoted them as helpmeets, burned them as witches, exploited and exhausted them as breeding mares. Their bodies denounced as sinful, in need of binding, restraining, covering and mutilating to make them right. Their minds miscast as weak and polluting, open to evil, for which they must be silenced, denied leadership and voice.

What was lost when Yeshua was parted from his Magdalene? As when Adam turned on Lilith, and Yahweh usurped his Asherah:

Everything.

☽

I returned to Cyprus, as I'd always known I would. If I must see out eternity—watch the same follies, the same cruelties, enacted over and again—I would rather do so here, in the wooded hillsides of Alashiya of old, among the almond groves and birdsong, beside the rushing mountain streams, where time feels at once both endless and unimportant. Where every spring I can wonder, as I did that first time, at the magic of renewal, as the wheatear chicks call for food and the tender buds of herbs unfurl from the black ground.

From this quiet corner of the world, I have seen it all.

I watched the rise to limitless power of those ekklesiai, the churches founded by Maryam and Yeshua in partnership. Stripped of all female influence, detached from an original creed of equality and harmony, thriving far from its place of birth, this religion became the tool of unanswerable might, of crushing aggression, of exploitation and war. I watched the successors of Kephas call armies to these lands to claim them from so-called infidels. Such a convenient religion, that affords all power to a heavenly Father, whose only desires accord with the earthly men who worship Him.

Once again, children were slaughtered in the name of this Father, wells poisoned, crops burned and livestock felled. God wills it, they cried, as they have for millennia. I watched the inheritors of this religion take their god to new continents, to crush His children, to annihilate other gods and goddesses there, too.

Again and again, I watched these pointless wars, the result of man's unrestrained desire for dominance and control. Has there been a single minute of peace, without war or bloodshed anywhere in this world since Adam first brought forth his burnished sword?

The notion of one god, a Creator who favoured only His followers—and half of them at that—spread across the world. Each of these one-gods commanding an army of the faithful. All intolerant in their righteousness. Incapable of co-existence. Disrespectful of difference.

And just as they dominated women and other men, so they plundered this earth. Their hoped-for afterlife shifted their gaze from this world. Why care for it? Why cherish it, if there is something better to come? Why take any notice of it at all, this mere blink before the superior business of eternity? The vision that Norea described to me on the ark, that Maryam had preached in Jerusalem, was realised. Green fields and forests shrivelled. Toxic seas, bereft of fish, frothed with waste. Skies scoured black with smoke.

Now what? Floods and fires are raging, seas are warming.

A new threat emerges: deadly viruses mutate from mistreated animals.

Humankind teeters on the brink of destruction.

What did they think would happen? Imbalance, disharmony, domination. The world was poisoned by greed, unrestrained by Wisdom. By those who do not respect the earth, have no concern for what it can sustain. Who do not nurture and protect it, who care nothing for the animals we live among.

They do not deserve this world, this glorious spinning globe, this once-perfect garden, this Paradise.

☾

I, alone, was guardian of Maryam's message. I waited for the world to catch up with it. I took to burying her scriptures wherever I went. To plant her words within the ground that would keep them safe. I trusted in the understanding of the earth to return them when the time was right. When men were ready, at last, for Wisdom.

I cannot say that day has yet come. So, still I wait.

Her words wait too. In leather scrolls and papyrus codices, tightly bound in sacking, sealed with wax in clay jars, buried deep within caves, below middens, beneath unmoveable boulders.

☽

It was not meant to be like this.

Had I never been banished at the dawn of time, had I never refused Adam, never shed my mortality, I would have had an ordinary life.

I would have been the first mother. I would have died, at the right time. I would have taken Eve's place in Sheol. What will happen to that grim place now?

As I reach the end of this account of my long and sorry failure, I find I have learned only this: that immortality has little to recommend it.

Who would choose such a fate?

Why do humans set themselves above the laws of nature?

Why can they, alone in all Creation, not accept an ending?

Part Six

MY END IS MY BEGINNING

PRESENT DAY

Now I saw a new heaven and a new earth,
for the first heaven and earth had passed away.

Revelation 21:1

The Quake

Autumn comes early here on the mountainside. In the far groves, golden oaks and whitebeams' leaves are turning.

The waterfall thunders behind my hut. The stream rumbles louder past my window than in the muted summer months. Lilies dress the valley before me. Coaxed out by the first rains, their purple petals shiver on the still-warm breeze.

Last week, the cranes arrived. They trumpet from the salt lake, where they graze upon the plentiful shrimp, before flying on to Egypt for the southern sun. The warblers too will soon be on the wing.

In my ancient days, this was not just the end, but also the beginning: the new year signalled by the autumn equinox. The tipping point, when day and night are equal, light and dark in balance. A magical time. The pause before fallow winter, when the seeds of spring's rebirth are held deep within the earth's embrace.

Beyond my doorstep lies my latest rose patch. Everywhere on my travels, I have carried with me the hips from the sacred garden in Uruk. Wherever I stop long enough, I plant their seeds and tend them. In every place, a re-creation of that first Paradise. I smell them now, the roses She first planted for my delight. Tonight, I will prune them hard, to protect from frost. A reminder to retreat into their roots, conserve themselves, that they may blossom again in spring. But I will not plant again. This is my final garden. I am too weary to move, too spent for re-creation.

In the valley, log fires are burning. Sometimes, I stroll down the hillside, and sit beside the villagers in the shady plateia. I talk with the old women dressed in black for their lost husbands. The children play; the men roll their tavli dice beneath the plane trees. I even go to the churches, for I love the smell—the same incense that Norea once burned on the slopes of Ararat—and the rituals, so much older than the religion. I sit there in contemplation. Not of he, whom the place honours, but she, his Magdalene, whom I revere. I light candles for those I have lost. For Asmodai, for Samael, for Eve. Norea and Aradka. Shaharu, Jezebel, and Maryam. For all of them.

☽

This morning, there is another pull, another reason to put aside my task—for I am writing. I write the same story, over and again. Each time it starts in a fruitful garden. A woman and a man live there in peace and harmony. Until the man rebels, disobeys the divine law of his Holy Mother, and tramples his wife underfoot. In each version, I devise new punishments for this first sinner, new torments to atone for his crime, new powers for this more righteous female Almighty.

But today I lay down my pen (this ingenious invention! Filled already with ink that flows as I write. No grinding of gallnuts, no mixing with ochre, no powdering of lead to bind) for down in the valley, it is the pomegranate festival. The scent of jams and soutzoukos boiling, the sharp alcoholic bouquet of zivania-making, coils up the hillside to my door.

I descend joyfully through the fresh pines and fragrant junipers, spurred to a loose-limbed run.

The tremor is mild when it comes. In the forest, I barely notice it. The trees, firmly rooted, merely brush the air. A dislodged rock rolls and gathers speed, splashing into the rushing brook. But in the village, all is in commotion. A tower has toppled, ancient stones cast upon the ground. Pomegranates pour from an upended truck, seeds glittering in the dust like spilled rubies.

On the black and white screen in the crowded kafenio, images flicker. From the quake's epicentre off the coast of Egypt, remote aftershocks are triggered in Israel, Syria, Libya; in Lebanon, Turkey, and Greece. The earth ruptures. Caverns are exposed. Crevices widened, hidden ruins and foundations revealed. In all those places, where so many centuries ago, I buried Maryam's words. Long forgotten, even by me.

Amid all this destruction, not a single life is lost. But everywhere, jars and pots are exhumed. Smashed urns disclose feathery scriptures. As if the earth exhales with relief: it is time.

The first to be deciphered is a cache of scrolls, discovered when the quake diverted a tributary of the Nile. In televised reports, I see the timeless backdrop of the long-submerged settlement, the unmistakeable silhouette of the bankside cliffs. The day I buried them comes flooding back: a cloudless dawn of rosy pink, a solitary ibis watching me, approvingly.

More discoveries come in quick succession. Unearthed from a cistern into which a shepherd fell, beside the barren slopes of the Dead Sea. From jars interred inside a cave, freshly exposed by landslip in the heights of Mount Lebanon. In the long-buried cellar of a Roman house in Tarsus. Beneath a cracked boulder in the desert of Wadi Rum.

More, many more, are seized by customs officials in Istanbul. Acquired from raids of black-market antique dealers in Cairo. Found beneath the tarpaulins of smugglers' trucks leaving Syria.

I had almost forgotten the power of Maryam's words; the amazement I felt myself nearly two millennia ago, when I first heard them. The shock and the glory of the revelation of her goddess. But even as the contents of these extraordinary scrolls and codices are breathlessly reported, as the world reels from these discoveries, the backlash begins.

Her words are disbelieved and mocked.

She did not write these scriptures, they say. These are not the words of a penitent whore. If she had written them, she had not done so alone, another was responsible. Her thoughts were plagiarised. Borrowed from other, wiser (maler) persons. Her notions were unjustified, weak. Her prayers, though she had a pretty turn of phrase, inconsequential, undeveloped. Women in the ancient world did not preach, they tell us. Females had not sufficient learning. Yeshua—Jesus, they call him now—had no consort, for he was not of this world, he was above it. When Jesus talked of Sophia, he meant no goddess but an abstract notion, the Wisdom of a male god.

I wonder: will a woman's message ever be heard? Or will it always be too weak, too angry, too impassioned? Too irrelevant for all mankind (by which they mean: for men)?

And yet.

Had these scriptures emerged in an earlier age, they would have been destroyed. Burned for heresy before they saw the light of day.

Now, maligned as they are, her words are aired.

And something strange happens.

They leap beyond those denouncing men. They soar above those who mock them from pulpits, who disclaim them from a balcony in Rome. They fly into the world and are read, discussed and debated. They reach those with open minds and breaking hearts. They find fertile ground with women, just as they did two thousand years ago in the agoras of Corinth, Athens, and Ephesus.

Her account of the resurrection—of the *ordinary deceit* she revealed—sparks a trail of gunpowder that lights ever greater targets. For all rested on this one extraordinary claim. As it explodes in the wake of Maryam's testimony, what is left but the questions she posed: Why do you yearn to live forever? Is it right? Is it natural? Why do you seek to be led, judged, and punished?

Across the world, women drink thirstily from Maryam's words, seek meaning in them—and hope. They look again at the past, from which they have been erased, misrepresented, and cruelly slandered. They want a better story. One in which they see themselves. They want a new ending. No more judgment and tyranny. No more conflict born from struggle for domination. A celebration of this physical, real world, not an imagined realm beyond it. They talk of regeneration, not eternal, spiritual life.

They seek missing women's voices from their histories and religions. Search for the philosophers they never heard, the economists who might have counted profit and cost differently. Re-examine the gaps in science made by men. They see the link between their lost goddesses and their lost power. The direct line from Eve's supposed sin and the claim that women are too gullible, too emotional, too weak to lead. They ask: how can we tolerate invoking a man's god, to justify men's laws controlling female bodies they do not understand?

They look at the ice that is melting and the forests that are burning and ask how things might be had humans never conceived of a god outside our world. Had they never followed prophets who cared only for an afterlife, a *better place*, than the only world we know. Had they instead adored a deity rooted in this earth, who loved this life, these bodies, this planet.

They feel the loss of the Mother. They look at the girls ousted from schools, the women missing from parliaments. They see girls cut and covered and sold to men old enough to be their grandfathers. They observe the male leaders who talk while the world burns. They ask: Is this what the want of the Mother has done?

Maryam's cry—be your own gods!—spreads. Like a second quake, radiating from those ruptures in the earth that revealed her scriptures. An aftershock that arrives in waves of protesting, demanding women, it rolls in to topple those towering theocrats who prosecute the worst abuses of the female sex. Scrawled on banners in Farsi, Pashto, in Arabic, it is hashtagged, Instagrammed, tik-tokked. Proclaimed alongside joyful reels of women reclaiming their bodies, dancing in the streets, burning their veils.

Reminded of what they had lost, women sought the goddesses of their ancestors—not only Asherah, but all the Mothers crushed by the jealous Father, wherever His mighty arm reached. Artemis, Gaia, Elat. Isis in Egypt, Shakti in India, Nuwa in China. Papatūānuku in New Zealand, Yemonja in Nigeria, Pachamama in Peru. Al-lat in Arabia, Hariti in Afghanistan. Their message is the same: honour women, for they bring and sustain life. In searching, women find their own worth; cast off their shackles, reclaim their bodies, assert their right to power.

And I see my own hand, the seeds I planted, in all this. For now that I look, I see this yearning for the Mother we lost never truly died. It retreated underground, returned to its roots, like my roses. There it lay; protected, nurtured in the rich, black soil. No matter how hard each stem was cut back, new shoots grew, fresh buds quickened. When

She was deposed, women reinvented her: as Chokmah in the Hebrew, Sophia in the Greek. Brigid in the west. Magna Mater in Rome.

I see Her in this modern age, too.

I see Her in the still-sacred trees upon the high places, in the holy grottoes of the earth. I remember Serah, child of Nahalath, bud of my vine, who brought my teaching out of the flood. I see Her in the ruins of those ancient places, where young women hoping to bear a child still bring cakes to the Queen of Heaven. She endures in the basalt stone that Damaris brought from Samaria via Sidon, that still stands, worn smooth from the adoring hands of three millennia, at the crumbling shrine here in Cyprus for all to see.

These are old truths, Maryam said. Older than the Father. They will never die.

I even see Her in the churches. For so beloved was She, even that stubborn new religion could not unseat Her. She became the Panagia. Depicted in countless icons, venerated in every household. The same goddess of mercy and Wisdom, of animals and the earth, of fertility and motherhood. She is Pantanassa, queen of all, Thalassine, of the sea. Yiatrissa, the healer.

Mary, the mother of God, the church calls Her.

But I know better.

She *is* God.

Asherah, Sophia, Mary. Al-lat, Shakti, Yemonja. Call Her what you will.

Incarnation of that ancient Spirit of Creation.

My Almighty. Mother of All.

☽

My writing takes a new direction.

It is pointless to rewrite the past.

It is not the beginning that needs to change, but the end.

I draw a thick red line through every page. In ink I mix myself from the leaves, barks, and beetles of the forest, I start again.

At first, I write, *I loved him. How beautiful he was in those days.*

For six weeks, I barely leave my table. I write furiously. It is a tale of betrayed love and righteous revenge. Of the folly of man and the consequences of his first, most egregious, sin. Of the lie that has poisoned all life ever since: that our Mother's Wisdom is dangerous; we must be kept from it. Or else.

Else what?

Return

It is midwinter before I look up again. My story is almost complete—only, I cannot quite glimpse the end. I place a paperweight of rough stone on the pages and watch fat, silent flakes of snow start to fall. As dusk descends, it settles on the frozen ground.

In the valley, they are celebrating the birth of their god. In the deep of the darkest night, midst the barren, cropless fields, hope and light prevail. The eternal miracle of life: a mother and a baby. Who cannot celebrate that?

As the peal of the midnight bells reaches me across the frosty night air, even I, bitter as I am, as old as time, can raise a glass. To them both. The mother and the child. To regeneration. A coming again.

Which is why I am so unsteady on my feet, unclear in my mind, and somewhat intemperate in my heart, when the door opens at the fading of the final bell.

He stands there, the full moon silvering his handsome, still dear face. Snow dusts his hair.

"There you are!" he says. As he did the first time we met. As if it were I who had been gone these four thousand years, and not he. I put a hand to the high back of the wooden bench to steady myself.

"You're supposed to say: *Here I am!*" he scolds me.

My glass drops to the floor and shatters into a thousand pieces.

"Come, Lilith, what a waste of good wine." He takes a broom from the corner and sweeps the shards over the doorstep into the chill night air. "Charming place you have here." He bustles into the kitchen, brings out two more glasses and a fresh bottle of the best wine, a maratheftiko. But he is soon defeated by its opening.

"How in the devil's name does this work?" He puts his eye to it, pokes ineffectually at the modern plastic cork.

I take a corkscrew and open the bottle; pour the wine. An intense rubied red coats the glass like blood as he swills it. Scents of sour cherries and summer violets fill the air.

"Stuck in my ways," he laughs. "Out of touch. Always had someone to do this for me," he points to the floor and mouths theatrically, "down there."

The wine revives me, soothes my jittery gut. He sets my glass on the table. His hair has grown below his shoulders. A three-day stubble grazes his chin. He is dressed, unaccountably, in an extraordinary mauve polyester outfit of the kind that was known thirty years before this current age, as a *shell suit*.

It jolts me from my stupor. "What on earth are you wearing?"

He looks down and grins. "It was hanging on a line when I emerged naked from the fiery pits. I rather like it. Tyrian purple—such a jolly colour! More importantly, aren't you going to greet me?"

I fall upon him, my Samael, my love, and rain a thousand kisses on his face and neck. I can't get his hideous garment off him fast enough.

☽

As we lie together in the warmth of my bed, Samael tells me how he was freed. How Hell shrank over the years, as humans stopped believing in it. "First *she* went," he says, our fingers entwined. "A long time ago."

"But you did not seek me then," I observe.

"Because she was replaced. By another lord of hell, a prince named Satan. A vaunting angel, who, like us, displeased the Almighty. But he—oh, he was a nasty piece of work, my Lil, not like us at all. Archfiend, a fallen cherub, he loved that place, its livid flames, the burning lakes, the stench, the mournful gloom. At least he did not want congress with me—not like the other." He shudders.

"Then he went too?"

"Indeed. But only after miseries untold and grievous suffering of all who dwelt there."

I can hardly bear to know, but I must ask. "What of Asmodai?"

He takes a deep breath, pinches the bridge of his nose. "Well, Lil. That's the thing."

Panic engulfs me. What horrors has my son suffered in that infernal realm? What tortures has he endured in that seat of desolation?

Samael puts his hand on mine. "After Satan went, I thought that place would cease to be. At last, our son would be at peace. Six weeks ago (in mortal terms, a blink of an eye to you and me) a violent convulsion struck our domain. The sky exposed, sunlight flooded those sulphurous halls, soft rain fell upon the fiery lakes. Fresh vernal air swept the boundless deep."

"The quake!" I cry. "It ruptured this world, too."

"*This is it*! I thought. All we have waited for. The end of that profoundest hell!"

"And?"

"And—nothing! Nothing changed. The wraiths lingered on in melancholy and pain. Only I could fly away, unstopped. But still, I could not leave. I never knew our son in life, dear Lil. In death, diminished though he was, I grew to love him. Through the changing fortunes of that place, I sheltered him, protected him from the worst. I could not bear to leave him, uncared-for, all alone."

"But you have left him! Why then are you here?"

"I am here to save him. To end his torment. For whatever it is that will finish that place—whatever might banish that tyranny, forever terminate that judgment and pain—only you and I can do it."

"We two? Why?"

"Because we started it. I started it! I should never have planted that wretched tree! My love for you set all this in motion—it is all my fault! Had you never tasted Wisdom, you'd never have rebelled against that fool, Adam. Never been banished from Eden. Never would Eve have brought His wrath and judgment on all mankind. Our son would not be trapped in eternal misery."

I kiss his dear, tormented face. "Could I have lived, unwise, unfree? You saved me. You fulfilled Her plan. And you'd have saved all humankind too if Adam had only listened! He is to blame, not you. He tasted Wisdom and refused it. Denied his other half and set himself above the world in mastery and dominion. He shares the blame with the god of man, who usurped His wife and cursed all women to inferiority to stop Her Wisdom spreading!"

Samael turned to face me. "How can we make it right, Lil? It cannot be beyond our wits. We brought Wisdom into the world, you and I. We rescued a goddess from the depths of Hell! What can we two not achieve—together?"

Through the window, the evening star, Asherah's own, rises in the east. Is this why I have failed, I wonder? All I ever wanted, my lifelong quest, was to avenge Her death. Bring Wisdom to humankind. That they might become their own gods and put an end to Hell. Maryam's words ring in my ears.

Two halves are needed to create. Two opposites, but equals fused.

To do what must be done, to create a better world—was all I ever needed my other half?

☽

Samael sleeps. On a bench outside, I clear my mind.

Revealed by the quake, Maryam's words sparked a revolution, as I always knew they would. Planted in the fertile earth, time was all she needed. The quake freed Samael too—yet still, there is a Hell. Her plan for us was not fulfilled. Something has been left undone. What is it Samael and I must do—together?

Across the inky sky, the evening star attains the zenith of its arc. I learn from the clever (though still Unwise) people of this modern age that it's but a ball of gas, shining bright across the universe. Stars aren't gods, nor people come and gone, as once we all believed. So far away some die before their light reaches us. Like Asherah, who's gone but shines upon us still, bringing light and warmth. And Wisdom.

What is Wisdom but consciousness? Awareness of reality. Free will, with responsibility and consequences. A child attaining adulthood, who brings forth new and helpless children themselves.

The jealous god denied these things. A Father who punished curiosity, derided choice, and free will. Obedience, perpetual childhood—Unwisdom—was what He required. "Send them forth!" He bellowed. I hear Him now, after all this time. His mocking Voice, His potent Fury unleashed. *The man has become like one of Us, knowing good and evil! Now, lest he put out his hand and take also of the Tree of Life and live forever, send them forth!*

Moonlight glints from the fresh crust of snow. Wind whispers through the golden oaks.

"Consider a tree," Maryam said. "Its fruit is abundant. It shelters the beasts of the field and the birds of the sky. All living creatures feed themselves from it. What is that tree but our Holy Mother?"

The neurons and synapses of my brain fizz and spark. Unseen, dark corners of my mind connect. Flint-sparks take; flames fanned, now spread. Wisdom itself creaks and stirs to life.

She is the gentle breeze and the violence of the waves.
She is the circling of the years and the guiding light of stars.
She is the Tree of Life. In perfect communion with the world.

At last, I see it: I know how my story ends.

The Tree of Life

"Be gone, dark Lord! Leave off thy pronged fork!"

"Wake, Samael!" I drip water on his face to rouse him. "You're safe, back in the world, with me!"

"What is it? What?!" He turns to the window, to the door. He is out of bed, pulling on his clothes, stumbling. One-legged, he hooks a shoe to his heel. "Must we flee?"

"No—sit, be still. We're not in danger. It's only—I must ask you: Did you plant the Tree of Life?"

"Did I—what?"

"In Eden! The Tree of Life! Did you plant it? You planted the Tree of Knowledge for my sake. To give me the Wisdom She intended for all humankind. But the other—the Tree of Life—did you plant that too?"

He sits, becalmed. Wipes sleepfulness from his eye.

"I did not. Was one not enough? Were you not satisfied? Should I have returned for more?"

"Then where did it come from? Not from Him. He wouldn't have planted that which He forbade. So, who did?"

"Well—I guess She must have done. Before She left."

I kiss and wrap myself around him. Triumph unimaginable! "Don't you see?"

He ponders. His neurons and synapses fizz and spark too, though at dawdling pace. "Frankly, Lil, I don't think I do."

"It means you didn't fulfil Her plan—only half of it. The Tree of Life was meant for us, too. What was it you overheard that day in the meadow where the wild sage grows? She said it's time to give our children the greatest *gifts*. She meant *both* trees for us."

It is their birthright, Samael murmurs, remembering Her words. *What loving parent would not step aside in time?*

"That's why we were banished from Eden—Eve and Adam too. To keep us from the real prize."

"Wait," says Samael, head in hands. "I still don't see. I've been away—I've missed a lot. So tell me in your plainest terms."

I sigh and fetch us both more wine. "The Tree of Knowledge gave us Wisdom. In *plainest terms*, of what is good and what is evil. That is: consciousness of opposites, wherein lies all understanding. It taught us that balance and harmony in all things is essential."

"But the greater gift is the Tree of Life?"

"The first showed us how to flourish in this world. The second would have *rooted* us to it. The Tree of Life does not grant eternal life! Its gift is so much greater than that. *Her fruit is better than gold.* For She *is* the Tree of Life, Samael! To eat Her fruit is to embody Her eternal virtues and qualities. They should have flowed through me to my children—to all humankind—for I was to be the first mother! Then we would have lived as gods: free from judgement and tyrannous authority. In harmony with each other and the world— not in domination over it. To delight in it—not yearn for another life beyond it. We would have lived forever—collectively, through regeneration; in nature's way, as all other creatures do; not individually, in the hell of a bodiless form. Our children would replace us. We would step aside."

"And He prevented it?"

"Of course He did! Harmony and balance, partnership and coexistence—what use are these to a power-hungry god and the men who serve him? He usurped His wife, as Adam sought to master me. He sets Himself above this world as He set Man above it too; imposed a hellish afterlife to enforce His authority against the wishes of His wife. But the path of domination and control, of denying half of all humanity, leads only to destruction. *Without one, both shall die!* It means the death of this world, the only home we have ever known, the only life we will ever have. Even now, they are on the brink!"

Samael's eyes are closed. He drains his glass.

"So, you see, don't you? You see what we must do? Because, Samael, I *am* the mother of all mankind! You made me so, through our beloved son. And you are their father! *We* are the first parents as much as Adam and Eve. If we eat this fruit—together—it will course through us to our living children. Her plan at last will be fulfilled. All that sets itself above the world will end—including Hell, including Him! We will save our son. Save them all! For they must become their own gods to truly live—embodied in this world, connected, in balance and harmony, to every other part of it. To see this world as heaven on earth. To save it. We will regain Paradise, my love—a better Paradise. By giving our children what She intended and He denies: reality."

"Oh no, my sweet, my heart's delight. Please tell me you don't mean—"

"Yes. We must go back there. Return to Eden."

"By Satan's ripe fundament, Lil. Please no. Not again!"

Paradise Regained

We travelled through unholy scenes, a Hell remade on earth—for slaughter and bloodshed reign again, here where the great project of Creation began. The ancient route, the cedar-lined highway I travelled countless times, now beats a troubled path from Lebanon, Phoenicia of old, through warring Syria and the ruins of Iraq. The cities I once knew—serene Palmyra, proud Ninevah, white-walled Mari—reduced to rubble. Their ancient temples, almond-scented avenues, delightful colonnades; all bombed and blasted to dust.

In refugee camps, women burned the burqas their enslavers had made them wear; nursed infants begotten by their rapists. The same misery, the same violence, the same horrors I had seen so many times before. How little has been learned. How triumphant is disharmony. How miserable is Unwisdom.

And by the roadsides, a new horror: the brutal crushing of those rebellions sparked by Maryam's scriptures. Bodies hung from bridges, dangled from cranes. Blindfolded, handcuffed; painted toenails brushing the traffic that passes below. The remnants of a banner curled from a wall, all that is left of Maryam's call to arms. *Be your own gods* it cries, mocking us, reproaching us for what is still undone.

)

So here we are once more, Samael and I, back where it started. At the hidden garden bounded by four rivers, untouched, untrod for five thousand years. You'd never know this once was Paradise. It is barren now, uncared-for, spoiled. The fig groves died, the soil eroded. No rain falls here anymore. The desert crept. Inching from the south, it stole away that sylvan scene.

No fields of swaying barley, no irrigating canals. No trembling leaves, no branching palms, no lofty shade. The fruits are gone, the balmy groves, the luxuriant glades. No gambolling kid, no sweet-eyed cow, no cooing dove. No wild sage meadow, no myrtle-crowned bank, no pool where once I swam and washed away the seeds of Adam's sin.

Uncherished, un-nurtured, all is gone.

What is left?

A denuded valley still veiled from oversight by stony hills. Only two trees remain: unexpected, out of place, quivering with life amidst the wasted hollow.

From one: slim-trunked, bright-leaved, the fruit still hangs. Shining, ambrosial, the rubied glistening pomegranate that once I ate and once I offered to Eve. The fruit that brought Wisdom into the world and a curse upon all women to ensure it could not spread. The other, a palm: tall and sheltering, heavy, drooping low with clustered dates. At its roots: a once-bright sword still sheathed within the ground. Beneath the tree, shaded by its cooling, fanning leaves, three figures sprawl in sleepy repose.

"You have got to be kidding me!" Samael declares. "How the hell are they still here? Why did they survive when all else is gone?"

Senoy, Sansenoy, and Semangelof, in shrouds of ancient linen, snore and snuffle gently.

I nudge the nearest angel. Senoy splutters, kicks like a dreaming dog. Samael aims a harder blow at Sansenoy, who whines and whimpers in his sleep. Semangelof wakes, and standing, stumbles backwards when he sees us there.

"Aha!" he cries when he gathers his wits. "You return to the scene of the crime, infernal demons of the night, Satanic fugitives, ye monstrous vassals, ye wanton brutes—"

"Give it a rest, thou pompous seraph!" Samael groans. "We've heard it all before."

Semangelof attempts his trick of old. He bares his teeth, but they're no longer sharp: yellowed, blunt, ground down with time.

"Pathetic," Samael scoffs. "What are you goons still doing here?"

Feeble Senoy, now roused, speaks up. "We do our job. We guard the Tree of Life."

"From human hands?" I idly ask. "Lest they should live forever?"

"Indeed," he nods. "As you well know."

"But not from us."

I circle the tree, one finger to its husky bark. "For we are already immortal."

Senoy looks to Semangelof in alarm. His eyes widen, he adjusts his filthy shroud.

"True," the senior angel admits. "You aren't forbidden. So what? You cannot want this fruit. What can it do for you?"

I pull the sword from the ground's embrace and toss it, hilt-first, to Samael. Though the blade is dulled by unfathomable time, he cuts a cluster of the lowest-hanging dates.

"The Almighty commands me to eat this fruit. I cannot but obey."

Semangelof splutters. "The Almighty orders no such thing! I think we know His desires, by now!"

"You cannot think I refer to *Him*. I mean, of course, *my* Almighty!"

"Vile blasphemy! Foul heresy! What evil calumnies spout from your poison lips! There is no god but He above! He made the heavens. He made the earth, the seas, and all that they contain. He giveth life and taketh it away. He is the Lord, there is no other!"

"Then, tell me, do: if there's no Other, why is He so jealous? *I am a jealous god,* He cries! Of whom, if He is the Only?"

The angels shrink like sun-scorched grapes. They gape in bewilderment and terror.

"You await Him, am I right?" They nod.

On cue, above, a faint glow brightens, a grating hum resolves into a chord. "Disobedient daughter," He says, in muted Voice. "You have returned. I see you drag a rebellious angel in your wake."

"He is my love, my other half. Not that You would understand that. We are here to finish what was started. To do what You have conspired to prevent. To fulfil the wishes of a better god than You."

An impotent rumble, a feeble flash of light.

"There is no god but Me!"

"So You say—a lot. Then tell me, why have You not destroyed this Tree, which terrifies You so? Whose gift does it bestow that You are anxious to withhold?"

The bright glow dims. It glitches, like a malfunctioning screen. "You cannot question Me!" He roars.

I draw myself to fullest height. "My Mother gave me Wisdom. I will question Whom I please."

"You have no Mother!"

"Oh, but I do. Of that this Tree is living proof. What's more, You have a Mother too. From Whom You sprang at the dawn of time. From Whom all life came forth. The Mother of us all, this earth."

The brightness fades to blackest void. Sparks fly, fizzle as they dissipate. A glow resumes of lesser strength. A heavenly, embarrassed Cough.

"But let us see. We will eat this fruit, we are not forbidden. If Your claims are true, naught will change, for we cannot claim immortality we already possess."

"And if *you* are right?" the Voice enquires. "What happens then?"

"My Mother's will shall be restored, Her plan for us prevail. Humans shall be their own gods. All that sets itself above the earth will end. Your thugs, Your hellish afterlife. You."

"And you?" He sneers. "You're immortal too. What place for you, a lewd demoness, what seat for your fallen angel in this bold new world?"

Samael and I exchange a glance. We have not talked of this. But in his eyes, I see he understands.

"Do You think we do not know?" he cries. "Happily, we step aside, to save our son. To save them all! What *loving parent* would not do the same?"

A deathly still. A breathless pause.

Then: "Go on," He taunts. "Eat it, if you dare. We'll see."

Samael offers me a handful of the ripest dates. He holds me close. "No one was ever loved more," he says. "No one has endured more than I for you."

How lucky I was to love and be loved. By an equal man, a worthy man.

He feeds me and I feed him. Sticky and sweet, the fruit tastes sublime.

We lie beneath the tree, hands tightly gripped.

Three faces peer over us.

"What's happening?" asks the wolfish one. His blunted teeth blur into vanishing lips.

"Should they look so . . . happy?" asks the second. The feathers of his wings loom large, each milky quill, each barbule sharp. I never saw the world so clear.

"I feel faint," says the last, the nervous one. "So very, very—"

In that instant, a final vision.

Dark caverns, exposed to light, collapse. Mournful shadows at long last laid to rest. Alighting from the shade that was once my son, a dove flies freely out of Hell. Within the earth, long-dormant roots probe the soil. Enriched, they sprout above the ground. Shoots swell, saplings bring forth boughs and branches. Trunks thicken, leaves unfurl. Buds unfold, fruits ripen and fall; a new tree grows.

An icy river flows onwards to the sea. The moon waxes, wanes, is reborn anew. Tides ebb and flow in answer to its luminous call.

I feel rocked, as I was upon the ark. Cradling my infant child, complete and whole and filled with love.

Rich scents fill the air, of violets, and bosky glades. Of myrtle by a dappled pool. Of rockrose resin and burning azallu.

Bees hum, wheatear chicks call out for food. My roses bloom.

The muted Voice sighs. A relinquishment, celestial relief. I sense regret.

I feel a faint pressure in my hand.

Then—

What is there at the end?

A better world. A better story.

Author's Note

There is no myth with more power, more longevity, and a more malign legacy than the opening chapters of Genesis in the Bible. Eve's creation from Adam's rib justified woman's inferiority for two and a half thousand years; her susceptibility to temptation the model for centuries of witch-burners who claimed women were easily seduced by the devil. Having led Adam astray, woman would never again be permitted authority over man.

Eve's punishment for her "sin" is telling:

In pain you shall bring forth children
yet your desire shall be for your husband,
and he shall rule over you

Genesis 3:16

She loses control of herself and her body. By coincidence, this is the ultimate goal of patriarchy: control over women, and specifically of their reproductive power. Here we see it delivered with divine sanction by a male god acting entirely in male interests. How convenient!

But there is something else going on beneath the surface of this myth that is less obvious to modern readers—a hidden message that was crystal clear to its original audience, and which explains a critical step in the evolution of patriarchy.

Israelites in the first millennium BCE would have recognised the fruit, the Tree of Life, and the serpent, as symbols of the Hebrew goddess Asherah, the wife of God (Yahweh). She was the latest and local incarnation of the mother goddess worshipped throughout the Middle

East since the paleolithic era. Her cult, once a mainstream part of the Hebrew religion—she was openly worshipped by King Solomon at Jerusalem in the tenth century BCE—was suppressed by the time monotheist scribes and priests finalised the opening chapters of the Bible around 500 BCE.

This powerful story of the forbidden fruit (representing the goddess's powers of fertility and regeneration), the separation of humankind from the Tree of Life (Asherah was symbolised by a spreading, fruitful tree), and the evil snake (one of Asherah's epithets was Lady of the Serpent) is the final nail in her coffin. The goddess's day was over.

From now on there would only be one god, and He would be male. The status of women in this new world order would suffer accordingly. The Genesis myth echoes a historical reality that took place across the Levant and beyond in prehistory—not the Fall of Man, but the Fall of Woman. Once equal, once powerful, once divine. Henceforth, a helpmeet, a vessel for reproduction in the service of men. Made from a man's rib, thus defective and malformed; weak and prone to evil.

I wanted to tell this story—the story of the Fall of Woman and the demise of female divinity—by subverting the very myths that served to enforce male supremacy.

Enter Lilith.

In Hebrew myth, Lilith was the first woman, created equal to Adam. But she was banished from Paradise and turned into a child-devouring demoness when she refused to lie beneath him. Eve, the woman who accepted her own subjection, replaced her.

Lilith is the creation of a patriarchal mind: a warning to women who dare to be equal, and a cautionary tale to men of the destructive power of female sexuality. She is demonised in the way all dangerous women in patriarchal societies are: she is wanton, lascivious, a baby-killer—a threat to family life. Who better to expose this dastardly plot? Who better to correct the egregious crime, the real sin at the heart of Genesis: the theft from women of their goddess, and with her, all female power and equality, their very humanity?

The idea came to me: of immortal, banished, *furious* Lilith, wandering the earth for millennia, seeking to overturn this great injustice. Her furies are my furies, for what were the consequences of this double loss—of Lilith, the equal woman, and of the ancient mother goddess who once bolstered women's dignity and power?

For in time, the concept of a sole, male god would come to dominate much of the planet. The entire Western world was built on the pattern of this creation myth: a Father who creates life without a Mother; who ordains man as superior, in possession of authority; woman as inferior, the ruled.

How different would the modern world be had this never come to pass? How would female power, female spirituality, female-centred philosophies have shaped the world, had they not been suppressed? What would a religion freed from androcentrism, equally influenced by women, look like?

This book is my answer to those questions. It is a howl of rage at the injustice and catastrophic consequences of a world built on the subjection of half the human race. It is about the tragedy of what was lost with the female deity: harmony, not domination; divinity rooted in this world—not above it, in the form of a punishing, paternal god; a worldview embracing the cyclicality of life, where death leads to regeneration in the physical world, not eternal life in a spiritual realm (if you behave). It is about the seeds of the ecological crisis we are now facing, which were planted in Eden when a male god gave man dominion over the natural world, as well as over all women.

Women deserve a better origin story than a fable that vilifies and slanders us, which ordains our inferiority. A myth that was wielded as a misogynist's charter to justify women's oppression, erasure, and abuse for two and half thousand years—and which *still* has power over our lives.

We deserve the origin story we *already had* before the rise to pre-eminence of a sole, male god. We deserve the equal woman, the powerful woman, the divine woman. We deserve Lilith.

Eve's Legacy

I permit no woman to teach or to have authority over a man; she is to keep silent. For Adam was formed first, then Eve; and Adam was not deceived, but the woman was deceived and became a transgressor.

Paul the Apostle, 1 Timothy 2:10-11

For the woman taught the man once, and made him guilty of disobedience, and wrought our ruin. Therefore, because she made a bad use of her power over the man, or rather her equality with him, God made her subject to her husband.

Saint John Chrysostom, 4th Century Archbishop of Constantinople

For it is true that in the Old Testament the Scriptures have much that is evil to say about women, and this is because of the first temptress, Eve . . . And it should be noted that there was a defect in the formation of the first woman, since she was formed from a bent rib, that is, a rib of the breast, which is bent as it were in a contrary direction to a man. And since through this defect she is an imperfect animal, she always deceives.

Malleus Maleficarum, "Hammer of Witches," 1487

Historical Notes

Lilith

The Hebrew myth of Lilith, Adam's first wife in the Garden of Eden, may have arisen to explain the discrepancy in two accounts of the creation of humankind in the Bible.

In Genesis 1:27 man and woman are created equal:

So God created humans in his image,
in the image of God he created them;
male and female he created them.

But in Genesis 2:23, God makes Adam first, from "dust," then fashions Eve from his rib. This woman is not equal. She is not made in God's image, but from Man—an astonishing reversal of the self-evident truth: that man is born from woman. Adam names her, as he names all other living creatures, signifying his dominion over her and all life on earth.

This at last is bone of my bones
and flesh of my flesh;
this one shall be called Woman,
for out of Man she was taken

The first written account identifying Lilith as the first woman— the equal woman—dates from the *Alphabet of Ben Sira* (c700–1000 CE). This is the source of the core elements of the myth: Adam's attempt to compel Lilith to lie beneath him, her refusal on the grounds of her equality, her flight to the Red Sea after uttering God's ineffable name, and the arrival of the angels Senoy, San-senoy, and Semangelof to talk her into returning to Adam. The mission fails, but one concession is extracted from the disobedient woman: she will harm no child bearing an amulet with the three angels' names.

Lilith's reputation as a demonic figure was already established in earlier Mesopotamian myth, as well as in the first-century CE Dead Sea Scrolls. She appears as a succubus and child-killer in the sixth-century Babylonian Talmud. Numerous incantation bowls warding her away from children and households have been found in Iran and Iraq, dating from the fifth to ninth centuries CE.

These elements inspired my Lilith's story, although she is quite different from the child-killing demoness and succubus of patriar-chal myth. My Lilith has a different reason for visiting babies in their cribs and an alternative explanation for her reputation as a seducer of sleeping men. She is the first woman as I see her: the equal woman, a heroine of power and dignity who will not be dominated. A woman of purpose and righteousness, defender of the female sex and the natural world, who will have her revenge for all that has been stolen from her.

The Fruit

In the original Hebrew, the fruit of the Tree of Knowledge was *peri*, meaning generic fruit. The apple didn't enter the story until 383 CE with the first Latin Bible, which played on the word *malus* meaning both evil and apple; earlier sources identified the fruit as a fig, a pome-granate, a grape, or even wheat. I chose the pomegranate because of its deep and abiding symbolism across the region. In Mesopotamian, Hebrew, and Greek myth, it represents female fertility, sexuality, abundance—and crucially, death and regeneration. It was linked to deities with roots as fertility/mother goddesses, including Ishtar, Hera,

Demeter and her daughter Persephone, Aphrodite—and for early Isra-elites, to Asherah, the Hebrew goddess who would be erased by later monotheists.

Samael

The fallen angel Samael may have started life as the Syrian deity Shamal. He is identified as the Angel of Death in the sec-ond-century CE *Targum Jonathan,* and the spouse of Lilith in the Zohar, a medieval work of Kabbalah. In the Hebrew *Book of Enoch*, he is "chief of the tempters." Samael's role in planting the Tree of Knowledge is described in the first-century CE *Greek Apocalypse of Baruch.*

Asherah

The existence of Asherah, the Hebrew goddess, was hidden for about two and a half thousand years. In 1928, thirteenth-century BCE cuneiform texts unearthed at Ras Shamra and Ras Ibn Hani in Syria revealed the complex mythology of Athirat, chief goddess of the Canaanite pantheon, wife of El and mother of all gods. Later finds would show Athirat was also worshipped in Judah and Israel—in the very Temple of Jerusalem—under her Hebrew name, Asherah, as con-sort of Yahweh. She was the wife of God.

We now have ample evidence of her central role in early Israelite religion, such as the eighth-century BCE inscription from Kuntil-let Ajrud invoking "Yahweh of Samaria and his Asherah," hundreds of seventh- to sixth-century BCE terracotta figurines of the goddess with full, milk-heavy breasts, and depictions of her as the stylised tree which symbolised her.

The suppression of Asherah's cult started in the first millennium BCE and intensified after the Babylonian destruction of Jerusa-lem in 587 BCE. Francesca Stavrakopoulou in *God: An Anatomy* describes a profound theological shift, in which the priests and scribes who shaped the Hebrew Bible crafted a new image of Yahweh, increasingly intolerant of other deities. The divorce would be final and comprehensive. Asherah's sacred shrines and images were destroyed. No longer Yahweh's consort, Asherah was presented as a foreign god—or even better, merely an object: *asherim*, the sacred wooden idols that represented the goddess, were re-imagined as "posts":

> *You must tear down their altars, smash their pillars, and cut down their sacred posts.*
>
> *Exodus 34:13*

And yet, glimpses of Asherah remain in every modern Bible. Here she is, under assault from Josiah's reforms in the seventh century BCE:

> *He brought out the image of Asherah from the house of the Lord, outside Jerusalem, to the Wadi Kidron, burned it at the Wadi Kidron, beat it to dust and threw the dust of it upon the graves of the common people. He broke down the houses of the male temple prostitutes that were in the house of the Lord, where the women did weaving for Asherah.*
>
> *2 Kings 23:6-7*

As Astarte, or Ashtoreth, "abomination of the Sidonians," the Book of Kings describes the "high places" King Solomon built for the goddess to the east of Jerusalem (2 Kings 23:13). She is the Queen of Heaven whose worship infuriates the sixth-century BCE prophet Jeremiah:

> *The children gather wood, the fathers kindle fire, and the women knead dough to make cakes for the Queen of Heaven, and they pour out drink offerings to other gods, to provoke me unto anger.*
>
> *Jeremiah 7:18*

Jeremiah also records the popular resistance to the attempts to quell Asherah's worship:

Instead, we will do everything that we have vowed—make offerings to the Queen of Heaven and pour libations to her, just as we and our fathers, our kings and our officials, used to do in the towns of Judah and the streets of Jerusalem. For then we had plenty to eat, we prospered and suffered no misfortune. But ever since we stopped making offerings to the Queen of Heaven and pouring libations to her, we have lacked everything, and we have perished by the sword and by famine.

Jeremiah 44:17-19

Mesopotamian Mythology

In Part Two, Lilith's journey to Sumer refers to the inextricable connection between Hebrew and Mesopotamian mythology.

Lilith herself started life in Sumer, first appearing in the historical record in the third-millennium BCE poem, *Inanna and the Huluppu Tree*. Here, a demoness called Lilitu sets up home in the trunk of a sacred tree—a story that shares elements with the later Genesis myth.

The biblical story of Eden also shares motifs with that of Enkidu and Shamhat in the Epic of Gilgamesh (c2100 BCE). Noah's flood is prefigured in the Gilgamesh poems, while the story of Cain and Abel has clear links to the rivalry of the farmer Enkimdu and the shepherd Dumuzi for the hand of the goddess Inanna.

My suggestion that the Asherah of this novel was originally a goddess of Uruk is based on the similarities and cross-identification of the great Semitic goddesses Asherah, Astarte, Ishtar, and Inanna, as well as a Sumerian inscription from 1750 BCE that describes the goddess Ashratum as wife of the god Anu. Asherah does not share all Inanna's qualities, but both claim the epithet Queen of Heaven and are linked to the planet Venus.

The priestess at Uruk is inspired by Enheduanna (b. 2286 BCE) High Priestess to the moon god Nanna at Ur, and the first named author in history. Her exquisite, intimate hymns to Inanna reveal the depth of women's devotion to the female divine over four thousand years ago.

Lilith's descent into the Underworld (Sheol in Hebrew tradition, Kur in Sumer) is inspired by *The Descent of Inanna* (1900–1600 BCE), in which Ereshkigal, Queen of the Underworld, hangs her divine sister's corpse from a hook in the wall.

The Curse of Canaan

The story of Noah cursing his grandson Canaan and all his descendants to slavery is one of the oddest in the Bible. The point of the story is clear: to justify the Israelites' (Shem's descendants) enslavement of the Canaanites (descendants of Ham). But what did the child Canaan do to deserve such an awful punishment? All we can discern from the biblical description is that his father saw his grandfather naked:

> *Noah, a man of the soil, was the first to plant a vineyard. He drank some of the wine and became drunk, and he lay uncovered in his tent. And Ham, the father of Canaan, saw the nakedness of his father, and told his two brothers outside. Then Shem and Japheth took a garment, laid it on both their shoulders, and walked backwards and covered the nakedness of their father; their faces were turned away, and they did not see their father's nakedness. When Noah awoke from his wine and knew what his youngest son had done to him, he said,*
> * "Cursed be Canaan;*
> * lowest of slaves shall he be to his brothers."*
>
> *Genesis 9:20-25*

In the Hebrew Bible, "seeing" or "uncovering" someone's nakedness is a euphemism for intercourse—this meaning is explicit in

Leviticus 20:17. Third-century rabbis in the Babylonian Talmud agreed Ham either sodomised Noah or castrated him. In *Hebrew Myths*, Robert Graves & Raphael Patai say the crucial passage has been edited out of the Genesis narrative, obscuring the mythical origins of the story and its similarities with contemporaneous Hittite and Greek tales of fathers castrated by sons. The curse for this heinous crime falls on Canaan, as Ham has already won God's blessing (Genesis, 9:1).

Jezebel

No biblical woman is more reviled than Jezebel, the ninth-century BCE Queen of Israel. Three thousand years after her death, her name remains a byword for immorality, wickedness, and harlotry. But what was Jezebel's chief crime? The answer is perhaps revealed by the prophet Elijah when he demands of King Ahab:

> *Now therefore have all Israel assemble for me at Mount Carmel, with the four hundred fifty prophets of Baal and the four hundred prophets of Asherah, who eat at Jezebel's table.*
>
> *1 Kings 18:19*

Jezebel worshipped the goddess Asherah, who was being slandered and erased from the Hebrew story by the authors of the Book of Kings, writing three hundred years after the events they describe. What follows: the battle of the gods between the polytheist and monotheist Israelites at Mount Carmel, will have grisly consequences for the goddess-worshipping queen.

Of course, Jezebel is no saint. She massacres the Yahwist prophets, and frames inoffensive Naboth to steal his vineyard. But she is no different to Elijah who slaughters the prophets of Baal. Why shouldn't she be as passionate, as devoted to her goddess, as Elijah is to Yahweh?

This is the Jezebel I wanted to write: the powerful, sometimes vindictive queen, the devoted priestess—and before it all went wrong, the beloved bride and the hope for Israel's future we glimpse in Psalm 45, which is thought to commemorate her marriage to King Ahab:

> *The princess is decked in her chamber with gold-woven robes;*
>> *in many-coloured robes she is led to the king*
>> *behind her the virgins, her companions follow.*
> *With joy and gladness they are led along*
>> *as they enter the palace of the king.*

Aramaic Names

I've used Aramaic names throughout Part Five: Yeshua for Jesus; Maryam for Mary, Yehuda for Judas, and the nickname Kephas (from the Aramaic for rock) for Peter.

Gnostic Gospels

Part Five is heavily influenced by the Gnostic Gospels, a collection of scriptures discovered at Nag Hammadi in Egypt in 1945. These texts, written in the earliest centuries of the Christian era, were sealed in a heavy jar and buried in the fourth century CE, when gnosticism—a belief in the divine spark within individuals, and the corruption of the material world—had become dangerously heretical.

Unsurprisingly, these scriptures offer a fundamentally different view of Jesus, his disciples and early Christianity than the gospels of the New Testament.

For me, the most astonishing text is *Thunder, Perfect Mind*, which inspired the hymn that Maryam hurls into the wind when she meets Lilith for the first time at the cave above Magdala. We don't know the real author (Maryam's authorship is my invention) but it is striking that the text voices a divine female figure that is entirely absent from later Christianity. It stunned me when I first read it. The line: *For I am the first and last* feels like a direct challenge to the male God who makes the same claim in Isaiah 44:6. But this voice goes on to make statements of unabashed womanhood; hounded, harassed, and slandered, yet still powerful. It felt to me like the voice of the lost goddess herself, speaking across the divide of two millennia.

The female divine figure appears throughout the gnostic texts. Indeed, some gnostics concluded that God was dual-natured, both Father *and* Mother. Followers of Valentinus, the second-century CE gnostic theologian, prayed to the "Mother of the All." Valentinus' disciple Marcus taught a eucharist in which wine symbolised not Jesus's blood, but that of the Mother, and prayed that her grace might flow into the drinker; this is the source of Maryam's alternative eucharist in my novel.

Mary Magdalene

Mary Magdalene is much more significant in the Gnostic Gospels than in the New Testament. In the *Gospel of Philip*, she is described as the *koinonos* (partner) of Jesus, who kisses her. In *The Dialogue of the Saviour*, Mary dominates the disciples' conversations. In the *Gospel of Mary*, she is asked to reveal teaching that only she knew.

An important clarification: the Maryam of my novel is no gnostic. Her spiritual beliefs are rooted in materiality, reflecting much older ways of understanding divinity incarnate in the world. My *Gospel of Maryam* is fictional and not to be confused with the gnostic *Gospel of Mary*. But I was moved by aspects of the gnostic scriptures, which reveal the diversity of belief in the early Christian era, the continued allegiance to the female divine, and the much more equal role of women in the movements that would be denounced as heretical from the second century CE onwards. Inspired by these ancient texts, my fictional Maryam is a prophet in her own right, bringing a message of harmony and love for this physical world from a female deity. Equal in teaching and in the movement she creates with Yeshua, she is the female half of a whole that more truly represents humanity than a religion comprising a Father-God, a Son, and a sexless ghost (who gets higher billing than any female). Of course, as a woman daring to assume authority, Maryam is denounced as a whore, just as Pope Gregory I pronounced the real Mary Magdalene a prostitute in 591 CE; the time-honoured method used to diminish or malign women.

Another gnostic text, discovered in 1773, is the basis of the conflict I portray between Maryam and Kephas. In the *Pistis Sophia,* the resurrected Jesus explains the mysteries of the divine female figure Sophia to the disciples. Mary's contribution to the discussion earns Jesus's blessing—but Peter is not happy. He complains that Mary "taketh the opportunity from us" and lets none of the men speak. Mary does not take this lying down. She tells Jesus she is afraid of Peter, because he threatened her and "hateth our sex."

In the *Gospel of Thomas,* Peter tries to oust Mary, saying that "females are not worthy of life." In the *Gospel of Mary,* Peter becomes enraged when he learns Jesus has given Mary secret teaching denied to him.

This conflict between Mary and Peter reflects the battle at the core of my novel: between a worldview of equality and harmony between the sexes—a desirable state coined as *gylany* by Riane Eisler—and the opposing urge of male supremacists to dominate women and brand them as inferior.

Chrestos, not Christos

In the early years following Jesus's death, he was known in the Greek world as Chrestos (the good man), not Christos, (Christ, the anointed man). Numerous records attest to this original form, including two of the earliest codices of the New Testament, the Codex Sinaiticus and the Codex Vaticanus. The second-century CE Roman historian Tacitus describes Nero blaming the Chrestians, not Christians, for the Great Fire at Rome. Inscriptions on tombs in Phrygia dating from the third century CE describe the deceased as Chrestianoi.

I owe my introduction to the *Chrestos, not Christos* epithet to Robert Graves' remarkable novel *King Jesus.*

Jesus and Sophia

Sophia is the Greek form of Chokmah, the female personification of Wisdom in the Hebrew Bible. She is the subject of Solomon's longing in the Book of Wisdom and speaks in her own voice in Proverbs 8. Sophia/Chokmah is the inheritor of Asherah; an echo of the lost goddess in the new monotheistic world. Now an aspect of God, the Spirit of God, or the Holy Spirit, she is no longer a goddess in her own right.

Yet, in the gnostic scriptures, she regains some of her former independence. Here, Jesus presents himself as a messenger of Sophia; it is *her* wisdom he brings to mankind, not his own. As the biblical scholar Elisabeth Schüssler Fiorenza points out, this explains the otherwise incomprehensible saying in Luke 12:10 and Matthew 12:32, that blasphemy against Jesus will be forgiven, but not against the Holy Spirit (Sophia).

Another clue remains in the New Testament suggesting Jesus's link to the lost goddess: at his baptism, as described in all four gospels, a voice from the heavens proclaims: "You are my beloved son, in whom I well pleased" (Mark 1:11). At the same time, the Holy Spirit descends and alights on him in the form of a dove—the ancient symbol of Asherah, and mother goddesses across the Eastern Mediterranean.

Scriptural Sources

The Nature of the Rulers; Gospel of Mary; Gospel of Philip; Thunder, Perfect Mind; Gospel of Thomas; Dialogue of the Saviour; Three Forms of First Thought; all from *The Nag Hammadi Scriptures,* edited by Marvin Meyer

Pistis Sophia, from the Gnostic Society Library, translated by G.S.R. Mead

The Complete Dead Sea Scrolls in English, translated by Geza Vermes

All bible quotations from the New Revised Standard Version

Acknowledgments

Lilith first came calling for me in the spring of 2019. I was research-ing another book, but the demands of the furious, vengeful first woman were very insistent, so I told my agent Ella Kahn I had a "quick" novella I wanted to get out of my system first. I hadn't got very far when the covid pandemic began, and in that strange, isolated, locked-down world, Lilith took over, bursting out of the limited scope I had initially imagined, to bestride 6,000 years of human history and hold the fate of the entire world in her hands.

My first and primary thanks are to Ella, who said, "Go for it!" and never once asked what had happened to the saner, more marketable novel I'd thrown over for my demanding heroine. I couldn't have writ-ten this book without Ella's encouragement and incisive eye; without her gently pointing out where I'd got lost and illuminating where the path led back through the thicket. Thank you, Ella, for your Wisdom.

I am immensely grateful to my editor Lauren Parsons, whose pas-sion and vision for this book has been so uplifting. I am thankful too to Vicky Blunden for her unwavering commitment to precision, and to everyone at Legend Press, particularly Ditte Loekkegaard for toler-ating my endless revisions, and Olivia Le Maistre and Lucy Chamber-lain, for such enthusiastic support.

I am thrilled that this book will be published in the US, Ger-many, and Turkey and so grateful for the tenacity of agents Allison Hellegers, Antonia Fritz, and Ayşenur Müslümanoğlu in finding the best possible homes for Lilith. My grateful thanks to editors Cordelia Borchardt, Holly Ingraham, and Kürşad Kızıltuğ for invaluable direc-tion and guidance.

The beautiful cover art is by Sarah Whittaker. I am in awe of her talent for distilling the essence of a novel into such an evocative, attractive design, and so proud and grateful it adorns this book.

Thank you, again, to Paul; I could not ask for a more insightful and encouraging first reader. Thank you to Sarah and Karen, dog-walking plot-untanglers, and of course to Lola, Winnie, and Brearley, without whom we would never have our weekly therapy/plotting workshops.

I am hugely indebted to the many scholars, academics, and translators whose work illuminated or inspired aspects of this book. Most notably these include: Eve Wood-Langford, whose fascinating book *Eden: The Buried Treasure* introduced me to a Unitarian approach to the biblical myth of Eden; Raphael Patai's ground-breaking *The Hebrew Goddess*; everything written by Elaine Pagels on the Gnostic Gospels, but especially *Adam, Eve and the Serpent*; *God: An Anatomy* by Francesca Stavrakopoulou; *Holy Misogyny* by April DeConick; *Did God Have a Wife?* by William G. Dever; *When God Had a Wife*, by Lynn Picknett and Clive Prince; and Margaret Starbird's *The Woman with the Alabaster Jar*.

The epigraph to Part Two is inspired by translations by Geza Vermes and Wilfred G. E Watson of manuscript 4Q184 of the Dead Sea Scrolls found at the Qumran caves in 1952.

The hymn my high priestess at Uruk cites is inspired by the poems of Enheduanna and other Sumerian texts translated in Betty De Shong Meador's *Inanna, Lady of the Largest Heart*, and *Inanna, Queen of Heaven and Earth*, by Diane Wolkstein and Samuel Noah Kramer.

The epigraph to Part Five and the hymn that Maryam recites at the top of the cliff in Magdala is inspired by the Nag Hammadi text *Thunder, Perfect Mind*, in translations by Hal Taussig, Marvin Meyer, Willis Barnstone, and George MacRae. Maryam's prayer: *I am the First Thought* is inspired by *Three Forms of First Thought*, translated by John D. Turner.